The Sticks

The Sticks

The Girl on the Glass
and the Boy on the Road

D. Austin Walker

For Beth

One

When the Stick girl came out, the light was so bright she could hardly stand it. Her instincts told her to remain perfectly still. That's what she did. She didn't squint or blink her black eyes. She didn't stretch or yawn. She didn't wiggle the fingers on her four-fingered hands.

Connected to her lay other stickers. Stick people. She had a vague memory of being with them in a dark box. There they had waited, all dreaming the same two dreams over and over. One, a nightmare of being in darkness forever, rejected. The other of light, of acceptance.

Her nose itched, but she resisted the urge to scratch it. Flat and motionless, she stared at the ceiling and waited for the world to tell her what she was.

As her eyes adjusted, a huge freckled face came into focus. Green eyes stared down, big as moons. Over the next few years, the Stick girl would be drawn to them. She would come to know the quirky workings of this person's heart and mind. Like her, a very different kind of girl. Those eyes would become the center of her life.

But some things are not forever. Sometimes they vanish into unbearable nothingness.

The Stick girl felt a sharp sting at each hand, then at her feet. She felt herself being lifted free of the other stickers. She heard plastic sliding on cardboard as they went back in the box. Sensing that they had been rejected and that she had been chosen, she felt two things at once: an urge to jump for joy and another to cry. An invisible new companion introduced itself. Guilt.

"I picked one," called the giant girl with green eyes, her voice raspy, sandpaper on stone. The Stick girl wondered if she could speak, too, but she didn't dare try.

Then a woman's voice. "Elizabeth, sweetie, that one's defective. Look at its mouth. Choose a normal one."

Her name is Elizabeth, thought the Stick girl. And, *What does that mean? Defective.*

A new giant spoke, neither Elizabeth nor the woman, in a voice like a songbird. "Yeah, Lizbeth, don't be a weirdo." Then quieter: "Weirdo."

Elizabeth's green eyes darted towards the voice. Her thick eyebrows bunched up like caterpillars ready to fight. "Mind your own business, Sophia!" She stared down at her sticker and whispered, "Are you broke?" The question arrived with the aroma of peppermint. The Stick girl, somehow knowing that she shouldn't reply, sent a thought instead. *Nope. I just woke.*

The second girl's face appeared. *Sophia.* She also had freckles, green eyes, and thick eyebrows. To the Stick girl, the twins looked exactly the same and completely different.

"Mine's perfect," Sophia said. "See?" She held up a second Stick girl, with a dress, pigtails, and a smile shaped like a crescent moon. The other Stick girl looked beautiful. Holding her by her arms, Sophia flew her away.

"I like mine better," Elizabeth called, showing a crooked grin. The Stick girl felt a tingle as a giant finger moved across her mouth. "She smiles like me."

In the distance, the woman called, "Honey, grab the Windex and paper towels."

A man's voice: "Yes, dear."

"Everybody got one? Let's stick 'em on the car."

Sophia: "Yes, Mommy."

Footsteps. The woman appeared over Elizabeth's shoulder. "Stop staring at it and come on before it rains."

"Sure thing, Mom."

Mom.

The Stick girl's view spun—ceiling, walls, windows. She felt herself being carried. A door opened to sunlight and a sky strewn with clouds. She saw trees, a yard, a house, and something that made her feel safe: an old white minivan, parked facing the street. The names of these things came to her as if they flowed from Elizabeth's mind to her own.

Running around the giant people was a giant four-legged creature, brown as dirt. *Dog,* the Stick girl thought. *We love him.*

The tallest giant approached, the *yes dear guy.* As he sprayed and wiped the minivan's back windshield, the Stick girl inhaled blue mist and thought, *Yum!* The man peeled away some paper from a Stick man and placed him in the lower left corner of the glass. "That'll work," he said.

Elizabeth gave him a high five. "Way to go, Dad."

Dad, the Stick girl thought. *Two dads. One stuck on glass and one that can move around.*

Next, Elizabeth's mom stuck a Stick woman to the glass. The sticker woman's hand overlapped the Stick dad's so that they appeared to hold hands. "There," said the woman.

Two moms. One stuck, one mobile.

Next, Sophia placed her Stick girl so that she held hands with the Stick mom. "I think I'll call you Sunny," Sophia said, "because you're so sunny, like me!"

"Seriously?" her dad asked. "You're naming your sticker?"

Her mom added, "Perfect, sweetheart."

Sunny, my perfect sister, thought the Stick girl.

Next, Elizabeth's turn. The Stick girl felt a tickle at the top of her head as a giant fingernail scratched at the corner of her paper backing. Until now, she hadn't realized it was there.

"I'll call mine...Lizzie," Elizabeth said as she worked. "Lizzie Lou."

"That's silly," her sister teased. "Lizzie rhymes with busy rhymes with fizzy. And Lou rhymes with...doo. You know," she giggled, "like dog doo?"

That's me. I'm Lizzie. I guess I'll do.

As the white paper came off, Lizzie could see both in front and behind. One way appeared clear, the other hazy (because of her sticky layer). It took only a second to switch from looking forward to back, just by thinking about it. Her family would eventually call this switching views *melding.*

Elizabeth carefully placed Lizzie's head on the glass. The Stick girl's vision momentarily went dark as a giant thumb smoothed her down. Lizzie felt pressure from her pigtails to her shoes—almost painful—and she was stuck. *I have pigtails and shoes,* she thought.

"Ha, I knew it," Sophia pointed as her face loomed close, "yours is crooked!"

"It is not!" Elizabeth exclaimed, and pushed her sister away.

Lizzie could tell that she wasn't exactly level with the other

Stick people. That didn't bother her. But sensing her knee-length dress for the first time, she thought, *This thing's uncomfortable.*

The giant mom touched Elizabeth's shoulder. "Sweetie, it is a little...off. Plus the smile is kind of broken. Why don't you go pick a better one? I'll scrape that one off."

But the girl examined Lizzie again and shrugged. "Nah. Straight enough for me."

As the humans turned away, Lizzie lifted her head to get a better look at the Stick girl next to her, Sunny. Unsticking was a lot easier than she expected. But the Stick mom shot Lizzie an angry look. She quickly flattened.

Yes, Mom.

And just in time, because one more family member needed to be placed on the back windshield—a Stick dog. The giant dad stuck him next to Lizzie. As the human smoothed out a bubble, the sticker dog looked over at Lizzie and winked. She liked him already.

Elizabeth knelt down and spoke to the giant dog who had been running around. "What do you think, Hershey? What should we call your sticker dog?"

The floppy-eared fellow's stubby tail wagged. "I'll call him Ups, like the lorry that delivered them," he replied in a British accent. "It was brown like me!" *A Mobile dog and a Stick dog,* Lizzie thought, *Hershey and Ups.* She didn't remember the brown UPS truck that had delivered her family in a box. But she figured that Hershey had made a joke.

"Wow, that's the most I've ever heard him bark," said the Mobile dad.

Then the Mobile twins kissed the top of Hershey's head, where he had a small lock of blonde fur. Lizzie could tell that none of them had understood his words. Apparently, Mobiles didn't speak Dog.

When the *Peeling* was over, the Mobiles all walked back into the house. The Stick family stayed on the windshield.

"What do we do now?" Lizzie asked, not at all surprised that her own voice had the same raspy quality as Elizabeth's.

"We're Sticks," Mom whispered. "Most of the time we stay stuck. That's our purpose. They're Movers. Their job is to move around."

The Stick dog's ears went up. "Really?" he asked. "That's their job?"

Lizzie and Ups exchanged a glance. "Why don't we call the big people something else?" she asked. "Movers sounds, I dunno, wrong."

"What do you suggest, oh crooked one?" Sunny asked. To Lizzie, her sister's voice sounded much like Sophia's, sweet to the ears, sour to the heart.

The *crooked one* shrugged. "I've been thinking of them as Mobiles."

"Movers, Mobiles, doesn't matter," Mom replied, "just hold the pose. That's an order."

The thought made the Stick girl fidget. "That's boring."

"No, it's glorious!" Sunny said, and gave her sister's hand a squeeze.

Lizzie snorted. "Are you sure we're related?"

Just then, a bumblebee buzzed right past Lizzie's nose. It hovered for a moment, then flew up and out of sight. Without a thought, the Stick girl freed her hand from her sister's, unpeeled, and raced up the windshield after the thing. By the time she reached the top of the minivan, the bee had vanished, but the world had appeared. The wider world. Endless streets, houses, and cars. Dogs in backyards and kids on a swing. A man riding a motorcycle, a woman watering flowers. Lizzie stared, searching her head for the names of these things, but finding none. Her ears—keen for a Stick person—picked up voices, slamming doors, and the rumble of traffic. In the distance, a jetliner silently inched its way across the horizon. From where she stood, it looked no bigger than the bee. *That one's so slow and quiet compared to the buzzer,* she thought.

"Hey, dummy!" The Stick girl turned to see her sister's face peeking up over the edge of the roof. "Get back down here!" Sunny demanded. "You're in SO much trouble!"

"Oh. Okay." Lizzie followed her back down onto the windshield.

"Young lady!" her mom began, peeling up to shake a finger at her. "Don't you EVER—" But the Stick woman suddenly flattened herself. "Lay down! Freeze!" she snapped.

With good reason. The front door of the house burst open and Elizabeth ran down the steps. She stopped a few feet away and stared at Lizzie. She said nothing, just grinned another crooked grin and made her eyebrows dance one more time.

Two

When the Stick family was again left to themselves, Lizzie mumbled, "I-I-I messed up. Next time I won't—"

"There better not BE a next time," Mom seethed. But that was all. No lecture.

Better not BE a next time, Lizzie thought. *Be. Be. Bee!* "Hey, that thing that flew by," she said, "I think it's called a—"

"Your person is weird," Sunny cut her off.

Lizzie closed her mouth. It appeared that nothing she had to say was worth hearing. She glanced over at the perfect Stick girl. "You talkin' to me?"

"Duh. Your person ran back outside, didn't she?"

For the first time in her life, Lizzie blinked. "What do you mean, *my* person?" Out of the corner of her right eye she could see Sunny shrug.

"Dunno."

"What Sunny means," Mom explained, "is that each of us has a big version of ourselves. A Mover—scratch that—a Mobile person. Isn't that right, hun?"

"Yes, dear."

"Each of us is connected to a Mobile," Mom continued, "but only one. That's the first rule about being a Stick person. One Stick for each Mobile."

"So..." Lizzie thought out loud, "that must be why I felt stuff when Elizabeth looked at me. And I felt nothing when that other girl did."

"Other girl?!" Sunny scoffed. "You mean Sophia. She's not just some *other girl*. She's the superstar in the family. And your girl has a broken voice." She glared at Lizzie. "You both do."

"No need to argue," said Dad. "Both of you are special and so are your Mobiles."

Lizzie peeled her head up just a little and sneaked a peek at him. *He'll always accept me,* she thought, *no matter what.* She rested her head back on the glass. But she couldn't stay silent. "Um, Mom?"

A heavy sigh. "Yes? Speak."

"How do you know all these things? Didn't you just come out of the dark thingy like the rest of us?"

"Out of the box, you mean, not a thingy. A dark box." Mom

cleared her throat. "Because moms know everything. Right, hun?"

"Yes, dear. Listen to your mother, girls."

Lizzie pressed on. "Ya know, when I came out of the—whatchamacallit—box, the first thing I saw was the ceiling. Pretty sure that's the first time I ever saw one. But I knew what it was *and* what it's called."

"Me too," said Sunny. "I knew it, too."

Lizzie looked up. "But out here the ceiling's called...sky. I think."

The Stick dog wagged his tail and added, "The girl next to me has a point."

"I'm Lizzie."

"Lizzie has a point," Ups amended. "I keep thinking I need to mark my territory. MY territory. Not someone else's." He barked a laugh. "But I have no clue what that means!"

"All in good time," Mom said. "We're still learning. If you know things that don't make sense, it's from being around your Movers. Or your Mobiles, if that's what you want to call them."

Kinda sorta makes sense, Lizzie thought. She closed her eyes and enjoyed the warm glass against her back. She was safely stuck with her family. It felt right.

Then, for no reason that Lizzie could figure, her dad laughed and blurted out, "Wanna hear a joke?"

"No!" the others all answered. At least on this point, the rest of them were in agreement.

When Lizzie opened her eyes again, she noticed that the sky had turned dark and the blue parts had disappeared. A powerful BOOM shook the air—as though the house had crashed into the minivan.

"Mommy?!" squealed Sunny.

"Hush, hush," Mom said with a soft chuckle. "It's just thunder."

"Thunder?" Lizzie and her twin both asked.

"Nothing to be afraid of."

They all stared at the charcoal, moving sky. After a few seconds, Ups asked. "What exactly is that? Thunder."

Dad lifted his head and turned to the Stick dog. "That's a good question, buddy. You see, our big people have big people of their own," he explained, "way up in the sky." Everyone stared upward." So big," he went on, "that none of us can see them. And that noise—" Thunder cracked again. "That's what they sound like when they play football." He looked away with a dreamy expression, then lay flat on the windshield. "Whatever that is."

"Oh," Sunny said. "So dads know everything, too?"

Lizzie grunted.

"Sounds like a bunch of hooey to me," Ups whispered. Lizzie sneaked him a pet on the muzzle.

"It *is* a bunch of hooey," Mom said. "There are no giant

giants, just the regular ones, the...Mobiles." Dad started to say something, but she silenced him with a wave of her hand. "Thunder is the sound of lightning, which is..." She seemed to search inside her head. "Which are lights in the sky, powerful ones. We might even see some."

All eyes turned to the sky again. Eventually, a flash illuminated the dark clouds, followed by another loud boom. Ups let out a whine. Sunny said, "So cool," but with a tremble in her voice.

Lizzie didn't care about the coming storm. Something else was bugging her. Something bigger, if not louder. "Hey, Mom," she began. She felt her mom's stare and quickly changed her tone, trying to sound as sweet as Sunny. "Mommy? I have another question."

"Go ahead, but this will be your last one for the day. After the thunder booms go away, we have a lot to do."

"A lot to do?" Sunny cut in. "Like what? We're stuck on this clear stuff—"

"Glass, dear. The clear stuff is glass."

"Okay, glass," Sunny said. "What's there to do besides hold hands and look at stuff?"

Mom patted the windshield. "Well, we need to inspect this beast and make sure she's road-worthy. Check the tires. Check the oil-change sticker on the front windshield. I'm making a list in my head."

Dad said, "I think I need to check the...wiper blades."

"We don't have to stay stuck all the time," Mom went on, "just when I say so. But absolutely, without question, we always have to be back *On Glass* before the Mobiles come outside. Understand? We'll know when they're on the way. We should feel it."

"Awesome," Ups said with a yelp. "I wanna run around the yard, like that big dog, Hershey."

Sunny shouted, "Yah!"

Lizzie grinned, relieved to know that her entire life wouldn't consist of standing by her family. Although they were starting to grow on her. Even Miss Perfect.

Mom said, "But don't be rude, Sunny." Lizzie glimpsed the Stick woman's hand as she lifted it and yet again wagged a finger. "You interrupted your sister."

"Sorry, Mommy."

"Lizzie. Make it quick."

Lizzie took a big breath. "What about the ones left in the box?" she asked. "The other sticky people. What about them?"

Silence followed, long enough that Lizzie wondered if keeping her mouth shut would have been better. She searched for a memory of the unchosen Sticks—a face, a name, the feel of their hands or feet. But like the blue parts of the sky, darkness had chased them away.

"They're gone forever," Mom finally said, her voice as flat as her family. "Don't think about the ones back in the box. Don't speak about them. Ever. They never existed."

A cool wind passed over the glass.

"Oh," said Dad.

"If you say so," said Sunny.

Mom: "I do."

Ups opened his mouth, then closed it without a word.

And Lizzie just stood there, stuck, as the first cold raindrop in her life trickled down her face.

Three

Three Years Later

The white minivan sat in the driveway, its hatch open. Lizzie, upside down on the back windshield, thought, *What's taking Sophia so long? My head's gonna explode!*

"Where *is* she?" Ups whined. "I do believe the blood is rushing to my head."

"Getting ready," Sunny replied. "She has to be perfect. Perfection takes time."

"Ready for what?" the dog scoffed. "We're driving out in the middle of nowhere. Nobody'll see her."

The Stick Mom and Dad added their two cents as well. But Lizzie stayed silent. Complaining would be doing something with them. She was done with that. Done with…everything.

"Do we have to keep holding the pose?" Ups asked. "Nobody's looking." Even upside down, the Sticks held hands, motionless: Dad on the left, then Mom, Sunny, Lizzie, and Ups. Exactly like they had been ever since the Chapmans placed them there three years ago. Nothing had changed. For the others, anyway. But for Lizzie? Everything.

"Hold your positions," Mom ordered. "The slacker could come out at any second."

"Don't call her that," Sunny protested. "Sophia's just—"

Lizzie cut her sister off with a turn of her head. *Just what?* she thought. *Say it. Lost?*

"A little like you," Sunny whispered. Lizzie felt her hand being squeezed.

Among the many things that had changed for the Stick girl was her memory. Her family, for example, remembered the Peeling clearly. To Lizzie, the details had grown fuzzy. She glanced down at a crack in the glass that ran beneath her leg, and sighed. If only she could forget that night, too. It had been about a year since the car crash. When the body shop had repaired and painted the minivan, they hadn't replaced the back windshield. Thus, the crack. Everyone knew why. Sophia had thrown a fit to keep the old windshield. If they installed a new one, the cracked one would be thrown in the trash, along with the Stick family. And those little sticker people were one of the few things that reminded Sophia of her twin.

It's been about a year since Elizabeth's death, Lizzie thought. *Since I killed her.*

Inside the van, the Mobile parents and their dog Hershey waited, too. The mom sat in the front passenger seat, talking non-stop—whether to her husband, to herself, or into her rectangle thing, Lizzie couldn't be certain. From the driver's seat, the dad gave two quick honks on the horn.

Finally, Sophia shuffled out of the house with a duffel bag over her shoulder and her phone to her ear. Lizzie closed her eyes. Sophia looked so much like Elizabeth: green eyes, caramel hair, freckles peppering her nose and cheeks. Lizzie thought she might break into tears if she looked at that face too long.

"Yeah, sucks beyond imagination," Sophia said into the phone.

Ms. Chapman stuck her head out of her window. "Move it!" she called. "We're late!"

The Mobile girl tossed her bag into the cargo compartment and switched the phone to her other ear. "Guess I don't have a choice," she sighed. "Yeah, Holly, wish you were going, too. Call you from the road, bruh." She slipped the device into her hip pocket and reached up for the hatch handle.

Please don't slam it, Lizzie wished. And to her surprise, the teenager pulled just enough for gravity to do the rest. The hatch closed with a soft click.

Then strangely, Sophia paused for a moment and stared at Lizzie. She hadn't done that since the day of Elizabeth's funeral. The Mobile's jaw dropped open, revealing a cavern of braces, which glinted in the sunlight. Lizzie couldn't fathom why someone with a perfect smile needed braces, unless it was to become even more perfect. Sophia examined the crack in the glass and the diagonal slash that ran across Lizzie's right leg. "You're peeling."

The thirteen-year-old moved even closer, until her face filled the Stick girl's vision. Sophia had plucked her thick eyebrows until they looked anorexic, and had filled in gaps with a pencil. Traces of dark eyeshadow hid in the fine creases of her lids. Her lips shone like a polished floor. Her hair, usually as fine as silk, had been slathered with some perfumy gel. To Lizzie, she looked a little like Hershey after he came out of a pond. At least she smelled better.

Sophia's giant index finger rose into view and pinned Lizzie's leg against the glass. The Stick girl's heart raced as a fiery sensation ran from her hip to her ankle.

Sophia bit her lower lip and squinted at the sticker person placed here by her dead sister. Her green eyes loomed even closer. "That's better," she whispered. Eyelashes, seemingly as big as an eagle's wings, sent a breeze across the Stick girl's face. She got a whiff of mascara, lip gloss, and Bubblicious. Then Sophia disappeared. Lizzie heard the van's sliding door open and close.

"Lizzie Louise! You broke character!" the Stick mom accused.

"Nope. Didn't happen," Lizzie replied, still trembling.

"You most certainly did. Completely unacceptable. Completely!"

"Now, dear—" Dad interjected.

"Don't *now dear* me."

"Leave my Mobile alone," Sunny growled into Lizzie's ear. "She's not yours."

The twins exchanged hostile stares.

"And your pigtails are drooping," Mom added. "Why can't you keep them like Sunny? At least make them even." Hurriedly, Lizzie fixed her hair. Like her, it never seemed to behave.

Her mom droned on, but Lizzie tuned her out. Before she could lose the moment, she closed her eyes and sealed that brief encounter with Sophia in her mind: the kind face, green eyes, and caramel hair. The pattern of freckles. A mental snapshot she could recall like a constellation. Unlike the last time she saw Elizabeth, the memory of this face filled Lizzie with warmth.

Four

As the van pulled out of the driveway, the Stick dad smiled up at the sky. "Looks like good traveling weather," he said.

Mom got a little more specific. "Eighty-four degrees Fahrenheit, twenty-eight point nine Celsius. Relative humidity forty-three percent. Wind from the northwest at three knots. Barometric pressure steady at—"

"Got it, Mom," Sunny interrupted, "clear and warm."

"Just reporting the facts," Mom shot back. "Of course, depending on our destination, the temperature could vary by plus or minus..."

Lizzie ignored them. Instead, she searched her mind for a clear, positive memory of Elizabeth. As usual, she unearthed a series of out-of-focus images and snippets of dialogue. Nothing she could hold onto. Although Elizabeth's personality had fully imprinted on Lizzie's being, the moments when this had happened now escaped the Stick girl's embrace. She felt awash in a flood of confusion.

Sunny tugged on Lizzie's hand, jolting the Stick girl out of her fog.

"Hey, space girl!"

"Huh?"

"I said, where do you think we're going? This trip? I swear you're getting worse."

"Oh. I dunno." Lizzie looked around at the khaki-colored houses. "Anywhere's better than Vinylville."

Her mom peeled her head off the windshield to make eye contact. "Don't judge. We can't all live in McMansions."

Lizzie didn't answer. She didn't mind that the houses in their neighborhood were small. Just that they all looked the same.

"So where?" Sunny asked. "Where, where, where?"

Ups wagged his tail. "Camping!" he shouted. "Woo-hoo!"

"Of course, camping," Sunny said. "But where to? Like, it could be Edisto Island or all the way to the Smoky Mountains."

"Or to Mount Everest," Dad suggested.

"Negatory," Mom countered. "I counted one tent, three sleeping bags, two coolers, a tarp, dog food, and a few dry goods. This family is not equipped for a major expedition."

"It was rhetorical," Dad replied.

"Re-what?" Sunny asked.

"Means he's flapping his gums," Ups said.

"Whatever. We should go to the mall," Sunny said. "Sophia needs new shoes."

She has too many already, Lizzie thought.

"The slacker doesn't always get her way," Mom replied. "It's spring break. No school. No malls. We may be gone for a whole week."

"A week!" Sunny moaned.

Lizzie closed her eyes. *That's enough time to get adopted. Or lost.*

"We Sticks are going to spend some time out in the sticks!" Dad said, a little too happy. "You know. The sticks? The woods?"

Ups pawed at Lizzie's hand. "Dad jokes."

"You're not funny, Dad," Sunny said. "Your jokes are as worn out as bald tires."

"But that was a good one!"

"Just stop, dear," Mom said.

He sighed. "I *used* to be funny."

Soon the minivan merged onto I-26. When the vehicle reached cruising speed, the road noise and vibration of the glass lulled the Stick family into a dream state, similar to sleep. Lizzie felt Sunny's hand go slack. She herself remained wide awake.

By Lizzie's count—she counted all the time—it had been four hundred and two days since the family's last road trip. The one that ended tragically. Although her good memories of Elizabeth had faded like fog on a windshield, the night of the crash remained all too clear.

The Stick girl watched the endless dotted lines on the highway, and worried it would happen again, that she would cause the death of someone she loved.

Why couldn't I just stay still? she wondered. She peeled up her head and took a long look at her family. As much as they irritated her, she still loved them. *My life's a wreck,* she told herself. *Theirs doesn't need to be. This trip could be the perfect time for them finally to be rid of me. And for me to escape.*

Five

When she could no longer bear the boredom of the highway, Lizzie *melded* from facing the pavement to facing inside the vehicle. Beyond the cargo area with its camping supplies sat Sophia Chapman, her head down. *I suppose she's texting Holly,* the Stick girl thought. Up front, the Mobile dad guided the van, his shoulders bouncing to classic rock. Next to him, Sophia's mom stared down at either her tablet or at a book. From this angle, Lizzie couldn't tell which.

The family's Boykin spaniel, Hershey, lay next to Sophia. The seat-back blocked him from view, but Lizzie knew he was there. In Elizabeth's seat.

Facing the van's interior, Lizzie could also see through the side windows. She watched other cars as they passed.

Characters, stuck to bumpers and back windshields, paraded by. Some of them noticed her and waved. A baby riding a skateboard shouted, "Righteous!" and pumped a fist. On the mud flap of a big rig, Yosemite Sam, the Looney Tunes cowboy, stood straddling the words "BACK OFF!" Noticing Lizzie, he drew his six-shooters and began taking pot shots at highway signs. With her free hand, Lizzie gave him a thumbs up. Next, a Jaguar XJ raced up from behind and zoomed around the van. As it did, the chrome Jaguar hood ornament let out an impressive growl.

Lizzie scrunched up her face. *How come they get to move around and none of their humans notice,* she wondered? *But I gotta stay frozen like a statue? One little look of surprise on my face and I killed somebody.*

Then a funky green Subaru Outback motored by. Dozens of stickers had been slapped on the car's backside: peace signs, rainbows, slogans, Mother Earth holding a bunch of baby animals, a chrome lizard-like creature, and more. Even a small family of Sticks. They all appeared to be having a party, dancing and laughing. And didn't seem to care if their Mobiles knew they were alive. By contrast, on the Chapman's minivan, the only other sticker besides Lizzie's frozen family was a AAA oval on the bumper. It didn't even talk, much less party.

Lizzie's grin faded. The Subaru Stick family—two women and a boy—had no noses, mouths, or fingers. No clothing. Their hands and feet were club-like. Lizzie's own family called their kind *Featureless*. Seeing them filled her with pity. *How awful to live like that,* she thought. She hoped they were simple-minded, unaware of their handicaps. The Featureless boy waved a fingerless hand. Lizzie looked away and grasped Sunny's hand more tightly, a normal hand with three fingers and a thumb. She glanced at the car again and saw a golden retriever–its long ears flopping in the wind–staring at her from an open window.

Not long after the Subaru disappeared from view, Lizzie's minivan passed a section of highway that had been trashed, literally. For about a quarter-mile, debris of human existence lined the break-down lane. Someone's stuff—clothes, toiletries, toys—had apparently fallen from a car's luggage rack. Mixed with this scattered junk lay a menagerie of bedraggled characters, some dead, but most alive: a Kool-Aid man, an Aflac Duck, a stuffed Elmo, an Exxon tiger, a trio of Chick-fil-A cows, and many more.

The sight of them filled Lizzie with dread. As much as she detested being stuck with her family, living in the actual gutter would be unthinkably worse. She quickly checked to make sure that the Mobiles inside the van weren't looking, then waved at the roadside rejects. None waved back, but some sat up and watched as the Stick girl vanished in the distance.

Six

Several hours later, Lizzie's family roused from their stupor. Dad covered a yawn. "Was I snoring?" he asked.

"I can neither verify nor deny," Mom reported.

"Kids?"

Sunny yawned. "I was out."

Lizzie said nothing.

They rode in silence. Finally, Sunny squirmed and let out a loud sigh.

"Sophia feels pressure in her tummy," she said. "Why does this always happen?"

The Stick mom and dad exchanged a knowing glance. "That's on a need-to-know basis," Mom said. "And believe me, you don't need or want to know."

"The Chappy daddy's hungry, " Dad added.

Mom cleared her throat. "Honey, that nickname seems so undignified."

"Yes, dear."

"But your assessment is correct. What kind of outfit are these Chapmans running? No sandwiches. No snacks for the road?"

Dad shrugged. "They're spontaneous."

"You mean unorganized, irresponsible, and endangering the mission."

"Jeez, Mom," Sunny said, "it's just a camping trip."

"Hershey's always hungry," Ups said.

"We're pulling over," Dad said. "Next exit has two gas stations, three fast-food joints, and a Hampton Inn."

"Please let us stop at the hotel," Sunny said. "Sophia shouldn't have to sleep in a stupid tent. Her hair can't take it."

"Negatory," Mom said. "This mission's a go. Ms. Chapman is dead set on getting in some tree-hugging time. I can feel it."

Hearing the word *dead*, Lizzie's right hand began to shake.

Mom and Dad whispered between themselves. They thought no one could hear, but Lizzie did. There *were* sandwiches in the blue cooler in the back. But because of what happened last year, there was no way anyone would be reaching over the back seat to get to them. Not with the van in motion. The last person who tried a move like that was in her grave.

Seven

Mom gave the family marching orders. Once the wheels stopped and the Mobiles were out of sight, the Sticks would scatter. Dad would crumb-hunt. Ups would gather intelligence on the family's destination. Mom would fill up the family's canteen from the squeegee reservoir. A sip of windshield washer fluid, if it wasn't too funky or watered down, would be refreshing. Sunny and Lizzie would check air pressure in the tires. After last year's accident, they no longer trusted this job to the Chapmans.

"And don't talk to any pirates," Mom warned. None of them had ever met a pirate, but the Stick mom insisted that a pirate would carve you to pieces with his sword.

The van rolled to a stop in front of pump 8 at a combo

Exxon and Bojangles Chicken. Once the Mobiles had all piled out, the Sticks climbed down, too.

Not Lizzie.

"We've got tire duty," Sunny called from the pavement. "Jump down." Lizzie didn't move. "C'mon, sis. I'm not mad about Sophia smoothing down your leg, if that's what you think."

Who cares if you're mad? Lizzie peeled off and made her way down. Near the right tail light she noticed how part of the paint didn't match the rest. She ran her hand over the area and felt a slight wave. She closed her eyes for a second and relived the moments after the crash: Flashing red lights. A man doing CPR. Sophia screaming hysterically. The face that Lizzie loved being covered with a sheet. Elizabeth's arm falling limp over the side of a stretcher.

When she reached the bumper, Lizzie stared down at the pavement and touched the tear on her leg, a habit. Back in the day, she could have leapt from the windshield, hit the ground rolling and sprung to her feet like a gymnast. She and Sunny had done that trick dozens of times. Sometimes, the yard gnomes next door cheered. But now as she leapt from the bumper, her right leg buckled. She sprawled onto the asphalt and scraped her palms. Sunny tried to help her up, but Lizzie pulled away.

"Hey, we help each other," Sunny said. "We're twins."

Are we? Really? Lizzie limped toward the front of the car.

"Good idea," Sunny called. "You get the front, I'll get the back."

With each step, the lower half of Lizzie's right leg folded. She felt more like an old woman than a thirteen-year-old. These days, she could feel people staring at her even if no one was around. When she reached the right front tire, she removed the plastic cap and pressed the tip of the valve. A jet of air shot forth and blew back her hair. *Hm,* Lizzie thought, *thirty-six PSI.* Like all Sticks, she could tell tire pressure without a gauge. *But what if I'm wrong? What if it's twenty-nine, or twenty, or twelve? It's not like we can pump up the tires ourselves. Or tell the Mobiles. Not like we can change a single thing.*

Eight

Back on the Interstate, Mom turned to Ups. "What's our destination? Any intel from the Black Army?" She meant the black ants, which normally cooperate with Stick people on all things tech.

The dog shook his head. "Their network's down. Somebody cut the lines. Surgeons, they said."

Mom grunted. "Insurgents, not surgeons."

"Oh, right," Ups grinned, "that makes more sense."

Mom said, "The Fire Empire is extremely dangerous." The Stick mom spoke to everyone, but fixed her gaze on Lizzie. "If any of you hear about or see one of their mounds, you tell me right away. Got it?" They all nodded.

"What if we see a line of them?" Sunny asked.

Her dad coughed and said, "Don't you worry about that, Sunshine, where we're going they're not going to–"

"Run," Mom interrupted. "And don't look back."

A shudder went through Lizzie. Fire ants. Fearing them wasn't being paranoid.

The Stick mom turned to her husband. "Crumb report?"

"Lots of goodies," Dad said, showing his bulging pockets. "For our entrée this evening, there's a Goldfish cracker, perfect condition. Then there's a meaty something or another, could be beef jerky, always good for a road trip. A cheese puff fragment. And check this out for dessert—a whole Skittle, barely melted! Yellow one."

"That's one of the good ones," Mom said.

"Plus, a bit of Hubba Bubba for the road. Strawberry flavor. Anyone?"

He passed the plug of ABC bubble gum down the line. Everyone took a chunk.

"You did good, hun," Mom said. She gave him a peck on the cheek.

"I claim the Goldfish smile," Sunny said.

"Why does she get it?" Ups protested.

"It's my fav," Sunny said.

The dog growled. "Mine, too!"

"Calm down," Dad said, "There'll be two smiles when we split the cracker. One for each of you."

I don't exist, Lizzie thought.

"Ups," Mom asked, "see anything suspicious?"

"Not a thing, but Hershey almost strangled himself on his leash."

"Oh?"

"Yeah. A golden retriever next door at the Subway," Ups explained.

"Noted. Girls? Tire pressure?"

"The back ones were thirty-six," Sunny said.

"Thirty-six PSI, spot-on. And the front?"

When Lizzie didn't reply, Sunny said, "Thirty-six. They were good, too."

And Lizzie thought, *why do we even bother? There's a freaking tire pressure indicator on the dashboard.*

"Can we eat?" Ups asked. "I'm starving."

"They'll feed Hershey this evening," Dad said. "You can wait too."

"The Chapmans are behind schedule and skipping lunch," Mom said. "Snacks only."

"That's their problem," Sophia said. "Let's eat."

Ups wagged his tail in agreement.

"Make do with your bubble gum," Mom said. "What do you think would happen if poor Mr. Chapman checked his mirror and saw us having a picnic?"

"Ha!" Ups laughed. "He'd run off the—" The Stick dog

stopped with his mouth open.

Lizzie stared at him. *Road. He'd run off the road.*

"At least we know where we're going," Dad said.

"We do?" Ups and Sunny asked.

"I heard Mr. Chapman asking his rectangle for directions to Gorges State Park. Remember? We went there three summers ago? It's beautiful."

"Road trip!" Sunny said.

"That means we still have hours of driving," Mom said. "The Chapman crew will have to set up camp in the dark, and so will we. You'll all have assignments."

"It'll be fine," Dad said. "You all remember the park, right? It's so pretty we called it Gorgeous State Park. And those waterfalls? One makes a rainbow and the other looks like a turtle?"

"Remember the night the skunks walked through the campsite?" Mom laughed.

Ups shook his head. "I don't remember that trip at all. For you guys it's been three years and a bit. For me?" He *woofed.* "Decades." A Stick dog could live as long as any Stick, but Hershey would not. Lizzie alone understood Ups' obsession with dog years.

As the sun inched toward the tree line, cars and trucks whooshed by on either side, some with their lights on. Lizzie melded toward the inside of the van so she wouldn't have to face the same way as her family. She counted stuff in the cargo area—tent, food, etc.—and discovered something that filled her with mischief: colored markers. Anything that could stain Sticks was considered hazardous. At dinner tonight, for example, they would handle the orange cheese puff and yellow Skittle with great care. Then they would wash with washer fluid from the canteen.

Markers were a whole other level of danger. Some would wash off, others wouldn't. As the minivan climbed into the foothills of the Appalachians, Lizzie grinned to herself. A crooked, devious grin.

Nine

Friday Evening

As the van bumped along the campground's dirt road in the dark, Lizzie's mood lightened. Unlike her sister, she liked the outdoors and detested the suburbs. Gorges State Park was indeed gorgeous, and big enough that she might find a chance to ditch her family for a while.

While the Mobiles unloaded their camping gear, the Sticks again waited with their feet skyward. Finally the hatch slammed closed.

"Feels like it's going to jar the fillings right out of my teeth," the Stick dad complained.

"We don't have fillings, dear," Mom pointed out.

"Technically, we don't even have teeth," Ups added, "just

white bars that look like teeth from a distance."

"Time to set up our own campsite," Mom said as the family unpeeled. "First thing, shelter. I saw a grocery bag stuck in the bushes a ways back. That should work."

"On it," Dad said.

"You're big and strong, honey, but you can't do it by yourself," Mom said. "You and I'll double team it. Girls, you search for firewood. There's nothing worse than a cold campsite."

"Except for being horribly burned," Sunny complained.

Mom dismissed her with a wave. "You know the kind of fire I mean. But don't wander far. There's squirrel nests everywhere. Keep your heads on a swivel for incoming acorns."

"Yes, sir," Sunny said. "I mean ma'am."

Squirrels didn't scare Lizzie. She wondered what their bushy tails felt like.

Mom went on. "Ups, as soon as the Chappies get that tent up, scout the terrain behind it and dig out a soft, level patch. I'm not sleeping on any rocks."

"Ten-four," the dog said. "I'm a digging fool."

Mom clapped her hands. "Chop-chop, let's move it."

Lizzie reached the dusty ground behind the van without falling.

"I'm not carrying any firewood," Sunny sighed. "Too heavy."

"Don't be silly," Lizzie replied, "she means funny-fire. You won't even break a nail."

"Right. We passed an empty campsite back there," Sunny said, pointing. "Let's start there."

"Pass."

"C'mon, Liz, you heard Mom. We have to."

"Yeah, but we'll cover more ground if we split up," Lizzie said. "You check the abandoned campsite. I'll see how far it is to the next trash barrel." Lizzie turned and began walking in the opposite direction.

"Aughh!" Sunny huffed.

Lizzie glanced back and saw her sister marching away. *Alone. Finally!*

Ten

Kicking at pebbles, Lizzie limped along the single-lane dirt road. This place seemed nothing like home, to the Stick girl's way of thinking, an automatic improvement. Before Vinylville had been built, all the trees had been cut down or bulldozed and new ones planted. They were still puny. Here at the campground, sycamores, oaks, and loblolly pines towered overhead, hiding the stars. Lizzie marveled at the broad boles and dizzying heights.

A wooded buffer lay between each campsite. As Lizzie approached the next site, sounds of acoustic guitar and laughter met her. An orange-and-yellow tent came into view. Two human women sat on a log, one of them playing guitar. Across from them, a teenage boy slumped in a canvas chair. Firelight bathed all three in flickering amber.

"Hello!" *woofed* a furry voice. Whiskers suddenly brushed Lizzie's face and a great black nose sniffed at her. A golden retriever's brown eyes, reflecting pins of firelight, examined the Stick girl.

Lizzie stepped back as a huge drop of slobber dripped from an enormous tongue.

"You're that dog from the highway, aren't you?" she asked. "The one covered in stickers?"

"I am?" The dog sniffed her own front legs.

"No, I mean the car," Lizzie said, "your station wagon. The one with all the stickers. I saw you in the back."

"Well, I take offense to calling it a station wagon," the dog replied. "It's an Outback. But yeah, I'm Daisy. As you can see, I'm oppressed." She shook her head and floppy ears to show that a rope stretched from her collar to a tree. "Silly people think I'll run off."

"Silly people," Lizzie repeated.

"Of course I *will* run off," said the golden, "but I always come back."

"Ah, well, good luck with that." Lizzie said. She hurried past, thinking *You're not the only one who might run off.*

No sooner had she passed out of the firelight and into the shadow cast by the Subaru, when another voice called.

"Psst! Chica! Hey! Little help, here?"

Lizzie looked up at the patchwork of bumper stickers that covered the rear end of the Outback. "Which one of you said that?" she asked.

"None of us outsiders," said a man on a bumper sticker. "But you'll find my fellows in need around the corner." He wore wire-rimmed spectacles and appeared to have a blanket draped over one shoulder. Where his body abruptly ended, a caption read, *Be the Change You Wish to See in the World.* "Our friends are in need of your kind charity," he urged.

"Yeah well, I don't know you or them," Lizzie said.

"My name is Mahatma Gandhi," he replied. "So now you do know me."

"You could be the President wearing pajamas," the Stick girl said. "I don't care."

"Ah," he replied with a half-smile, and said no more.

"Yo! Ola! A little help?" called the voice again.

Lizzie walked around the corner of the Subaru and looked up at a side window. Stuck inside stood the Featureless Stick boy, the one who had waved to her on the highway. *So sad,* Lizzie thought.

"What are you doing?" she called.

"We're stuck," he said. "Not sticker-stuck. We're locked inside, see?" Beside him, two Featureless Stick women waved and said something, but Lizzie couldn't make it out.

"You're Insiders."

The boy laughed. "Yes, very perceptive of you." He turned to the women and said something in what sounded like the Common Tongue—definitely not an ant language—but oddly, Lizzie couldn't understand it. He turned back to the Stick girl. "What d'ya say? Could you help us out?

"How am I supposed to do that? I'm just a—" She was going to say "girl" but didn't. "I'm just one person."

The boy pointed a fingerless hand. "There's a fingernail file down there. One of our Mobiles dropped it. That's all we need."

From behind the glass, the Stick women waved with way more excitement than Lizzie thought the situation called for. "Gracias!" they called.

Grass? Lizzie thought. She searched through the turf and retrieved a dusty metal file.

"Now climb up and wedge it under this window," the boy instructed.

Lizzie sighed. *Another chore.* "Can't you just—can't your bumper sticker friends help?" She could hear Hello Kitty and Mother Earth talking from the back of the car.

"Uh, actually, no. Kitty's arms are too stubby, Mama E has to watch her babies, and Papa Gandhi doesn't have any legs."

Lizzie didn't see how she could climb up carrying the heavy fingernail file. "Looks too hard," she said. She dropped the file and started to limp away.

"Oh, I see you're broken," the boy called. "Never mind. We'll wait for someone else."

With a *grrr* under her breath, Lizzie picked up the file, then climbed up the car just to prove she could. Once at the window, she pried the heavy glass with the fingernail file until the boy slipped out.

Seeing his Featureless face and hands up close, guilt washed over her. *I can't look at him,* she thought, and turned away. Just then, she slipped. He reached out and caught her. As he did, five fingers appeared on his hand. Lizzie pulled away and stared at it. *Freaky,* she thought. Not just that his fingers had grown right before her eyes, but that there were so many of them. She then watched as features appeared on the rest of his body. And not just normal stuff like a nose and mouth. Details and colors emerged that she had never seen on a Stick person—ears, lips, even a gold ring in one of his earlobes. Instead of normal black eyes, his blue ones stood out in the dim light.

"Whatcha starin' at?" the Stick boy asked.

Eleven

Lizzie glanced away, but just for a moment. "Ah...no, it's just that, uh." She couldn't help looking.

The fancy-faced Stick boy smiled. "What? Didn't know we could do that? Well, go ahead, look me over. We call it resolving. When we're On Glass, we're in display mode. Simple stick figures. But we get more complex when we're off."

Lizzie gave a little laugh. "Apparently." She examined him. Fingernails on five fingers. Fine hair. Blue eyes that all but glowed with color. Eyelashes. A necklace with a charm. Stripes on his T-shirt. Shoelaces. "Whoa, wait," she pointed, "is that a zipper?"

Now he laughed. "Yeah. Stop staring at it."

"I'm not. I wouldn't. No, I've just never seen one on a

sticker. I gotta go."

"Hey, not so fast. I was just kidding. Help me get my moms out."

Lizzie glanced at the two women behind the glass, one still waving, the other now giving her a hearty thumbs-up. "Moms?"

The Stick boy's eyebrows shot up. Lizzie could make out individual hairs on them. "Really? You really gotta ask?"

"Oh. Sorry. No. I've just never seen—"

"Anyone like us. Got it. And no hablas Español, either, I guess. It's all cool. Moving on. Now give me a hand."

Together, Lizzie and the boy pried with the nail file until the two women slipped out.

"Thanks so much, dearie, thanks bunches," the women said, as fine features appeared on their faces.

"You're a lifesaver," said the taller of the two.

"Don't talk about food, Thoma, I'm famished," the shorter woman said.

They climbed down. The Stick boy introduced himself as Nico. His moms were Mavis and Thoma. They had missed their opportunity to slip out of the car during the unloading, and were so grateful for her help. A little too grateful for Lizzie's taste. She tried not to stare at the extraordinary detail on their faces. *We should call them Super-detailed, not Featureless,* she thought. Feeling uneasy, she mumbled something about needing to find firewood and started to hurry away.

"Just hold on a sec, sweetie," said the short mom, Mavis. "You helped us; we'll help you. Yours isn't the only family that needs to build a fire. But first, we need to make our circle."

"Your what?"

"Our circle, of course. Doesn't your family make one? C'mon now, let's get this crowd off the car."

The moms and Nico began helping their friends down from the Subaru, except for Gandhi who was part of a bumper sticker and couldn't go anywhere. Nico introduced them: Hello Kitty, Mother Earth and her leafy baby animals, two Saint Louis Cardinals, and a peace sign hand named Ringo. They lived on the outside of their car. Lizzie bristled as each one gave her a hug. Lastly, a chrome lizard-like creature dropped to the ground, waved a shiny claw, and waddled away. He needed no introduction—the word DARWIN covered most of his body.

"Where's he going?" Lizzie asked.

Nico shrugged. "To find some primordial soup?"

Soup in the woods made no sense to the Stick girl, so she ignored the comment.

"Everybody in!" Mavis called. She nodded at Gandhi, who folded his hands and remained on his bumper sticker.

The characters formed a circle and held hands. Mavis and Thoma each grabbed one of Lizzie's. Weird people, she thought. Then checked herself. That's exactly what Mom would say.

Mother Earth lifted her voice in a long musical note,

something between a wolf howl and the trill of a songbird. It gave Lizzie a chill, a good one. The leafy Mother then thanked the wind and the rain and the dirt and the trees. She thanked the campfire and the Subaru and the stars. By the time she got around to thanking road signs and the stripes on the Interstate, a grin had crept onto Lizzie's face. Finally, Mother Earth said, "And so we are." To which the others all replied, "And so we shall be."

Will be what?

They released hands and closed in for a group hug. For a few seconds, Lizzie's eyes bulged. *These people are freakin' crazy.* They finally let go.

"Say, dearie, you sound a tad bit under the weather," said Mavis. "Would you like a throat lozenge?" She began digging through her pocketbook.

"Uh, no thanks, ma'am," Lizzie replied. "This is my normal voice. This is me."

"Well, okay, then."

The Stick girl stood beside Nico and watched as his family began making camp behind their Mobiles' tent. Unlike Lizzie's crew, no one hurried. No one gave orders. No one issued dire warnings about squirrels or pirates. Some split off to do various tasks, but they had no set time to regroup. Nico volunteered to find firewood.

"That's what I'm doing," Lizzie said.

"I'm just gonna walk to the next trash barrel," he said.

"No, you're not. That's where I'm going."

"So? I'll go with you."

"Not necessary. Go the other way."

"We kinda owe you for helping us out."

"But my mom wouldn't want me talking to—" Lizzie started to say "a Featureless boy." Then she realized how that would sound. "You don't owe me anything."

Nico flashed a smile, something he seemed to do easily. "Don't worry, we know what people like you think of us."

"People like us? What, my family?"

"Yeah, you know. Outsiders. Regulars. Your faces don't resolve. You guys think we're weird. Doesn't mean we can't hang."

Lizzie opened her mouth, but no words came out of it. So, even though all she wanted was to be alone, the two walked down the dirt road together, toward the next trash barrel. She focused on the ground; he looked at the sky, as the strumming of a guitar faded behind them.

Twelve

Ahead, an overflowing trash barrel loomed like a factory tower. Against it leaned a broken lawn chair too big to fit inside. As Lizzie and Nico approached, they passed another Stick family going in the opposite direction and holding a resealable sandwich bag over their heads.

"Pretty smart," Nico said, "a ready-made tent."

"I'd rather sleep under the stars," Lizzie said. "Did you see that bag? By morning, they're gonna all smell like chicken salad."

"Under the stars? Outside?" The Stick boy glanced up and gave a nervous laugh. "That'd be, like, terrifying. I mean, what if it rains?"

"What if it does?" Lizzie replied. This week, her family

would sleep in a tent to keep from getting dirt on their sticky sides. But she had slept outside her whole life.

As they walked, Nico caught Lizzie staring at him. She looked away.

"What?"

"Nothing."

"No, really, you were thinking something."

She stared out at the trees, anything but at his blue eyes. "Um, yeah. I was wondering what language you and your moms were speaking. It's not any kind of ant that I know of."

"Oh, you mean Español," he laughed. "Yeah, that's still the Common Tongue, just a different version of it. Lots of Mobiles speak it."

"Really?"

"My Mobile, Joaquin, he used to speak it when he was little. Back when he lived with his birth parents. Now, his moms are trying to teach it to him again. So, naturally, we're learning it, too."

"Oh," Lizzie replied. Any further questions would only prove her ignorance, so she went silent.

The overflowing trash barrel buzzed with activity, literally. Natives and campers alike, bugs and characters, were drawn to its wealth. A line of red ants stretched into the distance, each one carrying a crumb larger than itself. A trio of yellow jackets waged an aerial assault on a junk-food bag.

"A garbage truck will be here in the morning," said one of the jackets. "Whatever you're gonna get, you gotta get it tonight."

"Okay."

Lizzie and Nico scoured the ground around the barrel, but found nothing for a campfire. They stared up at the mound of trash above their heads. One of the yellow jackets hovered closer. "Whatcha starin' at?" it asked. "Not our burgers and fries, I hope."

"We're looking for fire," Nico said.

"Oh, that's cool. The real kind or the funny-fire?"

"What do you think?" Lizzie said.

"Hold on. I saw something." The yellow jacket buzzed higher up on the pile and returned a moment later. "Yeah, just the thing you want, right at the top."

"Thanks," Nico said.

"What's the best way up?" Lizzie asked.

"The chair," the jacket replied. "Hey, but first, could you help a buzzer open a bag?"

"Sure," they replied.

"I'll help," Nico said. "You go for the fire."

Lizzie scaled an aluminum pole that was a leg of the lawn chair. When she reached the rim of the barrel, a red bag with the words "Jalapeño Hot Chips" poked out of the trash. She pulled it out and examined its illustration of flames. *Perfect.*

Nico had finished helping the yellow jackets and climbed up to the rim.

"That's just what we need," he said. He reached for the chip bag but she pulled it out of reach.

"Get your own fire."

"Hey, that's not fair!"

"Oh, well." She turned the bag upside-down and began dumping crumbs over the side of the barrel. Below, dozens of red ants broke formation and ran to pick them up.

"Is your Mobile as mean as you are?" Nico asked with a scowl.

Lizzie gave him a look that could have melted glass. "Don't you ever mention her again." She held the chip bag farther away.

"Fine," the boy replied. "Good luck trying to climb down. Sliding down that chair pole will be tricky with your bad leg. Yeah, I saw how you limp. You'll bust your butt."

Lizzie glared at him. The last thing she wanted was for anybody to feel sorry for her. Grasping the bag by the corners, she leapt from the side of the barrel. The thing popped open like a parachute and she drifted to the ground, landing gracefully on her feet. She winced at the pain in her leg, but, at least, it didn't buckle. She carefully folded the bag into a manageable square, tucked it under one arm, and walked away.

Trying for all the world not to limp.

Thirteen

Red ants, yellow jackets, and rollie-pollies descended on the crumbs that Lizzie had shaken out of the potato chip bag. As she walked past the crowd, beneath all the munching and arguing, she heard a faint, muffled voice.

She turned to see Nico, who had slid down the lawn chair leg and followed her.

"Was that you?" she asked.

"Me what?" he replied. He leaned close, which made her a little uncomfortable.

She waved him out of her personal space. "No, not you. I heard something."

"Huh?"

"I heard someone calling," she said, "like they were in

trouble. Wait, there it is again."

"I'm not in trouble," said one of the yellow jackets.

"You're gonna be," replied one of the ants, shooing the flier away from the crumbs. Lizzie didn't speak *Red*, but she got the gist of his reply.

"Shhh!" she shushed them, but no one besides Nico paid her any mind. Lizzie looked all around, sure that she had heard something. Someone in trouble. "Everybody, be quiet," she said, her voice shaking a little. It made the Stick girl nervous to speak in front of people, so she almost wimped out. But someone somewhere around here was in a bad way. So she summoned her courage and raised her voice.

"Shut it!" she shouted. "Listen!" She clapped her hands three times, just like her mom. That did the trick. A hush fell. Everyone looked at Lizzie. She moved over to the litter barrel and put her ear against it. "Someone's inside," she said. She rapped her knuckles on the thick rusty metal wall.

A green beetle, a big fellow who came up to Lizzie's shin, strode towards her. "Move over, lightweight," he said. Lizzie stepped aside. The beetle ran at the litter barrel and head butted it. The metal wall resounded like a gong. Everyone waited. Then a faint voice came from the other side of the wall.

"Yep, we got a goner in there," said the beetle. He pointed a foreleg at the Stick girl. "You got good ears, kid."

"Who are you?" Lizzie yelled at the wall. A muffled response came back, but she couldn't make out the words.

"It's the tennis woman," said one of the yellow jackets. She turned to her winged companions. "We watched her get tossed in there." The other jackets nodded.

"And you just left her there?" Lizzie demanded.

The first jacket shrugged. "Happens. Go look in any trash barrel in the park. Or try dumpster diving sometime. Somebody'll be stuck at the bottom."

Lizzie looked around at blank faces, then watched as the crowd, except for the yellow jackets and Nico, scampered back to the crumbs.

"It's a Mobile world," Nico said. "At least we Sticks have windshields to go home to."

"But-but, that's not right," the Stick girl replied.

"Our kind are too little to move trash around," the leader of the jackets explained. "If we tried, some of that stuff could shift around. Then we'd be stuck. No, thank you."

"No, thank you!" the other jackets buzzed.

Lizzie pushed the folded bag—the funny-fire—into Nico's arms. "Hold this," she said, "and don't run off or I'll hunt you down." She walked to the chair pole and shimmied up. Behind her, the bugs resumed scavenging spicy potato chips. At the top of the trash heap, Lizzie pushed some of it around. They were right, it was heavy.

"You know there's all kinds of nasty stuff in there, right?"

Nico called up. "Come down before you ruin your sticky side."

Lizzie paused to look at her hands—both of them already littered with bits of debris. The fancy-faced boy was right. If she climbed into the barrel, it would take forever to get clean. Her mom would go ballistic.

The Stick boy voiced her thoughts. "What're your parents gonna say?" he called.

Yeah, well, nothing good. But then, what else is new?

Lizzie poked around some more. She saw some openings, but no clear path down to the bottom.

What would Dad do, she wondered? *He'd say "Listen to your mother." So, what would Mom do? She'd walk away. She'd say that the tennis woman never existed. To never mention her. And what about Elizabeth? What would SHE do?* Lizzie balled her hands into fists, felt the grit on the sticky sides, and opened them again. Her crooked grin made an appearance. *That girl never worried about getting a little dirty,* she thought. *If something needed doing, or was just fun—mud, grass, leaves, dirt—none of those mattered. And danger?* Lizzie almost laughed. *Elizabeth would scrape up her knees and elbows and hardly even notice.*

As the Stick girl began her descent, she looked up to see Nico walking toward her on the rim of the barrel, followed closely by the airborne trio of yellow jackets.

"I told you to wait on the ground," she barked.

"No, you said to hold the bag. But you're not my boss. I have a mind of my own."

"Where'd you leave it?"

"My mind? It's right here."

"Not funny. You know what I mean. My chip bag."

"Our chip bag."

"Whatever. Great. Now I gotta find more fire."

"Stop freaking. I left it with the ants."

"The Red Army? You can't trust them! Only the Black."

"I disagree. The Reds and I made a deal. They can unfold the bag and clean out the crumbs if they'll watch it for us. Nobody but us Sticks wants an empty bag, anyway."

"Are y'all going to fuss all night or are we going in?" asked the lead jacket.

Lizzie snorted. "Since when do you care?"

"Yeah, well," the jacket said, "this is our buzz, if you know what I mean. We saw how the trash went in. We know where it's stable and where it's not. Besides, you're both light as paper. We can lower you in."

Nico peered past Lizzie and into the chasm of discarded items. "Looks iffy."

The lead jacket shrugged. "Easy peasy," she said.

Lizzie tried not to grin. That was one of her dad's sayings. Only he would have added, "Lemon squeezy."

"I'm Sojourner," the jacket said. "And this is Cynthia and

Seth." Her companions nodded. "We don't mind the occasional charity air lift."

"Thanks, I guess," said Lizzie. She shook hands with their extended forelegs.

Nico said. "Nice wings."

For a moment, they all stared down into the cavern of trash. The muffled calls had come from near the bottom. Now, nothing. Only the helicopter sound of transparent wings beating the air. Lizzie wrinkled her nose.

"Yeah, it stinks to us, too," said Sojourner.

"But I thought—" Lizzie started.

Sojourner swooped right in front of her face. "You thought what, flatty? We can't smell? We ain't maggots, ya know. Now, let's go!"

Fourteen

As Sojourner lowered Lizzie into the barrel, darkness swallowed the patch of stars above them. The Stick girl found the yellow jacket's feet prickly. She had never felt Velcro, but had seen the Mobiles use it, and imagined the texture must be similar. From the rim of the barrel came Nico's echoey voice, asking if they were alright. "We're good," she called back, then flinched at the sound of her own voice, overly loud in the confines of the litter barrel. Despite what Sojourner had said about Sticks being as light as paper, Nico had been too heavy to lift. So Lizzie and Sojourner descended by themselves.

"I once saw a movie about Coast Guard dudes in a helicopter who rescued people," Sojourner said. "Made me want to enlist."

"Yeah? How'd that work out?" Lizzie asked.

"Eh, height requirement."

The jacket lowered Lizzie slowly, shifting left and right, forward and back, to keep open space below the girl's feet. The space was getting cramped. Lizzie bumped up against a styrofoam cup, then cringed as a bead of sticky soda slid down her arm. It had only been a few seconds and already this place creeped her out.

"So, you watch movies?" the Stick girl asked the yellow jacket.

"Love 'em! A fine Scorsese film is worth the risk of getting swatted. Know what I mean?"

"I guess," said Lizzie. "I'm more of a Disney—" She started to say, *a Disney girl,* but stopped short. Her family had watched just about every movie the Chapman twins had. The Sticks couldn't hear much of the audio through the glass, so they used to fill in the silence by making up their own dialogue. Often their versions were more entertaining than the originals. Lately, though, Sophia stared at the little rectangle she always carried.

"Anyway," Sojourner said, "I'm like the Coast Guard pilot and you're the rescue diver."

Lizzie wrinkled her nose as she passed a bag of rotting junk food. "Do all bees talk so much?" she asked.

"Watch your tongue, missy! I'm a jacket and proud of it. Don't lump me in with those nectar addicts."

"Sorry." Then she added, "Don't call me 'missy.'"

They had descended halfway down the barrel by now. The contents looked chaotic, but the jacket knew every turn. The deeper they went, the darker it became until Lizzie could see almost nothing.

"Okay, right under your feet are some plastic bottles," the jacket said. "I'm going to set you down."

"Yeah, I feel one with my toes."

"Don't slip. They had motor oil in them."

"I'm there, I'm good," Lizzie said. The jacket let go of her wrists.

A moment later Sojourner joined her.

"From here on, the trash is packed tight. I can't lower you. You gotta do that slithery thing you Sticks do."

"You mean bend?"

"Yeah, that's it. I'll be right behind you. But don't get your hopes up. That poor fool you're trying to save? Tennis woman? She's at the bottom. Probably pinned. We're wasting our time."

Lizzie sighed. Her back was already gritty with rust from brushing up against the wall. She could feel the slime of motor oil on her feet. Her mom would pitch a fit. Like most Sticks, Lizzie hated confined spaces. A windshield was her home. The sky was in her blood. The idea of being pinned under an avalanche of garbage filled her with dread. She could feel herself shaking. Her excitement about rescuing some stranger seemed stupid now. Sadness reached for her in the dark. The same sadness that had been choking the life out of her soul on the sunniest of days. She heard a rustling noise coming from somewhere below.

"Are there rats down there?" Lizzie searched the faint pins of light that shone from Sojourner's eyes.

"I don't think so. You ain't something they wanna chew, anyhow."

Lizzie began climbing down. *That slithery thing we Sticks do.* She had to push things aside and wedge herself between the wall and any number of random objects. The deeper they went, the nastier it smelled. And they had company. Lizzie had no great love for, nor prejudice against, cockroaches. Sojourner was less tolerant. She ran them off with little more than bravado and the threat of her stinger.

"What did you mean by tennis woman?" Lizzie asked.

"You know," said Sojourner, "a woman who plays tennis."

"Yeah, I figured. What's that?"

"Huh! I thought you Sticks were world travelers," the jacket replied. "She swats at a bouncy ball. You'll see."

Oh, Lizzie thought, *she means Yellow Ball.*

The Stick girl groped blindly for handholds until they finally reached the bottom. Sojourner could stand, but Lizzie had to crouch. A tall cardboard box blocked their way.

"So where are you, tennis woman?" Lizzie called.

"I'm right here," said a voice.

"Where?"

"Other side."

"Other side of what?"

"The box, of course."

Lizzie reached down and felt an antennae.

"Watch it," the yellow jacket said. "Those are sensitive."

"Sorry. I can hardly move. How are we gonna get to her?"

"Gimme a sec." The jacket got down on all six legs and searched the base of the box until she found a gap. "Through here," she said, and crawled beneath the box. Lizzie followed.

When she reached the other side, Lizzie could stand, but it was a tight squeeze between the box and a deflated swimming-pool float.

"Where are you? I can't see anything."

"I'm right in front of you," said the tennis woman.

"Oh!" Lizzie touched the surface of the box.

"That's my nose."

"Huh?"

"You just ran your hand over my nose."

Lizzie tapped the box.

"And that's my shoulder."

She tapped again and heard a *twang*.

"And that's my racket."

"You mean you're—"

"On the box? Of course I am. What'd you think? I was on the Wheaties cover last August. Lucky for me, my Mobiles are bacon-and-eggs people. Lots of us get thrown out in a week or two. I had months. Hey, I really appreciate you guys coming for me. I'm Serena."

"Hi, Serena. I'm Lizzie."

"And I'm Sojourner," said the jacket.

"So what's your plan?" the tennis woman asked. "You do have a plan, don't you?"

Lizzie didn't know how to answer. She had figured there would be some little action figure or paper person stuck at the bottom of the barrel, someone small enough to carry out. Instead, they needed to extract a whole cereal box.

"This is really brave of you," Serena said. "I've been worried. Tomorrow is, you know," her voice trembled, "trash day."

"Seven-thirty sharp," Sojourner added.

Brave, Lizzie thought. She felt the edge of the cereal box. For the last year she had been nothing more than broken. Certainly not brave. Now she had an impossible task and very little time. Staring up into darkness, she felt the oppressive weight of all that trash. *What would Elizabeth do,* she wondered?

Fifteen

izzie and Nico hurried back to their families' campsites on a mission: enlist everyone's help in rescuing Serena. Nico said his family wouldn't hesitate. They loved causes. But Lizzie expected pushback, especially from her mom. As it turned out, Mom agreed immediately. Once she heard the "parameters of the mission," as she put it, the Stick mom marshaled her family's efforts as if it was a military operation.

Nico's moms took some convincing. It had been a long ride; everyone was tired; they hadn't eaten dinner. They went all "circle of life" about Serena. Everyone has their time, they said. But then Nico got emotional. Raising his voice, he said it wasn't like them to ignore someone in need. He would go back to the barrel, with or without them. When Lizzie's family marched by, Nico and several of his extended family followed them (the lizard creature, Darwin, Mother Earth, and her babies). Pretty much shamed into it, Mavis and Thoma joined the group as well.

When they arrived at the barrel, both families were glad to see the folded chips bag with its illustration of fire. The Red Army had watched it dutifully.

The rescue party climbed the broken lawn chair—except for the Saint Louis Cardinals and the yellow jackets, who flew—and assembled on the rim. There they stared into a filthy abyss crammed with boxes, soda cans, oil cans, water bottles, a torn tarp, a broken umbrella, and several torn garbage bags spilling who-knew-what. Sunny pointed at a broken beer bottle and gave Lizzie a grim look. Trash bins back in Vinylville never got this stuffed.

Lizzie's mom gave a double clap. "Well, don't just stand there, let's get started."

They worked long into the night, pulling things out of the barrel. Characters from all over the campground heard about the operation and showed up to help. Besides the yellow jackets, hundreds of ants, rollie-pollies, and a variety of crawly creatures pitched in. Dozens of fireflies provided light. Everyone helped except the cockroaches. Every once in a while, work halted and everyone scattered as a flashlight came bobbing up the road—Mobiles on their way to the rustic shower.

Progress went slowly. Throughout the park, conversations grew quiet. Campfires faded. Lanterns were extinguished. Lizzie could hear tent flaps being zipped as Mobiles bedded down. The night grew chilly. The mood of workers turned glum. No one complained, but no one sounded hopeful either. Sunny tried to cheer everyone up. Lizzie was secretly ashamed that she herself was too shy and nervous—or not *sunny* enough—to rally them. By the time the gray of dawn crept into the eastern edge of the woods, the rescue party had managed to remove only a few water bottles, soda cans, and assorted loose paper trash. They couldn't lift any of the glass bottles. Couldn't even budge the wadded-up tarp. Wedged below it, a massive plastic lid from a cooler held it down. The garbage truck would arrive in an hour.

Violating her own rules on hygiene, Lizzie's mom climbed down to see Serena. The Stick girl leaned into the darkness and listened as she gave the cereal celebrity a pep talk. They were doing everything they could to dig her out, she said. Then their conversation grew too quiet for Lizzie to hear. When the Stick mom climbed out, she gave Lizzie a tight-lipped grin and touched her shoulder. "We're done," she said. "She made the call herself."

"No!" Lizzie screamed. At the best of times, the girl had a scratchy voice. Now it sounded raw. "There's still time," she said, fighting tears. "We can do this." She looked around. Half of the helpers had already left. The rest stood slump-shouldered and looking down.

"Honey—" Mom gestured at all the mess still stuck in the barrel. "You've fought the good fight but—"

"Don't sweet talk me, I'm not sweet. I'm bitter. Bitter like this stupid place." *Bitter like busted glass,* she thought. She turned to Sunny. "Hold this!" She shoved into her sister's hands the fingernail file she had been using as a pry bar. "I'm going in." She hopped down to the next level and climbed down.

"Sweetie!" her dad called.

"Elizabeth Ann!" her mom yelled.

Lizzie scowled up at her mom, who quickly covered her own mouth. "Don't you ever use her full name," the Stick girl seethed, then disappeared into the jumbled darkness.

Serena thanked Lizzie for trying so hard. None of the permanent characters like Sticks or bumper-sticker folk—*The Cherished,* she called them—had ever tried to save a disposable character before.

"You're not disposable," Lizzie said into the darkness.

"Of course I am, honey, I'm cardboard. They threw me out like I was nothing. Not even good enough to recycle."

"But you are good enough. You are."

Serena gave a little laugh. "Child, you don't even know me. I might have been a champion once, but not tonight."

Lizzie sat there in the blackness and just let her talk. When Serena first got tossed in, she had hoped that county workers might separate out the recyclables. The yellow jackets told her the truth. They would dump her in a landfill, an endless mountain of slowly rotting filth.

"I have no regrets," the tennis woman said.

"Then you're a better person than me."

The two ran out of words. Lizzie touched the cereal box, trying to capture its texture, its feel. Or maybe the essence of the superstar. Finally she climbed out.

Halfway up, she reached out blindly for a handhold and touched a broken bottle. She drew her hand back with a gasp. Suddenly memories rushed at her: another dark night, a screech of tires, the scraping crash of metal against metal. Elizabeth's face colliding with the back windshield, her neck bent at an odd angle. A streak of light, a shard of glass. Excruciating pain across the Stick girl's leg. A much worse pain across her soul. Then red lights flashing on blank faces. People shouting. Lastly, Elizabeth's face disappearing beneath a white sheet.

By the time she reached the top of the barrel, Lizzie's tears had dried. Sunny alone greeted her.

"Mom led everyone back and went to get breakfast started. Don't know about you, but I'm starving."

The twins climbed down.

As the east grew gray, the two walked along the dirt road, saying nothing. No doubt, their mom would insist on grooming before going to sleep. Hours of speck removal. Sticks took stickiness seriously. The danger of being ripped from the windshield was too real. Lizzie had made a bunch of trips to the bottom of the trash barrel, so she was speckled with all kinds of nasty stuff. As she and her sister walked, she rubbed at her aching leg. *Funny,* she thought, *it didn't hurt all night.* She felt old and exhausted and sad. Sunny kept urging her to come on. Finally, Lizzie stopped and stared at the ground.

"You go on," she said. "I need a minute. Meet you there."

Sunny touched her shoulder, nodded. Lizzie listened as her sister's footsteps faded. *A woman is gonna die,* she thought, *and all they care about is eating and getting clean.*

Sixteen

As Lizzie inched past the campsites, birds awakened the dawn. She hoped their happy songs would drown out the inevitable rumble of a garbage truck. Instead, her ears picked up a much more subtle sound. Quiet crying. It sounded exactly like Elizabeth.

Spooked but curious, the Stick girl followed a narrow path that led from the dirt road into the piney forest. She had to walk farther than expected. Fatigue crept in. In addition to her throbbing leg, her back and shoulders ached; her forearms and calves burned; even her fingers trembled. As much as Lizzie wanted to hear Elizabeth's voice again, haunting sobs weren't what she had hoped for. And dead people don't cry, so, apparently, Lizzie had exhausted her brain, too.

As she rounded a bend, on a huge boulder sat—not Elizabeth—but Sophia, still in her pajamas, her face buried in her arms. *Because-I'm-so-sunny* Sophia. The perfect Mobile. Sobbing like someone had died. The Stick girl had no way of knowing that she had been doing this pretty much every day for over a year.

Lizzie watched for a long moment, long enough that she felt guilty for invading the other's privacy. Even though she had never bonded with this human—not like with Elizabeth—Sophia's sobs spoke to the deep grief that Lizzie carried all the time. She shook off a chill. *Whatever her problem is,* she thought, *can't be worse than getting crushed in a landfill.* She felt an urge to get tough. She would tell Sophia to stop all that blubbering, to get herself together. She pictured herself marching right up to that boulder and demanding that the thirteen-year-old help dig Serena out of the trash barrel. But she didn't.

The last time a human had seen life in Lizzie's eyes, that person had lost their own life. The Stick girl turned to leave. But before Lizzie could slip away, Sophia looked up, wiped her eyes, and noticed the bedraggled Stick person. Walking in the forest, not stuck to glass. The Mobile's eyebrows bunched up.

"Are you really there?"

Lizzie turned. "Nah, you're seeing things."

Sophia let out a bitter laugh. "Obviously."

Lizzie fought the urge to run. "Why—why are you crying?"

"Don't be nosey."

Lizzie waited.

Finally Sophia sighed and pointed down the path. "My family all hiked to the Overlook."

"The what?"

"It's a cliff." She looked down. "I just wanted to be alone."

Lizzie took a deep breath. "Too bad. I need your help."

Seventeen

Lizzie rode in Sophia's hands back to the trash barrel. She didn't care how much trouble she was about to cause. She had spoken to a Mobile and the world hadn't exploded. Now as they rushed back up the path, she said one word over and over. "Hurry!" A few minutes later, Sophia halted in front of the barrel.

"This doesn't make any sense," the girl said. "It's Saturday. Trash day is Monday."

"Not everywhere, genius, only in Vinylville."

"Where?"

"You know. Our neighborhood."

Sophia laughed. "Vinylville? That's what you call our neighborhood? Ha!"

"Look at me, soldier!" Lizzie commanded, sounding like her

mom. The other obeyed. "What do you see?"

"Uh, a sticker kid talking to me?"

"Exactly. Only I'm not a kid. I'm as old as you."

"Whatever."

"And you're expecting things to make sense?"

Sophia's metal-mouth hung open. Lizzie almost expected to see a little locomotive come chugging out from her molars.

She pointed to the trash barrel. "She's in there."

Sophia peeked in. "A whole woman in there? In that nasty stuff? Ew!"

"Stop yapping. It's a matter of life and death."

"A little dramatic, aren't you?"

"I wasn't the one boo-hooing in the woods."

Sophia pouted. "But that...yuk! I'll smell like garbage." She sniffed at Lizzie and wrinkled her nose. "Like you."

Lizzie couldn't make up her mind whether to frown or grin. Sophia was just like Sunny. Girlie. Prissy.

Sophia let out a heavy sigh, then she pulled out the cooler lid as if it were nothing. Lizzie watched it clatter to the ground. Her family and friends had spent over an hour trying to move the thing.

"Who's in there again?"

"I told you. My friend. Her name's Serena."

"Like the tennis star?" The Mobile stuck her head into the trash barrel. "Hello?" Then after a few seconds, "I don't hear anything."

"She's at the bottom," Lizzie said. "She was up all night, so she might be asleep. Plus who knows, you might not be able to talk to her at all."

"Is she invisible?"

"That's crazy."

"Well, girl, maybe I'm crazy. Only you don't get to call me that."

Lizzie wanted to scream. "Just dig. And don't call me a girl."

Sophia started to pull out a leaking trash bag, then stopped. "I have some gloves back at the tent. I'll run and get them. Only take a minute."

"We don't have a minute!" Lizzie yelled. "Just do it. I swear you're as bad as my sister!"

"Your sister!"

"Yes, you're exactly like Sunny. That's how it works."

"I'm like your sister?"

"Right, now just pull out the rest of the—"

"Oh, then that means you're like mine. Right?" Sophia gasped. "Oh, wait. Can you... *feel* her?"

Lizzie played dumb. "Feel who?"

It was Sophia's turn to look stern. "You know who."

These days, Lizzie couldn't feel much of anything, especially her lost Mobile. "Yes, yes, I feel Elizabeth all the time," she said. "We're one. We're BFFs. We talk, we chat, we're like this." She held up two fingers side by side. "And right now she's saying to EMPTY THE FREAKIN' TRASH!" She looked off into the distance. "Tell her what?" Lizzie asked nobody there. "Okay... good idea." She turned to Sophia. "Don't be such a priss-pants!"

"Oh-ma-god," Sophia gasped, "you sound just like her."

"I did? I mean, of course I did."

Now Sophia looked into the distance. "Oh-ma-god, oh-ma-god!"

"What?!"

"Did you hear that?"

For an instant, Lizzie had the freaky feeling that Sophia had actually heard her dead twin. Then, the Stick girl heard the rumble of a heavy truck, followed by the crashing sound of a trash barrel being emptied.

"It's here!" they both said. Sophia shoved Lizzie into her pajama pocket and began pulling trash from the barrel. For some reason, she named each item. "Water bottle, water bottle, stinking junk-food bag, Coke can, rope, more rope, trash bag. Oh, yuk, it's peeing!"

"It's what?"

"Leaking."

Just then the garbage truck appeared around a bend in the road.

"Can you see her?!" Lizzie called. She had climbed to the top of Sophia's pocket and was hanging over the edge.

"Not yet! What does she look like?"

"She's a tennis woman."

"Tennis woman?!"

The truck pulled up right beside them.

"We're too late!" Sophia cried.

"Tip it!"

"What?"

"Tip it over!"

"They'll be mad!"

"I don't care!"

A bearded man dropped from the back of the truck and moved toward them.

"I'm trying," Sophia groaned, "It's heavy!"

"Hey, what are you doing?" the man yelled. "Get away from there!"

"TIP IT, SOPH!"

The thirteen-year-old kicked the broken lawn chair, which clattered toward the worker. Then, she pushed with all her strength and spilled the contents of the barrel onto the ground.

The sanitation worker grabbed Sophia by the wrist.

"Let go of me!" she shouted. With her free arm, the girl slapped his face. Still, he didn't let go.

"What's wrong with you?" the man demanded. "Pick up that trash!"

So Sophia let out a scream, like something out from a horror movie. The truck driver stuck his head out of the window. The other worker dropped her wrist.

"There!" Lizzie shouted. "Grab that box!" Sophia bent over the garbage and grabbed an empty Tupperware container. "Not that one, the Wheaties box! Yeah, get it! YES! Now run!"

Like some feral shoplifter bolting from a supermarket, Sophia sprinted into the woods with the empty Wheaties box under her arm. The sanitation worker yelled something, but Lizzie, bouncing around in Sophia's pocket, didn't catch it.

Sophia headed back to the boulder. She pulled Lizzie from her pocket and set her on top, then set the cereal box beside her. "*This* is what you had me dig through garbage for? A Wheaties picture? What a joke! I smell like an ogre's armpit!"

"She doesn't mean it," Lizzie said to Serena. The cardboard woman stared, unblinking, at the tennis ball hovering in her photo. "She's really nice when she's not being a royal buttocks."

Sophia leaned against the rock. "I could have been arrested. I could have been injured. I was assaulted. Did you see that big, hairy dude grab me?"

Lizzie smiled. "Actually, you assaulted him. You were awesome."

Sophia went slack-jawed and Lizzie read her reaction. Lizzie's funny little crooked smile matched Elizabeth's.

"I need chocolate," the Mobile said.

"For breakfast?"

"Mom promised chocolate-chip pancakes when they get back from their hike." She saw Lizzie's quizzical look. "On the camp stove. Little ones."

"I missed dinner and breakfast," Lizzie said. "Trying to dig her out."

"For real?"

"You should've seen us. Even my family. They were almost cool. Anyway, we can't eat yet."

Sophia rubbed her face. "If I've finally gone nuts like my mom keeps saying, I'm not going there without chocolate. And I'm not going to let my imaginary stick friend tell me what to do."

Lizzie crossed her arms. "First of all, who said we were friends? Second, I might be the one imagining you. Third, I've already been telling you what to do. And fourth, watch your step. There's a Black Army outpost right under your foot."

"What? Where?"

"Right there. That anthill. That's the good army. Or I always thought so. The Red Army did us a solid last night. Anyway, calm down. Fifth, we have to free Serena from her box."

"Do you always count stuff like that?"

"Always."

"Interesting. And this chick," Sophia pointed at the tennis player frozen in mid-swing, "does she still even play tennis?"

"Don't say 'chick'. That's demeaning."

"Whatever."

"And how would I know? Cereal people have a long shelf life. Her box could have been sitting in a pantry for years."

"So how am I supposed to free her?"

"Your Swiss Army knife," Lizzie said.

"My—?" The other drew the knife from her pocket and stared at it. "How did you—?"

"Elizabeth gave it to you for your birthday." Their eyes met. Lizzie gave her a grin. "You carry it everywhere."

Careful not to break a nail, Sophia struggled to open the sawtooth blade of the knife. She complained the whole time as she cut out Serena's cardboard figure. Halfway done, she fished out her phone and took a selfie so she'd have proof that she hadn't imagined it all. Lizzie ducked behind her at the last second so she wouldn't be in the picture. Sophia also kept swatting at gnats, mostly missing them.

"When did you get so clumsy?" Lizzie asked.

"Watch it," Sophia replied, scratching her arm. "They're sneaky buggers. That's why they're called no-see-ums."

"Ha!" Lizzie said. "I can see um just fine. Must be because you're so big."

"Bite me, smarty pants."

Lizzie snapped her fingers. "Just work."

When Serena finally lay by herself on the boulder, Lizzie stared at her motionless form and wondered if the tennis woman had died after all. "Don't forget that." Lizzie pointed at the yellow tennis ball. As Sophia carefully carved it out, the Stick girl caught Serena glancing over. Finally, Sophia laid the cardboard ball on the boulder beside the little woman in her tennis skirt and bandana.

"There." She turned to Lizzie. "Satisfied?" She took another selfie, then checked her gallery of photos. "Hey! Why aren't you in any of these? Now nobody will believe me."

"Camera shy," Lizzie said.

"Right. I think you're just a weird thought bouncing around in my head."

Lizzie started to reply. But suddenly Serena sprang to her feet, flipped up the ball with her racket and the side of her shoe (that little flippy thing that tennis players do), caught it, and dove off the side of the boulder. Sophia gasped and jumped back. Lizzie erupted in laughter. Serena hit the ground, rolled a couple of times, and sprang to her feet. The ground didn't slow her momentum. With a high-pitched little victory *hoot* that sounded sort of like a songbird's call, she raced off into the forest.

Lizzie smirked at the Mobile girl and crossed her arms. "Told ya," she said.

Eighteen

Lizzie felt like a queen riding an elephant. With just a whisper into the Mobile's ear, she could be heard. And she wasn't used to that. Her family had stopped listening, until Lizzie had stopped trying to explain what she felt: awful, confusing emptiness. Sitting on Sophia's shoulder, holding onto her long, caramel hair, Lizzie now jabbered whatever popped into her head—favorite kinds of pickup trucks, obscure road signs, growling hood ornaments, cartoon characters on mud flaps—while a baffled Sophia tried to make sense of it.

They were almost within sight of the campsite, when Lizzie insisted Sophia put her down. The Mobile stopped, but made no effort to lower the Stick girl.

"Yo. Sophia. Bend down."

Sophia craned her neck to see Lizzie.

"Can't I just, like you know, think you down?"

"Uh... no. No magic here."

Sophia gently took Lizzie's hands and lowered her to the dirt. "So, you're trying to say that you're real? Really real?"

"Yeah, no." Lizzie considered how to answer. "I'm only real in your mind," she said. "I'm a coping mechanism. A way for you to process the grief of losing your sister."

"You are?" Sophia's underfed eyebrows bunched up.

How can they be so enormous, Lizzie wondered, *and yet so skinny?*

"Hey, wait a minute!" Sophia's look turned angry. "I know what you're doing! Elizabeth used to do the same thing." She squatted down until they were face to face. Because Sophia tried to hope for the best in people, people had often said that Elizabeth had been the smart twin and Sophia the dumb, pretty one. Even though they made nearly identical grades.

"Okay, okay, I'm real," Lizzie admitted. "It only feels like I'm walking in a waking nightmare." She pinched herself, a habit she had picked up from her Mobile. "Yep. But listen, this is important. You can't tell anyone about me. Or about the tennis woman, either. Your family would flip out and so would mine."

"You mean..." Sophia glanced at the rear end of Nico's Subaru and the unflinching face of Gandhi. "You mean there's more of you?"

Lizzie scowled. "Now that is a dumb question. What'd you

think, I was the only one?"

Sophia batted her lashes the way Sunny did sometimes. Lizzie wanted to jump up and pluck one of those suckers out. "Then, that means—" the Mobile said.

"Yeah. My sister and you are the same. She thinks like you, feels like you, whines like you. Lucky me. Now, I have two princesses to deal with."

Sophia broke into a big grin. "This is so exciting! I can't wait to meet her. I mean I know we've already met, technically, but now I can talk to her!"

"No. Absolutely not. You don't listen any better than Sunny."

"Sunny?"

"My sister."

"She goes by Sunny? Oh, that is soooooo cute!"

"Of course it is, you named her. Jeez, girl, listen!" Lizzie raised her voice enough that Gandhi peered over his spectacles. "You can't talk to her. You can't tell anyone. You have no idea how much trouble I'd be in."

Sophia knelt down. "But I mean, this is awesome."

"This isn't open for discussion, soldier!"

Sophia drew back. The Stick girl had done a perfect imitation of Sophia's mom. "Oh," she said. "Your mom is like..."

Lizzie grimaced. "Like yours. So you get it? I'd get raked over the coals." She glanced up at the smoke of a morning campfire drifting through the trees. "Not real coals. You know what I mean. Plus, no one tells. No one. As far as I know, no Stick person has ever spoken to a Mobile before."

"Spoken on a mobile?" Sophia asked. She whipped out her phone. "Well, of course, you haven't, it's too big for you."

"Not that thing. Mobiles are what we call big people."

"Mobiles." Sophia stood up to her full, ginormous height, crossed her arms, and twitched her mouth in a pout that Lizzie recognized all too well. "Well, okay, I guess."

"You guess?"

"I said okay."

"Not good enough," Lizzie said. "Do the thing."

"What thing?"

"The *thing*. You know, that thing with your little fingers—" Lizzie dropped her voice, "—that *y'all* used to do."

"Pinky promise? Okay." Sophia reached out a pinky finger and hooked it around what she thought was Lizzie's.

"Ow, you just about knocked my arm off."

Sophia widened her green eyes. "How did you know about that?" she asked. "Our pinky promise?"

"I know *everything*," Lizzie said. She leaned forward with one shoulder and squinted. It was what she and Sunny called their smoldering look.

It was Sophia's turn to see her sister in the face of another. She blew out a breath that sent her bangs flying. "Deja vu!"

Nineteen

Lizzie trudged into camp like a refugee. Part of it was an act—the part on her face. In truth, saving Serena felt more worthwhile than anything she could remember. She had forgotten to be sad and, for a moment, felt almost worthy to be alive. But she couldn't let her family see that. As far as they were concerned, the tennis woman had been crushed in a landslide of garbage. Lizzie should look devastated. Her ragged appearance certainly helped. And she felt more exhausted than a tailpipe.

She skirted the clearing where the Mobiles had arranged collapsible chairs and a ring of stones. Embers still smoldered there with the remains of last night's campfire. Instead, she made her way around to the back of the big, blue, dome tent. There, the Sticks had pitched a makeshift tent of their own—a

Harris Teeter grocery bag with six bent willow twigs as supports. An empty ring of pebbles marked a spot for the funny-fire that Lizzie had never delivered.

Ups saw her first. "Where've you been?" he whispered. "You missed breakfast."

A moment later, her dad carefully wrapped her in a hug—not an easy thing when one side of both people is sticky. "Lizzie-Lou," he said quietly. "I'm so sorry." At first she bristled. Since Elizabeth's death, she had become as cuddly as a cactus. Then she remembered her secret and tried to relax. She even tried to cry. They had to believe that she was sad. The thing was, most of the time she really was sad, only not right now. Somewhere in the woods, Serena Williams was running free.

Lizzie's mom came near and stroked her hair. Then, apparently unable to help herself, began redoing the Stick girl's pigtails. "We all tried so hard to save her," Mom said. "We're very proud of you. I want you to know that."

A few fake tears trickled out of Lizzie's eyes as she squeezed them shut. But then she shuddered for real as self-loathing reared its beastly head. The warm tears on her cheeks triggered a special cruelty that she saved just for herself. *If you could see inside me,* she thought, *you wouldn't be so proud.* Suddenly she really did need to cry, but clamped it down. Finally, the trio broke apart.

"Give me a hand," her mom said to her dad.

"Yes, dear." They began hanging up candy-wrapper blankets that had gotten damp with dew.

Ups dropped a dirty ball (a wadded-up scrap of aluminum foil) at Lizzie's feet. "Wanna throw the ball?" he asked. "That always cheers you up."

"No, dog breath, that always cheers you up. Move, you're drooling on me."

"I do not drool." Ups curled up by the bread bag tent and began chewing his ball.

The Stick girl plopped down on a number-two pencil that her parents had converted into a bench. "Where's the princess?"

"Sleeping," Mom said with a glance toward the tent. "Try not to be loud." Lizzie listened for a few seconds and heard delicate snoring.

Dad pointed to the styrofoam-cup table in front of her. "Have some breakfast. Beef jerky, cheese puff, and Goldfish for dessert!"

Lizzie yawned. "Fish for dessert?"

"We're saving the yellow Skittle for tonight. The Thompsons invited us over for a cookout."

Lizzie didn't bother to ask who he meant.

Ups stopped chewing the ball. "I saved you my Goldfish smile. But...then I ate it."

"Thanks for trying, dude." The Stick girl picked up a fragment of orange cracker. "So, I'm confused. Whose is this?"

"Sunny's," her dad said. "She saved it for you."

Lizzie examined *the snack that smiles back.* "What's wrong with it?"

"Nothing, silly."

"She was being nice," Mom put in. "Give her some credit."

"Uh huh." *She always gets credit.* The Stick girl nibbled at a flake of beef jerky, dropped it, and started on the cheese puff. "What's with the Thompsons?"

Ups pointed a paw toward Nico's campsite. "The hippie people."

"Yeah, I know." Lizzie frowned at an empty ring of pebbles. "They took our fire, didn't they?"

Dad said, "Of course not. I let them have it as thanks for helping. We're going to share it."

"Figures. And our light, too, apparently." To build funny-fire, the family usually wrapped a fire illustration around a teepee of twigs and illuminated it with an LED, powered by a watch battery. Lizzie began munching on Goldfish. "Did you know they're Featureless?"

"Yes, wow, what a surprise!" her dad answered. "Off Glass, they have more detail than us. Did you see their colors?"

"Colors, schmullers." Lizzie brushed Goldfish dust off her fingers. "Sleeping-bag time."

Mom looked up from the clothesline. "We have to groom you first."

"But Mom—"

"You have filth smeared all over, front and back. No stickiness to you at all. If I don't pluck all those specks, you'll be waving in the wind. No one in my platoon is coming unglued."

Lizzie's mood—grumpy but happy—shifted like a breeze. *I am filthy,* she thought. *I'm the worst person in the world.* She had never endured a picking like the one her mom gave her this morning. Speck by speck, Mom gouged out the larger pieces with a toothpick. Then she used a glass sliver—from the same headlight that had injured Lizzie's leg—which the Stick mom kept in a pouch in her pocket. Once the girl's sticky side was clear, Mom scrubbed her front with water and a scrap of napkin.

Finally, Lizzie crawled into the grocery-bag tent. As she shimmied into her oak-leaf sleeping bag, she noticed a single pin of sunlight in the ceiling. She stared at its luminous beam as it crossed her leg. At last her eyes closed. That's when Sunny sat up.

"Morning, sis," her twin chirped.

"Mmm."

"Gosh, I slept well. Crazy dreams, though."

Lizzie could hear her, but her eyes were on strike.

"Mmm."

"Did you get the Goldfish I saved you? Did you smile back?"

Lizzie didn't answer. *If I lay still, she'll go shower someone else with sunshine.*

"I'm really sorry we couldn't save the Cheerios woman."

Wheaties, Lizzie thought. She rolled away so Sunny couldn't see the grin spreading in a crooked line across her face. *And I did save her. So there.* Then she felt Sunny's breath and smelled some kind of flower her sister had used as cologne.

"You tried something no one else had the guts to do," Sunny whispered. "No one *ever.* Least of all me." Lizzie felt a light kiss on her forehead. "You're my hero."

No other words could have cut as deep as that. *I'm no hero,* Lizzie thought, *I'm a freak.*

Twenty

Saturday Evening

When Lizzie stumbled out of the tent, she thought it was the morning of the next day. But the light of the setting sun looked all wrong. It seemed like time had sped up.

As her family got ready to visit the next-door neighbors, Lizzie said she didn't want to go. Her parents overruled her. "It's the least we can do," her dad said. "They helped with the rescue mission last night."

"The failed rescue mission," Lizzie said. "And fancy-face boy had to guilt his moms into it."

"Nico," Sunny repeated to no one in particular.

"Be nice to them," Mom said.

Lizzie blew out a sigh. *I'm gonna get our fire back,* she

thought. *I'm the one who found it.*

Nico's campsite was different from Lizzie's. Instead of a tent made from a grocery bag, the big family had built a long rambling hut out of twigs, leaves, and pine needles. Mavis, the more talkative of the two moms, gave the Chapman Sticks the grand tour. Their hut had twelve chambers. Each bedroom featured a window made from a Jolly Rancher wrapper that could roll up like a window shade. While Mom and Dad marveled at the pantry, Lizzie slipped outside.

"I thought you might try to escape," Nico said as she came out.

Lizzie studied the ground. "Big groups of people make me nervous."

"Ha! Yeah. M can talk the bark off a tree."

"M? That's what you call your mom?"

He shrugged. "Short for Mavis."

"Right. My mom would strip my glue if I called her by her name."

"Strip your glue. Good one," the boy said. He laughed, then quickly covered his smile with a hand.

"Hey." Lizzie pulled his hand down. "Why are you doing that?"

"Doing what?"

"Hiding your smile."

"My—what?"

"Don't hide your smile," Lizzie said.

"Says the girl who almost never smiles."

Lizzie crossed her arms. "I smile plenty. Except mine looks terrible. Like a crack in a sidewalk." Then, under her breath, "Compared to Sunny's."

Nico shook his head. "Not true. Your smile reminds me of a new moon. You know, that skinny-mini, crescent moon that floats in the sky at an angle?"

"Whatever." Lizzie twisted her mouth into a definite not-smile. "Still, you shouldn't put your hand up like that, not unless you're chewing food. Your smile is...pretty."

"Did you just call me pretty? Dude, I'm a dude."

"So? Dudes can be pretty."

Nico shrugged.

"Plus you just called me a dude," Lizzie added.

"Did I?" He narrowed his blue eyes. Lizzie looked skyward to avoid them. They were dazzling and she didn't care to be dazzled.

"Whoa!" she said and pointed up.

Nico looked up. "Double whoa."

"Way more stars than in Vinylville," Lizzie said.

"What-ville?"

"Nothing. Just our stupid neighborhood."

"Oh yeah? What's so stupid?"

"You know. Houses all look the same. Vinyl siding." She

looked up at the sky again to avoid those piercing eyes. She could still feel them as he spoke.

"Our Mobiles live in an apartment, Nico grunted. "They say the walls are made of paper." He turned his eyes to the stars again and Lizzie felt relief to know he was staring at something besides her. "I don't see how the place doesn't fall apart when it rains."

They stared upward in silence for a moment, then Lizzie shook her head and gave a grin. "Paper thin. It means you can hear through the walls."

"Oh," Nico said. He tilted his head. "What's wrong with that? We can hear through the windshield."

Lizzie shrugged, "Mobiles are weird."

"Mine sure is. How about yours?" When she didn't answer, he tried again. "Your Mobile's weird too, right?"

Lizzie bit her lower lip to keep it from trembling. "Was."

"Wa—" The question "Was?" didn't even make it out of the boy's mouth before he caught himself.

The Stick girl looked at the other. "Elizabeth was her name. She was weird in all the right ways," she said.

"Elizabeth," Nico repeated, holding Lizzie's gaze. "That's a pretty name."

Lizzie nodded. They both found other things to look at for a while. Soon they heard their families' conversation just on the other side of the hut door.

"You wanna go for a walk?" Nico asked.

"With you?"

He looked over each of his shoulders and nodded. "Duh."

"Don't take this wrong," Lizzie said, beginning to fidget, "but you're not my type."

"It's just a walk."

"Don't you have to ask permission?"

"You kidding?"

Lizzie glanced back at the door as she followed Nico from the campsite. When she passed a matchbox table where dinner was laid out, she broke off a chunk of Skittle. Then, the door squeaked open behind her and she ran for it.

Twenty-one

Saturday Night

Lizzie joined Nico behind a rock. "I thought you were right behind me," he said.

She held up the chunk of yellow Skittle. "A dude's gotta eat,"

"You rock," he said.

She punched him on the shoulder.

Nico raised one eyebrow then looked away into the distance. "This whole place is, like, Disney World or something."

Lizzie closed her eyes and tried to remember her family's Disney trip. She shivered as she recalled the feelings that Elizabeth had experienced on the thrill rides. She saw fireworks and heard the crowd. Lizzie and her Mobile had been so connected that while the Stick girl's body had been stuck in a parking lot, her spirit had soared with Elizabeth's. Now as she opened her eyes, the warm memory faded. In its place came the coldness that she seemed to always carry these days.

"I hear there's a waterfall," Nico said. "I've never seen one."

"There's two," Lizzie said. "The Chapmans camped here one other time. It's a *really* long trail."

"You actually got to see it?"

She shook her head. "Believe it or not, my mom was even more neurotic back then."

Nico jumped up. "Let's go explore," he said and tramped off into the woods. Lizzie watched him for a few seconds, then peeked around the rock toward the campsite. Her family and his had settled into chairs around the funny-fire. Lizzie didn't like the idea of following anyone. Much less following a boy and into the dark. But this time she did.

As they hiked, Nico talked about deep things, silly things, anything. *He likes the sound of his own voice,* Lizzie thought. They wound up looking up at the trash barrel where they had worked the night before. None of the crowd were there.

"Where'd they go?" Nico asked.

"No garbage, no pickings," Lizzie replied.

"Hm."

At an empty campsite, the two climbed atop a picnic table. Nico began doing a little Tai Chi.

"Whoever camped here last must've had a huge campfire,"

Lizzie said. She stared at a scorched place on the ground. Anything not to have to watch the Stick boy show off.

Nico switched to break dancing. Lizzie, out of other things to look at, watched him. Finally, her curiosity won out. "Where'd you learn that stuff?" she asked. "You make it up?"

Nico grinned. "Our Walk/Don't Walk person showed me."

"Your what?"

"The person at the crosswalk on the way to Joaquin's school."

"Who?"

"My Mobile's name is Joaquin. But I learned Tai Chi from our Walk/Don't Walk man. Or woman. Whatever they are."

"You learned martial arts from a crossing guard?"

Nico scratched his head. "I'm talking about the person on the post. You know? The lighted sign that tells people when they can go?"

Lizzie wrinkled her nose. "We call those guys the Electric Dot Man."

"Yeah, that's him. He's wild. Sometimes, he dances. You should see him do the moonwalk. The kids love it."

"Wait. He does this stuff in front of Mobiles?"

"Just for little kids."

"And he doesn't get caught?

"Well, sometimes a parent will see him and walk up and look real close. So he just flickers on and off and makes a buzzing sound. The grown-ups figure he's broken."

She grinned. "Smart. What about the hand that says it's time to stop?"

Nico shrugged. "They can talk in sign-language ABC's. But usually we just get a thumbs-up."

Just then, a firefly flew up and hovered. "I see you're doing better than I did tonight," he said with a wink at Nico.

"What? Oh, uh, no," the boy stammered. "We're just friends."

The firefly flew in the shape of a heart over their heads. "Love is in the air," he said. He and his glow-in-the-dark buddies were obsessed with finding a girlfriend. "I'm D.J. That's short for Don Juan," said the flier. His soft, greenish light pulsed on and off.

"Hi," the Stick boy said. "I'm Nico."

Lizzie hoped they wouldn't start talking about girlfriends again. She handed Nico the chunk of Skittle. "Hold this," she said. Then she tied off the hem of her skirt, did a handstand, and walked around in a circle upside-down. When she popped back to her feet, both the Stick boy and the firefly applauded.

"Not bad," said Nico.

"I used to do handsprings," she said. She looked down at her bad leg. *Before the accident.*

Nico looked in her face until she met his eyes. "And I was beginning to think you had no talent at all," he said. He punched her gently in the arm.

"Jerk," she said and punched him back, but harder. That was when Lizzie decided he *might* be okay.

Although Lizzie's afternoon nap had refreshed her, her muscles felt sore from last night's work at the barrel. Also, the diagonal tear in her right leg had begun to throb. In truth, it hurt all the time. She never admitted it, not even to Sunny. She figured if she ignored her pain it would go away.

This approach had not worked with her leg or with her heart.

Lizzie and Nico said goodbye and good luck to the firefly, then climbed down from the picnic table. They walked down the dirt road, then found a path. They took it without saying a word. Here, the forest on either side was carpeted with pine needles. It was easy walking. The trees were spaced far enough apart that the risen moon bathed the ground in light. Nico found a stick for a staff and walked along, jabbing it in the ground with every other step.

"You look like a shepherd," Lizzie said.

Nico chuckled. "If I'm a shepherd, that makes you a sheep."

"Haha, you're not funny," she said, but her crooked smirk played on her face. They continued down the path in silence until, finally, Lizzie said, *"Baahh!"*

Nico glanced at her. *"Baahh!"* he said.

For the next few minutes as they walked in the moonlight,

they spoke in one-word sheep sentences and barely-contained laughs. Finally, Nico stopped and pointed.

"What's that?" he said. He sounded serious.

"What? Where?"

"Shhh." He lowered his voice. "Could that be a, you know... bear?

"It better not be. Where?"

"Right there. Where I'm pointing."

Lizzie shook her finger. "If you're trying to scare me—"

"No, look."

Then Lizzie saw. And from this angle in this light it might have been a bear hunched over and eating. She snorted a laugh. "I know what that is," she said, and strode forward. Nico followed. When the two of them finally stood in the shadow of the boulder, he couldn't hide his embarrassment. He had mistaken a lump of granite for a large carnivore.

"So, let's climb this bear," Lizzie said. With a bad leg, no Sophia to help her, and carrying the Skittle, this proved quite a chore. Near the top, Lizzie let Nico give her a hand. He hadn't said anything else about her limp.

"Wow," he said, as they peered over what to them was a cliff.

Lizzie broke off a chunk of Skittle and held it out. "Hungry?"

"Really? You're lucky I haven't already bopped you over the head with my staff and stolen that thing."

"You're lucky you didn't try," she said. "Here. Taste the

rainbow." They ate without talking.

As they climbed down, Nico halted and asked, "Where'd that come from?" The Stick boy pointed at a Wheaties box with a hole in it the shape of a woman.

Lizzie opened her mouth to lie, but Nico's trusting look stopped her. So she told him the truth, all of it: tipping over the barrel, finding Sophia here at the boulder, lying to her family. When she was done, he just stood staring into the woods.

"So Serena didn't get taken with the trash?" He swallowed and blinked. Lizzie knew that meant he had a lump in his throat. "And you really spoke to a Mobile. That's incredible, that's—"

"A secret."

Nico nodded. "Not a word."

Back at the Thompsons' campsite, the families met Lizzie and Nico with barely a comment. Mom kept giving Lizzie looks, but not like she was in trouble. More like she thought Lizzie and Nico were boyfriend-girlfriend and she liked the idea. The dirty looks came from Sunny.

Mavis loaded up both teenagers with plates of food and they ate. Lizzie could feel her muscles warning that a day or two of soreness was on the way. She stared at the funny-fire in the middle of a pebble circle and tried not to think about how she could be in trouble if Nico didn't stay quiet.

The company was good, if a bit awkward because of their

differences. The Thompsons had a more laid-back approach to life. Every one of them was musically inclined. One of the moms, Thoma, played a dental floss guitar. Darwin, the lizard creature, showed remarkable talent on a xylophone made of hairpins. Hello Kitty blew single notes from a didgeridoo fashioned from the barrel of a Bic pen. Mother Earth danced all around the circle, shaking both her bottom and a tambourine that had once been an earring, while her baby animals danced at her feet. The peace-sign hand, Ringo, snapped his fingers, providing a perfect beat. And Mavis sang. That short little Stick woman sang like the stars above had filled her lungs. The two St. Louis Cardinals piped along with backing vocals and flew in and out of the campsite.

Nico cleared the floor with some surprisingly good break-dancing. Lizzie noticed her mom's shocked expression at the site of a Stick intentionally getting down in the dirt. But when the boy popped up with a handspring and the others continued dancing, he didn't appear to have picked up many flecks of debris. Mavis coaxed Dad to his feet for an unsightly but enthusiastic dance. Mom remained firmly planted in her chair until the Conga line got going.

As the line grew, everyone got pulled out of their chairs and into the dance, except for Ringo the hand, who still kept the beat, and Darwin kept playing those keys. Somehow, Lizzie ended up behind Thoma, the taller and quieter of Nico's moms.

Lizzie just about jumped out of her skin when she felt Nico's hands on her waist. She glanced back.

"I'm not getting frisky," he said. "Promise. It's just a dance."

Behind him, Sunny glared at her. Lizzie turned to the front and tried her best just to get through the dance. She wasn't completely lacking in rhythm, but every bounce made her right leg throb. At one point, she stubbed her toe against a stray pebble. That made her hobble worse.

If Nico's hands are on my waist, that means Sunny's hands are on his.

"I can help you with that, you know."

Lizzie snapped out of her thoughts. The voice had come from Thoma, the tall Stick mom in front of her in the Conga line.

"What? No, I just stubbed my toe," Lizzie said.

"I don't mean that," Thoma said. "I mean that." She nodded toward Lizzie's right leg.

"What do you mean?" Lizzie meant it as a question but it sounded more like a demand.

"How do you think we built our hut?" the tall woman asked.

Lizzie hesitated. "I dunno, pine sap? But you're not putting that nasty stuff on my leg. Melts all over everything."

"Not pine, magnolia," Thoma said, looking over her shoulder. "Magnolia sap is better, lasts longer. It's not a perfect fix, but I've seen it do wonders for injuries like yours." And she turned forward.

Lizzie finished the dance in a daze. The idea that she might walk normally again? She was afraid to believe it.

When the circle of dancers fell to the ground or into their chairs, Lizzie staggered, vaguely aware that the music had stopped. Whether by accident or because she unknowingly wanted to, she bumped into Nico.

"You okay?" he asked. Lizzie looked up and saw him standing with Sunny.

"I'm fine," Lizzie said. "It's just, your mom, the tall one—"

"Thoma? I call her Tee."

"Right, her. She just said something that blew my mind."

"Of course, she did," Nico laughed. It was genuine, but a little awkward. Maybe because Sunny was standing there with him? He glanced at her, then looked at Lizzie. "Welcome to my world," he said.

Twenty-two

Sunday Morning

After her mom's fifth attempt to rouse her, Lizzie wriggled from her sleeping bag and hobbled out of the tent. She collapsed, next to Sunny, onto the pencil-bench in front of the empty ring of pebbles. "Morning, sis!" her sister chirped. "Whoa, you look like, well, not great."

Lizzie squinted in the morning light. "Not all of us are morning people," she said. "I'm just sore. And hungry. Anything to eat?" Their mom, bustling around the campsite doing productive stuff, pointed to their table, the one she had made from the bottom half of a styrofoam coffee cup. Next to a pebble centerpiece, which kept the table from blowing away, sat an acorn. "Oh no," the Stick girl said. "I'm not touching that." She remembered eating an acorn, as bitter as a moth's wing, on their last camping trip.

"You were really dead asleep," Ups said, from where he lay on the ground. He gave a vivid impression of Lizzie's snoring. The groggy twin cast the stink-eye at the dog.

"Where's Dad?" she asked.

"Looking for something edible," Sunny said. She patted the acorn. "We hope."

While they waited, her mom and sister and dog gossiped about the Featureless family next door. Mom called them odd. Sunny preferred *exotic*. Ups was just confused as to why there wasn't a Stick dog with them.

Sure, they're weird, Lizzie thought, *but in a nice way.*

Tired of waiting for Dad, Mom fished out a small jar of pollen dust she had been saving. She mixed it with a dewdrop and made what southern Sticks call "cold grits." As with most Stick meals, they ate only a tiny amount—not enough pollen to sneeze at—but it filled them up.

Then Mom declared, "It's too fine a day to waste. The best thing for sore muscles—" She pulled Lizzie to her feet. "Is a brisk hike."

"Aw, c'mon, Sarge—" Lizzie began.

"Don't start that, Lazy Bones."

"But Sergeant Mom—"

"It's Mom or Mother, take your pick."

"Very well. Mother. And don't call me lazy."

"Then don't *be* lazy. Be Lizzie."

"As if."

"And what's that supposed to mean?"

Lizzie blew her hair out of her face. "Nothing."

As they marched through the woods, Lizzie's sore calves did feel a little better, although she wasn't about to admit it. The gash in her leg, however, soon started throbbing. Before long, she shuffled like an old woman.

"My leg hurts," she grumbled.

"Your leg always hurts," Sunny replied.

"And you're trying to steal my friend."

"Nico?" Sunny said with a grin she couldn't hide. "He's cute."

"I met him first. You can't have him."

"You have a friend?" Ups asked.

"Stuff it, runt," Lizzie shot back.

"Keep up, Lazy Bones," Mom called from up front. "You'll get attacked by a pirate."

"Jeez, Mom," Lizzie sighed, "they live on boats. We're in the woods."

Sunny returned to her new favorite subject. "I should get to be friends with Nico, too," she said. "You owe me. I helped you try to save that dead woman."

Lizzie stopped and looked down as her hands began to shake.

Sunny looked back and then stopped, too. "Sorry. I mean tennis woman."

"Yeah, you helped. Some." They continued walking. "Who says she's gone, anyway? Maybe the garbage truck drove right by and forgot to empty that one."

"Liz, dude," Ups said, shaking his head. "Get real."

Lizzie switched to her preferred mode of conversation: silence. She listened to her sister pepper their mom with questions: Where were they going? How long was this going to take? Were they marching in a big circle? The march went on and on. The sun climbed into the treetops and the chilly morning dampness vanished.

What's Sophia's school like? Lizzie wondered. *Will she tell her friend Holly about me? Will she go looking for Serena? Does she* like *me?*

She pictured the moment when she had realized that the trash in the barrel was too big for her rescue party to move. She had been pulling on the plastic lid of a soda cup and couldn't budge it. It had taken her and a platoon of red ants to pull the lid from the barrel. Lizzie had despised her weakness at that moment. Now, as they made their way back to the campsite, Lizzie swore that she was done being weak. She would never need anyone again.

Soon, they emerged into a clearing, but not the one with their tent. It was Nico's campsite. In front of the primitive hut,

Mavis, Thoma, and the Stick boy stooped over something. Seeing Lizzie and her family, the three rose to their feet.

"Namaste," said Mavis. She clasped her hands together.

"Namaste," Thoma and Nico repeated.

"No, we must not stay," said Mom, misunderstanding. She pointed back at the woods. "I just miscalculated our exit point."

"Whatcha doin'?" Sunny asked. She pointed at an arrangement of pebbles on the ground.

"Making a sundial," Mavis said.

"A mini Stonehenge," Nico added.

"Oooh, show me!" Sunny squealed.

The pebbles did indeed resemble the ancient formation in Scotland. The Chapman Sticks recognized it from a "Wonders of the World" book that the Mobile twins used to carry in the car.

"This is the coolest thing ever!" Sunny gushed.

"Here," Nico said. He bent down and picked up a robin feather and handed it to Lizzie's sister. "You can put on the gnomon."

"The what?" Sunny asked.

"It's the shadow-casting part," Nico said.

Together, she and Nico wedged it in the rocks.

"Gnomon," Sunny repeated. Her voice sounded like someone playing a flute in a dream, annoying Lizzie more than usual.

"Hypothetically functional, but you built it in partial shade," Mom said to Nico's moms. She glanced at her own wrist as though she was wearing a watch. "Well, we're on a schedule. Troops!" And she marched her family away.

"Come back after lunch," Mavis called. "We're making moccasins."

"Sounds fun!" Sunny called back.

It looked to Lizzie like her sister practically skipped away. "Keep moving," she said and poked Sunny in the back.

Before they crossed the narrow, wooded boundary between the two campsites, Lizzie, last in line and limping, glanced back. Nico met her eyes, smiled, and waved. When Lizzie didn't wave back, he got a confused look on his face. Then from behind him, Thoma appeared. The tall mom pointed at Lizzie's leg and nodded, as if the girl would know what she meant. And Lizzie did know. She knew with every step.

Twenty-three

Sunday Afternoon

Lizzie and her sister trekked over to their neighbors' campsite.

"Today, we're gonna make moccasins," Thoma declared.

"Yes!" Nico pumped a fist.

"We're gonna *make snakes?*" Lizzie asked, knowing better.

"Not that kind of moccasins," Mavis laughed. "They're soft shoes made of leather. We used to make them when we were kids." In truth, childhood was a fuzzy feeling the woman had inherited from her Mobile. "We use rhododendron leaves," she added.

"Leather is a crime against bovines," Nico explained, walking over between the twins.

Lizzie leaned over to him. "Guess that's a big no for bacon, too, eh?" He just flashed a smile in response.

According to Mavis, vines were either too thick or too weak to sew moccasins. Fishing string would have been perfect, but opening a tackle box for Stick people is like trying to pull the roof off of a school bus. Instead, they planned to use threads from the hem of a pair of cut-off jeans—ones belonging to Nico's Mobile, Joaquin—which hung from a clothesline.

The two Stick women watched as their son and his new friends tip-toed along the cord, plucked the threads, and let them drop to the ground. To distract the humans, Daisy, the golden retriever, barked at absolutely nothing on the opposite side of the campsite.

When the three Sticks climbed down, Sunny did a gymnastics-style jump and landed with her arms spread in a wide V. Seeing this, Lizzie hopped down, too, but her leg buckled and she had to plant her hands on the grass. Sunny and Nico both reached to help her up.

"Get off!" she growled. They backed off.

Next, the group hiked about a hundred yards to gather leaves. For Sticks, it was like a couple of miles, or as Mavis said, "About a Starbucks away."

During the hike, Lizzie lagged behind, limping. When they finally reached the tree, Nico turned to his taller mom and asked, "Why did we hike all the way here? Why this tree? We passed a whole stand of rhododendrons already?" Lizzie heard irritation in his voice—the first time she had heard a hint of rebellion.

"Rhododendron moccasins are good," Thoma explained, "but I prefer magnolia. They last longer."

"Mags put blisters on my feet," Nico argued. "I'm gonna go get the others." He turned and strode back toward the campsites.

Sunny watched him for a second then said, "Me, too!" and followed.

Lizzie now recalled something the women had said about magnolia sap, that it had healing properties, whatever. "We didn't come all this way for shoes, did we?" she asked.

"I prefer the thick moccasins," Thoma replied.

"As do I," Mavis agreed. "But as long as we're here, we might as well harvest a little sap, too, just for emergencies."

Resentment rose up in Lizzie. *How dare they?* she thought. She didn't want help, didn't want to owe anyone a favor. But she got over it quickly. These women weren't ordering or insisting, like her mom usually did. They were offering. And so the Stick girl helped them pick tiny magnolia leaves near the bottom of the tree. The women then bored a hole in the trunk with a computer screw that Thoma pulled from a pocket. Lizzie studied their work as they gathered sap with the top of an acorn shell.

As they hiked back, she asked them questions about birds they saw. She listened to the story of how Thoma and Mavis's Mobiles had met at a bonfire on the beach. She asked what it was like to be an Insider and Featureless, though she didn't use that word. They answered every question patiently, speaking to her like she was a grown-up. No guilt trips, nothing about chores. No comparisons to her sister. By the time Lizzie, Mavis, and Thoma entered the clearing behind the giant orange-and-yellow tent, the girl was certain that neither of these women would ever put her in harm's way. She might even let them doctor her torn leg with their funky home remedy.

Lizzie was in a good mood as she made moccasins with the group. Her sister and Nico stood shoulder to shoulder as they worked, but it didn't bother her so much. At sunset, they all high-stepped around the campsite in their shiny green kicks, which squeaked like new shoes.

That night, as the girls slipped into their oak-leaf sleeping bags, Lizzie whispered something to Sunny that would forever change their lives.

"My surgery's in the morning."

Twenty-four

As Lizzie watched her family eat breakfast at their styrofoam-cup table, Thoma sat with them. Sunny had blabbed that the tall Stick was going to patch Lizzie with a Band-Aid or something.

"Magnolia sap is the best for patching and repairing injuries," Thoma explained. "I've heard that rubber tree sap lasts longer, but it's much too thick and they don't grow around here, anyway."

"We've patched folk with it before," Mavis added, walking up. "Take a look—" She held out her arm. Lizzie's family closed in around the short woman for a better look. Lizzie had seen Mavis' elbow scar on the way back from harvesting the sap. A star-shaped light-brown patch, not quite the color of Mavis herself, marked the spot where an injury had once been.

"What did you use for the patch?" Lizzie's mom asked.

"A gold star," Thoma answered, "the kind a kindergarten teacher puts on a kid's schoolwork."

"I left it gold for a while," Mavis added, "but finally colored it in—close to skin tone as possible."

"I never even noticed it," Mom said.

"The sticky on the back of the star won't hold by itself?" Dad asked.

"Right." Mavis answered. "The magnolia sap helps it to stick *and* seals it. The sticker doesn't wear off as fast."

"You're gonna put gold stars on Sissy's leg?" Ups asked. Lizzie looked at the dog and felt a lump in her throat. *He hasn't called me Sissy in ages.*

Thoma shook her head. "Lizzie's injury is too big for stars. We have a strip that came off of Gandhi's bumper sticker a few weeks ago. We've been hiding it in the Subaru until we had a chance to repair him. But when he heard about your leg—" She glanced at Mavis, then at Lizzie. "He insisted we use it to patch you up."

The girl bit her lip.

"Tell him thank you for us," Mom said.

"Tell him yourselves," Mavis said. "He can't leave the bumper and could always use company." Dad and Mom both nodded.

"I'll tell him," Lizzie said. Then her colorless black eyes bore into Thoma's blue ones. "Are you gonna put me to sleep?"

"Yes," Thoma said, "You can't be moving around while I'm working. And I won't lie to you, it's going to hurt. The main thing—this is very important—you'll have to stay off your feet for a full twenty-four hours. It takes that long for the sap to set."

"Set?" Lizzie asked.

"To dry."

Lizzie nodded. She looked over at Sunny, then to Nico's moms. She didn't like the idea of being laid out on a table like a science experiment in front of a bunch of people. "Is everybody gonna watch?"

Thoma answered. "It'll just be you, me, and Mavis." She shot a look at Mom. "There's not much room in the hut and I don't need distractions."

"Nico's out gathering ivy," Mavis said. "Mobiles call it poison ivy. That's what we use for anesthetic. To put her to sleep."

Ups tilted his head to the side. "To put her to sleep,'" he repeated. "Not sure why, but I don't like the sound of that."

Lizzie looked at the dog and saw that his tail had become still. It just now occurred to her that she might never wake up. *Like Elizabeth,* she thought. *Would we be together? Or just gone?*

Twenty-five

Nico's moms had cleared out one of the rooms in their makeshift home, and had added a skylight to brighten it. Like other rooms in the multi-roomed hut, the windows had been covered with Jolly Rancher wrappers. For an operating table, they had built a raised bed out of rocks and reeds. Lizzie lay down and rested her head on a cotton ball pillow. *Ah,* she thought, *I need one of these for my sleeping bag.*

Through the skylight above her, treetops stretched toward a cloudless sky. Nico entered and laid a pile of ivy in a corner. As he passed the operating table, he gave her a thumbs-up. Mavis and Thoma appeared on either side, wearing makeshift surgical masks and gloves. Lizzie stirred, trying to get comfortable.

"Relax," Mavis said. "You're gonna be good as grits."

Grits. Lizzie rubbed her stomach. "I'm hungry."

Thoma finger-brushed hair out of the girl's eyes. "Good. That means we won't have to wear your breakfast." That brought a grin to Lizzie's face.

Nico, now masked and gloved and holding some of the ivy, moved into view. Lizzie's eyes darted to Thoma. "I thought you said there was only room for you and Mavis." She pointed a thumb at Nico.

"You want your mom in here, instead?" Thoma asked. The girl shook her head. "Well, all right, then." The tall woman took a single ivy leaf from her son and brushed it across Lizzie's face. A white haze passed across her eyes—like looking through her adhesive side. A few seconds later a tingling sensation swept over her face. Then numbness spread from her head to her feet.

"Wow, I didn't know you could smile like that!" Nico said. Thoma motioned with her head for him to step back. He disappeared from view, as did Mavis.

"How do you feel—do you feel?" Thoma asked.

Lizzie searched the ceiling with her eyes. "Fuzzy—uzzy—uzzy." Her voice sounded like when she and Sonny used to hide in a Campbell's soup can.

"Good—ood."

The sounds of the Chapman family campsite drifted into Lizzie's hearing: Sophia's parents talking, laughing, rattling tin cups.

She yawned and tried to keep her eyes open. The room bent sideways. *Nico's family never asked how I hurt my leg. Did Sunny tell them about the wreck?* Or maybe they knew without being told. Anyone could see the crack in the back windshield, and that there were two Stick girls but only one Mobile one.

Above her mask, Thoma's grey-blue eyes stared down. "This big tear on your leg—it was from glass, right?" she whispered.

Lizzie tried to nod but couldn't tell if she really did. "Uh huh."

"But not just that one time, was it? It's been torn over and over."

Even in her fog, Lizzie understood that Thoma knew about one of the things the Stick girl kept hidden. She tried to reply, but her tongue got lost. Thoma leaned close, put an ear next to the girl's mouth. She could see through the gauze mask to the pores on the other's skin. Such detail for a Featureless person!

I can see through the mask and she can see through me.

"I found a rock," Lizzie whispered back. Using a piece of quartz, the girl had scratched at the slice on her leg until it became an ugly, jagged tear. It showed how she felt inside. Torn. Looking into Thoma's eyes now, she wasn't sure that either of them had whispered anything at all, but she saw compassion.

As the echoes all faded and sleep overtook her, Lizzie desperately missed the human girl with kind green eyes and a crooked smile. She missed running, missed not hurting. Missed feeling whole. She missed the days when she didn't cover her smile with her hand, or with a scowl.

If I could run again, she thought, *I'd never stop. I'd run so far no one would ever find me.*

The room smeared; swaths of white filled her vision, as if some giant with a pencil had erased her.

Twenty-six

Monday Afternoon

Lizzie's bad leg stuck to anything that touched it: her bedding, her hands, the doorway to her tent, even to motes of dust. She soon bored of lying in the tent, and relocated to a spot in front of the dormant funny-fire. There she sat in a chair made from a bubble-gum wrapper—like a fold-up canvas chair that a Mobile might use—with her foot propped up on a twig shaped like the letter Y. If she moved around, the sap might sag or drip. The patch might peel off. Lizzie faced twenty-four hours of sitting still and avoiding dust. Doing nothing.

She heard whispers and turned to see the rest of her family huddled together. They quickly disbanded, each one giving her a thumbs-up or a little wave. Then one by one, they sneaked away toward Nico's campsite. *Wouldn't you know it,* Lizzie thought. *All this time I've been trying to ditch them. Now, they're ditching me.*

Alone, she shifted uncomfortably in the chair and adjusted her foot in the Y. From the angle of light slanting through the forest, she figured it must be afternoon. As the sun inched its way lower, a column of sunlight fell across the Stick girl's leg, like a spotlight focusing on her handicap and hope, and illuminating a nano world of dust. Armed with a pink wildflower petal that Sunny had given her for a fan, Lizzie tried to shoo it away, but only managed to stir it into chaos.

She stared at the darkened funny-fire that she had found at the trash barrel. She examined the petal. *Silly pink flower.*

Laughter echoed from the campsite next door. Sunny, Nico, her parents, and Ups must be having a good time. Probably Mother Earth and her baby animals were joining in, too. Lizzie watched as the two Louisville Cardinals streaked by overhead, headed in the same direction.

Maybe my limp won't be so bad. It was a lot to hope for. Hope didn't exactly shoot from Lizzie's fingertips these days. She hadn't thanked Thoma and Mavis, or Gandhi, who had given up a sliver of his bumper sticker for her patch.

In front of Lizzie loomed the Chapman's tent. The massive, blue dome reminded her of Stone Mountain, an incredible hunk of granite near Atlanta. She had glimpsed it from the Interstate on a trip. You could see it for miles. *Funny,* she thought, *the boulder where I met Sophia, the one where we freed Serena, is shaped like that, too. It's Little Stone Mountain.* A smile blossomed on her face and quickly faded.

Wonder when I'll see Sophia again?

Lizzie stared into the sun-dappled forest. Beyond these hills —what her dad called the foothills—stood the oldest mountains on earth, like Lizzie, worn by time. She shook her head, trying not to contemplate their vastness. They could swallow up someone as small as her. If she wandered in, she might never find her way out.

Yet something had already swallowed Lizzie: Elizabeth's death. Every time the minivan started, the Stick girl felt a darkness of spirit. The meaningless of life. Nothingness. She had lost the person who had brought her into the world. Sunny was all she had left. And yet, these days not even Sunny understood her. No one knew what she was or what she had done.

Hershey, the Chapman's dog, strolled into Lizzie's camp, carrying a ball in his mouth. He was the *family* dog. Everyone loved him, but no one had babied the floppy-eared brown fellow more than Elizabeth. Now, the sight of his huge, brown eyes made Lizzie's lower lip tremble. She willed it still.

"All by your lonesome?" Hershey asked in his British accent.

Lizzie nodded toward the sound of voices. "They found the joy of my company too much to bear," she said.

He placed his ball on the grass in front of her. "Me, as well."

"Your family ditched you, too?"

"I could've tagged along," the dog replied, "but they're boring."

"Even Sophia?"

Hershey shook his head; his ears did a floppy dance. "Her most of all. She's sick with a fever."

"Whoa. What?"

The spaniel winked. "Boy fever."

"Oh. You got that right."

Hershey sniffed at her leg, then lay down. "Under the weather, are we?"

"I had an operation," she explained, fanning at the dust cloud he had created. "I'm still sticky."

"Aren't you chaps *supposed* to be sticky?"

"Well, yeah, but—" She twisted in her bubble-gum chair and turned her right leg over so he could see the long patch on the backside. "Check it out."

The dog looked close. "Very clever. Do you think it will work?"

Lizzie shrugged. "Feels stiff."

"Ah well, don't give up, dear heart."

"I just hope it helps me keep up with Sunny."

Hershey laughed. "What a fool's errand," he said.

"Yeah, I get it. I'll never be as good as her."

"Poppycock! That's not what I meant. The two of you are different, that's all." He stared at her leg. "Does it hurt?"

"Starting to. They sprinkled something on it for the pain, but it's wearing off."

He grunted. "You'll survive."

They sat in silence for a few minutes, then the dog said, "My natural urge is to lick your wound. Dog slobber does wonders for your immune system, you know."

"Please don't."

"If you change your mind, the offer stands." His tongue lashed his nose.

"So," Lizzie said, "I've been wondering something. About you."

The Boykin rolled onto his side and did a big lazy stretch. "I'm an open book."

"Why do you talk like that?"

He raised his head. "Begging your pardon? Dogspeak? We of the canine tribe have difficulty with the Common Tongue. I am, as you well know, fluent in Black Ant, Chipmunk, Squirrel, and Bird Chirp. The Common Tongue is quite easy to understand, as are Mobiles themselves. It's producing the sounds that I find difficult."

"You can't count Squirrel," said Lizzie. "They just have an accent."

"Some say we dogs are the most multilingual of all

mammals. It's our big secret. Like the fact that you Stick people are alive, is yours."

That's not my big secret, Lizzie thought.

He went on. "Besides, do you suppose that my two-legged servants would allow me to loll about the house all day if they knew? They'd put me to work answering emails or some rot." Lizzie nodded and let him talk. "The only thing that would send me to Crazy Town faster would be breaking The Code." The Cat Code was a mystery to other species. Only cats spoke Cat. And they showed no interest in communicating with any but their own kind.

"Hershey," Lizzie said.

"Yes?"

"I was talking about your accent. "

"What accent?"

"That British thing you do. *Bloke this* and *bloke that.* Everyone else in the family sounds like they're from South Carolina."

"You mean like they just crawled out of the marsh?"

Lizzie laughed. "Yeah, I guess. And that includes me. But you sound like you just stepped off a double-decker bus."

"Oh. That accent. BBC America."

"Huh?"

"It's on the telly. Like the movies you used to watch in the van. Or the stuff they watch on—what do your people call them?

I call them mobile devices.”

“Every tool they use is a Mobile device,” Lizzie said. “They’re Mobiles.”

Hershey sighed. “No, dear heart, the ones they carry.”

“Oh. So, a telly is like a rectangle?”

“But different. If you turn on the telly, it just keeps going and going without anyone having to tap the screen at all.”

“That sounds awful.”

The dog shuddered. “You have no idea. Long before you came out of the box, the Chapmans went away for a weekend. This was back in the days of their Volkswagen Beetle, before the minivan.”

“They had another car?”

“Certainly. Anyway, they went on holiday and left me at home.” Hershey paused for effect.

“No!” Lizzie said, exaggerating her shock.

Hershey nodded.

“They’d never!” Lizzie let her mouth hang open.

“And me but a pup, still missing my mum.”

“That was horrible of them.”

“Yes, a bit dodgy of them, but I suppose they had their reasons,” the dog said. “Back then, I was prone to car sickness.”

Lizzie winced. “Ew!” She had never actually seen or smelled throw-up, but Elizabeth had. Of all the things that the two girls had shared, their revulsion for partially digested food was the worst.

Hershey waited as Lizzie held her stomach, then he continued. "They left me food and water. And we have a dog door, so there was no problem getting out."

Lizzie nodded. She knew that dogs marked their territories, but didn't understand how things worked. Sticks don't go to the bathroom.

"Still, that's awful," she said.

"Yes," he said, "except I wasn't entirely alone. They left me with BBC for a babysitter."

"That telly thing?"

"The bloody thing played for three days."

"Couldn't you turn it off?" she asked.

He held up his paws. "No thumbs. So I watched and watched. Masterpiece Theatre, Dr. Who, Graham Norton, Sherlock, Absolutely Fabulous. And there was a show about a flying circus snake—I think—that one's a bit fuzzy."

"And people on the telly thing—they talked like you?"

"Ding-ding, good guess, you win the prize. And I got hooked. After the first day I didn't *want* to turn it off. And I most definitely didn't want to sound like I was from South Carolina. To this day, I still sneak into the den late at night to watch a spot of BBC."

"That explains a lot," Lizzie said.

"So if you ever hear Sophia's mum and dad having a row

about which one of them changes the telly in the wee hours? Well, that would be me."

"Oh, I almost forgot," Lizzie said. "I met somebody who shares your tennis ball obsession. A cardboard woman, but very tough. You'd call her cheeky."

"You don't say."

"Her name's Serena." Ths Stick girl looked into the woods. "Running around here somewhere."

"Smashing," said Hershey. "I'll watch for her."

Lizzie stared at a patch of orange between the trees as more and more sounds of laughter drifted from next door. It seemed like everytime she looked away, she barely missed something in the corner of her eye. "What are they up to? Just tell me."

Hershey opened his jaws for an enormous yawn. "Tent sliding."

"Tent what—? Oh!" Something white had just streaked through the orange, accompanied by the unmistakable happy-squeal of her sister.

"Sliding," the Boykin repeated.

Next, Lizzie saw Ups race down the side of the tent, riding on a sock, screaming his head off. She started to get up.

"Don't be daft," the dog warned. He touched her head with an enormous paw. "You'll pick up all manner of debris."

Lizzie sat back. "But they're having fun without me."

Hershey nodded. "The story of every dog's life."

The girl stared through the trees at the patch of orange canvas. Sunny climbed up a string. Then Nico flew past her on his way down, his legs splayed in a wide V. Instead of a sock, he appeared to ride a leaf.

Lizzie examined her leg again. The jagged edge, where she had cut it herself with a piece of quartz, had been trimmed smooth. The whole gash had been covered by a long strip of bumper sticker material. The color matched, but undoubtedly it would scar. Maybe she might not limp so badly. Then again, running? Running had been Elizabeth's thing, her passion. It had been *her* thing, too—Lizzie's—and she wanted it back. *If I could run again,* she thought, *I'd just keep going and never look back.* She settled into her chair with a groan.

"So," Hershey asked with a twinkle in his eye, "what do you think of Daisy?"

"She's too tall for you," Lizzie said.

The dog raised his head. "That's a matter of opinion. Not to mention a stereotype. You of all people should know better."

"Don't get me wrong. It's not like you're a toy breed. But—"

"Though I have been wondering," Hershey kept talking, "why doesn't that family have a Stick dog? Peculiar."

Lizzie shrugged. "They probably stuck on their Sticks before they got Daisy."

Hershey nodded. "I guess." He looked into the distance with a dreamy expression. "Ah, Daisy. She's just the bird for me."

Lizzie grinned. "Think she likes you back?"

Hershey lay his head down. "Dog knows. She didn't even notice my butterscotch." His *butterscotch* was a streak of gold on the crown of his head, the only blonde place on an otherwise brown dog.

Lizzie sighed. "I know the feeling."

Hershey cocked his head. "You're not pining over that boy."

"Heck, no. Didn't say that."

"But that's what you meant."

Lizzie shrugged.

"Lizzie Lou!" Hershey growled. "We both know you're not crushing on a boy."

She stared at the orange patch in the distance. Ups, her Stick dog, flew down on a banana peel, howling like a wolf. "It's just that when Sunny's around, I'm invisible. Like I'm transparent."

Hershey lay his chin on the grass right before her. "Ah well, but you and he could be good friends." The Boykin stayed with the girl for more than an hour, until the Mobile dad called him. The dog jumped to his feet. "Yah!" he said, and snatched up his tennis ball. "Fetch time!" He bounded away. Just before disappearing around the corner of the tent, he turned to her again. "One more thing. The Chappies forgot insect repellent. Expect a trip to the nearest market sometime soon."

"Thanks for the heads-up."

And the dog was gone.

Lizzie closed her eyes. A slash of sunlight passed ever-so-slowly across her face. A reddish glow on the inside of her eyelids called her to nap. She felt the magnolia sap slowly tightening, drying. She heard her sister and Ups arguing about whose turn it was. The voices slipped away. New voices drifted to her from a dream world, where everyone spoke with a British accent and ate butterscotch.

Twenty-seven

When Lizzie opened her eyes, she saw Sophia peeking from around the corner of the blue tent.

"You shouldn't be here," Lizzie said, sitting up.

"And you should be plastered to our car window," the Mobile replied. She stepped around the corner and approached. "Where's your family? I wanna meet them."

"You can't. I already told you. Besides, they're off having fun while I'm stuck here."

"That's funny. You're a sticker and you're stuck."

"I don't think it's funny."

"Is that them climbing on the cute boy's tent?"

"How can you see them? Alarm bells should have gone off in Sunny's head before you even looked their way."

"Don't know about that, but I see 'em right now. Weird

game. Looks like fun."

"Duck down, quick! They can't see you looking."

"If you say so." Sophia got down on her hands and knees. "You know, when I tell people about you, they're gonna put me in therapy."

"You're not gonna tell anyone," Lizzie said. "I made that clear. What's therapy?"

"That's when you pay a grown-up to listen to you."

Lizzie blew out a breath. "Grown-ups listening? That's crazy talk."

"Exactly." Sophia scratched at a mosquito bite on her arm.

"You need to leave," the Stick girl said.

"Ha. You wanted me around when you made me dump out the trash."

"I didn't make you. But if I did, it was a mistake."

"The mistake was me hallucinating you in the first place," Sophia said.

"Ha-lucy-nating?"

"Seeing things that aren't there."

"Oh. Well, that's not nice."

"You're kind of a jerk, you know that?"

"Then why do you want to be around me? Go."

"Not happening."

Lizzie crossed her arms. "Anyway, maybe you're the one who's not real. Ever think of that?"

Sophia twirled her caramel hair. "I'm the real girl. You're just a copy."

"No, I am."

"I am."

"Me."

"No, me."

They both fell silent. Their eyes widened. Sophia and Elizabeth, more than once, had called each other "just a copy." Lizzie had never heard them, but she had felt it.

"Okay, *maybe* you're not a jerk," Sophia said. "Just, I dunno, a pain in the butt. But if I'm seeing things—and obviously I am—I wanna take a good look before some psychiatrist puts me on medication."

"I'm not going away," Lizzie said. *At least not yet.* She put her face in her hands, then ruffled her own hair.

"Hey, I didn't realize you could do that," Sophia said.

"Do what? This?" Lizzie took a handful of her white hair and let it fall to her shoulders.

"Yeah. I thought your hair was, like, all flat and stuff. Plasticky. And your pigtails are out."

"I'll have to tie them back up when my mom gets back. Sometimes I twirl it, too. Or chew on it."

"Please don't. It causes split ends."

No kidding, Lizzie thought. *Sunny says the same thing.*

"And your dress. It moves like cloth, too. Oh, and that's

another thing. Why do you and your sister and mom wear dresses? You never heard of leggings? I hardly ever wear dresses. And Mom only wears them on date night. And my sis? To her, dresses were like torture."

"Exactly."

Sophia sat back on her knees and crossed her arms. "Anyway, I got a bone to pick with you. That's a saying."

"I just fell off a minivan, not a turnip truck."

"You got me in trouble."

"How so?"

"With the park rangers, that's how. Remember the garbage man?"

"The one who grabbed your wrist?"

"Yeah. He told the park rangers I was vandalizing the park."

"Meaning?"

"Vandalized. Damaging stuff." Sophia got in Lizzie's face again. "He blabbed that I was tipping over trash cans."

"Well, you were," Lizzie said.

Sophia's mouth dropped open revealing her cavern of periodontal work. "Only because you talked me into it."

"Maybe you shouldn't be such a follower," Lizzie said.

"Maybe you shouldn't be such a little turd!"

"Follower!"

"Turd!"

"Follower!"

"Turd!"

"Follow—"

Suddenly both girls cringed as Sophia's mom called from the other side of the blue tent.

"I'm fine," Sophia called back.

"If she comes back here, it'll ruin everything," Lizzie whispered.

"No, if she comes back here she'll see me talking to myself." Sophia arched her anorexic eyebrows. "You're very elaborate for an illusion, you know that?"

"Whatever. It's my fault you got busted for dumping trash. Why not? Everything's my fault."

"Exactly," Sophia said. Then she looked unsure.

Lizzie did her best impression of her mom's finger wag. "Just don't be checking out the back windshield. If you do, Sunny will sense it. Then she'll tattle and I'll be in big trouble."

"If you say so."

"Well, okay, then."

"You might be interested to know that we're running low on TP," Sophia said. "The stinky smelly ladies' room is out."

"Sure. Whatever that means."

"It's— You know, TP? Toilet paper?"

Lizzie furrowed her brows. "Paper? Plan on doing some homework? I thought you were on spring break."

Sophia laughed. "You never heard of toilet paper? Don't

worry about it. I'm just giving you a heads-up that we'll be going to the store soon. We need TP and bug spray."

"I already know, but thanks."

"Like probably tomorrow. Hey wait, how did you know?"

"Her—Her—" Lizzie caught herself. She was going to say that Hershey had told her. "Heard it somewhere. Anyway, so what did they do? The rangers?"

"One of them was nice," Sophia said, "the younger one. He asked if I was looking for something in the trash."

"You were."

"Yeah, but not like I could say I was fishing for an empty box of cereal."

"Good point."

"He might even be cute if he wasn't ancient." The two exchanged a look. "Thirty," Sophia clarified.

"Eww," Lizzie said.

"But there was this bald-headed older one—thinks he's big stuff. Ranger Frowns-a-lot."

"That's a weird name."

"Not his real one. I just call him that. He's got a creeper mustache." She held a finger across her upper lip. "Like a caterpillar."

"Like your eyebrows used to be," Lizzie said.

"Hey, that's mean!" Sophia glanced up.

"Don't worry, your new brows are much more...something.

Stylish?"

"Are they ugly?"

"No, they're as adorable as a line of black ants. You were saying?"

"Oh yeah. Ranger Frowns-a-lot tells my parents that I've been—" She put on a deep voice and did air quotes, "destroying the habitat."

"What did you do?"

"Lied, of course."

"Next time, tell him you were looking for your retainer."

"Like *that'll* work," Sophia scoffed. "I don't *wear* a retainer. I still have my braces, see?" She bared the metal.

"Yeah, but he might not know that stuff."

"How do *you* know that stuff?" Then quickly, "Oh right. Sorry." Elizabeth had worn a retainer.

Lizzie waved her off. Sophia continued.

"If he catches me, they'll kick my family out of the park. That's what he said. Not that I wanna be out here in the sticks for a whole week to begin with. My folks will ground me for the rest of my life." She seemed to notice for the first time that Lizzie's leg was propped up. "So what's with your foot?"

"Not my foot, my leg. I had surgery." Lizzie twisted in her chair again and showed the Mobile the patch. She explained about the crunchy neighbors and the tree sap.

"Shoulda used superglue," Sophia said.

"It's locked in the van."

"Oh well. Lemme know next time you need it," Sophia said. She pointed at Lizzie's wildflower petal. "Petty color. Pink's my fav."

"Of course, it is."

Sophia didn't seem to notice the sarcasm. "One more thing."

"What's that?"

"I turned over another trash barrel."

"What? But you just got through saying..." Lizzie's voice trailed off when she saw the devious smile turning up the corners of Sophia's mouth. *A perfectly straight smile, like Sunny's.*

"I was curious," the Mobile said. She saw the blank expression on Lizzie's face. "About cereal-box people. I wanted to see if I could make another one jump up and run into the woods."

Lizzie laughed and kept an eye on the orange patch of tent as first her mom, then her dad, went sliding down the canvas. "Did you find any?"

Sophia shook her head.

"Next time, just smile at them," Lizzie said. "That should do it."

"Haha. You mean they'll be scared by my braces. Anyway, all I could find was an oatmeal box."

"Does that count as cereal?"

Sophia waved her hand, maybe. "So I grabbed this oatmeal box and took it back to the big rock."

"Little Stone Mountain. That's what I call it."

"I like it. So I ran to Little Stone Mountain with this little old Quaker dude on a box."

"I'll take your word for it."

"Then I cut him out with my knife, like we did with the tennis woman. Only he didn't do anything. He was only a, um, a head."

Lizzie grimaced. "What do ya mean, a head?"

"They only show him from here up." Sophia held her arm across her chest. "I thought maybe he had arms inside his jacket or something? And maybe he'd walk away using his arms?"

"That would have been funny."

"Wouldn't it, though. But he just lay there."

"Too bad."

"Yeah."

An awful thought occurred to Lizzie. "You didn't, you know, wad him up, did you?" Sophia shook her head. "Good." Lizzie imagined the poor Quaker Oats man—his head anyway—lying there on the boulder, blinking up at the trees and striking up conversations with passing insects.

"Then I got to wondering if he has a body somewhere," Sophia added. "Like on some other box, waiting around for his head to show up."

"You really are a weird Mobile," Lizzie said. "Your twin sister was weirder, but you're not far behind."

"Anyway, I was wondering…. You don't have a little cheat sheet, do you?" the giant girl asked.

"You lost me."

"You know, like a list of Stick people and cereal people and stuff."

Lizzie made a show of turning out the pockets of her dress. "You're on your own."

Sophia sighed. Just then, her mom called again from the other side of the tent. "I gotta book," the Mobile girl said. She turned to leave, then quickly squatted back down. "Can we hang out sometime?" It sounded a little pathetic.

Lizzie didn't want to sound too eager. "Why don't you hang out with your dog?"

The other grimaced. "Why don't you hang out with *your* dog?"

"Yeah, okay, never mind," Lizzie said. "If my parents saw you and me together, they would have a fit."

"So you keep saying."

"But if we're sneaky…"

"I can be sneaky," Sophia said.

Lizzie doubted that, but went on. "If it's daytime, just hoot like an owl."

"That's dumb," Sophia said. "Owls sleep in the day."

"Exactly. So if I hear an owl in the daytime, I'll know it's you."

"Ah," Sophia said. "And your folks aren't smart enough to figure that one out?"

"I hope not." Lizzie blew on the back of her knuckles, "I *am* the smart one, you know." It didn't look as cool as she had hoped.

"Jerk. So where ya wanna meet?"

"Trash barrel?" Lizzie suggested.

Sophia shook her head so hard it turned her hair into a haystack. "Ranger Frowns-a-lot is watching the barrels. Might arrest me."

"They don't arrest kids," Lizzie said.

Sophia put her hands on her hips. "I'm not a kid."

"Or thirteen-year-olds. Come to think of it, that's too near the road."

"How about Little Stone Mountain?"

"Perfect," Lizzie said. "LSM it is. But remember, it takes me a lot longer to walk there. You're like, ginormous."

Sophia giggled.

"What?"

"It's just, I've always wished I was taller."

"So you'll *hoot* if it's during the day," Lizzie said. "What if it's dark?" It wasn't like her to plan ahead, but she didn't want to be left moping around the campsite if Nico and Sunny ditched her again.

"I have a little flashlight," Sophia said. She searched her pockets and found her knife, but not the light. "It might be in the tent. Anyway, I'll find it. If it's dark, I'll hide back there," she pointed to the woods, "and flash it on and off three times. Then two times. Then three times. That'll be our signal."

Lizzie nodded. "Three flashes, then two, then three. And we meet at the rock."

"Right."

"At Little Stone Mountain," they said together, and laughed. That twin thing again—thinking of something and saying it together. They both quickly looked down. When Lizzie met Sophia's eyes again, she wondered if the girl could remember the last time she had laughed like that with Elizabeth.

"I'm s'posed to stay off my leg until tomorrow morning," Lizzie said. "I'm still sticky. It's... icky."

"What ev," Sophia said, "I'll hoot you tomorrow. Or flash you tomorrow night."

"Not sure why, but that sounds...wrong."

Hearing her mom call again, Sophia jumped up, stirring up dust. Lizzie fanned at it with her wildflower petal.

"Bye, imaginary friend," Sophia said. She disappeared around the corner of the big blue tent.

"Bye, imaginary friend," Lizzie said to no one at all.

Friend.

She dropped her petal and closed her eyes. Sunlight and shadow took turns painting her face. And she slept.

That evening, Sunny and Ups kept whispering about their tent-sliding adventure. They called it Slip 'n' Slam. Lizzie repaid them with a heavy dose of silence. Her dad promised her that she could try it later that week if the patch worked. Sunny kept primping her hair in the reflection of a sequin.

"Making yourself pretty for Nico?" Lizzie asked, unable to hold her tongue any longer.

"Don't be silly," her twin replied. "I'm already pretty. Besides, we're just friends."

Lizzie grunted. She told herself she didn't care. *Maybe I have my own new friend,* she thought. As darkness fell, she stared at the forest. Tomorrow night, she would watch for a blinking flashlight. Three flashes, then two, then three.

Twenty-eight

With her oak-leaf sleeping bag open and her leg propped up, Lizzie slept fitfully. Over the years, she had often dreamed of flying in a paper airplane, a fantasy common to Sticks. Tonight, though, the plane crashed again and again into the side of a mountain. Each time her eyes blinked open, she touched her leg to see if the magnolia sap had dried. Each time, it felt a little less tacky. Before daylight, she crawled out of the tent.

She walked a slow circle around their site. Her right leg felt extremely stiff, almost as if she had been glued to a popsicle stick. Not a good sign.

Last night's funny-fire lay dark. The LED light had been turned off when the others went to bed. Lizzie squinted up at the Chapmans' mountainous tent, a black silhouette against the tree line. What would it be like to slide down a mountain on a sock?

She remembered the helpless feeling she had at the trash barrel. She had been powerless to free Serena without the help of a Mobile. So much of Stick life centered around them. Lizzie, with her bad leg and no Mobile of her own, felt torn in more ways than one. Who was she without a Mobile? The most helpless Stick of all. She hated that.

But maybe her leg would loosen up if she worked it. Maybe she would be able to keep up with Sunny. Maybe get some of her old life back. Or even better, a new one. *If I could run,* she thought, *I'd run away and never look back.*

Holding a tiny river pebble on her stomach (to her the size of a football), she began doing crunches. After two sets of fifty, her abs burned, but in a good way—a hurt very different from the pain she had sometimes inflicted on herself with a piece of quartz. She let the pebble roll aside, stood up, and looked around. Her family's campsite seemed so small and insignificant, no place to become a new you. So, not knowing where she was headed, Lizzie limped into the world of massive trees. As the forest swallowed her, she felt no fear, just a determination that she was done being helpless.

She heard Sunny calling in that irritatingly cheerful voice—the one that never got old to anyone other than Lizzie. Then a second time, louder. *Jeez, how can anyone be so peppy in the morning? If Mom wakes up, I'll have to explain why I'm in the woods.* Of course, whenever her parents demanded an explanation, they never seemed to listen. So the Stick girl tried to run. It had been ages since Lizzie had moved any faster than a hobble. Now she did so awkwardly. The patch felt stiff and alien, but her leg felt strong, so she kept going. Sunny's calls faded.

Being so small, she didn't have to worry about getting slapped by branches, but some rocks and clusters of leaves had to be climbed. Roots had to be hurdled. She still limped, but only because she was used to it, not because she had to.

Soon Lizzie moved beyond the hardwoods and into a growth of pines. Straw carpeted the ground instead of leaves. The brush thinned out. Gazing at pencil-straight trunks, black against a gray horizon, she slowed to a walk. Somewhere a mockingbird sang. Before long, the woods came alive with birdsong.

As the morning sun slanted through the trees, green, blue, and gold revealed themselves. Ahead, a brown bunny sat next to a narrow trail.

"Hi," said Lizzie as she approached.

Saying nothing, the bunny darted down the trail. Then eight tiny bunnies burst from hiding and followed their mother. Lizzie watched their bobbing white tails disappear, then raced after them. They outran her, of course. They disappeared into the forest and she never saw them again. But Lizzie kept running.

After a few minutes, she realized she wasn't limping. She felt her old running rhythm coming back. Her stride felt strong. Although the sap was still somewhat stiff, she could feel the patch becoming more limber. She regretted doubting Thoma. *Thank you,* she thought.

Encouraged, she turned on the speed, pushing herself. Fire sprang into her lungs, but she growled back at it. She literally growled like a wild animal. And ran like she would never stop.

Eventually, Lizzie halted on the muddy bank of a small creek. Panting, she threw her hands behind her head and walked in circles. She took off her leaf sandals and wiggled her toes in the mud. Her mom would kill her, but she didn't care. Eyes closed, she tilted her face into a sunbeam. She took the scrunchies from her pigtails and stuffed them into her dress pockets. A breeze lifted her hair, cooling the sweat on her forehead and the back of her neck. She dipped her hands in the water and tousled her hair. It became as wild as she felt.

The creek looked too deep to wade, so she slipped her sandals back on and tightened them snugly. Then she turned and ran parallel to the water. Her legs wanted more. *She* wanted more. Lizzie couldn't remember the last time she had felt any hope for the future. Now as it rose in her, it vied for attention with her constant companion: guilt. *Why should I feel good again? Elizabeth never will. But it feels SO good to run!*

The creek snaked on and on. The Stick girl had to detour around reeds and briars whenever they edged the water. She met frogs, turtles, minnows, dragonflies, and a wide variety of birds—robins, cardinals, goldfinches, red-winged blackbirds. The sky became a vivid blue. Blanched clouds sailed above the treetops. The deep shadows of the forest grew lighter. The undersides of leaves glowed a luminous green. The creek shimmered in a hypnotic dance.

Lizzie became hyper-aware. She felt the texture of the soil through her thin moccasins—each pebble, each dip and rise of the terrain. Her ears—sharp to begin with—processed the tittering, the buzzing, the wind—as if in an added dimension. Each inhale brought smells of wildflowers and earth, even as the air seared her shallow lungs. Her blood (Sticks have their own kind) rushed through her limbs, pounding in her ears. As Lizzie's body came alive, a long-dormant fire in her soul ignited. She felt herself waking from a long, dark time in her life. For months, she had told herself, *I just wanna run away.* Now she thought, *I just wanna run.* Without seeing the difference.

The creek grew suddenly narrower and faster, outpacing her. Finally, the Stick girl skidded to a stop. A silver ribbon of water scattered into diamonds as it spilled over a sheer cliff. Gulping air, she stood on the rocky ledge. She laced her fingers behind her neck and peered over. Unafraid.

In the hills below, faraway trees waved their branches as if saying hello. But Lizzie longed to see more than trees. She searched the tumbling slow-motion clouds. Every direction. For just a glimpse of Elizabeth's presence.

You can't have abandoned me forever. Not when I feel like this.

But the dead girl's face did not appear. Not the crescent of an eyebrow in a morning moon. Not the curve of her chin on an outcropping of rocks. Neither the forest nor the sky nor the twisting stream below gave any sign. The wind's soft whisper carried no voice, no laughter.

Yet Lizzie clearly recalled Elizabeth's fierce spirit, her quirky sense of humor, those kind, mischievous green eyes.

Elizabeth's heart had stopped beating forever, but Lizzie's beat on. She felt like a bear rising from hibernation. Rising alone. *I will never stop looking for you,* she swore. Then and there, she decided to be her own person, whoever that might be, however that might look. No matter what her family or anyone else might think. No matter what they called her. She would be herself in ways that Elizabeth never had the chance to be. She owed it to her own self, if not to the dead. She would be true, inside and out. Without apologies.

Not far from the cliff where Lizzie stood, the rock wall jutted out to a point called Gorges Overlook. There, a middle-aged couple with boots and backpacks stood gazing out. Lizzie approached, careful not to be seen. Soon the couple turned away and walked toward a trailhead. Lizzie followed them as far as a sign that read RAINBOW FALLS 3.2 MILES. They disappeared around a turn.

The Stick girl propped her right foot against the signpost and examined the patch on her leg—not coming loose, not wrinkling. The seam looked clean. Hearing footsteps, she ducked behind the post. A teenage girl in jean shorts, T-shirt, and sneakers approached. Not just any girl. Sophia.

Lizzie started to call out, but got an odd feeling and decided not to. Sophia drifted like a ghost toward the cliff. At the edge, ran a stone wall, topped by a metal rail. The Mobile girl gripped it with both hands, vaulted up, and stood there, nimble as a cat. Lizzie's breath caught in her throat as Sophia stared down at the sheer drop for what seemed like an eternity. Lizzie thought *please don't jump, please don't jump.*

Instead of leaping to her death, Sophia dug her mobile phone from her pocket, propped it up, and did a handstand. Lizzie let out her breath as the teenager pivoted away from the edge and dropped safely to her feet. Sophia then retrieved the phone and thumbed through it. Although Lizzie couldn't see the screen, she knew exactly what the other was doing: scrolling through selfies.

The smell of campfires greeted them as Lizzie shadowed the Mobile back to the big blue tent. The Stick girl watched the other disappear through the enormous zippered door. She herself moved out of sight, sat down in the grass, and began picking at the mud on her feet, wondering if she had almost witnessed the death of the second twin.

"It's never going to come out like *that*," said a familiar voice.

The Stick girl looked up to see Hershey, his stubby little tail wagging. The Mobiles often called him Hershey Bob. Hershey, because he was brown as a chocolate bar. Bob, because of his bobtail.

Lizzie grunted. "You got a better idea?"

"Allow me." Hershey then licked off most of the mud in seconds.

"Thanks, Hersh."

"You're quite welcome. And I'll bet you thought dog slobber was only good for the common cold." He walked away.

When Lizzie reached her own campsite, everyone was up, but no one questioned her. Sunny, redoing her own pigtails, just flashed her a grin. Ups wagged his tail, but didn't even pause in whatever he was chewing on. Her dad gave her a thumbs-up and a goofy nod. And the Queen of Control Freaks just glanced at the mud stains on her feet and turned away, without so much as a scowl.

Exhausted in more ways than one, Lizzie went back to bed. Asleep in an instant, she dreamed of flying in a paper airplane— right off of Gorges Overlook.

Twenty-nine

A high-pitched, whistling sound pierced the warm afternoon air. Lizzie flung back her sleeping bag and scrambled out of the tent. Sunny jumped up from her chair. Their dad frantically pulled on his shoes. Ups ran into the clearing. Mom waited at the corner of the big tent, snapping her fingers and blowing on a reed whistle. Since the Mobile mom was the one who actually drove the minivan everyday, it was the Stick mom who could sense when her keys jingled. The Mobiles were about to go to the store, which meant so were the Sticks.

"This is not a drill!" Mom barked. "Repeat, this is not a drill! Fifteen seconds to Glass. Fourteen, thirteen..."

Lizzie grabbed her shoes and raced barefoot to the minivan. She out-ran everyone but her mom, who pulled her up onto the bumper. Lizzie climbed the rest of the way on her own. She slipped on her shoes, dug her scrunchies out of her pockets, put up her pigtails, and smoothed her dress. She stuck herself, being careful to make sure the crack in the glass fell precisely where the gash in her leg had been. Her family climbed up beside her. Sunny took her right hand. Ups stilled his tail. They smiled, they sealed, they froze in their pose.

"Your piggies are crooked," Sunny whispered.

Lizzie's left hand instinctively shot toward her pigtails. But Mom growled, "Don't!" Lizzie dropped her hand and froze.

Two seconds later, the van's great hatch whooshed upward. The Sticks hung inverted, smiling, and watched as the Mobile dad threw an armful of empty water jugs in the cargo area. The hatch boomed down and Lizzie's family stood upright again. Doors slammed. The motor started. Hershey, tied to a stake beside the tent, waved goodbye as the van pulled away. Moments later, they left the park's dirt road and pulled onto the blacktop.

"How's that leg holding?" Mom asked. "Not fully dry, is it?"

Lizzie glanced down at her patched leg. "I guess we'll see." As the van accelerated, the Stick girl stared at road stripes flashing by faster and faster. Sunny tightened her grip on Lizzie's right hand.

"How about it?" Mom asked.

"Still good," Lizzie replied, but she felt a moment of panic.

When the sap had dried, it had left a small area of non-sticky surface on the back of her leg. But would it make her float?

"Approaching cruising speed," Dad reported. And then, "Okay, we're there. This is as fast as we're going to get on this curvy road. Lizzie-Lou? Any you-know-what?"

"Float?" she asked. "No, I'm stuck." Sunny unpeeled a little and gave her a look. "Really," Lizzie assured her, "I'm good. I'm flat as a possum on a freeway."

"Hurrah!" Ups shouted.

Sunny squealed, "Yah, Lizzie!" Although something about the tone of her voice sounded fake to Lizzie.

"I never doubted you'd stick," Mom said. "Not for a second."

But Lizzie could hear the relief in their voices. For a long time, her parents had warned them about the terrible danger of floating. Of being lost to the road. To Lizzie, it just sounded like how she already felt: lost. But now that she could run again, now that she had a friend—maybe two friends—the awful risk of it hit home.

For Stick people, float is like cancer. A rear windshield wiper sometimes pulls up a Stick's edge. Once float starts, it spreads. A Stick person will either be lost to the road, or worse, scraped off by their Mobiles. Neither Mom or Dad had known how to fix Lizzie's leg. Ever since the accident they had fretted over her, even as she grew distant from them.

Maybe now they'll stop acting like I died, too, she thought.

A dump truck rushed past the van in the opposite direction. Lizzie heard the whine of rubber on pavement, followed by the shush of air brakes as the rig slowed for a curve. With horror, she noticed something white stuck to one of those massive tires, flashing with each rotation—like a neon sign flashing the word *death*. A cloud of dust settled on the Stick family. They all expected what came next. From inside the minivan, the Mobile dad squirted both the front and back windshields.

"Blue shower!" Dad shouted. The family all closed their eyes until the mist and wiper had done their work.

For over a year, Sunny had often squeezed Lizzie's hand to reassure her. It annoyed the Stick girl worse than bubble gum stuck to a tire. She had never really thought about how much she loved her for it. Now, Lizzie squeezed back. Without looking, she knew her twin's cheeks had tears on them, probably mixed with wiper fluid. There's mist on my face, too, Lizzie thought. But just mist. Still, Lizzie wondered about that fake sound in her sister's voice. Did Sunny secretly hope to be rid of her?

When the minivan rolled into an Exxon station, Dad looked at Mom and shook his head. "Gas stop only."

"This is a rolling stop," Mom announced to the others. "Hold your positions."

Mr. Chapman got out of the vehicle and began unscrewing the gas cap. A moment later, Sophia's door slid open. She hopped out and circled around to the rear hatch.

"Want me to fill up the water jugs?" she called.

"Nope, sweetie, that's okay," her dad replied as he lifted the gas nozzle from its cradle. "We'll do that at the apple stand."

"You sure?"

"Yeah, kiddo, get back in the car."

"Whatever," Sophia said. But she lingered at the hatch and stared at the Sticks. *Go away,* Lizzie thought. *Go!* Finally the girl got back in the van.

"What was that about?" Ups asked.

"I felt her staring at me," Sunny said.

"Me, too," Lizzie added, to blend in.

"I thought she was going to scratch me," Ups said. Then he scratched behind one of his own ears.

Mom peeled up enough to make eye contact with Lizzie. "She was staring at you. Again."

Lizzie's mouth hung open for a second. Then she fell back on sarcasm, which she figured everyone expected. "Guess I just have one of those faces," she said.

"I'll bet she noticed your new leg thingy," Sunny said. "You gotta figure somebody would."

"That must have been it," Dad said. "Good thing she didn't pick at it."

But Lizzie's mom gave her a long, hard look. "Go ahead and fix your piggies. They're a mess."

They were back on the road within five minutes.

Their next stop, the "apple stand," turned out to be a large and very old country store. Its tin roof gleamed in the afternoon sun. A faded sign read BABY BEAR'S TRADING POST. And in smaller letters: FRESH APPLES, CIDER, BOILED PEANUTS, SUNDRIES. The Chapmans piled out of the van. Sophia's dad again momentarily inverted the Stick family as he retrieved the water jugs.

Lizzie watched the Mobiles cross the parking lot. A little bell jingled as they entered the store.

"Their leader has a long shopping list," Mom announced, referring to Ms. Chapman. "That'll give us fifteen minutes, maybe even thirty."

"Yes, ma'am," the girls and Ups all said. Everyone unpeeled.

"Chop-chop!" Mom clapped her hands twice and they all picked up the pace. "You know what we need. Food, string, anything good that'll fit in your pockets. Plus, our tent has a hole in it. If it rains, we're in trouble. Look for something to patch the bread bag."

"Like that woman's star sticker?" Sunny asked.

"Yeah, that'll work. Now, gravel is tricky to walk on. Allow extra time to get back. Any questions?"

As they climbed down, Ups said. "Hershey hates being tied up."

"They couldn't exactly leave him in the car," Sunny said.

"That would be cruel."

"Oh, phooey, it's only April!" the Stick dog argued back. "They could roll down the windows and leave him with water." As he landed in gravel, Ups turned to Lizzie, who looked like the only one still listening. "Better yet, what would be wrong with letting him go in the store? Sniffable place, I'll wager."

Lizzie shrugged. "Mobiles are weird."

The family made their way with difficulty across the gravel expanse and into a flower bed. Then, they split up. Ups headed under the porch, toward a crawl space that ran beneath the building. The Stick parents circled to the back of the building for some dumpster diving. Sunny hung close to her sister.

"What are you, my shadow?" Lizzie asked. At that, the other stalked away toward the other end of the porch. Lizzie waited until she had disappeared, then darted into a clump of monkey grass. Soon, a red SUV pulled into the lot. Doors slammed. A man, a woman, a little boy, and a stroller crossed the gravel. Lizzie cocked her head at their appearance. They all wore matching Mickey Mouse T-shirts—odd, since they were hundreds of miles from Disney World. Even the baby in the stroller wore a Mickey onesie. The moment their feet clomped up onto the porch, Lizzie ducked out from the grass and followed. The steps were tall, but she climbed them easily. Before her leg patch, this would have been a chore. Ahead, the strangers hesitated at the door as the mom wiped the boy's face.

From behind a rail post, Lizzie looked up and down the long porch. Bushel baskets of apples ran from one end to the other. An elderly couple rocked gently in rocking chairs, their eyes closed. An unfinished game of checkers sat between them on a barrel. They were either dead or asleep. One of the two let out a snore. Asleep.

At the door, the little boy tried to squeeze inside at the same time as the stroller. The dad handed a diaper bag to the mom so he could pick up the kid. This gave Lizzie an opening. She ran between the mom's legs, underneath the stroller, and inside Baby Bear Trading Post.

I'm an Insider now, she thought.

Beside the door, loomed a vast tower of postcards. Lizzie slipped through the metal racks. On the darkened inside, she peered up at a wire frame, like standing in the lobby of a cylindrical hotel. Perfect for climbing and for scoping out the store. She had almost reached the top when the walls began to move. She held on tight as her legs flew sideways and the ceiling spun.

Then it stopped. Then it spun. Then it stopped again.

As Lizzie regained her footing, a window opened nearby. Someone had taken the last card from a slot. A giant bearded face appeared. The man raised some reading glasses to his face and read aloud a corny poem about getting old. Chuckling, he gave the rack one last spin as he carried the card away. Flapping like a lawn flag, Lizzie glimpsed the inside of the store as a blur. When the postcard tower came to a halt, her window now faced a wall.

Thanks, Bubba, you ruined my view.

So she climbed to the very top and poked out her head. Now, she could see everything. The Inside was amazing. There were no trees, grass, sky, or street. No cars, only Mobiles. And Lizzie had never seen so many things: row after row of jackets, T-shirts, food, health and beauty aids, sunglasses. Even more stuff mushroomed from crates and half-barrels. A city of footwear dominated an entire corner.

Shoe Land, Lizzie thought, *Sunny would love it.*

In a large window, dozens of wind chimes swayed lazily. On the back wall hung a yellow kayak. To Lizzie, it traveled up the wall.

No one seemed to be looking her way, so she stood up. Ceiling fans whirled overhead like drone propellers. Air conditioning vents pumped out cool air. But Lizzie wasn't chilly. As an Outsider, she could endure extreme temperatures. It was in her blood.

Time and tourists had worn The Baby Bear's plank floor. Right now, dozens of shoppers with woven baskets shuffled through the aisles. A queue inched past a cash register.

Lizzie spotted Sophia on the far side of the building, standing in front of a glass cooler and tapping at her phone. To reach her, the Stick girl could climb down the postcard tower and creep along the bottoms of shelves. But by that time, Sophia would be gone.

To her left, the bell jingled again as two young men walked into the store. One wore a baseball cap, the other a rumpled fedora. At the same time, the little boy in the Mickey shirt broke away from his parents and rushed at the postcard rack. Lizzie gasped as the boy's eyes locked with hers. Then he spun the rack and laughed like it was the funniest thing in the world. Again, Lizzie's world whirled. At first, she held on for dear life. Then with a glance at the dude in the fedora, she let go and launched herself.

Thirty

Having landed on the brim of the hat, Lizzie peaked over the edge. Directly below spilled a profusion of lanky dark hair. She smelled suntan lotion and sweat. Back at the postcard rack, the Disney mom grabbed the little boy's hand. With the other one, he waved at Lizzie. She didn't wave back.

Sticks didn't try to hide from babies, but with little kids, it was iffy. The older they got, the more risky it became. According to Stick lore, the world itself would end if human adults ever discovered them. Lizzie doubted that. Compared to Sophia doing handstands on the edge of a cliff, riding around in some guy's hat didn't seem that dangerous.

She crawled to the front of the fedora. *This must be what it's like to ride a camel,* she thought, *bouncy and hairy.*

Of course, Fedora Dude couldn't see her unless he looked in a mirror. But his friend might. Or others.

"Dude," Baseball Cap said, "let's check out the paddles."

"Go for it," Fedora replied. "I'll find butane and bug spray."

Lizzie kept an eye on Sophia. Still punching away at her phone, the thirteen-year-old wandered from the dairy case toward the back of the store—by chance, not far from the butane. So when Fedora Dude bent to pick out a bottle, Lizzie leapt from the hat and onto a shelf right in front of her friend.

Sophia looked up from her phone. "Oh, hello there. Didn't *imagine* I'd see you here."

"That supposed to be a joke?"

"Eh. Imaginary friend humor. Can you believe it?"

"Believe what?"

"One bar!" She shoved the phone in front of the Stick girl. "See? One bar and still no wi-fi. We're not even in the jungle. It's a store, for God's sake!" She went back to tapping.

"I don't get it. What's wifey?" Lizzie asked. "Like your mom is your dad's wifey?"

Sophia laughed to herself. "Not wifey, you goof, wi-fi. I thought you knew everything. It's a better signal. Which obviously doesn't exist in hick land."

"Yeah? Then what are you doing?"

"Oh... Um... One sec."

Lizzie waited.

The other read something on her phone and grinned. "I'm texting Holly. She's asking her folks for a puppy. She says if they don't let her have one, she's gonna kidnap Hershey."

"That would suck. So how are you two talking? I thought your rectangle didn't work."

"Yeah. Barely. It's either one bar or no bars." She shoved the phone in her back pocket. "So. Were you saying something?"

"Nope. How's your life of crime going?"

"Huh?"

"Garbage tipping. Still getting grief from Ranger Frowns-a-lot?"

Sophia shook her head. "No new vandalism. No incarceration in my future. How's your leg?"

Lizzie stretched and flexed it. "It's great. I actually went for a run this morning."

"You're kidding. Where to?"

Lizzie thought about the Overlook. "Just the woods," she said. "Met some bunnies."

"Cool," said Sophia. "Bunnies would be okay. I just don't wanna run into a bear."

"Whoa. That could happen?"

"Duh. We're near a bear preserve. What I'd really like to meet is a buck. You know? A deer?"

Elizabeth had once seen a ten-point buck in the forest. Lizzie closed her eyes for a second and tried to summon its image—a shadow of a memory—but couldn't. "That would be awesome," she said.

Just then, the four-year-old Disney fan galloped around the corner. His tiny cross-trainers squeaked to a stop. Then he pointed at Lizzie and shouted, "There you are!"

"Put me in your pocket," Lizzie said to Sophia.

"Huh? You'll get squished." She started to stuff the Stick girl in her back pants pocket with her cell phone.

"No, genius, your shirt pocket."

"I don't have one."

The four-year-old stood at Sophia's feet now, peering up at them. "That's mine!" he yelled.

"Just hide me and scare the bejesus outta that kid!" Lizzie said.

Sophia looked around frantically, then stuffed the Stick girl under her arm. Lizzie heard muffled voices from that dark, warm, and somewhat smelly location.

"Gimme my li'l people!" the little boy demanded.

"I think I hear your parents calling," Sophia said.

"It's mine!" the boy insisted.

Sophia bent down, bared the metal in her mouth, and growled. The boy ran away, calling for his mommy.

A moment later, Lizzie blinked into the fluorescent light of the Baby Bear's women's room. Sophia closed a stall door, sat down, and placed Lizzie on her lap.

"Your armpit? Really?"

"I couldn't think."

"Next time, just tear me in pieces and swallow me whole," Lizzie replied.

"You're kidding."

"Ya think?"

"Was it gross?" Sophia asked.

"Just—" Lizzie looked around the bathroom stall. "What is this place, anyway? It's shiny."

"It's the girls' room," the other said.

"Girls' room?" Lizzie looked around. "Doesn't look like a bedroom."

"It's not. This is where girls..." Sophia lowered her voice, "...do their business."

"What, like a Walmart? Since when do you run a business? You're not even good at math."

"I don't." The teenager fake-laughed. *"Doing* your business is nothing like *running* a business. I mean—" Her face had turned red. "Remember how I said we were low on toilet paper?"

"Yeah."

"Well, this is it." She pulled the tissue roll and handed the end to Lizzie.

Lizzie tore off a square. "Hey, wow, this stuff could be useful."

"Yeah, well, you got that right. This room is where we use it. Rooms like this. And this white chair with the water in it is a toilet."

Lizzie frowned. "Okay. Weird. That really doesn't explain—"

"You don't wanna know. Let's just say, there are worse smells than underarms, okay? Leave it at that."

"Worse?" Lizzie laughed. "I can't imagine anything—"

"Shh! Someone's in here."

Lizzie heard the door of the next stall open and close. Clothes rustling.

"Does that chair you're sitting on have a hole in it?" Lizzie whispered.

Sophia nodded and placed a finger to her lips.

"That's weird. Why are we here, anyway?"

"Shh!" Sophia gestured with her head toward the stall wall. "We're hiding from a boy."

"That kid? I thought you scared the applesauce out of him."

"I did, it's another one."

Lizzie nodded toward the next stall. "Is he in here?"

"No, of course not. Boys don't come into the girls' room."

"Oh. How come?"

"Cuz they're boys, silly."

Lizzie thought about it for a moment. "And I'm guessing that girls don't go in the boys' room. Assuming there is such a thing."

"You're smarter than you look. Boy-boys don't go into a girls' room or girl-girls into a boys' room, but it's okay for a boy-girl or a girl-boy to use each other's. Long as they aren't, like, old and creepy."

Lizzie rubbed her face. "That's really confusing."

"Sounds like it, but not really. Just trust me, it would be icky if a boy came in here. I wouldn't feel comfortable doing my business."

Lizzie asked, "But what if he only looked like a boy and wasn't really?" And she thought, *Or what if a girl only looked like a girl?*

"Oh, that's a boy-girl. Like when she has boy parts but feels like a girl."

The Stick girl nodded. Then frowned. "What do you mean by *parts?*"

Sophie grunted and laughed at the same time. "You know. Parts?" Lizzie only stared back. "Oh, wow, you wouldn't know about that stuff, would you?"

Lizzie waved her hand. "Never mind. Are you going to start your business now?"

"What, with you here in the stall? Ew! No."

"But I can help. My dad says I'd be good at running a business."

"Lizzie, it's not that kind of business. We're just hiding. Not from the Mickey kid, from Subaru Boy. The one from the orange and yellow tent."

"You mean Joaquin?"

"Is that his name? That's so cute! Wait. How do you know his name?"

"Long story. Is he trying to start a business, too?"

Sophia sighed. "No, it's my hair."

"Why would he be after your hair?"

"He's not. You're so weird, you remind me of Elizabeth. I mean, I don't want him to see me with my hair like this." She combed it with her fingers.

"Like what? Brownish-yellow?"

"Seriously? I look like a lion threw up a hairball."

Lizzie laughed. "You could shave it. I'd *kill* to shave my hair."

"And these shorts make me look like a cow. And my makeup." Sophia hid her face in her hands.

"But you're not wearing any."

"Exactly." The other uncovered her face. "I'm a walking atrocity."

"No, you're not, you're beautiful."

"Stop. You're just saying that." Sophia looked close at the Stick girl. "Really?"

"No, I mean, yes. I mean, I'm not just saying it and, yes, you really are." She held Sophia's stare. "So you don't want him to see you?"

"I'd die."

Lizzie flashed back to Sophia doing handstands at the Overlook. "Well, we don't want that to happen. But seriously, he's always staring at his mongo-size rectangle, anyway. I'm surprised he doesn't run into something."

"That's called a laptop." Sophia sniffed the air and wrinkled her nose. Unlike her, the woman in the next stall wasn't there to hide. "We need to get outta here."

"Oh-ma-god!" Lizzie cried out loud. "What is that god-awful smell?"

"Shh!" Sophia scooped Lizzie up and placed her on her shoulder. "Hide under my hair."

"My word!" said a woman's voice. "How many people are over there?"

"It's like a garbage truck full of dead rats!" Lizzie screamed. "I'm gonna die of stink!"

"Sorry, ma'am," Sophia called. She stood up and marched out of the stall, then stood at a mirror for a moment pawing at her hair.

Lizzie, holding a hand over her nose, poked her head out from a hairy amber curtain. "Forget your hair, move your feet, girl! What on Dog's green earth is that smell?!"

Sophia laughed. "That," she nodded at the woman's stall, "is doin' business."

Thirty-one

Lizzie held onto Sophia's locks—like fistfuls of rope—a snow-white face floating in a curtain of caramel. *Good thing she doesn't wear pigtails anymore.* The Stick girl had taken little notice of Joaquin at the campsite. Now, as they maneuvered around the store trying to avoid him, she got a good look. Like the Stick boy, Nico, he was lean with cappuccino skin and loose curls of black hair. His blue eyes shone so brightly that Lizzie thought they might burn her retinas if she stared at them. She looked down to see Sophia's reaction, but the girl hid as she ducked behind a display of bird books.

"Oh-ma-god, he's right there. What do I do?"

Lizzie glanced around. "Use people as shields."

"Do what?"

"Hide behind people until we can reach the door."

"Oh, okay. How about that old lady?

"Too short."

"Who then?"

Lizzie pointed. "Next lane over—"

"Next what?"

Lane was the closest word to *aisle* that Lizzie knew. "Tall dude in the cowboy hat."

"Handlebar mustache?"

"Yeah, him. Stay right behind him and act like you're shopping."

Sophia did as the voice in her hair directed. As the tall man meandered down the aisle, the petite teenager shadowed him. Joaquin, too, kept moving around the store, all the while tapping his laptop with his thumbs.

Lizzie chuckled and whispered, "Cowboy's gonna think you're checking out his butt."

"I am not!" Sophia replied. At that, the man turned and gave her an odd look.

The teenager gave a nervous little *hehe* and went around him.

"Where is he?" she whispered urgently.

"The cowboy?" Lizzie asked.

"No, Joaquin."

"I dunno, we lost him. Hold up. Lift me up on that bear."

Sophia turned to see an eight-foot growling grizzly bear standing on his hind legs. His front paws reached toward the ceiling, claws extended. "Yikes!"

"Don't be a wuss. He's stuffed," Lizzie said. "Make it quick, but look casual."

Pretending to stretch, Sophia plucked Lizzie off of her shoulder and dumped her roughly onto the bear.

"Hey, watch the merchandise!" Lizzie complained.

"What are you, a delicate flower?" Sophia shot back.

More like a weed, Lizzie thought.

She climbed to the tip of the grizzly's outstretched claws and peered around. Joaquin stood at the back of the store, taking a photo of the levitating kayak. Lizzie also noticed that Nico and his family—the Stick boy, his moms, Mother Earth and her baby animals, the peace-sign hand, and the rest—were browsing the lanes. The Louisville Cardinals had perched in the wind chimes and dream catchers. Astonishingly, no one else noticed any of them as they tumbled and darted about like an elite acrobatic troupe.

Lizzie started to climb down from the bear. Then, from over by the cash register, the four-year-old terror spotted her. The kid pushed past a woman and charged toward the bear.

"Catch me!" Lizzie called down.

"Do you see him?" Sophia asked.

"Just catch me!"

Five minutes later, Lizzie and Sophia held their breath as the little boy passed by them for what must have been the twentieth time. The Stick and Mobile girls both lay hidden in a huge bin, beneath a mound of discounted items: down parkas, boots, fishing hats, fur-lined gloves, scarves, woolen socks, tarps, and a pair of skis.

"This was a bad idea," Sophia hissed.

Lizzie heard herself sounding like her mom."Pipe down and do what I tell you."

They listened as the boy's parents finally captured him and carried him screaming from the store. Sophia shifted and stirred. "Let's get up."

"Whoa, you surprised me!" said a boy's voice. "Are you on sale, too?"

Lizzie glimpsed the last thing in the world either she or Sophia wanted to see right now: Joaquin's blue eyes.

"Uh. Hi," said Sophia. "I'm just...shopping."

"Uh." He waved the pair of gloves he had just removed from her face. "Yeah." He looked around as if for an exit. "Me, too."

"Half-price," Sophia said with a weak laugh. "You should buy those. You're cu—I mean—they're cute."

"Think I will. Bye," he said. The boy placed another pair of gloves back over Sophia's face.

"Kill me now," the Mobile girl whispered. In the darkness, Lizzie sensed her humiliation. They waited until his footsteps had faded, then Sophia erupted from the bin, spilling merchandise onto the floor. The Stick girl held on as the Mobile bolted from the store. Back at the minivan, she stepped off of Sophia's shoulder and sealed herself onto the back windshield.

"Later."

"Later."

Sophia walked around to her sliding door, tried the latch, and said a bad word.

"Locked?" Lizzie asked.

"Yep." The other groaned. "Joaquin thinks I'm a weirdo. My life is over."

Don't say that. Anything but that.

Lizzie said, "So he found you hiding like a terrorist in a box of discontinued knitwear. No biggie."

"No biggie?! Are you kidding? Now he thinks I'm weird."

"You are weird."

"Ahh! You're no help."

"Um, I meant that as a compliment."

"And he hates me."

"Not true."

"Is too."

"Look, he bought the gloves, didn't he? And it's April. Think about it."

"Oh." Sophia's face brightened. "He did, didn't he?"

"Like an Eskimo buying ice."

"Don't say that. That's racist."

Lizzie wrinkled her forehead. "You might be right. Sorry. But the gloves were a good sign. I think he's into you. Anyway, get it together. Your folks are on their way out. Mine, too." The Stick girl returned her dad's wave as her family started across the gravel. "And whatever you do, don't look at me. They'll freak if they find out we were together."

Sophia didn't reply, but at the sound of a soft *thud, thud, thud,* Lizzie melded to see her bumping her forehead against the side of the van. Lizzie's breath caught in her throat. "Don't!" she pleaded in a whisper.

Sophia looked up, startled, reminding Lizzie of the worst day of her life. Of both their lives.

Thirty-two

ack at the campsite, the Sticks enjoyed a sesame-seed lunch. One seed each and they were stuffed. Soon they became sleepy and lolled about, dozing. But Lizzie had already taken a nap before the trip to the trading post. She had no desire to spend the day lying around the campsite. She had just started over to Nico's to see what he was up to, when she heard a single *hoot*. Faint but clear. She looked back to see her dad waving at the woods. "You owls should be sleeping," he said. Then he yawned and took his own advice.

Sophia sat on Little Stone Mountain, arms crossed. "Where have you been?" she demanded.

Lizzie held up her hands. "Whoa. I can go back if you want."

"Don't you dare. I have been waiting and waiting."

The Stick began climbing the boulder. "Hey, little help?" Sophia lifted her to the top. "I told you it would take me longer than you," Lizzie added.

"Yeah, well, why can't you be like a regular imaginary friend and just pop onto my shoulder when I say so?"

Lizzie thought back to when she had just come out of the box. She herself had had an imaginary friend named Toop-toop, a tiny elephant that used to sit on her shoulder. But Toop-toop had never popped there instantly. She flew there.

Looking up at Sophia now, something sad occurred to her. And not for the first time. *No one sees the real me. Not my parents, not my dog. Even Sunny acts like I'm just her reflection. Or worse, her shadow.*

"Tear me in half," Lizzie said.

"Huh?"

"You heard me."

"Why would I do that?"

"If I'm not real, it doesn't matter."

"I—" Sophia's mouth dropped open.

"Right?"

"I guess not."

"So do it."

"Hm. Okay, why not." She lifted the Stick girl by both arms again.

"Not like that," Lizzie said. "You'll just tear off my arms. That'll hurt like the dickens and make me even more of a cripple."

"That's a bad word," Sophia said.

"True, but I'm a bad imaginary friend. Hold my waist so you can rip me right down the middle." Sophia adjusted her grip. "Yeah, like that." Lizzie winced as she waited to die.

"Wait a minute," Sophia said. "Don't turn this around on me. I'm the one who's upset. Besides, this feels wrong. Like I'm killing my sister all over again."

"*Again?*" Lizzie asked. "What's that supposed to mean?"

Sophia placed her back on the rock surface, gently. "Nothing."

"Look at me," Lizzie said.

"I don't want to talk about it."

"Neither do I. Look at me, anyway."

Sophia met Lizzie's stare.

"I'm a person," the Stick girl said. "Maybe not who you want me to be, but I'm me. I'm not going away and I can't just pop up whenever you want, because I don't live in your messed up brain. I live on the back windshield. Got it?"

"Got it."

"And don't ever say that you killed your sister. You didn't."

"But—"

"No buts. You didn't. The accident wasn't your fault." *It was mine,* Lizzie thought. "There's even a word for it. Sir, something."

"Survivor's guilt," Sophia said. She couldn't look down without looking at Lizzie, so she looked into the woods. They were both so quiet that the wind in the leaves seemed loud. Finally Lizzie spoke.

"Now tell me about this boy."

Sophia shrugged. The sadness on her face played tug-of-war with a dreamy-dopey look. "I dunno. He's just..." She looked up into the sunlit leaves. Dreamy won.

"Holy moly, boy fever," Lizzie said under her breath. "Hershey was right."

"What'd you say?" Sophia asked.

"Nothing."

"Oh, no you don't. It was something. You said, 'Hershey was right.'"

"No, I said he's bright. He's a bright dog."

Sophia studied Lizzie until the Stick girl looked away.

"He's not that bright," Sophia said. "He can't even catch a ball."

"Maybe he can't see too good." Lizzie's words came out before she could catch them. She bit her tongue. Hershey had complained for months that his vision was going dark around the edges. Of course, he could never tell the Mobiles. *And he is bright,* Lizzie thought. *He's the smartest dog I know. That*

British accent of his does make him seem even smarter, though.

"Hershey can't see?" Sophia asked.

"I didn't say that. I said maybe."

Sophia seemed to process the info slowly. "How. Would. You. Know that?"

"I am a keen observer of the canine condition," Lizzie said, amazed at her own knack for pulling a fib out of thin air.

"Right."

Things were complicated enough. She didn't need Sophia trying to talk Dog. *When you want to change the subject,* Lizzie told herself, *ask the other person a question they want to answer.* "What's up with you and this boy?" she asked.

Sophia sighed. Then she described Joaquin, but not how Lizzie had expected. Instead of saying he was tall, cute, handsome, or hot, she described him as quiet, caring, and thoughtful. He loved nature. He treated his moms with respect and they trusted him. They let him do tons more stuff than Sophia's folks let her, but he didn't take advantage of it. Eventually, Sophia got around to his blue eyes and bronze arms. But one thing she said about him confused Lizzie.

"I've never seen a person of color with blue eyes."

Lizzie remembered the first time she saw all of those details appear on Nico. Features and color. She and her own family were completely white, except for their black eyes. Even her hair was white. Nico's family had all kinds of colors, especially the red cardinals. She looked at Sophia, with her beige skin, pink lips, green eyes, and caramel hair. All of the Chapmans had beige skin. Sophia's dad had blue eyes. Did that make them *people of color*?

Sophia had a serious case of boy fever. *What boy wouldn't want to be her boyfriend,* Lizzie wondered? Stick boys were always acting sweet to Sunny, too. That's how boys and girls were. *All except me,* Lizzie thought. She finger-combed her tangled white hair until her pigtails came the rest of the way out. *I'm the only odd one.*

She and Sophia came out of their own little worlds.

"Whatcha thinkin' about?" the Mobile asked.

The Stick girl shook her head. "Nothin'. You?"

"Trash. I was thinking about trash."

"You've been barrel-dumping again?"

"Course not. Can't. Look." Sophia lifted a plastic trash bag that had been sitting on the other side of Little Stone Mountain. "I picked up all this. 'Bout a third full."

Lizzie grunted. "Becoming a hoarder?"

"Hey, don't hate. That's a real thing, I mean an illness. I think. No, I have to."

"Have to what?"

"Pick up trash. Ranger Frowns-a-lot told my dad I have to pick up a whole bag of garbage."

"Eh, that should be easy. Just go to the barrels—"

"No, it has to be litter. Or else he's gonna write my dad a citation."

"Ah."

"It's supposed to re-habituate me."

"Rehabilitate."

"Yeah, that. Smarty pants." Sophia shook the bag and it *clanked.*

Lizzie grinned. "What's in it?"

"Soda cans, beer cans. Hey, wanna see a trick? Watch this." Sophia rummaged in the bag, then placed a Budweiser can on the boulder. "Step back," she warned, and Lizzie did. The Mobile stood up on the boulder, truly gargantuan at this angle. A second later, she stomped the can flat. A loud *crack* sounded, followed by a spray of beer droplets.

"That was your trick? You got stale beer all over me!"

Sophia sighed dramatically, then cleaned off Lizzie with her shirttail.

"Great. Now my folks will think I've been drinking," Sophia complained.

"No, they won't," Lizzie said. "You've been picking up beer cans. But Mom will think I took a bath in the stuff."

Sophia sniffed at Stick girl. "You do stink."

"Thanks. At least we Sticks don't eat too much and then start a *business*," Lizzie mumbled.

"You mean *do* their business. No, I guess not."

"Gross," Lizzie said.

"I agree. Very gross."

The girls looked at each other and laughed. Same laugh, same time. This time, it seemed natural to Lizzie.

"You got an empty Sprite can in there?" Lizzie asked. "Stomp one and maybe I'll smell a little better."

Sophia found a Sprite can and Lizzie stood next to it while the Mobile stomped it. Again air and droplets blasted her.

While she waited to dry, Lizzie told Sophia about her morning run, about meeting bunnies and dragonflies, and the little stream sparkling in the morning light. She admitted how afraid she had been that the patch on her leg wouldn't work. And then described how strong she had felt running again. She failed to mention that she had seen the other doing a handstand on the edge of a cliff.

There was the big thing left unspoken, too: how she could no longer feel Elizabeth. Lizzie and Sophia were as different as any two people could be. But they had their loss in common. On the day the two first spoke, Lizzie had claimed—had lied—that Elizabeth's ghost was her best friend. Since then, Sophia had not asked about it. She probably knew it was a lie. Lizzie had seen dead animals on the highway. She understood what dead meant. But she still looked for the shape of Elizabeth's face in the clouds. Everywhere. Now it seemed childish.

On the way back to the campsite, Lizzie rode on Sophia's shoulder while the other dragged the trash bag. When they got to the dirt road, they passed a trash barrel. Sophia turned around and pointed. "If we turned that barrel on its side, I wonder if I could walk on it? You know, like log-rolling."

"Isn't that how you got in trouble?" Lizzie asked.

"I'm not gonna really do it. I was just wondering."

"Whatever. What's log-rolling?"

"It's a lumberjack thing," Sophia said. "I saw it on YouTube." She described it and Lizzie could sort of see it in her head. In the water, Sophia explained, a log would just spin. But if you walked on a barrel on dry ground, it would move. If you walked forward, it would move backward. And if you walked backward, the barrel would move forward. "Don't you think so?"

"There's only one way to find out," Lizzie said.

"Oh no-no-no," Sophia replied. "I'm not tipping over that barrel."

"Not you. Me." Lizzie made Sophia dig out one of the un-crushed soda cans—a Dr. Pepper—from her trash bag. Then the Stick climbed up on it and tried to walk forward. At once, the can rolled backward and Lizzie fell. "You're right," she said, picking herself up.

"I'm not a dummy."

"You were *never* dumb," Lizzie said, thinking of Sunny. She climbed up and tried again, this time with Sophia holding her hands for balance.

They worked at it until Lizzie got the hang of it. She could move forward by walking backwards, and backwards by walking forward. If she took smaller steps with one leg, she could turn the soda can. And if she walked forward with one leg and backwards with the other, she could turn it in a circle. Lizzie fell off a bunch of times, but before long she could maneuver the can like an acrobat in Cirque Du Soleil.

"Too bad I can't try that with a barrel," Sophia said as she walked and Lizzie rolled down the dirt road.

"Yep. Too bad. Sticks only."

When they got near the clearing of Sophia's campsite, Sophia asked, "Mind if I blink you after dinner? With my flashlight?"

Lizzie grinned. "I'm getting used to having a stalker."

"Haha."

"It's boring around here, so yeah, whenever. Just not in the morning. That's my running time."

"Deal," Sophia said. They bumped fists and parted ways.

Lizzie skidded into camp on the Dr. Pepper can as if it was a sports car. Nico's family heard the commotion and came over to see what was up. Then the Cardinals flew off tweeting about it and word spread fast. Characters from all over the campground, as well as local insects, gathered behind the big blue tent as

Lizzie rolled around on the can and did tricky moves. Then someone discovered three more soda cans at the corner of the tent (Sophia had placed them there). And so everyone took turns learning to roll around on soda cans. But no one could do fancier tricks than Lizzie. Some were calling her the Pepper Stick. Sunny was pretty good too. They called her Sunny Delite, even though her can was a Mellow Yellow.

As daylight faded and stars appeared, it turned into a party. They had can races. Then they stacked the cans in a pyramid and competed to see who could climb the highest before it tumbled down. Lizzie's mom brought out potato-chip fragments on an enormous Pringles lid. The crowd completely consumed a Life Saver for dessert.

No one asked Lizzie how she had discovered can rolling, but Sunny kept giving her a hurt look. Lizzie remembered staring at Sunny like that—jealous, accusing—after Elizabeth's death. She knew what it meant. Sunny could no longer feel Sophia.

Sunny couldn't, but Lizzie could. While the Stick girl ate crumbs, she tasted Sophia's hamburger and sweet potatoes. While the Sticks gathered around the cold LED light of funny-fire, Lizzie felt the warm embers of a real campfire. And when a little flashlight in the forest blinked on and off, Lizzie didn't even need to see it. She felt Sophia waiting for her. Something drew Lizzie to Sophia, just as it had once drawn her to Elizabeth. It was all she could think about. So, as Lizzie sneaked into the woods, she had no idea she was being followed.

Lizzie met Sophia just beyond view of the campsite. She was glad not to have to walk all the way to Little Stone Mountain. She thanked the girl for setting out the three extra soda cans. Then she went on to tell her about the fun they had had with them.

"You weren't watching us, were you?"

Sophia shook her head and almost knocked Lizzie off her shoulder. "Nah. I wish."

"Please don't," Lizzie said. "If they find out you know about us, it'll be bad."

"If you say so."

"And another thing. Make sure the back window of your tent stays zipped closed."

"How am I supposed to do that?"

"I dunno. Just do. I mean, we can usually sense if y'all are going to do something where you might notice us. You know, like if your dad is thinking about opening the back hatch, my dad will feel it. But it would be a real pain to hide if your mom zips open that window."

"Could you do that? Hide that fast?"

"Maybe. We're like super-hiders."

Sophia did a duck-lips face and glanced down at the Stick. "That sounds like something someone says right before they get caught."

They had been on the dirt road for a few minutes. They passed many campfires, plus an occasional bobbing flashlight.

"Where are we headed?" Lizzie asked.

Sophia pointed ahead. "To look at that board. Before I die of boredom."

Not far from the ranger's station stood a glass-enclosed bulletin board. The girls took turns reading the notices out loud: a missing cat, a warning about not feeding bears, a map of the park, and ads for Baby Bear's, guided tours, and a river outfitter. Of greatest interest, a flier for a dance.

"Friday night at The Pavilion?" Lizzie read. "What's that?"

"Must be the Visitor's Center. You've seen it, the big place with the gift shop and the, um, business rooms, as you like to call them."

"A dance, huh?" Lizzie said. "Hm."

"Hm," Sophia said. Then she yawned. "Okay, so, nothing here. I'm ready for my sleeping bag."

"Me, too." Lizzie stifled a yawn of her own. And they went back to the campsite.

Thirty-three

Wednesday Morning

Lizzie again rose before the sun. No crunches this time. She quietly tied on her moccasins, stretched her sore calves, and jogged into the forest. She had gotten more exercise in the last two days than in months. Strangely, her face also felt sore. As the dark woods turned gray, she puzzled over this mystery, never suspecting that the muscles in her mouth and cheeks hurt from smiling.

The bunnies didn't show up this morning, but Lizzie felt them watching. When she reached the stream, she crouched down and splashed her face with the cold water.

Sunbeams streamed through the treetops. A light breeze ruffled Lizzie's white hair. Birdsong grew all around. From somewhere far away, the *caw* of a crow echoed. Morning broke like any morning. But to Lizzie, this day lay balanced on a scale. On one side, sat grief and depression. On the other, hope. It could go either way. Above floated the unknown, a tiny speck that could tilt the scales.

Lizzie had spent most of her life stuck on the back windshield of a minivan. Elizabeth, too, had felt imprisoned by a role that everyone expected her to play. But here in the mountains, anything could happen.

Lizzie didn't run all the way to the cliff. If Sophia was doing handstands on the rail again, the Stick girl didn't want to watch. Instead, she veered off onto a narrow trail that snaked around in unexpected turns. Eventually, the path seemed to disappear.

As Lizzie wandered around searching for a way, she recalled her mom's biggest worry: getting lost. One wrong turn, Mom always warned, and she might not make it back to the minivan. She'd be lost forever. To Lizzie, that sounded better than being told what to do every minute of her life. Besides, the Chapmans would be camping here all week. The Stick girl felt no real danger. As if to confirm her confidence, the trees suddenly thinned out. She emerged from the woods and into a grassy meadow.

Before her, row after row of giant vehicles—ones that made the minivan look small—gleamed in the morning sun. She walked toward them. Gazing around she thought, *So these are RVs. What's that stand for? Rolling vacation?*

Lizzie could hear the muted talk of people inside their houses-on-wheels. This seemed weird. These families had travelled to the great outdoors only to stay indoors. With the sun now up, her own Mobiles were probably bustling around their campsite, poking at last night's campfire. Or walking to the shower cabin to do that *business* thing. So what was the point of a Rolling Vacation?

Ahead stood the most rickety road whale imaginable. Lizzie paused to marvel at it. The tires were slick. Rust covered the wheel rims. Tall weeds grew underneath. A bumper sticker on the back bumper read PIERRE'S SEAFOOD. A hole in the sticker, the shape of a person, suggested that someone had cut out a character, presumably a guy named Pierre. As Lizzie moved on, she noticed that plastic had been duct taped over a broken side window. Maybe the owners had abandoned the thing. But if so, why hadn't the rangers had it towed away?

Then, a small voice with a bad French accent broke through her thoughts. "Geeve me your loot if you want to *leeeeve*," he said. "Be quick about it." Out strode a pirate. He wore high leather boots, silver breeches, a purple waistcoat, and a white shirt with ruffles. A green plaid bandana held back his long dark hair. A wisp of mustache clung to his upper lip. He stood with one leg forward in a kind of fighting pose. In one hand, he held a sword, which he pointed at Lizzie's stomach. He held his other hand high, behind him, as if he might call down lightning or catch a falling apple.

Lizzie stared down at him. He came barely to her knees and was paper-thin. "Well, aren't you the fashionista," she said.

The little pirate twirled his sword with a flourish. "Madame, neither your flattery nor your tears will save you. Hand over all your money and jewels and I *may* let you live." His French accent slipped away like a bad odor.

Lizzie fished through her pockets. *Nope, nothing. Sorry, little dude.*

"Then we shall dance zee dance of dueling deaths!"

Lizzie covered her mouth to keep from laughing. "Where'd you come from, a bag of croissants?"

"Oh, so you think you are funny? Then take this! And this!" He sliced the air several times, then reached as high as he could and thrust the blade through her middle.

"Ow!" she screamed. "Give me that thing!" She snatched the sword. "You just poked a hole in me!"

"It has been your misfortune to cross paths with Cap'n Nobeard. That's me. The most notorious pirate on the high seas!" He leapt for his sword, but Lizzie held it out of reach. "Give it to me! It's mine!"

"No way, bucko."

"But a pirate must have his sword!"

"Not if you're going to poke holes in people." Lizzie rubbed her side. "This really hurts."

"It does? May I see?"

She showed him the pinhole of light that shone through her. If she had had kidneys, the wound might have been fatal. The Stick girl doubled over. "Ouch. I don't even know if this can be repaired."

"You could cover it with a belly button ring, eh?" suggested Cap'n Nobeard. He looked closer at the hole in Lizzie's gut. "Although it is a tiny bit off-center. Tell you what. I'll let you keep your loot."

"Hello? I already told you, I don't have any."

"Any what?"

"Loot! Or a belly button, for that matter." Lizzie examined the little sword with its silver blade and ornate golden hilt. "I oughta break this thing in half."

The pirate clasped his hands over his heart. "You wouldn't! I didn't mean to jab you. It's just that, I'm supposed to be, like, well you know—" He puffed out his chest and attempted a fierce look.

"Tough?" Lizzie asked. "I don't think so. And that fake French accent? Please."

"But I'm dashing, don't you think? We pirates have a flair for the dramatic." He spun in a three-sixty, swept off his hat, bowed, and smoothed his mustache.

"Yeah, you got the drama going on, I'll give you that."

"Come. Let's take a closer look at your injury."

She followed him underneath the cab of the RV and sat down in the grass. The vehicle's grimy radiator hovered overhead like a mother ship.

"But first, please, my steel baby?" He held out his hands. Reluctantly, Lizzie returned his sword.

"No poking."

"No, never. At least, not again." The pirate sheathed it and examined her puncture. "Ooh, that's bad," he said. "Wait just a sec." He skipped (yes, skipped) around one of the front wheels and out of sight. Lizzie heard a *whoosh*. He reappeared holding the head of a white wildflower with a yellow center. He plucked one of its petals and placed it over the puncture. "We press it against the wound, like so." The Stick girl held the velvety-soft petal in place.

"A petal? But that's not going to—"

"Fix it? No," he said, "but it's chamomile. Good for the pain."

"That's not... bad," Lizzie sighed. The pinprick of fire in her side began to cool. "I've heard ivy works, too."

"True, but it makes you drowsy."

The two sat down in the grass and made small talk. Lizzie held the velvety, white petal against her belly as the pain subsided.

From a nearby RV, a Mobile emerged and clomped down the steps. Cap'n Nobeard turned to look. Lizzie stared at the pirate's profile, and at the hilt of his sword.

"Fancy," she said.

"It is a treasure." He drew it, polished the handle with the tail of his coat, then slid the sword back in its sheath. "It was part of my bumper sticker. Of course."

"Your sticker?"

He nodded toward the back end of the RV.

Lizzie remembered seeing the RV's bumper sticker with the person-shaped hole in it. "That was you. The seafood restaurant?"

"Pierre's," he said.

"But how?" She had never heard of a bumper sticker character who had been cut out of their rectangle.

"I cut myself out," the pirate said, twiriling his sword, "with my wicked blade." Lizzie gave him a doubtful look. "Not really," he admitted. "Chip freed me with a sharp rock."

Lizzie examined his precise edges. "For real? Chip did this work with just a rock." She and the pirate both meant a chipmunk. *Chips* all share the same name.

The other nodded. "He was a talented art student, specializing in sculpture."

"So, if you came from that bumper sticker, that means your name is…"

"Pierre, at your service." He tipped his hat. "Pierre's features the finest dockside dining and endless crab legs."

Lizzie nodded as if she knew what he meant. "So if your real name is Pierre," she said, "why do you go by Cap'n Nobeard?"

"Because I had no beard in high school and I don't need one now!" He laughed at what Lizzie assumed was supposed to be a joke.

"You went to school?"

The pirate rubbed his smooth chin. "Of course. Didn't you?"

Lizzie frowned. "Home-schooled." Then she added, "Well, you don't need a beard. Pirates don't have to be fierce. It's okay to look..." She searched for the right word. "Fabulous." That brought a smile from him. She glanced up at the greasy underbelly of the RV. "So, how come you're still hanging around this rust bucket?"

He pointed up. "Loretta needs me. My Mobile. She's like a thousand years old. Sometimes she falls. Forgets things. Someone has to watch her. Anyway—" the little pirate thumped the front tire with his fingers, "what's a captain without his ship?"

"Sure." The Stick girl glanced at the bald tire. "It's quite a...." She hesitated to call the junker a ship.

Cap'n Nobeard wagged a finger. "Not it, she. A ship is always a she."

Lizzie scowled. "Sounds like a stereotype."

"You have a point. Still, she's a remarkable vessel."

"Right." Lizzie got to her feet, as did the Cap'n.

"Feeling better?" he asked.

"Peachy." She thrust the petal into his hands. "Been a blast, but I gotta go."

"Must you?"

"Ah, yep. Afraid so."

"Next time–" the petite pirate began.

"Next time don't poke a hole in me," Lizzie quipped.

"Of course." He then promised that, on Lizzie's next visit, he would plunder Loretta's sewing box for a straight pin and teach the Stick girl to sword fight. That actually sounded fun, so she promised to return later that week.

As Lizzie jogged away, the tiny swashbuckler blew her a kiss, waved the petal, and called, *"Adieu, bon voyage!"* Still not sounding very French.

I met a pirate, she thought. *How do you like them apples, Mom? I met one and lived to tell the tale! Now, what can I use to make a belly button ring?*

Before she had run very far, she stopped at a kiosk and memorized the park map, noting the location of the RV campground. After staring at it for a moment, she slapped her forehead. *RV. Of course. Remarkable vessel.*

Thirty-four

When Lizzie reached her campsite, she saw her sister, dog, and Nico standing at the top of the big blue tent. She watched as Ups sat down on a sock and then slid down, *woo-hooing* loudly. At the bottom, he face-planted in the grass. Just as quickly, he hopped up and brushed himself off. Lizzie folded her arms to hide the hole in her stomach.

"Looks fun," she said.

"It's a blast. I'd tell you to give it a try, but that'd be fewer turns for me."

"You're so thoughtful, Ups. Where's Mom and Dad?"

He shrugged. "Not here."

Works for me, Lizzie thought.

From the top of the tent, Nico waved a sock like a big thick flag. "You up for this?" he called.

Lizzie showed him a grin. "I guess," she called back. She turned to the dog. "Any trick to this?"

"Uh, no. Yeah. Take off your moccasins. They're slippery."

"I thought slipping was the point."

"Well, duh, on the way down, sure. Not when you're climbing up. And here." He undid a yarn harness from his waist. "Tie this around your middle."

Lizzie took it and nearly fell down from the weight. Ups laughed.

"Heavy, huh? There's a big pebble inside. It keeps us from floating. You know—" He waved a paw like an airplane.

"Got it." Lizzie tied the loose ends of yarn around her and looked down. It looked like some kind of dorky fanny pack, but the heavy stone also covered the sword hole in her stomach. *Good.* Ups handed her the sock. She threw it over her shoulder, then kicked off her magnolia-leaf sandals.

"I gotta run," he said. "Got some serious exploring to do. Hey, watch." The dog pointed toward the top of the dome. Lizzie watched as Sunny sat down on a sock, gave a little push, and began sliding. She pushed a second time and picked up speed. She raced down the canvas screaming like she was three instead of thirteen. Near the ground, the slope leveled out. As Lizzie's twin reached the grass, she let go of the sock, did a somersault, and landed on her feet. She held up her arms and arched her back like a gymnast. Lizzie ran up to her.

"That was amazing, sis!" But Sunny didn't even look at her. She snatched the sock off the ground and began climbing back up.

Lizzie turned to Ups. "What's her problem?"

He shook his head. "Dunno. The Princess of Ever-loving Sunshine has a rain cloud over her head. You going up, or what?"

It looked like Sunny and Nico were waiting for her to climb, so Lizzie started up. The tent wall was steep and slippery. She could see how it would be impossible to climb wearing magnolia sandals. About halfway up, the big sock got in the way and she slipped back a little.

"Maybe you should go on another nature walk," Sunny called down.

Nature walk! Lizzie thought. *I'm a runner!* She glanced at her patched leg. It looked and felt strong. *Lizzie* felt strong. She kept climbing. As she reached the top, Nico held out a hand to help her up. Lizzie acted like she didn't see it and stood up on her own.

Without looking at her, Sunny took another turn. Halfway down, she stood up like a surfer. At the bottom, she finished the ride with a cartwheel.

"She sure likes to push the limit," Nico said.

"She's pushing my buttons," Lizzie said. "Why are we up here, anyway?"

The Stick boy scratched his head. "To slide?"

"No, I mean what's wrong with your tent?"

"Oh. You haven't heard? Check it out." Nico nodded toward his campsite.

Lizzie gazed over at the orange and yellow tent. She had a good view of it from this height. But something was odd. It was moving. Shaking. Leaning. A few seconds later, the whole thing collapsed from view. Lizzie could hear Mobiles gathering poles and pulling up pegs. She could even see the tops of their heads. She turned back to Nico.

"You're leaving?"

"Not exactly. Our Mobiles are hiking to the Ray Fisher campsites."

"Where's that?"

Nico grunted. "In the middle of nowhere."

Lizzie closed her eyes and visualized its exact location on the park map. Sites that the map called *primitive*. She opened her eyes. "That's hardcore."

"That's my family," the other laughed. "Hardcore granola-heads."

Lizzie gestured at the woods. "This isn't nowhere enough?"

"Yeah, but you gotta hike to Ray Fisher. No cars allowed," Nico said. "Our Mobiles are worried that Daisy will get hit by a car. They're making Joaquin leave his laptop and iPhone. He's, like, always on it."

"Chit-chatting with friends?" Lizzie asked.

Nico shook his head and laughed. "You mean chatting? Texting? No, nothing like that. He's kind of a nerd. Coding. That's all he does. Codes apps."

The Stick girl nodded. "If you say so." *Still,* she thought, *Sophia will think Joaquin and his family are leaving for good. She'll freak.* "What about the Subaru?" Lizzie asked.

Nico glanced around. "Half the sites here are empty anyway, so the rangers said we could leave the car here for a couple of days. "

"You're going, too?"

He nodded.

"How's that gonna work?" She looked through the trees but could not see any of his family—Mother Earth and her babies, the Cardinals, Darwin, or the moms.

"Stowing away in the backpacks," Nico answered.

"Ha. Try not to get squished by a bag of granola."

"Wanna hang out when I get back?"

Lizzie looked down. "Guess so."

From the ground, Sunny called, "You sliding or what?"

"In a sec!" Lizzie shouted back. She gave a little growl.

"Well, then, I'm coming up." Sunny started to climb again.

Nico said, "Listen, you need to be careful."

Lizzie looked over at his campsite just to avoid watching Sunny climb. "Don't worry about me."

"You? I'm not. I'm worried about her." He nodded at Sunny, who was half-way up.

"I bet you are."

Nico sighed. "Lizzie Stick, for someone who's supposed to be smart, you don't see very much."

"Sunflower, that's what my dad calls her. Sunflower."

"Yeah? If you ask me, that one's wilting."

"I guess that's what happens to a flower if it doesn't get enough sunlight. Or in her case, the spotlight."

Nico shrugged and shook his head. "I dunno. Something's not right."

Sunny was getting near the top. Lizzie gave Nico a dark look and poked her finger in his chest. "Sisters fight," she whispered. "That's normal. But *you* better not hurt her or you'll wish you'd never been stuck."

"Me?" Nico gave her a grin that made it hard not to like him. "I'm harmless as a puppy." He sat down on his sock just as Sunny reached the summit. "I'll see you—both of you—in a day or two," he said. The girls watched as he slid down, landed on his feet, and disappeared into the trees.

Ups, too, had run off to the woods. That left just the twins. As they looked at each other, Lizzie saw more anger in Sunny's eyes than ever.

That's when a simple game of sliding turned into a contact sport. Each one tried to outdo the other. Instead of pushing off with their hands, they made running starts. And no more feet-first. They dove headlong down the side of the tent, going faster and faster. Sometimes they slid standing up. Sometimes they did handstands. They went all X Games with their landings too, doing flips and making up tricks. Instead of giggles, they grunted at each other. When one of them wiped out, the other just laughed.

On the last slide, Sunny reached the summit just as Lizzie started down.

Lizzie got a running start and leapt face-first. As she did, the wind gusted behind her. She hit the canvas sliding faster than ever. As the ground rushed at her, she vaulted into a twisting triple somersault and landed on her feet. *There's no way Sunny can beat that one,* she thought. She turned to flash a wicked grin at her sister, but just as she did Sunny plowed into her. The two went tumbling through the grass in a tangle of arms and legs.

Lizzie felt like she had been smacked with a fly swatter. She staggered to her feet.

"What'd ya do that for?"

"Me? You won't get out of the way!"

"Just forget it," Lizzie said. "I'm done with you."

"You're what?"

"Done," Lizzie said. "Done with this game." She started walking toward the bread-bag tent.

Sunny followed her. "That's not what you said. You said, 'I'm done with *you*,' meaning me."

"I did not."

"You did, too."

Lizzie wheeled on her sister. "Just drop it. What if I did? You've been done with me for what—a year?"

"I have not!"

"Oh, yes, you have!"

"No, I haven't!"

"Right. How long did you try, Sunny? How long until you left me alone to wallow in—whatever this is." She thought for sure Sunny would shoot back with "Self-pity!"

"I've been trying everyday," Sunny said, scrunching up her face. "Everyday!" Lizzie saw tears in her eyes. "For a year and a month and twelve days."

Lizzie's mouth fell open.

"Yeah," Sunny said, "I know how long it's been. Sophia counts the days and so do I. Only today I counted by myself. Because I can't *feel* her. I can't feel my own Mobile anymore!"

Lizzie wanted to hug her sister, but her own hurt and anger stung too much. So what if Sunny couldn't feel Sophia? Lizzie couldn't feel Elizabeth anymore, either. Some days Lizzie felt incredibly sad. On others, she felt nothing at all.

"Welcome to my world," Lizzie said. She turned and walked into the forest. *Why would I say such a thing?* she wondered. *I'm a terrible person.* For once, she wished their mom would tell them to knock it off.

Sunny followed. "Where'd you go last night?"

"For a run," Lizzy replied. She didn't look back. Her own eyes had turned glassy with tears.

"At night?"

"It's called a night run."

"I saw you," Sunny called. "I saw you with *her.*"

You're crazy, Lizzie thought. But Sunny was right. Lizzie had been with Sophia. She stopped and spun around. Just as she did, her sister tackled her.

Thirty-five

"**Y**ou stole her!" Sunny screamed as the two again rolled on the ground. "You stole my Sophia!"

Lizzie landed on top of Sunny. "You stole my friend!" she yelled back. "Nico was my friend, first!"

"I did not."

"You did. You batted your big eyelashes and—Ow!" Sunny pulled Lizzie's hair and flipped on top.

"He's still your friend, genius. But you had to go and show yourself to a Mobile. *My* Mobile! And now, I can't feel her! I might never feel her again!" Sunny's tears fell onto Lizzie's face, which was shocking, since Sticks are nearly bone-dry to begin with. And the look on Sunny's face was not just anger or sadness. It was blank. Like all the life had been drained out of her.

Lizzie had never been good with words. Now, she proved it again. "Sucks, doesn't it."

Screaming, they tore at each other as they rolled around in the dirt and leaves. They had always shared so much as twins. Now their sorrow mingled like oil stains on a highway. Finally, exhausted, they lay still, side by side, panting and looking up into the branches.

"You took... my sister," Sunny mumbled.

"I what?"

"You... you took my Lizzie Lou."

"Now I know you've lost it. I *am* Lizzie."

"I know who you are. First I lost Elizabeth, then I lost you."

"Hello? *You* didn't lose Elizabeth, *I* did."

Sunny gasped, trying to choke back sobs. "When Sophia lost Beth... I lost her. It crushed us. I felt..." Her voice faded into a soft moan.

To Lizzie, losing Elizabeth had been an intense personal tragedy. But her whole family had been affected. Now she realized that Sunny felt that loss almost as deeply as she did. Lizzie stared at her. Her sister reminded her so much of Sophia crying at the boulder. What Sophia felt, Sunny felt. Lizzie searched for words.

"But you're always so... sunny."

Sunny nodded. "I am. I try. I try to be happy so everyone else will be, too. Especially you, 'cause you're broken. But it takes all I've got. I don't have enough sunshine for both of us. I'm sorry." The tears in both girls' eyes brimmed like a mountain lake in spring after the winter thaw. "And I just can't —" She buried her face in Lizzie's shoulder.

"Do it alone?" Lizzie whispered.

They lay there, sweating, sticking to each other, tears streaming. Finally, they rolled apart and sat facing each other with their legs crossed—two Stick girls, powdered with dirt and leaves.

Lizzie told Sunny about how she had met Sophia. About how they rescued Serena Williams from the trash barrel. She told about their adventure in Baby Bear's Trading Post.

"And get this," she said. "Joaquin found Sophia hiding in the discount bin."

Sunny gasped. "If someone saw me like that, I'd just die."

"That's what Sophia said."

Lizzie also told Sunny about meeting Cap'n Nobeard, the pirate. She showed her the stab wound in her gut.

"Oh-my-god, I can see daylight through you!" Sunny exclaimed.

"Poked a hole in my dress," Lizzie said with a grin.

"No big loss, eh?" Sunny asked. "You've complained about that dress ever since our Peeling."

Lizzie sighed. "I wasn't made right."

Sunny took both of her hands. "You were absolutely made

right. You're the completely different-from-me identical twin you're supposed to be."

Lizzie grinned and wiped a tear. "That doesn't make any sense, but thanks."

"You're just a tomboy," Sunny said. "Or something different. But you're you and that's all you need to be."

As the afternoon light slowly turned reddish gold, the twins held hands and talked and threw little twigs at each other and laughed. Lizzie shared more stuff that had been on her mind. She only held back one little detail that lay buried in her heart. It was about the night that Elizabeth died. That was something she couldn't even whisper to herself.

Sunny opened up too. She told Lizzie how she felt about Nico. "It's not a crush if he feels the same way, right?" She and Nico had walked to Bearwallow Creek. They had sneaked inside the Visitor Center. They had held hands, but Nico hadn't gotten up the nerve to kiss her yet. Sunny said she was about to get up the nerve for him.

Lizzie made a face. "Yuk. You're just thirteen." Then, seeing Sunny's frown: "Maybe it'll happen at the dance."

"Dance?"

"Oh, right, you don't know." Lizzie described the flier that she and Sophia had read at the bulletin board. "While the Mobiles have their dance party, we can have one of our own."

She told Sunny she was glad for her and Nico. "Now we've

got to find a way to get Sophia and Joaquin together."

Sunny sighed. "His family just left on a long hike. They might not even be back for the dance."

"Don't worry, they'll be back."

"How do you know?"

Lizzie punched her sister in the arm. "I don't think Nico can stay away from you for that long." That brought a smile to Sunny's face.

"But you said the dance is Friday night," Sunny said. "We'll be gone by then."

"Yeah, but remember—half the campsites are empty. The rangers might let us stay longer. If our Mobiles want to. We just need to convince them."

Sunny got a dreamy look on her face. "He's sweet, isn't he?"

"Sure. Sweet as a melted Gummy Bear. But listen—" Lizzie ruffled her sister's hair. "Forget about him for now."

"Why's that?"

"Because while he's gone, you're gonna spend some time with Sophia." Lizzie made her eyebrows dance. "Face to face."

"Huh?"

"Yeah. You're going to meet her at a secret place we call Little Stone Mountain. You're going to talk to her—"

"But—"

"Just like you talk to me. Not like a scaredy-cat little Stick girl who stares back from the windshield and never says a word."

Sunny didn't say anything back. She just squeezed her sister's hands.

By the time the girls appeared before their parents, they had picked most of the dirt, grass, and rock fragments off of their sticky sides. Most, but not all.

Mom said, "You're both dirty," but nothing more.

Lizzie figured their mom knew they had been fighting. So the girls kept working to remove the remaining dirt from each other, using a brush made from chipmunk fur.

Not long before sunset, a certain sleep-deprived owl hooted. "That's the signal," Lizzie whispered. And she sent Sunny off to Little Stone Mountain, while she herself stayed at camp.

It was unusual for Sunny to go for a walk by herself. It looked as if Mom and Dad might follow her. To distract them, Lizzie asked if they would show her Bearwallow Creek. So the three of them hiked the short trail to the creek. Lizzie had never seen water so powerful. It scared her. To hide her fear, she inched forward and stretched out her foot to dip a toe in the water. But Mom thrust an arm in front of her.

"No, you don't, soldier! Watch." The Stick mom plucked a dandelion and tossed it in. Lizzie watched as the current pulled the seed-puff downstream, between two immense boulders, and beneath the surface of a white blur.

"Okay. I get it," she said.

Her dad said, "C'mon, Lizzie Lou, it's getting dark. Let's get back."

Lizzie laughed, then he laughed, and even Mom let out a chuckle. But it was the kind of laughter that covers something. As they hiked back to camp, Lizzie saw them glancing at her. *They're afraid, too,* she thought. *Afraid of losing me.* And for the first time she realized that they had been carrying that burden for a while. Just like Sunny. For a year, a month, and twelve days.

Thirty-six

Wednesday Evening

Over dinner, Lizzie and Sunny sent messages back and forth with hand signals, winks, and whispers. Mom watched, but left them alone.

"So, you like her?" Lizzie asked.

"She's amazing!" Sunny whispered back. Her eyes bulged with wonder. "She picked me up and walked around, I mean—wow!"

Lizzie laughed. "Wait 'til you get stuffed in her pocket. That's no fun. Any news about Joaquin?"

"Sorta. His family walked over to let Sophia's parents know they're out of here for a couple of days. Oh, did you know he's adopted? Yeah. Anyway, Joaquin's moms gave Sophia a pair of boots, you know, some used ones they had. Maybe like a thank-you gift? Or maybe because they're so ugly they didn't want them. Clunky things."

"Who cares, boots are boots. But did Joaquin talk to her?"

Sunny shook her head. "Hardly even looked at her. Just sat there tapping away at his mega-rectangle. What'd Nico call it?"

"Laptop."

"And now Sophia feels all fluttery."

"So—you can feel her again?"

Sunny flashed her perfect crescent-moon smile and nodded.

The loser in Lizzie's head spoke up. *Guess I just lost another friend.*

"And guess what?" Sunny whispered. "She wants to meet us after her folks are snoozing."

Lizzie stared. "And you're up for sneaking out? You radical!" They bumped fists.

After dinner, Lizzie and her family sat by the funny-fire and listened to the night. With the Stick and Mobile families next door gone, the campground was fairly quiet. She could hear the Chapmans' conversation and the crackle of their campfire. A motion picture of their stretchy shadows flickered across the branches. Slowly, their fire died. The Chapmans retired to their sleeping bags. Lizzie saw the side of the big blue tent bulge as someone rolled against it.

"About that time," the Stick dad said with a yawn.

As the Stick parents and Ups crawled into their bread-bag

tent, Sunny asked, "Can we sit by the fire and talk? Me and Lizzie? Sister time?"

Their mom looked out from the tent entrance. "Permission granted, but don't stay up long. You need your rest. Don't forget to put out the fire." She disappeared inside. After a while, Lizzie could hear her parents both snoring. She stared out at the forest, waiting for three flashes of light, then two, then three.

"Mom snores worse than dad," she whispered. She looked over and saw Sunny's lips moving silently. "What the heck are you doing?"

"We're counting. One-ninety-five, one-ninety-six. Don't mess me up."

Lizzie read her lips. *One-ninety-seven, one-ninety-eight, one-ninety-nine, two hundred.*

Sunny slipped on her moccasins and stood up. "C'mon."

Lizzie glanced at the dark woods. "But the signal."

"She's not out there. C'mon."

Sunny switched off the funny-fire light, Lizzie grabbed her moccasins, and the Stick girls tiptoed away. Sunny led Lizzie around the big tent to the clearing in front. Sophia sat on a cooler with her back to them, warming her feet by the remains of the real campfire. Sunny tapped her on the leg.

Sophia bent down to their level. "You scared me!" she said quietly.

"Sorry," Sunny whispered back.

"What happened to the signal?" Lizzie asked. "I thought we were going to meet at Little Stone—"

"Shh!" Sophia pointed toward her tent. "Somebody's still awake. I couldn't signal 'cause I left my flashlight in there. Come on up." She lifted the twins into her lap. The campfire's embers still glowed red hot. Neither Lizzie nor Sunny had ever been so close.

"Real fire, oh that's so cool," Lizzie said.

Sunny differed. "Oh no, no, no. This is so not cool at all."

"Stop your whining, I won't let you melt," Sophia said. She glanced back at the tent. "And keep your voices down." She started counting again silently. Both Sticks read her lips. And Lizzie thought: *Sophia must be a two-hundred girl. Elizabeth used to count to eight. Like, all the time.*

Somewhere around 150, Sophia stopped counting. "I think they're asleep."

Lizzie listened. "They are."

"You're sure?"

"Well..." Lizzie stretched her hands toward the fire's warmth and breathed in the smoky smell. "Your dad doesn't snore, but when he's out, he whistles through his nose. He's doing it now. Your mom's sawing logs. Even you can hear that. And Hershey —well, he's not asleep. His breathing hasn't changed yet. I'm sure he's onto us, but he won't even thump his tail unless he senses we're in danger."

"Hershey never snitches," Sunny added.

Sophia's mouth hung open. "What's that supposed to mean? And how can you hear all that?"

The twins glanced at each other and ignored the first question. Sunny whispered, "If Lizzie says she hears it, that's the way it is."

The instant they left the campfire, Lizzie missed its warmth. Sophia had forgotten her little flashlight, so she walked down the road in darkness. Lizzie rode on her left shoulder and Sunny on her right. A dark wall of trees stood against a star-sprinkled sky. The dirt road wound like a frozen gray stream. When they passed some people with flashlights, the twins quickly hid behind Sophia's hair. Sunny hadn't been under there before. She looked around at the dark curtain and started to say something, but Lizzie placed a finger over her lips. When the people had passed, the twins came back out and took their places on each shoulder.

"Where we goin'?" Lizzie asked.

"I know where," Sunny said.

"You both know," the Mobile added.

Lizzie grunted. "Not me."

Sunny leaned forward and caught her sister's eyes. "Try."

Sophia nodded. "Like she said. You're both mine now. Or I'm yours. Whatever."

Lizzie squeezed her eyes shut and concentrated. She didn't

get any words or images, but when she opened her eyes, she said, "The cliff."

"Exactly."

"Why there?"

"Why not?" Sunny and Sophia both asked.

Lizzie sighed. As long as the giant girl didn't get too near the edge, what did it matter?

A swollen moon flooded the clearing, revealing Gorges Overlook and making the Sticks glow white. Sophia walked up to the rail.

"Not too close," Lizzie warned.

Sophia craned her neck to see her. "You saw me? Here? Right here on this rail?"

"Maybe."

"What're you guys talking about?" Sunny asked.

Sophia blew out a breath. "Your stalker sister saw me—"

"Doing handstands," Lizzie interrupted. She pointed at the rail. "On that."

All three peered down at the sheer drop.

"No way!" Sunny gasped.

"Jeez on a grilled cheese!" Sophia defended. "I was just taking a picture."

Lizzie crossed her arms. "Right. Could have been your last."

The Mobile girl pulled out her phone and showed them a series of dramatic selfies.

"Impressive," Sunny said, "and stupid."

Sophia sighed. "I guess. And my stupid phone's got like zero signal, so I can't even post these."

Both Stick girls stared at her.

Sophia pocketed the phone. "I got it out of my system, okay? Pinky swear." She offered her little finger.

"Careful," Lizzie said, as the twins fist-bumped it, "her pinky swears are like getting hit with a pencil."

Sophia looked from one sister to the other. "Hey! This is like a movie where there's an angel on one shoulder and a devil on the other."

"That makes me the angel," Sunny said, smiling.

Lizzie glanced at her sister and grinned. "I'm the devil."

Sunny hugged Sophia's neck, or at least as much of it as her arms could reach. "Don't jump!" she called in a melodramatic voice.

Lizzie pointed down. "Hehehehehe, jump!"

"Don't jump!"

"Jump!"

They went back and forth, laughing, until Sophia promised not to do anymore potentially lethal handstands. Then they grew quiet and stared out at gray hills blanketed in moonlight.

"I wish Lizbeth was here," Sophia said.

"Lizbeth," Lizzie repeated. "I forgot you used to call her that." She stared up at the moon, wondering if Elizabeth's light had gone dark forever.

On the way back to the campsite, Sophia suddenly stopped in the road. "Hey, I almost forgot, we're going whitewater rafting tomorrow."

"Who is?" the twins asked.

"We are. My family. First thing in the morning. That means you two, too."

"Well, of course," Lizzie said. "Our family goes everywhere yours does."

"No, silly," Sophia said, "I mean I'll take you with me in my pocket. In the raft."

Sunny squealed with excitement and clapped her hands. "That's so awesome!"

But Lizzie's eyes narrowed. *Ice-cold water rushing over sharp rocks*, she thought. *Oh, boy.*

Thirty-seven

Before daylight, Lizzie slipped out of the tent and into her moccasins. She stared at the shadowy forest. *Easy to get hurt running in the dark,* she thought. *Plus there's the rafting trip.*

No one in her family had ever been left behind when the van rolled out. Lizzie didn't want to be the first.

She bent down and massaged her sore calf muscles. They felt beefy, at least for a Stick. But her arms... *Puny! Pathetic!* Then she realized what she was doing—criticizing herself. Again.

I am not pathetic. I am strong. I am smart. But it was hard to hold onto good thoughts. She raised her arms and flexed her biceps like a dude. *I'm getting stronger,* she told herself. Then she had an idea, a way to make sure she really was getting stronger and not just lying to herself. But it meant she had to wake Sophia.

Lizzie tugged open the zipper to the big blue tent and climbed in. Three Mobiles lay sleeping in cloth cocoons. Their chests rose and fell with each breath. Hershey opened one eye, saw Lizzie, and went back to sleep.

Trying not to make a sound, she tiptoed between the mountainous forms until she found Sophia, and climbed up. *Mobile ears are weird looking,* the Stick girl thought as she looked down into one of Sophia's. Then she whispered "Wake up" into it. The giant girl yawned and mumbled something that Lizzie couldn't understand. Then the Stick girl had to duck as a massive hand took a swipe at her. As if she was a mosquito. It took several more tries to wake the teenage giant.

Outside the tent, Sophia lifted Lizzie to eye level, smacked her lips, and blinked in the dim light. "What."

Lizzie started to make a comment about morning breath, but decided to get right to the point. "I need to get into the minivan."

"You what?" The Mobile girl glanced at the dark sky and sighed. "What time is it?"

"Time to do what I tell you."

"Uh-uh. I think it's o-dark-I'm-still-asleep."

But a minute later, the dome light blinked on and the door

chime sounded as Sophia climbed onto the driver's seat. "This better be, like, life and death," she said tossing the keys on the floorboard. She set Lizzie on the flat surface underneath the front windshield.

"So this is inside," Lizzie said. "It's so quiet."

Sophia grunted. "Yeah? Not when the radio's playing some retro junk. Or my folks are jabbering about politics. Why d'ya think I keep my earbuds in?"

"Ha! You should try a few hours of highway noise. Or my mom's lectures." Lizzie gazed up at the sloping front glass. "Wow!" Then she knelt down and felt the rippled texture of the dashboard.

Sophia thumped the steering wheel. "Hello? Why are we here?"

"I told you," Lizzie said, "I need some stuff."

"What stuff? Where?"

"From the vault. Um, the uh...you call it the glove something."

"Glove box?"

"That's it. Which makes no sense at all 'cause it's not shaped like any box I ever saw, plus you don't keep any—"

"Just—what d'ya need?" Sophia began rummaging in the glove compartment.

"The first-aid kit," Lizzie said. "There's Q-Tips in there. No, no, put all those back. I just need one."

"You gonna clean out your ears?"

"You'll see. No, don't close it. I need the Superglue. It's way in the back. Right corner."

Sophia dug around and fished out a small tube of glue. Then Lizzie made her collect four quarters from the change tray in the center console. She instructed Sophia to glue two coins on each end of the Q-Tip.

"Careful. You're dripping."

"I never said I was crafty. What am I making?"

"A barbell."

"A what?"

Lizzie held up her skinny arms. "I need to pump some iron."

"Ew."

"Once that dries it'll be perfect for doing bench presses and curls. The exercise kind, not like curly hair."

"You're weird." Sophia placed the tiny barbell on the dash to dry, then pointed the Superglue at Lizzie. "You need some?"

The Stick girl leapt onto the rearview mirror and clung to it. "Don't get that anywhere near me."

"Why not? Might help you stick better."

"Put the cap on. Quick."

"Jeez," Sophia said, "it's no biggie, it wears off. I stuck my fingers together when I was a kid."

"Yeah, well, I'm not you," Lizzie said. "Superglue's dangerous. If I scratched my nose, I'd be stuck that way."

Sophia laughed. "It'd be funny if you got stuck scratching your butt." Getting only a scowl for a reply, she capped the tube, then tossed it in the glove box. "My bad."

Still hanging from the mirror, Lizzie swung around to the shiny side. "So that's what I look like."

Sophia laughed. "You've never seen yourself?"

"'Course I have. Just never this close. We use the side mirrors. Sunny's, like, addicted to her reflection."

"Nothing wrong with liking how you look," Sophia said. "Don't you?"

Lizzie looked away from her own image and shook her head.

Sophia leaned close. "But you're pretty. You look just like your sister."

Lizzie crinkled up her face. "Lucky me." She swung onto the other's shoulder.

Sophia flashed a smile at the mirror. "Well," she said, "I have something you might like. In the back of the car."

Lizzie *melded* from looking forward to looking toward the back of the van.

"Whoa, I didn't know you could do that!"

"Oh sure," Lizzie said, "it's called melding. NOT to be confused with melting." She tried not to show fear as she and the Mobile girl exchanged a look. "So what's back there?"

"You'll see."

All *Outside* Sticks were curious about the inside, from the gas pedal to the spare tire. But for Lizzie, the cargo area was the last place in the world she wanted to go. It was where Elizabeth had died.

Where I caused her death.

Sophia climbed into the back seat with Lizzie on her shoulder.

This is where she used to sit, Lizzie thought. *Right here.*

Sophia leaned over the back seat to grab something from the far back.

Lizzie closed her eyes. An image very much like this—a waking nightmare—had played over and over in her mind. Like Sophia, Elizabeth had reached for something in the cargo area. At that moment, a car had plowed into them from behind. Elizabeth's head had collided with the back windshield. Lizzie had been looking into her eyes at the split-second that the light went out of them.

I killed her.

Sophia sat up straight, then turned on the dome light and held up a set of sixteen markers. "Ready to put a little color in your life?" she asked.

Lizzie grinned. "You want to draw on me? No way. Mom would kill me."

"Suit yourself." Sophia tossed them in the back. "Okay, well, how about this?" She pulled a plastic wheel from her cup holder. "Remember when my dad ran over my skateboard?"

"Yeah, genius, you shouldn't have left it in the driveway."

"You sound like him. Anyway, I saved one of these. You can use it for your workout."

Lizzie examined the wheel. "What am I supposed to do with it?"

"You flip it. End over end. Like this." Sophia demonstrated. "The high school football team flips big tractor tires in practice. S'posed to turn 'em into hunks, I guess."

"Mm-hm. Football players?"

"Hey, don't judge. Anyway, give it a try." She set Lizzie on the seat.

Lizzie grunted as she lifted and flipped the skateboard wheel. "Whoa! Sucker's heavy. I love it."

Sophia grinned. "And I bet your barbell's ready." She started to climb up front.

"Wait," Lizzie said. She had felt a chill.

"What."

"I dunno. Gimme a minute."

Strangely, Lizzie felt a *presence* in the far back of the van. Not Elizabeth's ghost. She knew the only thing living back there was her own guilt. Still... something was there. So she took a big breath and climbed over the back seat.

The cargo area looked and felt ordinary—flat and empty except for the box of colored markers. She walked slowly around the floor. "Weird," she said. "I can feel..." She looked up at the windshield and her own place there, a Stick-shaped clear spot in the dust. Beyond that, she saw the first gray light of dawn. Then she knelt down, reached into a crease in the carpet, and drew out a broken necklace. Sophia and Lizzie gasped. Together they examined it. A silver chain with a charm hanging from it: half of a heart. Letters engraved on it read "ters" and "ever."

Sophia reached inside the collar of her pajamas and pulled out an almost-identical necklace. The letters on its charm read "Sis" and "For." The Mobile girl fitted the two charms together into a single heart and rubbed her finger over the completed message. Lizzie ran her hand across it, too, feeling the sharp edges of the letters. As one, the girls read the words aloud.

"Sisters Forever."

Elizabeth had lost her necklace the moment she lost her life.

Lizzie dodged a giant teardrop.

"Sorry, I'm sorry." Sophia sniffed and ran the back of her hand across her face. "I kinda think you should have this," she added. She held up Elizabeth's charm next to Lizzie—about the size of the Stick girl's head.

"Thanks, but it's a little big. Could you wear it for me?"

Sophia showed a sad smile as she draped both necklaces over her own neck.

"I wanna believe she's not gone, gone," Lizzie ventured. "Know what I mean?" The other nodded. "Long as you have that necklace, you still have her."

"Not this," Sophia said, shaking her head and scattering tears. She tucked the chains inside her pajama top. "You, Lizzie Lou. Long as I've got you."

Light streamed through the trees as the Stick girl returned to her own campsite, carrying her new barbell and rolling the skateboard wheel with her foot. A light wind rustled the branches. Birds sang. Nearby, campers gathered wood.

Lizzie did sets of eight. Eight bench presses, eight curls, and eight squats. She flipped the skateboard wheel eight times. Eight, eight, eight, and eight, over and over until the muscles burned in her arms, shoulders, and back. Lizzie pumped iron even after her family woke up and sunlight cast long shadows across the clearing. She stopped only when her dad touched her elbow and said, "The Chappies are heading somewhere. Time to get On Glass." Then she put away her gear and walked to the van.

Thirty-eight

During the hour-and-a-half trip to the Nantahala Outdoor Center, the Sticks held hands and smiled. Lizzie knew that Sophia had fallen into a funk. But, like Lizzie, the Mobile girl had mastered the art of hiding her pain. She laughed at her dad's bad puns. She petted Hershey. She answered her Mom's questions and acted interested in the conversation. But Lizzie knew better. Both Lizzie and Sunny could sense Sophia's dark mood.

"She's upset because of a necklace," Sunny reported.

That's my fault, Lizzie thought.

"And worried that she won't see the blue-eyed boy again."

"Joaquin," Lizzie said. *Also my fault,* she thought, even though that made no sense.

The highway miles rolled by: fenced pastures with horses,

cows, and ramshackle barns. Bird houses with *See Rock City* printed on them.

"She's bored," Sunny added.

My fault.

Descending into a valley... "She's angry."

My fault.

Passing a fruit stand... "She's hungry."

My fault.

Climbing back into mountains... "She's confused."

My fault.

"She's lonely, she's angry, she's sad."

My fault, my fault, my fault.

Nantahala Whitewater Adventures lay in the crook of the river it had been named after. The gravel parking overflowed with tourists. As soon as the Chapman family left the car, the Sticks *de-glassed.* Meaning they climbed down.

"Listen up," Mom barked. "The Chapmans won't be first in line, not even close. It's just past O-nine-hundred. Our intelligence indicates that there will be a delay before our Mobiles deploy downriver. Ups, fill in the details."

"According to Black Army reports, our people will have to stand in line for life vests and paddles first," Ups said. "Then they'll watch a training video. Could be an hour before they even get in a raft. The trip itself takes about two hours. Afterwards, the Chappies will be bused back here. They'll deflate their raft and hand in their paddles. All told, about three and a half hours. The Black Army rates the restaurant dumpster here as Four Crumbs," the Stick dog added.

Mom clapped her hands for no reason. They were already paying attention. "I want all Sticks *On Glass* by twelve hundred. You knuckleheads need to start back to the rendezvous point at eleven hundred."

"Rendezvous point?" Sunny asked.

"The minivan," Lizzie whispered.

"Got it?" Mom demanded.

"Yes, sir," they all said.

The twins caught up with Sophia on the back porch of the center, in line for a life jacket, behind her parents. Lizzie and Sunny untied her shoe laces, then darted behind a post. When she bent down to tie them, they waved. Sophia whispered the last thing either of them expected.

"What are you two doing here?!"

"We're going rafting," Lizzie and Sunny said together. "Like you said."

Sophia glanced around nervously. "I didn't mean it literally," she whispered. "You're supposed to stay on the windshield."

"That's no fun," Lizzie said.

"Not a bit," Sunny agreed.

Lizzie shook her head. "We're going with you—"

"—like it or not," they said together.

"Just put us in with your rectangle," Sunny suggested.

Sophia frowned. But, a moment later, she crammed the Stick twins into her hip pocket, in a plastic baggie with her iPhone.

"Ouch! My left foot is like folded over and stuck to itself!" Sunny complained.

"I'm squished, too," Lizzie groaned. "But at least we're not stuck back at the—hey, look!" The screen had lit up. "Wonder what these funny shapes mean?"

"They're apps." Sunny pointed. "Look, this one's for texting. This one's for taking pictures. This one's for posting them so everyone in the world can see them."

"Everyone?" Lizzie asked. She would never admit it, but she was jealous that her sister knew so much.

"And this one," Sunny raised one eyebrow, "is for sending messages that only one person can see. See?"

"You mean Holly," Lizzie said. "Sophia's BFF."

Sunny cleared her throat. "I like to think that *I'm* her BFF." She pressed the green telephone icon, then scrolled down a list of names. "Check it out," Sunny said, pointing at the word *DAD*.

"Why would she have her dad's number?" Lizzie asked. "They live in the same house. He's standing right beside her." She slapped the name with the palm of her hand. The twins heard a mechanical purring sound.

Then, on the second ring... "Hello?" A man's voice.

"Hello?" replied Lizzie.

"Who is this?"

"Nobody." The Stick girl punched the red button.

Sunny gave her an angry look. "I think you just called—"

Suddenly the phone disappeared as Sophia snatched it out of her pocket, nearly ripping out the twins with it.

"At least, we've got some air," Lizzie said. She and Sunny listened as Sophia and her dad talked about their rectangles. The Chappy Daddy didn't understand how—if Sophia had butt-dialed him—some stranger could have been on the line.

"Probably some scammer," Sophia told her dad.

After long waits, the family collected their life vests and paddles, watched a safety video, and filled out the required paperwork. Before climbing into the raft, Sophia switched the twins and phone to her front pocket. Sunny managed to unfold her foot. Both Sticks were glad to have a little breathing room. And now Lizzie could hear the river guide. She learned how to turn by paddling forward on one side and backward on the other, kind of like riding a soda can. If you fell overboard and couldn't reach the raft, you were supposed to swim with the current and head for the river bank. Fighting the current would just tire you out. *Maybe that's why I feel like I'm drowning,* Lizzie thought. *I'm always swimming against the current.*

The yellow raft glided smoothly through the water. The river guide and Sophia's dad sat in the bow, her mom and Sophia in the back. Peeking out, Lizzie watched Sophia's skinny arms move forward and back in an easy rhythm: reach, pull, reach, pull. Her dad paddled at a different speed. Their paddles kept smacking with a sound that echoed across the water. The inflatable boat started to spin in a circle. Instead of calling out instructions, the pimple-faced teenage guide put his efforts into telling Sophia about a goal he had scored in his recent soccer game. Finally, the Mobile mom had enough of drifting and spinning.

"When I paddle, you paddle," she told the guide. "When I wait, you wait. Now stroke. Stroke. Our side, then theirs. Stroke. Stroke." First, the guide and Mom paddled. Then Dad and Sophia. As they fell into a rhythm, the raft straightened out. Listening, Lizzie grinned. The Mobile mom seemed more like the Stick girl's own mom than ever.

Lizzie looked down to see her sister playing with the giant mobile phone again. "You're not supposed to mess with that thing. What are you up to?"

"I'm chatting with Holly," Sunny replied.

"You're what?"

"It's okay. She thinks I'm Sophia. Did you know that girl calls her Soph? Oh, look. We got three bars."

"Show me!"

While the Chapmans paddled, the Stick girls carried on a

slow conversation with Sophia's best friend. Typing takes longer when you have to slap each letter with your hand. After a while, Holly apparently got tired of the delays. She typed, "Hold on, Facetiming you."

Lizzie and Sunny looked at each other and exchanged arches of their eyebrows. *Facetime?*

A moment later, the phone vibrated. Shocked, the Stick twins lost their feet and tumbled around in the plastic bag. Finally Lizzie reached up and pounded the green camera icon with her fist.

"What was that?" Sunny asked as they got to their feet.

Lizzie shook her head. "I dunno, it just—AIGHHHH!"

A teenage girl leered at them, so close to her phone that her nose looked bigger than the rest of her face. Her braces looked even more scary than Sophia's. When Holly saw the Stick twins, she screamed so loudly that both of them fell down again. Lizzie scrambled to her feet and smacked the red button. The monstrous face disappeared. Lizzie helped Sunny to her feet. Then, for a moment, the sisters just stared at one another.

"That thing was...horrible," Sunny said.

"I'm pretty sure that was Holly."

"Sophia's Holly? But her nose! She was *all* nose! Her BFF is a nose?"

"Sure looked that way."

A second later, the seal on the plastic bag popped open and

Sophia peered down at them.

"Did my phone buzz?" she whispered.

The twins shrugged. Sophia bunched up her skinny eyebrows. She started to pull out her phone. Then her mom said something and the teenager went back to paddling. Lizzie stared at the sky through the open bag. She and her sister inhaled deeply and didn't have to say what they thought. *Fresh air!*

The girls sat in the bottom of the baggie and crossed their legs. With the bag open, they could hear Sophia and her mom arguing. Tomorrow morning, Friday, the mom insisted, they would head home. Back to air conditioning. A week was more than enough time to swat mosquitoes, she said.

"That's not fair," Sophia complained. Lizzie could picture the pout on her face. "The dance isn't until Saturday."

Lizzie sighed. Since when was anything fair?

After a few minutes, the Chappy Mommy began barking out orders again.

The Stick twins looked up. "You hear that?" Lizzie asked.

"More fussing?"

"No, something else. Listen."

"Wait. Yeah. Sounds like rain. I hope she closes the bag."

"Not rain." Lizzie gave Sunny a frantic look. "Rapids! Hold on!"

Sunny screamed as the floor of the raft—and the plastic bag

—began bouncing. They could hear the Mobiles screaming, too. Staring at the opening in the baggie, Lizzie visualized the dandelion puff she had seen pulled under by a small stream. This was an actual river.

"We gotta seal this thing!" she yelled.

"How?" Sunny yelled back.

"I dunno." She pulled herself up onto the phone and reached for the seam. But zippered bags aren't made for closing from the inside. She lost her balance and fell onto her sister.

"Hey!"

"Stand up!" Lizzie ordered. "Climb on my shoulders!" But neither of the girls could stay on her feet for more than a few seconds.

Then Sophia's hands appeared above them. In an instant, the bag zipped shut and the roar of the water became muffled. The bag, however, continued to bounce. The twins held onto each other.

"I think I'm gonna throw up," Sunny said.

Lizzie scowled. "You know we can't do that. But Sophia might." She could feel the Mobile girl's stomach churning like whitewater. Nothing frightened Lizzie more than throw-up.

The humans all paddled fiercely, even Sophia and the teenage guide, as the raft tossed.

"She's afraid of the river," Lizzie said. "Can't blame her."

"And furious at her mom," Sunny added. "Friday night is

her last chance to meet Joaquin."

"Yeah, hear that?" Lizzie asked. "They're still yelling at each other. No, wait, they just stopped."

In the middle of the Nantahala Falls rapids, the mother-daughter argument abruptly ended. Lizzie felt something inside Sophia go numb. The Stick girl watched in horror, as the Mobile girl released her paddle and let it slip over the side of the raft.

Thirty-nine

Thursday Afternoon

The Chapman parents stood on their knees, digging their paddles into the angry river with a ferocity unlike anything Lizzie had ever seen. First, the floor of the raft trembled, then the whole thing tilted as they raced around a giant boulder, the mom pushing away from it with her paddle. Meanwhile, Sophia sat with her arms crossed.

"She doesn't care!" Lizzie called. She pointed to Sophia's unbuckled life vest, the straps dangling.

"I know!" Sunny called back.

Suddenly, the bow of the raft rocketed skyward. The front half left the water, then landed with a great splash, drenching the Mobiles. Over the roar of the river, Lizzie could hear the mom calling out, "Dig-dig-dig!"

The river's roar, already loud, grew deafeningly louder. Lizzie glimpsed a second raft ahead of them as it tipped into a nosedive and disappeared. "Hold on!" she shouted. The twins hugged each other as their raft raced toward the same drop. Sophia's parents and the guide screamed as they went over the edge.

The raft plunged into a cauldron of boiling, white foam. Lizzie expected the blue sky and dark green tree line to reappear at once, but it didn't. She saw Sophia's knobby knees, then shoe strings writhing like sea serpents. The twins stuck together as their plastic bag did cartwheels underwater. The rocky river bed rushed by. Then the dark underside of the raft. Then white again.

As the bag broke the surface of the water, Sunny shouted, "Look!" Sophia's life vest floated past, like a whale passing the window of a submarine. "No, no, no, no, no!" Sunny cried. Lizzie held her as she began to sob.

The plastic bag bobbed along. Eventually the current slowed. Lizzie wiped away her sister's tears, but more kept flowing.

"She's okay," Lizzie said.

Sunny nodded and placed a hand over her heart. "I can still..." She fought back tears again.

"You can still feel her," Lizzie said. "So can I."

Sunny pawed at her face, smearing tears forehead to her

chin. "That was— That was the worst thing—in the world," she sniffed. "And that's what you..." Sunny squinted into Lizzie's black eyes. "That's what you went through with Elizabeth. Only it never stopped." She hugged Lizzie. "I'm so sorry."

"It's okay," Lizzie whispered back. "I've got you."

The two spent several minutes unsticking from each other. Then something in their surroundings changed. Leaves floated by. "We stopped moving," Lizzie said. "I think we're caught in something. Look."

The plastic bag had lodged itself in a clump of wax-myrtle branches sticking out from the bank.

"Maybe we won't float all the way to the ocean, after all," Sunny said.

"I'm just glad there was enough air for us to float at all," Lizzie said. "Speaking of which, it's getting stuffy again. Let's open it up"

"Can we?"

They pulled at the plastic zipper, without success, until they exhausted themselves.

"That ain't workin'," Sunny said. "Any other great ideas?"

"We could yell our heads off," Lizzie suggested. "Not that anybody's gonna hear us."

Sunny snapped her fingers. "A call for help, right, but not that kind." She turned on the smartphone. "Let's see...." She poked around until she found a list of recently-called numbers.

"What are you looking for," Lizzie asked, "Holly's number? That won't do us any good."

"Not hers," Sunny pointed at the screen, "his." The Chappy Daddy answered on the second ring.

"Who is this?" he demanded, sounding even angrier than the first time the Stick twins had called.

Sunny cleared her throat and spoke in a fake-deep voice. "This is, uh, Fred. I'm a hiker. Hiking my fool head off today. I just found this phone down by the river. Thought I'd see if I could locate the owner."

The twins heard Sophia's dad cover the phone. In a muted voice, he said. "Sophia, honey, someone found your phone."

"Oh-ma-god!" Sophia practically yelled into the mouthpiece as she took her dad's phone. "Who is this? You found my phone? Was it empty? The bag, I mean. Did you find anything else in it?"

"It's me," Sunny said.

"Oh."

"And me," Lizzie added. "Now, before you say anything else, just take a second, play it cool."

After a pause, Sophia replied, "Uh, thank you. Sir. Thank you," Then, in a whisper: "Where are you guys?"

"Still in the bag," Sunny said. She mopped at her face. "Sweating. Somewhere." She looked at Lizzie.

"We're on the bank, caught in some branches," Lizzie said.

She looked at the river. "When I look out, the water is flowing to the left."

"Okay, good, same side as us," Sophia whispered. "How am I supposed to find you?"

Lizzie laughed. "Cheese puffs, Soph! Don't you have an app for that?"

"Oh, yeah," Sophia laughed. "I'm on my way." Then in a louder voice: "Thank you, sir. I understand you have to continue your, um, hike. You're going to leave the phone where you found it? Well, I appreciate you calling. Yes, you have an awesome day too."

After about half an hour, the Stick twins heard footsteps. Then Sophia's hands scooped them up. Fresh air flooded in. The Mobile girl's smiling face came into view, wet hair still plastered to her head. "Found it!" she shouted to her parents.

"You found *us*!" Sunny said.

"You're hurt," Lizzie added.

Sophia touched a blood-red scrape just above her left eyebrow. "That's nothing," she said. "Look at this." She showed them her elbow, where a strawberry of raw flesh oozed blood. Her legs were also crisscrossed with scratches. "Now, stop yapping and hide on my shoulders. Quick, before they see."

"You're all beat up," Sunny said. "So why are you so happy?"

"You're safe," the other replied. "Plus, I didn't lose all my new selfies."

The twins exchanged a look. "Seriously?" they asked.

Clinging to ropes of wet hair, they rode on her shoulders as she, her parents, and the young guide—still bragging about his soccer stardom—hiked back to their starting point. The current had carried the capsized raft downriver. Other guides would fish it out. The Stick girls, meanwhile, had plenty of time to describe their adventure. They said nothing, for the moment, about Sophia dropping her paddle and not fastening her life vest.

As the minivan climbed up and down the North Carolina mountains, the afternoon light aged to a soft gold. Luminous green leaves passed overhead. Sunlight slanted through the trees, sparkling in Lizzie's eyes and washing her family in dappled light.

Lizzie held Sunny's hand without complaining. Inside the car, she knew, Sophia had no one to hold onto. Her twin was dead, and she might never meet her crush. It wasn't hard for Lizzie to imagine the girl's loneliness and frustration. She knew her own all too well. The plan to pack up and roll out in the morning seemed like one too many injustices in a world already full of them. So Lizzie began scheming a way to keep them from leaving.

Forty

After dinner, the girls watched the dark woods for Sophia's signal. When the flashlight never blinked, they sneaked around the big, blue tent and peeked under the flap. No Sophia. They finally found her at Little Stone Mountain. There, the two confronted her about what had happened on the river.

"Why'd you let go of your paddle?"

"It was wet. Slipped out of my hand."

"And you unbuckled your life vest."

"It was itchy."

"Right before the rapids?!"

"I wasn't thinking."

"But we were yelling our heads off for you to put it on."

"I didn't hear you."

"Then we saw it float by, like you slipped out of it."

"The current snatched it. It was crazy, I was just struggling to swim. My stupid boots, they were too heavy."

The twins exchanged a hurt look. "What would have happened to us if you had drowned?" Lizzie asked.

Sophia tilted her head like a dog puzzling over his next move in a game of chess. "You would have disappeared. Poof!" She made a mini-explosion with her hand. "Along with every other crazy idea I've ever had. And I've had a few."

Lizzie switched to the issue that had upset the girl to begin with. "Your family's not going home tomorrow," she said. "We won't let them."

"Right," Sophia said, and blew out a breath. "Like my imaginary friends have any say in the matter."

Sunny gave a frustrated, girly growl. "I can't believe you're still stuck on that! Tell us this: can imaginary friends dial a phone? Huh?" The Mobile's frown went slack. The other smirked. "Think about it."

Lizzie explained that they planned to disable the minivan. In the morning, the Chapmans would be unable to leave. "If the car won't start, your family will be stuck here. And if your parents let you go to the dance and Joaquin is back from the wilderness—"

"That's a lot of ifs," Sophia interrupted.

Lizzie grinned. "Better than a poke in the eye with a sharp— well, you know."

The twins rode back to the campsite on Sophia's shoulders. Along the way, the giant girl explained why she was carrying a roll of toilet tissue.

"Ew!" Sunny said. "You're making that up!"

But Lizzie backed up the Mobile. "I swear, it's true. When humans do their business, it smells worse than— You know how bad it stinks when a junk car trails blue smoke? Way worse."

When they reached the minivan, Sophia opened the driver's door and popped the hood. As she peered at the dark engine, she whispered, "This is useless. I can't see what I'm doing. And my flashlight is in the tent. Should I go get it?"

"Too risky," Lizzie said. She looked at her sister. "How about fireflies?"

"Past their bedtime," Sunny said.

"Then we'll wake them."

A few minutes later, two green-glowing volunteers hovered over the engine compartment. Sophia stared at them for a moment, amazed, then listened as Lizzie instructed her how to switch around the spark-plug wires.

"Are you sure this won't break the car?" the teenager asked.

Lizzie shook his head. "Nah, but your dad will be stumped."

"I mean, we can't afford a new one. After all, we live in— what'd you call it?"

"Vinylville," the twins replied.

The Mobile narrowed her eyes. "Hey, how do you know this stuff, anyway?"

"Owner's manual," the Sticks said, again in unison.

"That's really irritating," Sophia said. "Both of you answering."

"We know," they said.

The giant girl tugged at the spark plug wires until she had unplugged all six. "Now what?" she asked.

"Put 'em back on," Lizzie said, "but different."

Sophia worked at it awhile, then squealed, "Ouch!"

"What?" Sunny asked.

"I broke a nail!" Sophia replied.

Lizzie thought, *of course, you did,* but said nothing.

When the girls had finished their sabotage, Lizzie thanked the fireflies for their help.

"Happy to help a legend," they replied. Which, to Lizzie, made no sense. And to Sophia, sounded like faint buzzing.

Tired, the three girls should have headed to their sleeping bags. But now that there was a real possibility of going to the dance, Sophia had one more thing she wanted to do. She sat in the driver's seat and rummaged through the console.

"What are you looking for?" Lizzie asked.

"This." The Mobile held up a black tube and pulled off the cap. Lipstick.

"Ah," Sunny said.

Sophia flipped down the sun visor and lifted the little door that covered its mirror. A soft yellow light washed her face as she began applying Cherry Berry first to her upper lip, then to her lower. She smacked them together and turned to the twins.

"How do I look?"

"Fabulous," Sunny said.

"Grown up," Lizzie said.

"Bet you wish your BFF was here," Sunny said. "Holly."

Sophia looked from one Stick to the other. "Hm. Yeah, I do. But you know what?"

"What?" they asked.

"She's gonna love you two. We'll all be BFFs together one day. You'll see."

"Think so?" Sunny asked.

"I know so. Maybe we'll all live in a psych ward, but if so, we'll rock that place."

Seeing the thirteen-year-old's face transformed by a splash of red lipstick gave Lizzie an idea. "Remember those markers?" she asked.

A moment later, Sophia began coloring Lizzie's hair. "How many colors do you want?"

"All of them," Lizzie said. "But don't get it on my neck."

"Got it." Sophia colored each strand of the Stick girl's hair. It took a while. Then she leaned back and admired her work.

"Okay, you're all done."

Lizzie ran her fingers through her multi-colored locks and peered into the mirror. "What d'ya think?" she asked.

"You look amazing!" Sunny said. "Mom's gonna tear you to pieces." She edged her way in front of the mirror. "Me next. Just my lips, though." She tilted back her head.

Lizzie grunted. "Copycat."

Sophia began painting Sunny's lips with a red marker.

"She's gonna tear us both to pieces," Lizzie laughed.

"No, just you," Sunny replied. "I'll wipe mine off."

Sophia drew back the red marker and froze. "Um…"

"Are we done?" Sunny asked.

Sophia cleared her throat. "You know this is a Sharpie, right? I said that."

"Sure," Sunny said. "But for a marker, it's really not all that sharp."

"No, you don't understand." Sophia said. "Sharpies are permanent markers. Permanent. Not. Washable."

"Or wipeable," Lizzie added.

Sunny's mouth dropped open. "Oh, well, Mom'll just have to get over it."

As Sophia finished coloring Sunny's lips, she got a funny look on her face. "I got a signal for a few minutes this afternoon," she said, "just one bar. And I got the strangest text from Holly. She claimed that she and I were texting during the rafting trip. So I read the previous messages and saw this whole weird conversation that I don't remember. She even says we Facetimed each other. But that's impossible," she paused for effect, "since I was busy paddling for my life. Either that, or looking for my phone."

The Stick girls looked at each other, then answered in unison. "Holly's nuts."

Forty-one

Friday Morning

Lizzie woke up before daylight to the sound of drizzling raindrops pelting the bread-bag tent. It made her want to stay curled up in her oak-leaf sleeping bag. Gradually, the dripping sounds slowed, then stopped. The next sound she heard was anything but dreamy.

"What have you done to your hair?!" Mom demanded. The Stick girl opened her eyes and looked into her mom's outraged face.

"It's nothing," Lizzie mumbled. She rolled over and pulled up her sleeping bag. But an instant later, her mom pulled it off and slung it away. "Mom!" the girl protested.

Her mom kicked her sleeping husband. "Honey!"

Lizzie's dad grunted. "Em?"

"Get over here."

"What?"

"I need you over here, that's what."

He crawled toward her.

"Look at your daughter."

The Stick dad took in the situation: Lizzie curled in a fetal position, his wife hovering with her arms folded, the rainbow hairdo. He pointed at his daughter, grinned, and nodded.

"Ow!" he said. Mom had poked him.

"It's not funny," she said. She rubbed Lizzie's hair between her fingers. "This is permanent."

Dad looked confused. "What? No!"

"Yes. Look. Feel it for yourself. It doesn't come off."

Lizzie's dad touched her hair, then looked at his fingers. "Lizzie-Lou!" he said.

Mom shot questions at Lizzie. "What do you mean by this? Why would you do such a thing? Who gave you markers? Are you *on* something? Who were you with last night? Was it that boy?"

Sunny, who had been listening, sat up. "Leave Nico out of this. His family's not even here."

"Oh, my word!" Mom shouted. She pointed at Sunny's bright red lips.

Ups, who had been outside the tent, entered through the flap and looked at the two girls. "Smashing!" the dog said.

Mom shot him a look. "The only thing that's gonna get smashed is these two," she said, pointing at the twins.

Sunny rubbed her face. "It's just a little lipstick," she said.

"No, it's permanent marker. That means it won't come off!"

"We know what it means," Lizzie said. She tried to crawl out of the tent.

"Oh, no, you don't, young lady!" Lizzie felt a tug on her right foot. "You started this trouble and—"

"Don't call me that." She kicked free and jumped out of the tent, her mom close behind her. The girl found her moccasins, but they were soaking wet, so she dropped them.

"You've talked your sister into trouble again, haven't you?" the Stick woman accused. "Remember the book of matches? The ones you found last winter? Remember?"

Everywhere Lizzie turned, her mom cut her off. "Nobody got burned, just...sooty."

"It was dangerous," Mom said, "and irresponsible. And now this!"

Lizzie turned to face her mom, nose to nose. Mom stood a head taller. She always would. And she would always be there, telling her what to do.

"Okay, it was me," Lizzie said. "I got the markers."

"From where?"

"I stole 'em from a hobo. A homeless guy."

"From a what? Are you lying to me?"

"I mean a pirate."

"A pirate!"

"And I did my hairdo myself."

Her mom grasped a handful of Lizzie's hair. "I don't think so. You had help."

"Sunny didn't do anything. While she was asleep I sneaked in and did her lipstick."

"You did not," Sunny objected, emerging from the tent.

Lizzie shrugged. "Might as well have. I get the blame."

Mom's face couldn't turn red, but her expression showed barely controlled fury. "No one's blaming anyone."

"'Cause I'm the *bad* twin," Lizzie added.

"I didn't say that." The Stick mom let go of the girl's hair.

"You didn't have to." Lizzie turned and walked away, but her mom shadowed her.

"Do you understand what a permanent marker does?" Mom demanded.

"Deja vu."

"It marks you *for life*. Everywhere we go, you'll stand out."

"What's so bad about that?"

"We won't blend in."

"Afraid to be seen with me?"

"You'll be the girl with weird hair."

"Or the boy."

"And people will notice you."

Lizzie stopped. Her mom almost ran into her.

"Maybe I wanna be noticed." She willed herself not to shout, or cry. "I don't want to look like other girls because I'm *not* like them."

"You—" Her mom shook a trembling finger in the teenager's face, out of words. This was Lizzie's chance. The Stick girl turned and sprinted barefoot into the woods.

As her mom's calls fell behind, Lizzie slowed to a walk. *If Sunny so much as broke a fingernail, Mom would climb a mountain to help her. But she wouldn't follow me down this path, even if I was on fire.*

Raindrops dripped from the leaves, sparkling in the morning sun. If Lizzie hadn't been so angry, she might have appreciated the beauty. The prickly ground now made her wish that she had worn her moccasins, wet or not.

There's no going back. Maybe ever. Well, that's what I wanted, right?

She moved off the rocky path and crunched through dead leaves, instead. Soon she came to the stream, now swollen with runoff. She stared, astonished that it could have doubled in size. Then she spotted a flash of bright green in the distance and walked toward it. A moment later, she buried her feet in a bed of lush moss. A breeze stirred the branches, showering the moss in a variety of greens, light to shadow and back again. The Stick girl might have stood there all morning, but a bird's cry caught her attention. Not a regular birdsong. A song of fear and sorrow. Searching the tree limbs above her, Lizzie found the two Louisville Cardinals, members of Nico's family. One of them, the male, stretched out his wing at an odd angle.

"Are you hurt?" Lizzie called.

"It's them," the female cardinal called down. She pointed with her beak, as only a bird can, toward what could have been a tree or a cloud. Lizzie understood better than she should have.

"The others don't accept you. The other birds."

The cardinals nodded.

"Can I help?"

"We'll be okay," the redbirds said in voices like flutes. The male could still fly. He just needed to gather his strength and courage, they explained.

"Never be ashamed of how you're made," Lizzie said. "Inside or out."

They looked back with sad eyes. "You, too."

Forty-two

Lizzie sculpted a pair of clumpy shoes out of soft green moss and curly vines, and headed back toward the path. Dead leaves provide shelter for many tiny creatures, so Lizzie had company who didn't appreciate her plodding feet.

"You crushed my house!" complained a beetle.

"Oops. Sorry."

"Get off my lawn!" croaked a toad.

"Just passing through."

"You're ruining my roof!" yelled an earthworm. He didn't have a fist to shake, so he wriggled his whole body.

"My bad."

And then a voice from above. "Hey, whatcha *titch-cha-cha-titch*, whatcha doin' down there, fly-girl? *Titch!*"

Lizzie looked about, but saw only shimmering leaves and a starburst of sunlight. "Who's that?" she called. The Stick girl believed she could face even a hawk or a bear, but the *titchy* stuff sounded just like the squirrels back home, and none had been friendly.

"It's *titch-cha-cha* me!" A small squirrel landed in front of her. Lizzie had never met one, personally. Back in Vinylville, the fluffy-tailed birdseed bandits often threw acorns at her family, probably because Sticks are friendly with birds. This guy looked different—smaller, skinnier, and with loops of skin hanging from his arms and legs. Still, she shrank back.

"You're not going to eat me, are you?"

"I dunno, *titch*. Do you, *titch*, taste good?"

"Nope. Like a monarch butterfly."

"Yuck! Then I guess I won't chew you up and spit out your bones, *titch-titch-chah!*"

"Yeah, that'd be hard to do, since I don't have any." To demonstrate, the Stick girl bent her arms double. "I'm Lizzie," she said.

"*Titch-titch!*" The squirrel sniffed her arm and wrinkled his nose. "Monarch, eh?" He didn't sound convinced. "I'm Jayla." Then to Lizzie's surprise, he hugged her. It was only a quick hug, but for a second it seemed like she was wrapped in a prickly blanket. He stood back and smiled a big buck-toothed smile. Lizzie felt silly for having been afraid.

"Isn't that a girl's name? Jayla, I mean?"

The other rubbed his chin with his front paw. *"Titch!* What are you, the name police?" He then began running in circles around her. Each time his face went by, it took on a different, zany look: eyes crossed, tongue sticking out, cheeks squished in, lower lip stuck out. Jayla made the Stick girl laugh so hard she could barely stand up. Finally, he stood panting before her.

"Hey, what did you mean?" she asked.

"What? *Titch-titch.*"

"You called me something. A fly girl?"

"Maybe I did, *titch-cha-cha.* What are you doing down here?"

Lizzie looked around at the ground. "Where else would I be?"

"Flying!" Jayla spread his limbs. *"On the, titch-titch,* wind!"

The Stick girl spread her own arms. "I don't exactly have wings."

"You don't need 'em. Look at me. I got wrist bones made of *car-car*-cartilage and skin I can stretch like a kite. But you—" the other examined the almost paper-thinness of her arms "—fly girl, from head to toe, you're built for the air." The flying squirrel knelt down. "Climb on, I'll show you."

Ride a squirrel? Mom would have a cow! Lizzie thought. Perhaps for that reason, she hopped on and clung to Jayla's back as he scaled a towering pine. She voiced no complaints as he began swinging back and forth on the uppermost branch. When he let go, the small squirrel stretched out, wrist to ankle, like a furry kite. Before Lizzie knew it, she was soaring. Glancing back, she watched her moss shoes tumble away. Her legs trailed like streamers.

Jayla guided them over, under, and around foliage, letting out a series of mad, bucktoothed laughs. The Stick girl screamed, too, somewhat out of fear, but mostly for the sheer thrill of the experience.

Instead of landing lightly on the ground, as Lizzie had hoped, their flight ended abruptly at a maple trunk. The little squirrel stuck to it like spaghetti to a wall, his claws digging into the bark. He caught his breath, then scrambled upward again to the highest point.

Lizzie climbed off his back and stood with wobbly knees on a slender, bouncing branch, forty-plus feet in the air—mountain-heights to a Stick person.

She felt a grin spread across her face. "Teach me."

Jayla smiled, his eyes as full of life as a pool of minnows. *"Cha-cha-chah!"*

"The trick," he said as he led her out to the tip of the branch, "is to commit to your, *titch,* plan of action. Just throw yourself into the air." It sounded a little crazy.

"What if I crash and die?" Lizzie asked.

The squirrel waved a paw. "No big deal. If the wind *cha-cha-*

changes, change with it. Land somewhere else. Just try not to *tichy-hitchy*-impale yourself on anything sharp."

"Right."

"Watch me." Spreading his arms and legs, the flying squirrel tilted forward, his feet quivering the branch as he abandoned it. He glided downward, spiraling in circles around the tree and landed lightly on his feet. "Like that!" he called.

That looked easy.

Lizzie tried it. Spread-eagling, she leaned forward into thin air. Then panic took over. Scrambling to get her feet beneath her, she twisted awkwardly and plummeted. She didn't hit any branches, but landed hard on her butt. "Ouch," she said, rubbing it.

Jayla offered her a paw. "*Cha-cha*-child, you gotta commit."

"Gotta commit," Lizzie repeated with a nod.

They climbed back up. The Stick girl went first. This time, when fear assaulted her, she fought it. She told herself, *I'm thinner than cardboard, this ought to work*, and relaxed. Instead of tumbling like wadded-up paper, she glided downward. "Hey, I'm doing it!" she yelled.

"Control where you go!" Jayla called. "Use your *hitchy-*hands!"

And Lizzie discovered that, with just a little tilt of her hands and a slight turn of her ankles, she could swoop left or right, easy as eggs. Her flight looked better than her landing, though.

A gust pushed her into a tangle of briars. Fortunately, none of them tore her.

Jayla landed close by and helped her out. "When you land, turn your palms up, like an air-*pah-pah*-plane putting down its flaps." He demonstrated. "That'll slow you down. And put out your landing gear."

"Flaps," she wiggled her hands, "and landing gear." She glanced at her feet. "Got it."

To her credit, Lizzie tried over and over. Soon she rode the air in any direction she chose. The discovery of her body's aerodynamic form seemed miraculous. Until now, she could never remember feeling natural in her own skin. Of course, gliding was half work and half fun. You had to climb before you could fly. But once you got a sense for finding updrafts—and the openings between branches—travel by air seemed effortless. She had always heard that Sticks were made for the road. That might be true of others. Lizzie was made for the sky.

She imagined soaring off Gorges Overlook, or flying like a great jet, leaving white streaks across the blue.

Jayla broke into her thoughts. "The *ta*-tallest thing around here is the *pitchy-titchy*-power-line."

"Oh yeah? What's that?"

"Girl? You don't know what a power-line is? *Pow-witchy-titchy-pow!*"

She thought about it. "Telephone poles?"

Jayla waved away the idea. "That's small *pah*-potatoes. Hop on, I'll show you the Tower of Power!"

Forty-three

The flying squirrel bounded from branch to branch, gliding when he could. Lizzie clung to his coarse fur like some rodeo cowgirl. Eventually, they reached an enormous clearing that ran as far as she could see. They stopped. She slid off. High above, high voltage lines stretched between gargantuan towers. If Mobiles looked like giants to Sticks, these would seem like giants to the giants.

"You gotta be kidding," she said.

"What?"

"We're going up there?"

"Yep." The flying squirrel rested his paws on his hips. "Just lemme...rest a sec."

As Lizzie waited for him to catch his breath, she made conversation. "That's a very fine tail."

The squirrel took his slender, pointed tail in hand. "This thing? Well I am kinda *atchy*-attached to it." He nibbled on it with his buck teeth. "The Grays say we fliers have scrawny, little rat-tails."

"That's mean," Lizzie said. "Who's that? The Grays?"

"Our cousins. They're snobby about their great big tails."

Lizzie nodded. "The acorn throwers. They're just jealous. I mean, who'd want a tail so big and fluffy that you can't even fly?"

"Right-right," Jayla said. "Clumsy climbers can't fly like us!"

The last word in his statement caught Lizzie's ear. *Us.* For a long time, the Stick girl had felt alone. Now, she not only had Sunny and Sophia, she had joined an elite group—fliers. She stared along the immense power-line trail. Each tower stood on its own, but it took all of them to carry electricity to distant towns. Maybe she, too, wouldn't always stand alone.

"What about birds?" she asked.

"Ha! Don't get me *star*-started about those bomb droppers," Jayla said. "Gotta admit-bit, though, I'm a *bitchy*-bit jealous."

Lizzie wondered what he would think of Sticker birds, but she didn't get a chance to ask.

"Let's get going," the fly-guy said. "Race ya to the top!"

"What?! You expect me to climb all the way up—?"

"Nah, I'm kidding. Hop on." And she did.

Until now, Lizzie had been fairly impressed with the flying

squirrel's speed and stamina. His climb to the top of the Tower of Power, though, astonished her. The little fellow scrambled up near-vertical beams, then across, then up again. Over and up, over and up. The trail below them narrowed to a ribbon as it snaked through the mountains, tower to tower. After too much looking down, she buried her face in Jayla's reddish brown fur.

"Dizzy, Lizzy?" he called.

"Are we there yet?" she replied.

"Nope-a-dope," Jayla reported, "about a fifth of the way up."

"Oh, wow!"

The climb went on and on, so high up that Lizzie didn't dare take in the view. Jayla paused several times to catch his breath, seeming more exhausted at each stop. As he finally pulled himself up onto the very highest crossbeam, his whole body trembled beneath her.

"You okay?" Lizzie asked.

"Will be...in a...*min-min*-minute."

Lungs heaving, the squirrel rolled over, pinning Lizzie's right leg. It didn't hurt, exactly, but it had only been a few days since her surgery. If she tried to pull her leg out, the patch might tear. So she waited. A wise choice. The wind would have snatched her right off the tower.

As she waited, her eyes followed the thick, black, power cables stretching toward the next tower. She closed her eyes and felt the sun on her face. The insides of her eyelids filled her vision. The blustering wind shushed and faded, again and again. She had never heard the ocean—only experienced it through Elizabeth's feelings—but she figured it sounded like this. The great tower creaked with each gust. In her imagination, it became a wooden ship.

"I'm getting up," Jayla announced. "Careful, hold on." Lizzie gripped his fur. They both crouched, bracing themselves against the wind.

"Ready?"

Lizzie crawled to the edge and forced herself to peek over. "No, no, not yet! It's...whoa, that's a long way down! You do this a lot?" She looked up at the flying squirrel, who held up a single claw. Lizzie shook her head. "Are you serious? This is your first time?!"

Jayla nodded. "My *brotta*-brother said it couldn't be done. Said nobody could climb this high."

"Now, you tell me." They both stared into the void.

"Hate to admit it," said the squirrel, "but my insides are jumpy-bumpy."

"Yeah, well, this is my first day flying. If you're nervous, how am I supposed to—"

"You'll be fine. The air's the air. Same principles."

"If you say so."

"I do. And oh, yeah, if you wanna go really, really fast, make yourself like an arrow. Like this." He clapped his arms to his sides.

"Sure." *Like I would ever wanna do that,* she thought. A long moment passed. The Stick girl let go of his fur. "I think I'm ready."

Jayla gave her a look that somehow combined both joy and fear. Then without another word, he straightened himself like a pencil and dove over the edge, yelling, "Woo-*hitchy-hitchy-hooooo!*"

Lizzie watched Jayla plummet, his arms plastered to his sides, his toes pointed skyward. Then the little squirrel unfurled his wings of skin, and did a great loop de loop in the air. He glided on and on. She lost sight of him in a stand of tall pines.

The wind whipped unexpectedly. Lizzie lay flat and gripped the edge of the beam; her legs flapped like banners. *I'm not ready,* she thought, *I can't do this. Yes, I can. No, it's crazy. Don't be a wuss, get a grip!* Then it occurred to her that climbing down would be no less of a challenge than gliding. She was sure to get swept off. So when the wind settled again, she gathered her courage and stood up and ran toward the edge. As she dove into open space, yet another gust seized her and she tumbled upward. The world spun, sky to ground. Stretching her limbs, she halted the spin and began gliding.

I'm doing it, she told herself. The wind pushed with far more power than she had felt in the forest, but an unexpected thing happened. Her fear of falling vanished.

She rode forceful swells of wind, like a small child body-surfing great ocean waves. Her hair transformed into swirling tongues of rainbow-colored fire. And a real smile—a crooked one—spread across her face. She spiraled, she weaved, she zigzagged. She did loop-de-loops, recalling the thrill that Elizabeth had experienced on a roller-coaster. She straightened into an arrow and dove with astonishing speed. Then she spread her limbs and came out of it, floating on the wind with a carelessness that she found surprisingly relaxing. With a flick of her wrists and feet, she flipped over on her back. Above, pillowy clouds sailed on endless blue. *There's my ocean,* she thought, *my very own.*

Forty-four

Friday Afternoon

Lighter than a flying squirrel, Lizzie stayed aloft longer than her new friend. Gravity finally did deposit her in an ancient red oak, deep in the forest. The Stick girl stood on a massive branch, so high up that she couldn't see the ground. She had no idea how to find Jayla. After a short rest, she glided down to the forest floor. On the way, she practiced banking and turning, to avoid branches.

At the base of the oak, Lizzie stared into a world shrouded in deep green, darker and more quiet than any woods she had explored. A place fit for thinking. Her breathing slowed until she could hear the dull thud of her own heart (Sticks have hearts; they're just very flat). She watched a single leaf twirl lazily to the ground, and walked toward it. Thoughtfully. There was a time for running. This wasn't it.

Questions paraded through her mind, like mourners past a casket. *Why is glass clear? Will I always be stuck with my family? Where do the roads end? Why did Elizabeth have to die? What am I supposed to do with the rest of my life?* None with an answer.

Beyond this island of peace, she knew, the busy world marched on. Sophia's dad fussing over the van's engine. Nico's family trekking back to their campsite. Sophia freaking out about what to wear to the dance. Sunny, helping her freak out. Ups chasing something through the brush, squeezing the last bit of fun out of this vacation. Mom, furious about Lizzie running off, about her hair. Maybe she and Dad would be arguing. But at least they had each other. Everyone had someone. Sunny had Nico. Sophia had Joaquin, or at least hoped to. Hershey had Daisy. Even fireflies looked for love and found it.

Lizzie wished she was someone else.

She stood at the fallen leaf. A large drop of water clung to it. Strange, since the rest of the ground seemed dry. The Stick girl leaned close. Her own reflection peered back, distorted.

Who are you, she wondered? Or what? Maybe, one day, I'll find out.

One day was today.

An hour later, Lizzie found herself at the RV park. She had

unfinished business with the petite pirate, Cap'n Nobeard. After the quiet, old-growth forest, the clearing with its rows of motorhomes seemed unreal, or too real.

As she approached the dilapidated RV, she observed a large, black-and-white cat with white mittens sleeping under one of the tires. Some cats will chase stickers, so Lizzie kept an eye on him as she walked past.

"Ahoy! Ye scabby land-loving swine!"

Lizzie looked up. The Cap'n stood peering over the edge of the RV's roof.

She pointed at the Sylvester lookalike and mouthed the words, "What about the cat?"

The Cap'n shrugged. "Ye have no more to fear from him than from a mackerel flopping around on the deck."

"Okay. How do I get up?"

"This way." He walked toward the rear of the RV. "There's a ladder,"

Lizzie climbed carefully, since the old rust-bucket had grimy black soot covering its back end. She already had a lot of dirt and tree bark to pick off. Cap'n Nobeard offered her a hand as she climbed onto the roof. She ignored it, not because she was too proud to take his help, but to keep from pulling the tiny pirate overboard. She did accept the handkerchief he offered for cleaning up.

"Welcome aboard," he said, sweeping off his hat and

gesturing toward the rooftop. There wasn't much to it. A defunct air conditioning unit stood in the center, not far from the yellowed bubble of a skylight. Over the cab, a small plastic ship's wheel had been glued near the bow, if you can say that an RV has a bow. The pirate gestured at her hair. "You are a colorful one today."

"Oh, you like it?" Lizzie asked.

"Love it!"

"You don't sound very French today, Cap'n."

He clasped his hands together. "I'm taking a break."

"If you wanna work on your accent, there are apps for that," Lizzie said.

The other hung his head. "If only. See, my ship is truly grounded. No cell phone signal, no internet, no cable TV, no satellite."

"No sea," Lizzie said, then wished she hadn't. "Hey, but you've got that." She pointed at the ship's wheel and walked toward it. "That's awesome."

"What's a ship without a wheel?" he asked. Half her size, he had to jog to keep up.

When they reached the front, Lizzie peered over the edge at the cracked windshield. Even the windshield wipers were tattered. *He should name this thing the Titanic.*

"So what brings you to these waters?" he asked.

She looked around at the flat roof. "You tell me."

He rested his hand on his sword handle. "I said I would teach you sword fighting, didn't I?" he asked.

Lizzie shrugged. "Then I guess that's why."

"I made you a blade," he said, then ran to the yellowed skylight and disappeared into the vehicle's interior. A moment later, he returned holding two sewing needles and two pencil erasers. His own sword remained in its sheath, which he removed and set aside.

"Your saber, Mademoiselle." He tossed her a weapon.

Lizzie marveled at its sharp point. Her parents would never allow her to come close to such a dangerous thing. The non-pointy end had a button as a hilt, attached with a thin strip of duct tape. She swung the sword wildly. "Alright, pirate matey dude, let's do this!"

"Easy there," said the Cap'n. "We have to make it safe."

"Safe? I got a freakin' sword! There's nothing safe about it!" She sliced the air several more times.

"Hand it back. Just for a second." She did so, then watched as he affixed erasers to the sharp tips of both needles. "I figured these would work better than carrots," he said. "There."

Lizzie took her sword, now blunt. "What fun is that?" she asked.

"More fun than getting poked." He pointed at the hole in her stomach.

He laid down his needle and had her do the same. Then,

over the next half-hour, the Cap'n taught Lizzie how to stand and move forward and back—things she thought she already knew. He used terms like *advance, passe avant,* and *retreat.* Only then did he show her how to use a sword. He used fancy words for fighting, too—*press, parry,* and *riposte.* After they had been at it for an hour, the Stick girl asked if they could remove the erasers and have a real sword fight.

The pirate shook his head. "You know just enough to hurt yourself. Or me."

"C'mon, Cap'n."

Just then, the door to the RV creaked open and an even creakier woman's voice called the name *Powderboo.* Lizzie heard coughing and the sound of someone clanking down metal steps. The Cap'n ran to the edge of the roof and peered over. Lizzie joined him. They lay on their stomachs and watched as an elderly woman tottered across the small yard.

"What's a powderboo?" Lizzie asked.

"An escape artist," the other replied. When Lizzie frowned, he added, "The cat."

"Oh."

"Boo?" the woman called. "Time for your medicine." She searched for several minutes, but the cat didn't respond. *It's right there under the wheel,* Lizzie thought. With shaky hands, the woman removed her eyeglasses and mopped sweat from her forehead. The Stick girl hoped she could make it back inside without keeling over.

Cap'n Nobeard hopped to his feet. "Be right back," he said, then ran across the roof and around the corner of the AC unit. He came back carrying a piece of mirror almost as big as himself.

"What's that for?"

The Cap'n looked away with a hint of shyness. "Usually it's for signaling my friend, Eric. He lives on a Windstream in lot 37."

"Eric, huh?"

"But it's also good for cat-wrangling."

"Ha!" Lizzie made a doubtful face. "You can't make a cat do anything."

"Watch." The Cap'n aimed the mirror's reflection at the ground. A sliver of light danced on the grass right in front of the old woman's feet. A few seconds later, Powderboo emerged from hiding and pounced onto the light.

"There you are, naughty boy!" The woman scooped up the cat. Lizzie watched her ascend the steps and carry him inside.

"Impressive," Lizzie said. "You speak Cat too?"

"Haha, Mademoiselle makes fun," the pirate replied. "I am not a miracle worker, just amazing."

"Yeah? Let's see if you can amaze me in a fight!"

Still using rubber tips on their swords, the two sparred for the better part of ten minutes.

"You're a natural," the Cap'n said, "but you're no match for my skill."

"I could totally kick your butt if this dumb thing wasn't so heavy," she replied.

"Think so?"

"I know so."

"Very well...." Nobeard removed the eraser from his sword and tossed it away; Lizzie did the same. "En garde!" he called, and sliced the air.

The pirate advanced and lunged. Lizzie parried and counter-attacked. She couldn't help but admire his footwork. By comparison, she moved like a zombie with broken ankles. Until now, he had taken it easy on her.

The needle in her hand did feel so much lighter with the eraser gone. She found that she could manage more complex attacks. Still, she never got close to cutting him. Not that she wanted to hurt her friend. Finally, frustrated, she mounted a series of aggressive moves. She didn't know what she would do if the tip of her blade actually injured the Cap'n. She never found out.

In an indirect attack called a coupé, she overextended herself. One second, she thought she had skewered the little guy. The next, she watched in shock as locks of her own hair fluttered down like a rainbow snow flurry. She lowered her sword.

"What did you do!" she demanded.

"That was a flick," he said. "I already showed it to you. Were you paying attention?" He kept his guard up.

"That was my hair! You just cut my hair!"

The Cap'n pursed his lips. "Maybe."

Now Lizzie went at him with all her might. She lunged and almost fell on her face. The other parried and stepped aside. A second later, more hair showered down. This happened three more times. With each attack or riposte, Lizzie felt more winded. Finally, she could no longer continue. She stood panting with her hands on her knees. "You're good," she admitted.

"You're good, too," he said.

"Right."

"I mean it. You have potential. And your new look is an improvement."

"My new—" Lizzie grasped at the ends of her hair and couldn't see it. A storm cloud grew on her face. "You've ruined my hair," she said, "my brand-new rainbow hair!"

"Ruined? I think it's marvelous."

Lizzie's anger faltered. "I oughta—what?"

Cap'n Nobeard nodded. "Not ruined, just *changed*."

That little word buzzed into Lizzie's ears like a gnat. "Show me," she said.

The little pirate led her to the air conditioning unit where he had stashed his mirror. Lizzie stared at her reflection, turning her head one way, then the other. She brushed what little hair remained behind her ears, and felt the bare nape of her neck. *Me and Sunny might still look like twins,* she thought. *Twin brother and sister.*

"It's still a little too long on the sides," she grinned.

"I agree," said the Cap'n. "Let's fix it."

He put away his needle and drew his regular pirate sword. Then he had Lizzie climb up on top of the AC unit and hang by her legs. What remained of her rainbow locks hung down. The pirate then proceeded to fine-tune her hairstyle.

"You almost done?" she asked. "The blood's rushing to my head."

"You have blood?"

"Um, I think so. I'm starting to get dizzy."

"I have no blood," he said, "I'm a straight bumper-sticker guy."

She laughed. "If you're straight, then I'm a prom queen!"

Cap'n Nobeard started to reply, then broke into a huge smile, instead. When the two of them stopped laughing, he finished up with the trim, then scraped the back of her neck smooth. "Okay, Stick warrior, you can look," he said.

Lizzie got to her feet and again stared at her reflection. The Cap'n had chopped the right side in cascading layers that barely covered her ear. He had turned the top into a riot of rainbow spikes. A blue lock curled across her forehead. She turned her head and gasped when she saw a swath of close-cropped scalp revealing her left ear. She took a step back, then another. Something seemed off. She stepped back again and again until she saw herself from head to foot.

"You mowed it real good," she said. "But something's still bugging me."

Nobeard looked her up and down and nodded. "It's the dress," he said. "It's hideous."

Lizzie smiled.

With a snip here and there, and with the aid of a hot glue gun and a toothpick, the Cap'n transformed what had been a standard Stick dress into a pair of pants and a tank top. Gone were the puffy sleeves and billowing hemline.

When he was done, Lizzie gazed at her reflection, flexed her muscles, and did tough-guy poses. You couldn't tell that she had ever worn a dress. And she couldn't stop grinning. Until now, she had never gotten a good look at her newly toned-up bod. She looked over at the Cap'n, clasped her hands on top of her head, and made her biceps jump like a pair of sub-woofers. *Look out, world,* she thought. *I'm one bad dude.*

Forty-five

As Lizzie jogged back to the campsite, she didn't worry about what anyone would think. It didn't matter. She had found herself. Himself. Whatever she had found, no one could take it from her. Him. Them. Whatever.

To make good time, she ran along the park's main road. Running barefoot felt good. Without her moccasins, she still avoided rocky ground, but, in the soft grass, her feet now felt as strong and tough as the rest of her.

As the sun raced toward the horizon, so did her shadow. With pumping arms and legs, and close-cropped hair, it looked like any guy's shadow. Staring at it, she no longer felt embarrassment and revulsion about her body. *So this is how normal people feel.*

Without a swishing dress slapping her legs, or pigtails bouncing into disheveled chaos, each step filled her with strength. As great a feeling as it was, though, she didn't kid herself that it would last. She still had to face her parents. Her family's only responsibility was to stand beside each other on a windshield. Their image was their job. The new Lizzie would mess that up.

As she entered the campgrounds, she could hear conversations at the tents. She smelled dinner being cooked over open fires. Before reaching her own site, she slowed to a walk. When she entered the small clearing behind the blue tent, Ups saw her first.

"Whoa, you look like a dude!"

Lizzie gave him a little grin. It evaporated when Mom and Dad emerged from the bread-bag tent.

"What have you done?!" Mom demanded. She stepped forward and pointed. "First, the piercing! Then you ruined your hair! And now this? Really?!" The Stick mom shook with anger. "Your dress is destroyed. You look like a boy!"

"Mom, I am a boy."

"No excuses!"

"I'm not making excuses."

"This time you've shamed your family so bad that I don't know if I can—"

"This time? You've been ashamed of me all along?" She

glanced around, hoping Sunny would come to her defense, but she was nowhere to be seen.

Mom pointed a shaking finger at the blue tent. "The Chapmans will think their car's been vandalized. They may scrape you off! They may—" She lowered her voice to a horrified whisper. "They may scrape us *all* off!

"But Mom, listen—"

"Sticks stay where they're stuck," she interrupted. "We don't change. That's why humans leave us alone, because we remind them of when their kids were young."

Lizzie looked from one parent to the other. Dad stood looking down, wringing his shaking hands.

"Dad?"

Suddenly, her father marched forward and seized her shoulders. "What have you done with my daughter?!" he yelled. He shook her—not enough to hurt physically. It just hurt her heart.

Now Lizzie's words came out shaky. "What are you ta-ta-talking about? I-I *am* your daughter. I'm still ma-me, La-La-Lizzie. I just loo-loo-look da-da-different." She searched his face for understanding and found instead a crazy look in his eyes.

She waited for her dad to yell, or maybe even hit her, although he had never done anything like that before. Instead, he released her and his face went blank. "I don't know you," he said with a flat voice.

"But, Daddy—"

"I. Don't. Know. You." He turned away.

Lizzie's face twisted as she fought not to cry. She remembered that voice. Mr. Chapman had sounded just like that the night Elizabeth died. Like hope would never return.

Dad went back inside the tent. Mom followed. Lizzie could hear bitter whispers. "I don't care what you always suspected," her dad said. "That's not my little girl. I don't know what that is!"

So I'm no longer a person. I'm a that.

Ups appeared around the corner of the tent, his tail drooping. "Dude," he said.

Lizzie tried to smile, but was afraid it would turn to tears. She walked away rubbing her shoulders, but she didn't hang her head. *I don't have any reason to be ashamed,* she told herself. *It can't be wrong for me to be me.*

When she was out of sight of her tent, she stopped and looked up. Although the sun had already fallen below the tree line, the sky was a raging fire. *I could go live in the woods,* she thought. But as much as she enjoyed her morning run, she knew she wasn't equipped to live there.

There was always the road.

From her earliest memories, fear of becoming wheelless had been ingrained in her. For a Stick, being without a windshield meant you had no purpose. Without a purpose, you were trash. Destined to die. As bad as Lizzie felt right now, she didn't want to die. For a long time, she believed that she deserved death, or, at least, pain. Now, staring at the molten clouds, she fought against that lie. It was so seductive. So tempting to let the weight of blame just crush her. *When I'm crushed, there's no more struggle. A crushed Stick is invisible. Nobody bothers with it.*

If only Elizabeth's face would appear in the clouds.

"Why won't you answer me?" Lizzie called out to the sky. "Why did you leave me? I can't do this alone, I can't." A rare Stick tear trickled from her right eye and rolled down her cheek.

To her left, a quiet electric whir brought her back to reality.

"Hey, fella," Sophia called from the minivan's window. "Who ya talkin' to?"

Lizzie brushed away the tear. *Fella?*

Beside Sophia, Sunny waved. "Hey, dude."

"Hi," Lizzie said. "Mind if I come in?"

"Funny," Sophia said with a smirk, "I could have sworn you were coming out."

Once inside the car, the three exchanged stories. First, Lizzie. She told them about making shoes from moss, meeting Jayla, the flying squirrel, and the amazing experience of gliding from the Tower of Power. She described learning to sword fight with Cap'n Nobeard, how he had styled her hair, and designed her new sportswear.

"Look at those muscles!" Sunny said. "I saw you walking our way and I said—" She glanced up at Sophia. "Tell her what I said."

Sophia laughed. "She said 'Forget Nico, I wanna meet *him!*'"

Lizzie gasped. "You did not!"

"I did."

"She did," Sophia confirmed.

"And when I realized it was you, of course, I just—" Sunny placed her hand softly on her twin's shoulder. "Sis, you look so happy."

Lizzie bobbed her head and looked away. "Uh, wow. You shoulda seen me fifteen minutes ago." She described Mom and Dad's reactions.

"They're crazy, you look *amazing!*" Sophia gushed. "Don't be too hard on them."

"Hard on them? I think you got it backwards."

"Their whole life has been about never changing," the Mobile explained. "Give 'em time, they'll catch on."

"What'd you expect?" Sunny asked. "Mom freaking out is just a normal day."

"That's not it. It's Dad. As far as he's concerned, I'm...dead." Her voice trembled as she said it. But when she glanced down at her hands, they remained still.

"Don't say that!" Sunny and Sophia said together. Lizzie looked away, afraid she would fall apart.

"Come here," Sunny said and pulled Lizzie into her arms. Lizzie buried her face in her sister's shoulder and passed through several waves of dry sobs. Plenty of pain pouring out, but no waterworks this time. Sunny rocked her like a baby.

"I'd hug you," Sophia said, "but you'd get stuck to me."

"You're stuck with us, either way," Sunny said.

Lizzie wriggled out of the hug. *A little bit of touchy-feely goes a long way,* she thought.

"So..." Lizzie said, a little afraid to ask them the next question. "Would you two be offended if I used 'he' and 'him' instead of 'she' and 'her?'"

Sunny and Sophia exchanged a look.

"Why would we be offended?" Sunny asked.

Sophia agreed, "It's your life."

Lizzie looked down. "I guess some people won't care one way or the other." He met their eyes. "But to others, I'm a freak. They'll see my very existence as a threat to their beliefs."

"That's their problem," Sunny and Sophia said together.

"What do you think about *they* and *them*?" Lizzie asked.

"They who?" Sunny asked.

"Them who?" Sophia echoed.

Lizzie sighed. "That's what I thought. I meant the pronouns, *they* and *them*.”

The others shrugged. “Completely your choice.”

Lizzie thought for a moment. “But they and them are plural.”

“So?” Sophia said. *“They* doesn’t have to be.”

Lizzie groaned. “I think I’ll stick with *he* and *him*.”

“Don’t call yourself anything because of what others think,” Sunny put in.

The Stick *boy* shrugged. “He and him just feels right.”

Sunny nodded. “Suits you. He and him it is.”

“You’re gonna need to grow a thick skin,” Sophia said. “Like, be nice to people who accept you and ignore the ones who don’t.”

“Hey, I can be nice.” Lizzie glanced toward the big blue tent. “But it’s not that easy. The way Mom sees it, the Chappy Daddy may get out the scraper.”

“No!” Sunny gasped. “He’d never!”

“Chappy Daddy?” Sophia asked. “My dad? Nobody’s gonna hurt you while I’m around. Got it?”

“Got it,” they answered. Sophia poked Lizzie on the arm, then said, “Ooh, wow, you really are muscle-y.”

“Thanks.” Lizzie understood that, to some people, him being a *he* instead of a *she* wouldn’t make any sense. It didn’t have to. It made sense to him.

“What about Lizzie?” Sunny asked.

Lizzie got a confused look. "What about me?"

"Not you, your name. Are you gonna change it? To a boy's name?"

"Hm, I don't know. Maybe." He looked away for a long moment. Sophia broke the silence.

"Can we PLEASE talk about the dance now? This is Sunny's last chance to spend time with Nico. Maybe even get her first kiss!" Sunny let out a squeal. Instead of saying something sarcastic, Lizzie managed a laugh.

Sophia fanned herself with her hands. "And my last chance to meet Joaquin!"

Lizzie twisted up her face, confused. "But wait, you already did, remember? At Baby Bear's?"

Sophia hid her face. "No, no, no. Oh, no! That embarrassing encounter with me looking up from the discount bin?" She peaked out. "That doesn't count."

Lizzie gave a shrug. "I'd count it."

Sunny shook her head. "Nope, doesn't count." She glanced outside at the fading light and quickly shifted gears. "Oh-ma-god! What time is it? We're late!"

"Oh-ma-god!" Sophia repeated, checking her phone.

Lizzie couldn't suppress a smile. For the first time since he climbed in the car, he noticed that Sophia wore make-up, clean clothes, and a French braid, bound at the end by a pink scrunchie. Sunny still wore red Sharpie lipstick, not that she had a choice.

"Wait, what happened with the van?" the Stick boy asked. "And with the dance?"

Sophia explained that her mom had tried to turn the minivan around, so they could load it more quickly in the morning, only to discover that it wouldn't start.

Sunny added, "You should have seen *our* mom. She was blowing a fuse that you weren't On Glass."

Lizzie faked a yawn. "Oh, well."

"And *my* mom called for a tow," Sophia continued. "About an hour later, this ginormous guy shows up. Dude takes one look under the hood and fixes the thing, just like that." She snapped her fingers. "Of course, the greasy tattooed rat just had to tell my folks that someone switched the wires. And my dad— he says the stupidest things—he yells, 'What the helicopter!' Completely clueless!" She paused to laugh. "But my mom, she leans over the engine and picks up something. Then she turns real slow and gives me the stink-eye. Wanna know what she found?"

"What?" Lizzie asked.

"My broken nail! See?" Sophia held up the hand with the missing acrylic nail.

"Busted!" Sunny said.

"But instead of taking away my phone, like always, all of a sudden she started being sweet. Like, freaky sweet. And she gave me the green light to go the dance!"

"Wow, I'm happy for you," Lizzie said. "I hope you two have a blast. I think I'm grounded for...ever."

Sunny took Lizzie's hands. "Did Mom and Dad actually say you were grounded? Because, earlier, they said we can go to the dance. So you're going. They can make your life miserable later."

Lizzie let out a sigh. "Point taken."

"Then you'll go?" the others asked.

"I guess. I just don't see how we're not going to get stepped on or be seen."

Sunny and Sophia explained that, while Mobiles partied inside the Pavilion, non-humans would do the same around back. Lizzie yawned as they switched to girly talk.

"This mascara is clumping," Sophia complained. "I hate it. According to Holly, Mom bought me the cheap stuff. She keeps the Revlon for herself."

"So selfish," Sunny said.

"Speaking of which, how is she?" Lizzie asked.

Sophia's gaze didn't leave the rearview mirror. "My mom?"

"No, genius, Holly."

"Oh, I dunno. We're in no-signal territory." The Mobile flashed her phone as proof. "But I don't get it."

Lizzie grunted. "What's not to get? Even Sticks know what a cell tower looks like. There's none for miles."

Sophia brushed away the comment like a mosquito. "Not that. I mean, Joaquin's always tapping away at his laptop, while I'm at zero bars. I'd LOVE to know who he's chatting with."

Lizzie laughed. "Funny. I actually know the answer."

Sophia leaned close. "Who? Does he have a girlfriend?" She glanced at Sunny. "Is he talking to gamers?"

"Boyfriend?" Sunny ventured.

"Nada," Lizzie answered.

"That means nothing," Sophia said.

"I mean no one," Lizzie amended. "He's not chatting, he's coding. That's what Nico says."

The giant girl scrunched up her face. "Wow, he's a nerd!" Her emaciated eyebrows went up. "A hunky nerd! This is good."

"Very good," Sunny agreed.

Lizzie asked, "How's that a good thing?"

The two girls replied, "No girlfriend!"

Lizzie considered it. "Hm."

"Oh no!" Sunny exclaimed and pointed at the mirror.

"What?!" the other two asked.

"I have a speck on my neck! Get the tweezers!"

Lizzie laughed. "I thought it was something important."

Sunny scowled. "I have to look perfect."

The spiky-headed twin shook his head. "Y'all need to chill. I have specks of tree bark and who-knows-what all over me. Look around. This place is Hillbilly Central. It's only a dance." Sunny and Sophia gasped at him. "Besides, we don't wanna get there on time anyway," Lizzie continued. "Show up early and you're desperate. Show up on time and you're predictable. But show up late, everyone sees you walk in. That's how you make an impression. Even I know that."

Sophia waved the tweezers. "She has a point."

"*He* has." Sunny nodded at Lizzie. "You gotta point."

"Besides," Lizzie said, "they're only boys."

"Only boys!" the girls exclaimed.

Lizzie leaned back and put his hands behind his head. Doing so, he felt his new pixie cut on the right and his buzz cut on the left. He watched his sister and friend doll up themselves, and thought, *They're trying to be the prettiest girls at the dance. Something I'll never have to worry about again.*

Forty-six

When the girly-girls were done fussing over their looks, they all got out of the van.

"Think your fancy boy knows how to dance?" Lizzie asked his sister.

"I don't care," Sunny said, "long as he asks me to slow dance."

"Never mind your sticky boy," Sophia put in, "I need you two to spy on Joaquin."

Good grief, Lizzie thought. "I'll help," he promised. "I don't dance anyway. But if Mom and Dad show up, I'm outta there."

For the rest of the walk to the Pavilion, Lizzie only half-listened to their small-talk. It was hard to empathize. They were looking for the love of their lives, or, at least, their first boyfriends. Lizzie needed the world to know that her hair and clothes were more than a fashion statement. She *was* a boy. *He* was. Lizzie didn't want to threaten or offend anyone. If they were offended, that was their problem. He just wanted to be.

The Visitors Center loomed before them. Lizzie had never been this close. Unlike the small ranger station near the front of the park, this building had been designed for tourists. Supporting a high ceiling, massive wooden beams jutted out over the entryway. A man-made waterfall cascaded down a stone facade. Lizzie could see an information counter and a gift shop. Beyond that lay a large open area with a huge stone fireplace. That's where the dance would take place. Lizzie noticed streamers hanging from the ceiling and chairs lining the walls. A row of tables stood laden with refreshments.

"My party's inside," Sophia announced. She set the twins down on the sidewalk.

"Ours is around back," Sunny said. All three of them took a deep breath and wished each other luck.

The Sticks watched as Sophia disappeared into the Center.

"She's so beautiful," Sunny said.

"Yep," Lizzie nodded.

With one of the twins looking like a hillbilly prom queen, and the other like the lead singer in a punk-rock band, the two Sticks eventually reached the back porch. Gathered underneath one of the picnic tables were dozens of sticker characters, along with a few locals—a stuffed bear who had escaped from the gift shop, several yellow jackets, a cluster of black ants, and a pair of chipmunks. A trio of Monster High dolls stood in a corner, whispering and giggling. A tie-dyed Peace Frog sticker sat swaying to the music.

"Mood lighting, huh?" Lizzie said, pointing upward. Fireflies hovered overhead.

At one end of the gathering, a band stood on a stage–an overturned KFC bucket–playing bluegrass. Band members included Mavis and Thoma and a quartet of crickets. Nico played percussion, running a toothbrush over a scrap of Velcro. Colonel Sanders bobbed his head to the beat. Because he was upside down, his handlebar mustache hung in the wrong direction.

Sunny took Lizzie's hand and led him forward.

Many in the crowd stood nodding or tapping their feet in time to the music. Only a Barbie sticker, doing ballet, had ventured onto the dance floor. A Stick boy stepped up to the twins. He was younger than them and wore a baseball cap turned sideways.

"Hi, I'm Lazy," he said.

Sunny turned away.

"Yo," said Lizzie, dropping his voice an octave. Then in a normal voice, "Hi."

"We just got here," said Lazy.

Lizzie glanced at the boy's sagging pants. "Us, too."

"Not to the party, I mean the park," Lazy clarified. "My family just rolled in. We're camped right near the—" He turned to face a little Stick girl, who tugged at his arm. "What do *you* want?" Lazy asked her.

"Mom says pull up your britches," said the girl. "Says she can see your butt."

"Cannot!" replied Lazy, but he pulled up his pants, anyway. "Now take a hike, Kiss." The girl turned up her nose and marched back to her parents.

"Did you say her name is Kiss?" Lizzie asked.

"Uh, yeah."

"Then that makes you guys—"

"Right," the boy answered. He looked embarrassed. "We're the Ass family." He pointed to others nearby. "That's my dad Jack, my mom Smart, and my drooling little brother over there, he's Dumb."

Lizzie grinned. "Which makes you Lazy Ass."

Sunny let out an exaggerated sigh. "Go away, kid."

Lazy shuffled away. Sunny turned to Lizzie with a smirk. They both glanced in Lazy's direction and, thanks to his sagging pants, saw more of his backside than they wanted to. "EWW!" they said together and laughed.

"What's so funny?" asked a voice. The twins turned. Three teenage Stick boys stood there—triplets—tall with broad shoulders. They wore red sweaters with the letter C on the front. Sunny and Lizzie both groaned. Team Sticks always thought they were better than everyone else, as if their glue didn't stink.

"What's the matter, can't you talk?" one of them asked.

"What do you want?" Lizzie answered.

Another triplet answered, "Same thing we always want. We wanna WIN, WIN, WIN!"

His brothers took up the chant: "We wanna WIN, WIN, WIN! We wanna WIN, WIN, WIN! Gooooooooo Coyotes!" They kept it up until others in the crowd shushed them.

One of the Team Sticks pointed at Lizzie and laughed. "No one told us this was a costume party!" He exchanged fist bumps with his brothers.

Lizzie took a step forward. "Just say what's on your tiny brain, knuckle-dragger."

The boy sneered. "You're weird."

"Really weird," said another. Then, to Lizzie's relief, the three walked away, elbowing each other and laughing.

"Jerks," Lizzie said under his breath.

"What do you expect?" Sunny asked. "Team Sticks treat everyone like an enemy."

Lizzie looked around. The crowd had grown. "Is everyone gonna hate me?"

Sunny hooked her arm in Lizzie's. "You've got me and Sophia. Just be friendly and let the chips fall wherever.

Speaking of which, I'm starving. Let's eat. Then we'll spy on Joaquin and Sophia."

"But we came here so you could see Nico," Lizzie said.

"I do see him." She pointed. "He's on stage. And as long as he's up there, we can't talk, much less dance. Besides, he should try to find me, not the other way around."

Lizzie said, "Never thought of it that way."

Sunny batted her eyelashes. "Which is why you're you and I'm me."

Forty-seven

unny led Lizzie to the refreshments table, a paper plate. Other characters circled it, feasting on peanuts, potato-chip crumbs, and a whole Fruit Roll-up.

"I'm gonna get me a bite of that sticky, fruity thing," Lizzie said, "and there's nothing Mom can do to stop me."

"Go for it," Sunny said. "I'm on the chips." The two split up. Lizzie pulled off a piece of Fruit Roll-up and bit into it.

"Delish!" said someone standing nearby. Lizzie turned to see Mr. Peanut, dressed in a coat and bow tie, and wearing a glass monocle, which made one of his eyes look larger than the other. He was a paper label, of course, from a jar. Lizzie wondered how his monocle could be made of real glass, but thought it would be rude to ask.

"See any napkins?" Lizzie said, glancing around.

"Allow me," said the other. With a dramatic gesture, the tall peanut man fished a handkerchief from his breast pocket and offered it to Stick boy.

"Thank you, sir." Lizzie took the handkerchief and rubbed at his mouth. "Did I get it?"

"Almost," said the peanut. "Still a spot there." He pointed at one corner of his own mouth. "No, the other side. That's it. You got it." The Stick boy returned the handkerchief to its owner. *Real cloth,* Lizzie thought.

"You might want to save some room for those." Mr. Peanut pointed with his walking cane at pieces of peanut on the plate. "No allergies, I hope?"

"None," Lizzie replied, "I love peanuts. My dad made us eat acorns earlier this week."

"How dreadful. By the way, you sound hoarse," the peanut said, clutching his own throat. "You aren't contagious, are you?"

"What, me sick? No, no, nothing like that." Mr. Peanut turned to walk away. "Hey, wait," Lizzie said. "Please don't take this wrong, Mr. Peanut, but..." He didn't know quite how to ask his question without sounding dumb.

"Yes, young man?"

Young man.

"Where did you come from? I mean, you're not a big square label, you're—" Lizzie made a curvy gesture with both hands to indicate the other's shape.

"I've been carved," said Mr. Peanut. "Believe it or not, a Mobile helped me." They both glanced toward the large windows of the Visitor Center. Lizzie could just barely see people's heads inside. People dancing. "There I was, so deep in a trash bin that I could barely see the sunlight," the lanky legume explained. "Then along came a Mobile girl and tipped over the whole thing. I and my dry-roasted companions—" he pointed with his cane at the peanut fragments "—went rolling out. Then I fainted."

"But what about the Mobile?" Lizzie asked.

"The girl?" Mr. Peanut asked. "Oh, yes. When I came to my senses, she had vanished. I was alone in the woods, sans jar. Oddly, on top of a rather large stone."

Little Stone Mountain.

"And my shape had been perfectly trimmed, as you can see." Mr. Peanut removed his top hat and bowed deeply.

Lizzie smiled. "Good to meet you."

The other shook Lizzie's hand firmly. "And you as well, young fellow."

Lizzie turned and walked away. A firm handshake felt good.

In just a few minutes, the crowd had nearly doubled. About halfway to the stage, Lizzie began bumping elbows with others. People were sort of dancing, sort of just standing. He turned sideways a couple of times to squeeze through. But then he noticed that he didn't really have to. People were moving aside to give him room.

They don't want to touch me. Maybe they think I'm contagious. Touch the freak and you might turn into one.

Then someone grasped his hand. Lizzie looked up to see Sunny. Lizzie couldn't hear her at first for the loud music.

"Let's get to the windows," she said.

"What?"

"The windows," Sunny pointed. "Let's go!"

Lizzie allowed himself to be pulled out of the crowd. Several people gave them funny looks. With the crowd behind them, he asked, "So, what's the deal?"

"Two more songs in this set, and the band will take a break," Sunny said. "When they take the stage again, Nico will sit the next one out. Then we can dance!"

"And you know this... how?"

"Sojourner."

Lizzie scratched his chin. "Who?"

"You know." Sunny pointed in the distance at a trio of hovering yellow jackets. "Your bee friend."

"Oh. Cool. But she's a yellow jacket."

"Whatever. C'mon!"

Lizzie followed Sunny to the Visitor Center wall. They were just about to begin climbing the stones to look in the windows, when someone whistled. The twins exchanged a horrified look, recognizing the whistle as that of their own mom. Whistling at the whole crowd. A Mobile was approaching. The music stopped. Everyone dropped to the ground, except for the chipmunks and ants, who scattered.

Lizzie fell flat on his face. Then, as footsteps drew near, he *melded* to see upward. Ranger Frowns-a-lot squatted with a grunt. His face flushed pink as he examined the litter beneath the picnic table. From his brass belt buckle, the etching of a bald eagle whispered to Lizzie, "Help me!" The Stick boy felt sorry for the captive bird, but had no idea how to help. It wasn't as if Sophia could steal the ranger's belt. He gave the raptor a grimace. *I would if I could.*

The ranger un-holstered his walkie-talkie. Static crackled as he thumbed a button on the side.

"Someone was back here, alright. Probably teenagers. Over."

Static crackled again and a voice said, "Any damage? Over."

"Just made a mess, is all. Looks like they had a bucket of chicken and what-not. I'll clean it up. Over."

The other voice spoke again. "Do it tomorrow, chief. You're missing the party. Over."

"Maybe you're right," said Frowns-a-lot. "I just hope raccoons don't get into it. Over."

"Ten-four," the voice from the walkie replied.

The ranger walked back inside. Under the picnic table, the music and dancing started back up.

"Give me a boost," Sunny said as she and her twin stood up.

"What if he comes back?" Lizzie asked.

"Eh, we'll play dead again. Lighten up, it's a party."

Lizzie and Sunny climbed up the stone wall to the window sill and peered in at the Mobiles. Like their own party, about a third of the people were dancing. A band stood at one end, playing. The twins spotted Sophia, drifting around the room at exactly the pace needed to keep her parents on the opposite side.

"Oooh, there's Joaquin!" Sunny squealed. The Mobile boy stood stuffing his face with snacks, while simultaneously tapping away at his laptop.

"Whoa, look at him eat!" Lizzie said.

"Thirteen-year-old boys are disgusting," Sunny replied. She glanced over. "No offense."

"None taken."

Sophia inched her way around the room. Eventually, she and Joaquin stood back to back.

"That's bold," Lizzie pointed.

Sunny did a little *grrr* sound. "He's right there, standing by our beautiful Sophia, and he won't even look up!"

Lizzie shook his head. "I don't think Joaquin's coming up for air. His mind is on that bowl of chips. And coding."

"Yeah, you said that before. What in the world is coding, anyway?"

"No idea," Lizzie replied. He flew a hand over his spiky head.

"Bunch of numbers and squiggles. Nico can't even read it."

"She should just bump into him. That's what I'd do."

"Or tackle him," Lizzie laughed. "Then he'll have to talk to her."

Instead, Sophia stepped up to the food table, right beside the boy. But just as she did, Joaquin turned in the opposite direction and wandered away.

"Wow. Horrible timing," Lizzie said.

"Painful."

At the outside party, the music ended. Sunny began climbing down from the sill.

"Where are you going?" Lizzie asked.

"You know."

"Oh." Lizzie watched as his sister descended the stone wall. As if on cue, Nico descended the KFC bucket stage.

When Sunny jumped to the ground, she looked up at Lizzie. "You coming?"

"In a minute." Lizzie watched Sunny and Nico weave through the crowd toward each other like they had built-in GPS. By the time the music started back, they had found each other. The band played some lively mountain music and the two began dancing. *They do make a cute couple,* Lizzie thought, and turned away, *but if they're about to kiss, I don't wanna to see it.*

Instead, he watched the Mobile party inside the Pavilion. Sophia kept trying to meet Joaquin, with no success. Suddenly, the Mobile girl broke off her attack and turned away. She looked anxious, but Lizzie couldn't tell what had distracted her.

The Stick boy climbed down to rejoin his own party. He had barely edged his way into the crowd, when Sunny and Nico came dancing up holding hands. Sunny did a twirl, then held out Nico's hand to Lizzie.

"Your turn!"

Lizzie waved them away. "No, no. Not me."

"I insist," Sunny said.

"I don't dance."

Nico grabbed Lizzie's hand. "Then *I* insist!" Bouncing on his toes, he led Lizzie toward the stage.

"I really don't know how to do this," Lizzie shouted over the music.

"Neither do I!" Nico shouted back. "Just move."

Lizzie tried to bounce to the music. *I'm terrible. Everyone's looking at me.* Nico took Lizzie's hands and they slowly circled the dance floor. Then, before Lizzie knew what was happening, the song had changed to something slow, and Nico was holding him as they swayed slowly with the other dancers.

"I am *not* putting my head on your shoulder," Lizzie said. Then added, "Your dancing doesn't suck."

"Hm, an insult with a compliment. You're getting better."

"Just remember what I told you. I'll tear you to pieces if you hurt my sister," Lizzie said. He started to make a fierce face, but it morphed into a smile.

Nico put his head on Lizzie's shoulder. "I won't hurt her," he whispered. "Promise."

"You know," Lizzie said, clearing his throat, "you're not exactly my—"

"Not your type."

"Yeah."

As the song ended, Nico looked in Lizzie's eyes and said, "I like the new you."

"Ha. Not a new me, just the real one."

"Alright, then, I like the real you." They separated.

"I may not kill you after all," Lizzie said. "Least not tonight."

"That's awfully kind of—"

But Nico never finished that thought. The door to the atrium burst open and Sophia rushed out, so fast that no one whistled a warning. Ranger Frowns-a-lot flew from the door right behind her. The characters underneath the picnic table all dropped to the ground.

"You!" the ranger shouted, pointing at Sophia. In his other hand, he held a metal pole, the kind with a sharp end for picking up trash. "You trashed our picnic area!"

Sophia sprang atop a picnic table and did a handstand. "Me?"

"Get down from there!" he shouted. "You could hurt yourself! The park can't be held liable!"

Sophia regained her feet, then jumped to the nearest table. "You're not afraid of a little lawsuit, are you?" Ranger Frowns-a-lot chased, but the thirteen-year-old dodged him. She jumped from table to table, then disappeared around the corner.

"Run for it!" someone yelled, and the characters scattered.

Lizzie and Nico sprang from the ground. "Find your sister and get out of here," Nico said. "I gotta help those two." He pointed at Ringo, the peace-sign hand, and Darwin, the chrome lizard creature, his slowest family members.

Most of the characters had cleared out by the time Lizzie found Sunny. The two grasped hands and ran. "I think Sophia was helping us get away," Lizzie said. "Did you see that pointy trash poker?"

"Yeah. Now the Chappies will get kicked out of the park for sure."

"Doesn't matter," Lizzie replied. "They're heading home in the morning, anyway. The car's fixed, remember?"

Soon, the lights from inside the building fell behind. The sisters ducked behind a shed.

"Hey, hey," said a voice that Lizzie recognized, but not in a good way. "It's the hottie and her freaky sister-brother." The three Team Sticks stepped up, their red sweaters almost glowing in the light cast by parking lot floodlights. "Or is that brother-sister?"

"I'm not in the mood for fools," Lizzie warned.

"Whoa-ho!" said one of the triplets. "He-she is 'not in the mood.' What? Is this National Fag Day?"

Balling up his fists, Lizzie took a step toward him.

"Take it back," Sunny said, and stepped up next to her brother. To Lizzie's surprise, Sunny had picked up a pebble, one big enough to hurt someone.

The Team Stick reached out and ruffled Lizzie's brush-like rainbow hair. "What happened here? You got to playing with crayons? Then got run over by a lawn mower?" The other Team Sticks laughed and slapped him on the back.

Lizzie felt rage rising. He looked around for anything he could use as a sword and saw nothing. Sunny took another step forward and poked the Team Stick in the chest with her pebble. "You're an idiot," she said.

"What's with those pants?" one of the others called to Lizzie. "We should call you Patches."

"Hey, Patches!" they began calling.

"What are you, a boy or a girl?"

"I don't think it's anything."

"It's an *it*."

"And you know what *that* rhymes with!"

Lizzie looked at Sunny, both of them ready to kick some butt. Even outnumbered and outsized.

The brothers grinned at each other. "He, she, or it?'

"Good one, Bobby!"

"Good one!"

Suddenly, Lizzie was surrounded by them, with Sunny on the outside, looking like she was about to bash someone with that pebble.

"He? She? Or it?" one boy called.

"He? She? It?" called the other two.

"He! She! It!"

"He! She! It!" his brothers called back.

They lunged at Lizzie, getting in his face, grabbing at his hair, his clothes.

"He! She! It! He! She! It! He-she-it! He-she-it! He-she-it!"

They chanted faster and faster, until their words blurred into an obscenity. Lizzie tried not to lose control of his emotions. They were morons. Probably couldn't count higher than a football score. Their leering faces zoomed in and out of his field of vision. But his mind did a trick. Another face replaced theirs: her dad's. Instead of "He-she-it," Lizzie heard his dad's voice, saying, "I. Don't. Know. You." Lizzie's anger melted into shame. Tears welled in the corners of his eyes. Then, as the tears burst, his dad's face disappeared and the Coyotes became themselves again—hateful, small-minded Team Sticks.

Sunny had pushed her way into their midst. "Leave my—

Leave my— Leave 'em alone!" she yelled, as if the word *brother* wouldn't quite come out. She swung the pebble and one of the Team Sticks fell away, screaming. Again Sunny swung. Lizzie ducked. But they encircled his twin. Sunny swung her pebble wildly and screamed insults that Lizzie thought he would never hear from the Sunflower.

"Grab it!" one of them yelled.

"Grab her!"

"I got her. Ow! She bit me."

"No she didn't, I did!" Lizzie yelled. Then he felt something hit him from behind. He lost his feet. He could see Sunny kicking her feet as one of the Coyotes lifted her. Lizzie tried to stand up but fell back down. One of the Team Sticks now held the pebble. Another one held Sunny in a bear hug. Then, pain exploded in Lizzie's gut as the third one kicked him. He tried to grab the Coyote's foot, but got only an empty shoe.

"What should we do with them?" one of them asked.

"Let's put 'em under a rock."

"Too heavy. We'll never lift it."

"I know," said the one who had kicked Lizzie, "Let's cut off the hottie's hair so she looks like the freak."

"Oh, man, that's so perfect!"

"Then we'll cut her dress into a pair of pants."

"Hey, let's tie them to a cat's tail! Remember that cat we saw at the dumpster?"

Then suddenly, one by one, the Coyotes disappeared into the air. *I must be dreaming,* Lizzie thought. Until he looked up.

"A cat's tail?!" Sophia yelled. The giant girl held the three Coyotes by their heads. "That sounds like an excellent plan." She squatted down to Lizzie and Sunny's level. "What d'ya think?" The twins both nodded. "But that's a nasty trick to play on a cat," Sophia said. "I could just pull off their arms and legs." She turned the Coyotes upside down and held them by their feet. "Or I could tear them right down the middle."

Instead, the twins watched as Sophia wadded up the three screaming boys—sticking them to themselves—and thumped them into the woods.

"C'mon, imaginary peeps," she said, lifting Sunny and Lizzie onto her shoulders, "let's get out of here."

Forty-eight

Late Friday Night

The three sat on the rail at the edge of Gorges Overlook, staring out at the moon as a bank of clouds rolled past it. Lizzie touched the back of his head and winced.

"That's gonna bruise," Sunny said.

When Sophia leaned closer for a look, the moonlight revealed tear streaks on her face. "I had no idea Stick people could do that. Bruise."

"You left the party," Lizzie said. "But why?"

"Not just the party," Sunny corrected. "She left Joaquin right when he was walking up to her. Right when he got up the nerve to talk to her."

Lizzie looked up at Sophia. "Oh, jeez."

"I saw that ranger staring out the window," Sophia

explained. "Like he might have noticed all y'all under the picnic table? Then he went to a broom closet and got a pokey stick."

"She means a death stick," Sunny said. "A trash picker."

Sophia shrugged. "So, I did what I had to do."

Lizzie watched the moon as it slipped fully behind the clouds. "That was really brave of you."

"It was stupid. I can hear my shrink already."

Lizzie did a double take. "You're gonna shrink? Like, to our size?"

"How is that even possible?" Sunny wondered.

"You guys! Not that kind of shrink. My therapist, I call her my shrink. I know what she'll say."

"Oh," both Sticks said.

"I'm using my hallucinations as an excuse to push people away." Sophia blew out a breath that made her hair fly. "Maybe she's right."

"Are we back to that again?" Sunny asked.

The Mobile shrugged. "Gotta admit, this is crazy."

"Look," Lizzie said, "whatever your shrinker says, on behalf of hallucinogens everywhere, thank you. What you did took guts." She paused. "So, did you get in trouble with Ranger Know-it-all?"

Sophia let out what might have been a laugh or a cry or both. "You mean Frowns-a-lot. Who knows? I don't care what he tells my parents. We're leaving in the morning."

Sunny sighed. "Told ya."

"And I'll never see Joaquin again." Sophia stared up at the night sky as her body shook with new sobs.

Of course, it's the boy, Lizzie thought. *Couldn't be a monster or an earthquake or an army of demon-stickers. Those I could handle.*

"Joaquin called me crazy," Sophia sobbed. "When I got near him, I heard him say it under his breath."

"You sure about that?" Sunny asked.

The Mobile girl nodded. "He said, 'Loco bueno.' That means 'crazy girl'. I think."

The Stick twins exchanged a glance. Lizzie said, "I don't think so."

"Nico taught me a little Spanish," Sunny said. "The word for girl is niña or chica. Bueno means good."

Lizzie snapped his fingers (not easy for a Stick). "He was talking about the food, not you, Soph. Whatever he was eating was crazy good."

Sophia smeared at her eyes with the back of a hand. "Crazy good, huh? Come to think of it, he did have a mouthful. Kinda gross, actually. Doesn't matter. I missed my chance." She dug a napkin from her back pocket and blew her nose. "If Elizabeth was here, she'd know just the right thing to say," she said.

Lizzie grunted. "Fat chance."

"What?"

"You heard me. Elizabeth absolutely would *not* know the right thing to say."

"What are you saying?" Sunny and Sophia both asked.

"Just what I said. Elizabeth never knew—" he did air quotes "—the right thing to say. She blurted out whatever came into her head. When it comes to touchy-feely stuff, she was clueless. If she was here, she might just punch you, like this—" He punched his sister in the arm.

"Ow!"

"Or she might say that there's not a boy on earth good enough for Sophia Chapman. And that if he didn't have the grits to walk up and talk to you, then he missed the boat, sister, and don't you waste another tear on him. And he should have grown a pair, whatever that means."

"But he did walk up," Sunny objected.

"Then he shoulda walked faster," Lizzie said.

Sophia sniffed, glanced at the soaked napkin, then passed her forearm over her face. "How'd that first part go again?"

"This?" Lizzie punched Sunny again.

"Hey! What'd I do?"

"Yeah, that," Sophia laughed. She looked at Sunny. "Sorry, sweetie, but see what I mean? Just the right thing to say."

Lizzie grimaced. "But she's not here. She's not anywhere, far as I can tell."

"In a way, she is." Sophia reached down and ruffled Lizzie's short-cropped rainbow hair. "She's in you."

"I guess so. I just wish I felt her, you know, better." *At all.*

"Feel this!" Sunny punched Lizzie in the arm. He took it without flinching. Some silence passed. They sat on the edge of the abyss and watched the moon slowly emerge from the clouds, bathing the Jocassee Gorge in cool light.

Sophia recounted adventures she and Elizabeth had had as kids, forts they had built out of blankets, and one in the woods. Things that Elizabeth had said to her and to no one else. Lizzie told of how Elizabeth had felt, what she had dreamed. It hurt both Sunny and Sophia to hear how guilty Elizabeth had felt about everything. Sophia's tears rolled in waves.

"I need to tell you something. There was this one time–" the giant girl choked out the words, "—when Lizbeth and me were on the bus. And there were these kids from our grade that liked to tease anyone who was different. And they started on her. Giving her a hard time. Calling her names."

"What names?" Sunny pressed.

Sophia squirmed. "You know."

Sunny shook her head, no. Lizzie remained silent. He knew. He could feel what was coming.

"They called her the D-word," Sophia said. "And the F-word. You know, the three-letter one?"

Sunny looked from Sophia to Lizzie.

"Dyke," Lizzie said, "and fag."

"Lizzie!" Sunny put a hand over her own mouth.

Those words had struck Elizabeth like poison arrows. At the time, Lizzie had also felt their sting. But tonight, when one of the Coyotes had used one, Lizzie hadn't blinked. He wasn't immune to people's ignorance, but maybe he had begun to build up a resistance. He would need it.

"What did Elizabeth do?" Lizzie asked. "I know she didn't just take it."

Sophia fought back a tearful laugh. "She shot paper wads at them. Then, when we got off the bus—they live in our neighborhood—she tried to fight them. But the biggest girl pushed her down and scattered her homework."

"What did you do?" Sunny asked.

Sophia suddenly became interested in throwing pebbles into the abyss.

"What?" Sunny insisted.

"Both of us, me and Holly. See, those girls were real popular and—"

"No excuses," Sunny said.

Sophia stopped throwing pebbles. Her shoulders slumped. "Nothing. I did nothing. When we reached our stop, I ran home before Lizbeth even got off. I didn't see the pushing and stuff. But when she got home, her pants were dirty and her papers were a mess. The worst part, I got mad at her. Like it was her fault. Because they were so popular. And she didn't do anything wrong."

After a pause, Sunny said, "That was awful." Sophia nodded. Lizzie rested her hand on Sophia's giant hand. Their eyes met.

"You hurt her bad," she said.

Sophia bit her lower lip and mouthed the words: *I know*.

"But she forgave you."

Sophia's shoulders shuddered and she seemed to come even more unhinged. She mouthed *I know* again, then sniffed and brushed at her eyes. "Then at least one of us did. I've never forgiven myself."

"We forgive you," the Sticks said.

They moved closer to her, embraced her, hugged her, if you could call it that. She was too big for them to put their arms around. Lizzie knew more than she wanted to about holding on to blame. It felt good to offer grace to someone else.

Between sobs and hiccups and sniffles, Sophia quietly confessed one more thing. "I still haven't been to see her since the funeral. To her grave."

They held her for a little while longer. Then Lizzie asked a question that had bothered her ever since the first day she was stuck. "Do you know what happened to the others?"

"What others?" Sophia asked.

Sunny realized what Lizzie was asking and shot her twin a dark look. "Mom said not to ever talk about that."

"Mom doesn't know everything," Lizzie replied. "She said

the first rule of being a Stick is we can only bond with one Mobile. Ever." She gestured at Sophia. "Obviously, not true. So. What happened to the ones who went back in the box?"

Sophia stared at the twins. "I have no idea. I never thought about it."

"It's been bugging me ever since we lost Elizabeth," Lizzie said. "It's why I couldn't leave Serena at the bottom of the trash barrel."

Sophia said, "You think they could still be somewhere in the house? Like in a closet or the attic?"

Lizzie shrugged. "Maybe you could find out." Sophia nodded.

Sunny took her sister's hand. Or brother's hand. "You really are one of a kind."

Lizzie stared at the clouds as they passed over the moon again and again. The rain held off, but teardrops fell, no matter how hard Lizzie fought to stop them. Memories of Elizabeth—and the possibility that dozens of Sticks were still living a nightmare of endless darkness—they were too much. The twins finally rode back to the campsite on the Mobile's shoulders. Behind them, like a mountain climber, the moon searched for hand holds and carefully scaled the stars in the North Carolina sky. Well before sunrise, the cool, night air dried away the tears from the rail.

Forty-nine

Saturday, Early Morning

In darkness, Lizzie woke to the sound of footsteps. He sat up and looked over to see Sunny, already awake.

"It's her," Sunny whispered.

"Where's she going?"

"Not sure. I think she's heading for the river."

Lizzie frowned. "I don't like it."

The two crawled out of the bread-bag tent, careful not to wake their parents. Outside, Sunny said."She's moving fast. We need to roll. Like, actually."

As they rolled down the dirt road—Sunny on a Sprite- and Lizzie on a Dr. Pepper can—Lizzie asked, "Is she running away?"

"Not everybody wants to do that," Sunny replied.

Lizzie nodded. "Plus, there's nowhere to run."

Without another word, they rolled to the Overlook. But it was deserted. They hopped off their soda cans, scaled the stone wall, and peered over the edge. "You don't think—" Lizzie began.

"What? That she did a cartwheel off the cliff? Not a chance."

"So where?"

Sunny pointed.

Rutted by erosion, the rocky Rainbow Falls Trail followed a steep descent. The moon had fallen below the western horizon and the sun glowed faintly on the eastern, so the twins could see very little as their soda cans accelerated. Less than a hundred feet down the trail, Lizzie hit a gnarled root and went flying. He had the presence of mind to turn the fall into a glide, but his DP can tumbled down a steep embankment. A moment later, on foot, he caught up with Sunny, who sat in the dirt, rubbing her elbow. Lizzie could hear Sunny's Sprite can, further down the trail, ping-ponging off of rocks.

"Guess we're both runners, now," Lizzie said, and pulled his sister to her feet.

Soon the trail split. The twins veered right, continuing on the Rainbow Falls Trail marked by orange. Sophia's parents had hiked this trail earlier in the week, and had slid down Turtleback Falls, a gentle waterfall a half-mile beyond Rainbow.

"Maybe she wants to slide off Turtleback," Lizzie suggested.

"No way," Sunny replied. "We have waterparks back home. Plus the water's ice-cold. Maybe she just wants to see the rainbow at sunrise. They say you can really see one."

The trail to Rainbow Falls snaked downward for more than a mile, then followed the Horsepasture River. For the Sticks, it was like running a marathon. By the time they could hear running water, both were exhausted. Gasping, Sunny rolled onto a bank of moss and lay on her back. Lizzie sat down on a rock. With the sun just now at the tree line, they still had the trail to themselves.

"I've run this far before but... not all at friggin' once," Lizzie said as she caught her breath. "How we doin' with the... runaway?"

"Not good," Sunny said. "She's way ahead of us."

Lizzie sat up. "Gotta keep going." He tried to stand up but a painful cramp shot through his calf. He screamed, then took a minute to stretch it out.

"You okay?" Sunny asked.

"Will be."

"One more question."

"Shoot."

"Have you ever heard of a bunny rabbit eating a Stick?"

"Killer bunnies?" Lizzie laughed. "Don't think so. Why?"

Sunny pointed. "There's one staring at us."

Lizzie sat up. A brown bunny sat beneath some foliage and

stared out at them. Not the same one that Lizzie had met on her first run in the forest.

"Can you help us?" Sunny asked. "Did you see a giant girl go by here?"

"They don't talk," Lizzie said, "at least, not the Common Tongue."

Sunny got to her feet and took a couple of steps forward. The brown bunny drew back but didn't disappear. "Don't be afraid. We could use your help, ya know? You feel like a morning run?"

Lizzie watched as the bunny cautiously stepped out from the brush.

"You know Rainbow Falls?" Sunny asked. "I'll bet you do. Well, we need to get there, real fast."

Lizzie had ridden on the back of a flying squirrel, dived from an electrical tower, and been swept down a river, but from now on, this ride would define the word fast. The twins clung to the beast's back as he rocketed through the forest. The bunny veered off the main trail and onto ones that only he could see. He ducked beneath boulders, danced along the edge of sheer drops, and tore through previously invisible tunnels of leaves. Near the end of their mad journey, he raced down a hillside so fast that Lizzie thought they would land in the river itself. The bunny suddenly stopped next to the wooden deck that overlooked the falls.

The Stick twins tumbled off of his back. The bunny then turned and bounded back up the hill and out of sight. They didn't even have time to thank him.

The two walked to the edge of the deck. The falls lay below them and to the right. A steep embankment fell from the viewing deck to the river. Boulders more massive than any Lizzie had seen lay piled up there. The falls spilled from an impossibly high cliff, cascading with a violence that sent a chill through Lizzie.

Sunny pointed. "There she is!" Wearing yesterday's clothes, Sophia hopped from boulder to boulder, heading toward the bank of the river.

"Sophia!" the twins yelled, with no response. Lizzie figured that Sophia couldn't hear them over the sound of the water. Just then, the sun topped the tree line, washing the waterfall in dazzling white, and the arc of a rainbow sliced through the mist.

"Wow," Sunny said.

"Yeah, it's beautiful, but no time," Lizzie replied. "C'mon!"

They descended the same steep trail that the Mobile had taken. But by the time they reached the boulders at the base of the falls, Sophia had disappeared.

"Sophia!" Lizzie yelled through the roar of the falls. "Sophia!" She turned to Sunny. "Getting any vibes?"

"She's sad. And she's angry. And scared."

"Angry at who? Us?"

"I don't know. I just know that all those feelings together don't add up to anything good."

"Well, where did she go?"

"There!"

Sunny pointed to the opposite bank. Sophia had crossed the river and was hiking toward a rock face to the left of the falls. She must have gotten there by crossing an enormous tree that bridged the river. The twins hurried toward it.

Climbing the rough boulders to reach the tree provided enough of a challenge. But when the two finally stood atop the ancient log, they were met with a more daunting task than Lizzie had imagined. A slippery bridge with no rails, spanning a turbulent caldron.

Fifty

Although plenty wide, the water-soaked log was slick, and curved like a dome. Clouds of mist gusted from the falls, soaking Lizzie and Sunny, and making it hard to see. Crawling, the Stick twins inched forward.

"It's too hard, I'm gonna fall," Sunny said, peering down at the rushing water.

"Don't say that, don't look down, just keep moving."

The words were barely out of Lizzie's mouth when a wave splashed up from the river. It washed across their bridge, knocking them flat. Their sticky sides had no effect on the damp surface. Lizzie could feel the water pulling him toward the edge. Clawing at the wood, he glanced at the torrent of white water below.

Sunny screamed something, but Lizzie couldn't make it out

because of the water's roar. Both of them stopped sliding as they found handholds in the rotted, pock-marked wood. They lay flat as the water finished draining from the log. Then they scrambled back to the top, where they crouched on hands and knees and caught their breath.

Lizzie said, "Give me one of your scrunchies."

Without asking why, Sunny undid one of her soggy pigtails and handed over the band. Lizzie twisted it into a figure eight, then wrapped one end around his foot. "Loop this around your wrist," he instructed, and Sunny did so. "Now if one of us falls, we both do," Lizzie said.

Repeatedly, the river splashed over the log. Now, though, they were expecting it. They stayed low and tried to make sure they had some kind of hand-or foothold at all times. Although Lizzie warned Sunny not to look down, it was hard not to, even for him. Glancing again and again at the deadly water below, Lizzie had never been more scared.

When they reached the other side, they removed the scrunchie that had bound them, and looked around for Sophia. They spotted her climbing the rock face next to the falls. The twins yelled her name, but the thunder of water absorbed their calls.

"What's she thinking? She's got no rope!" Sunny moaned.

"And no common sense! If she slips, she's dead."

"Wait. She stopped. What's she doing?"

Lizzie gazed up at the girl, who now held on with only one hand. He looked at his sister and sighed. "Taking selfies!"

Sophia had made it about a third of the way up. If she slipped, it would be like falling from a seven-story building, with only a riot of rocks waiting to catch her. Before Lizzie could decide what to do, Sunny began climbing.

"Hold on," Lizzie said, pulling his sister to the ground.

"We gotta get her!"

"Look at yourself," Lizzie scolded. "Your adhesive has dirt all over it. Plus, you're soaked. I'll go."

"Not a chance. No one's picked your glue in days." Sunny picked a fleck of rock off Lizzie's back to make her point. "You'll be doing good if you can stick to the windshield. You're twice as dirty as me. "

"Yeah, but I'm twice as tough."

"No, Lizzie, you just think you are."

Lizzie looked up. The sun had risen. Sophia's red shorts shown like a driveway reflector. "She's moving fast. Maybe we should just let her climb."

Sunny stared upward. "I'm not sure if she's heading for the top or just after the ultimate selfie. I haven't felt her this depressed in...in a year."

"Oh." Lizzie looked long into his sister's eyes. Then he laced his fingers together and offered her a boost. Sunny nodded.

"Together," they said.

Although Sophia had a big head start, Sticks are great climbers, so Lizzie and Sunny began to close in on her. Still, thick mist from the falls rolled over them, and the rock face got steeper the higher they went. Lizzie knew that Sunny was afraid of heights, so he was impressed that his sister didn't complain. She just focused on grabbing the next outcropping of rock or sprig of grass. Lizzie himself looked down several times. He figured if the wind did sweep them off the wall, they could glide down. But for Sunny, it would be her first time flying. Assuming they didn't get pulled into the falls or land in the river, they would survive.

The Mobile was about three-quarters of the way to the top when she heard their tiny voices calling her name. "Are you crazy?" Sophia called. A minute later, the twins reached her eye level, one on either side. "What the fudge?!" she asked over the roar of the falls. "What are you guys doing here?"

Lizzie gave her a scowl. "You know why."

"The question is what are *you* doing here?" Sunny demanded. "You're gonna throw yourself off a cliff over a boy? For a boy?!"

"No, of course not. Why would you think that?" Sophia patted her hip pocket. "I just want the perfect profile pic."

Don't lie to us, Lizzie thought.

"I mean...I would never do that," Sophia went on. She looked down. Then, seeing the sheer height, she gasped. She grabbed for a better hold. Loose stone and dirt spilled down the wall. She started to shake. "I would never do that to my family. Or to you." She looked from one Stick to the other, first at Sunny. "I know what it would do to you." Then, at Lizzie. "And what it's already done to you."

"Well?" Sunny asked.

"Okay, you gotta admit they're gonna be great selfies. Even better than Holly's Grand Canyon profile last year." Sophia glanced down again and shuddered. "Or maybe I wanted to look Death in the eyes."

Lizzie rolled his eyes. "Well, I hope you got a good look."

Sophia made an embarrassed face. "I think I peed myself."

The twins returned confused looks.

"You know, like when Hershey marks things?"

Sunny looked horrified. "Ew!"

"Oh," Lizzie said. He recalled the girl's room at the trading post, and wondered briefly if the boy's room was identical.

"How are your hands?" Sunny pointed.

Sophia blinked back tears as she held one out. "Not great. Honestly? I don't think I can make it."

Lizzie said, "We're all gonna make it." He glanced down. "But you're kinda stuck. There's nothing to grab right above you. Sit tight, I'll go scout it out." The Stick boy scrambled away to the left and returned a moment later. "Over there, there's a ledge," he reported. "C'mon."

From that point on, the Stick twins guided Sophia and they made steady progress. Hope rose in Lizzie that everything would be okay. Hearing the grunts and heavy breaths of Sunny and Sophia fighting for the summit, he felt more connected, more at peace, than he had since Elizabeth's death. Life was a fight, but at least not one he faced alone. Then, within sight of the top, Sophia's foot slipped. At that moment, Lizzie had been admiring the sunrise. For a second, sunlight glinted off a piece of quartz and blinded him. He shielded his eyes with one hand. Then the falls, the wall, and the horizon all tilted.

Lizzie heard Sunny scream his name. Felt the wind pushing him. Saw droplets of water racing toward him. Heard the roar of the falls grow as if someone had twisted a volume knob.

Glide! Fly!

But Lizzie did not glide. He did not fly. He fell.

Swirling air currents flipped him, pushed him away, and then sucked him right into the thundering falls. Like being hit by an icy truck. Downward-racing water surrounded him. For a timeless moment, a constellation of sunlit drops dazzled him, iridescent crystals traveling through morning light.

Dark green murk suddenly enveloped Lizzie. He could see nothing. Felt only chill. For thousands of years, Rainbow Falls had been drilling a deep pit in rocks. As Lizzie plunged deeper and deeper into the basin, black replaced green. Numbness replaced the cold. His feet touched smooth stone.

The world lay as perfectly still as a Stick person in a box. Lizzie saw no bubbles, no fish, no waving plants. An emptiness turned him inside-out, so profound he couldn't fight it. An unbearable nothingness.

So this is where she went.

Images projected onto the walls of his mind. Faces without names. Stick people holding hands, a flying squirrel, a tiny pirate. A yellow jacket buzzing the trash. Ants and Skittles, a jaguar, a cowboy. Red lights reflected from a guardrail. Glass scattered like diamonds on a highway. A face being covered. A black dress. Empty eyes.

Time meant nothing. Only being. And Lizzie had almost stopped being.

Then, better images: Elizabeth riding a scooter. Playing hide-and-seek in the yard. Shooting hoops in the driveway with her twin. In front of a mirror, flexing her arms. A crooked smile, curious green eyes. Lizzie had soaked her up, like a white cloth sopping up grape juice, forever changed.

Maybe she's inside me.

Then nothing at all.

Fifty-one

A geyser of water sprayed from Lizzie's mouth. Gasping for air, he shut his eyes against the sun's glare. He wiggled his fingers and felt sand, felt cold droplets on his face. *I'm alive.* He blinked his eyes open and turned his head from side to side.

He lay on a small beach littered by piles of dirty brown foam. Beside him, a branchless tree trunk reached for the river's edge, as if it had died trying to find water. A forest stretched toward a blue sky strewn with charcoal clouds.

He tried to sit up, but failed. Instead, he lay looking up at the fast-moving clouds. It would have been better if he had passed out because, seconds later, he felt the first bite. True to their name, fire ants felt just like scalding fire.

To Mobiles, fire ants give painful stings and poison that

leaves an itchy rash. They didn't give anything to Lizzie. They took. Once they realized they had found their favorite nectar, adhesive, thousands of them swarmed the exhausted Stick boy.

Screaming, swiping at them, Lizzie writhed in the sand. With the last of his strength, he turned onto his stomach and began crawling toward the river. He never got there. More and more swarmed him. In the longest few seconds of his life, the horde tore at his body, stripping him of glue. He could do nothing but lie there while they pulled him in all directions. His ears filled with their eerie screeches. When they had devoured his glue, they tore at his body, their mandibles like red-hot knives cutting away tiny bits and strips of skin.

They left as quickly as they had swarmed.

According to windshield lore, glue held together a Stick's mind. "Your glue is you," every Stick child learned. There was some truth to that. Convulsing, Lizzie now went over the edge of hysteria, like the anguish of a year ago, and, if possible, even worse. Then he had lost Elizabeth. Now he lost himself. His higher thought processes scattered like a flock of frightened birds. What remained for the moment: guilt. *I deserve this,* he thought, over and over. *I deserve this.*

When Sophia and Sunny found him, seemingly eons later, he looked dead.

"Ohmagod, Lizzie! Lizzie!" Sunny cradled her twin's head in her arms. Sophia's giant head hovered like a mother ship, her forehead creased with worry. Lizzie saw his sister and friend as if through dirty film, their faces smeared. Their voices echoed nonsense.

As Sophia lifted him, fire shot through Lizzie's body. He cried out.

"He's alive!" the other two both exclaimed.

To Lizzie, their words circled like vultures, sounds that made no sense.

Without glue, Lizzie's nervous system lay exposed. As Sophia scrambled up a steep incline to the trail, each move sent a jolt through him. The giant girl then raced up the rocky path. Voices, without meaning to Lizzie, ricocheted through the treetops. Orange blazes on tree trunks flashed by like stripes on a highway. Angry clouds streaked overhead. Lush green ferns danced before the Stick boy's eyes long after they had passed. The eyes of small creatures, either real or imagined, stared at him through the leaves. The dark entrance of a hollow tree grew until it filled his vision.

Voices again, but whether they were talking about him or not, Lizzie had no idea.

"He's passed out again!"

"Then wake him up!"

"C'mon, sis', stay with me, dude."

Then two human screams, one high-pitched, one low. The world tumbled.

"What the heck?!" Sophia yelled.

"I was coming to find you. Your parents sent me."

To Lizzie, nonsense. *Find yind, send mend.*

Words and images faded in and out. The giant girl. A boy's tan face.

"Next time just punch me. What are you doing here, anyway?"

"I'm sorry...I just turned the corner and...they sent me to find you."

"I don't need finding. I'm on my way."

"Okay...but they told me to...and your dad fixed your car."

Then a flash of red came from the girl's pocket. An object. The Stick boy fought a wave of pain to place it, but its meaning flew away.

"Take this!"

"But your parents said I'm supposed to bring you back."

"Do what I say. Take it!"

Day whay say tay.

The red something passed from one giant's hand to the other's. The giant girl said something else, followed by the boy's incredulous answer.

"You want me to do what?! Are you loco?"

Loco boco roco hoco.

"Just do it!"

"But why?"

"I can't tell you."

"But why?"

"I need time…just a little time."

Lizzie felt the giant girl crying. In his simplified thoughts, despair replaced guilt.

Who is she? Nobile? Bobile? Mobile?

"I can't leave you here if you're gonna hurt yourself," the human boy said.

"I'm not!" Sophia replied.

"Then why are your fingers bloody?

"I was climbing, that's all."

"Okay, then promise me."

"I promise."

"Say the words."

Words birds.

"I promise, I won't hurt myself. Anymore."

Of all the weird words, these cut into Lizzie. He was vaguely aware of air passing through holes in his body. There was movement. Lizzie saw a giant boy running away.

Green? Steam? Jean?

Joaquin.

"One of the front tires," Sophia yelled after him, "make sure it's a front one."

Lizzie noticed Sunny's face for the first time since Sophia and Joaquin had run into each other. "We're gonna fix you," she said. *Ix foo.*

"Who?" His own voice sounded alien, like tires skidding on pavement. "I look...like you?"

"Not so much right now, Lizzie Lou. Not so much." Sunny's face disappeared. "Ready, Soph?"

"I lost my boot when I collided with that idiot! How could I have lost my friggin' boot?!"

Then light and sound faded.

Lizzie awoke to find an enormous, red belt—a dog's collar—strapped across his midsection. He looked around. The forest flew by in a green blur. He now rode a great, brown beast. Floppy ears waved in the wind.

Dog. We love him.

"Hey, you're awake," said a voice. A Stick girl's face appeared. *Sunny.*

Lizzie tried to ask, "What happened?" It came out as, "Whappa?"

"You got attacked by the Fire Empire," Sunny replied, "but me and Hershey are gonna get you help."

Fifty-two

Overwhelming pain swept over Lizzie, a wave so severe that it almost caused him to black out again.

"How far?" Sunny called.

"Getting close... to the... trailhead," the Boykin replied. As the steep incline went on and on, Lizzie could feel the dog's body tremble, could feel his lungs heave. Looking back, the Stick boy could see the rocky trail spotted with blood, and knew that the dog must be running his paws ragged.

When they reached the trailhead, the ground leveled out. The campsite lay another half-mile away. Hershey dug in even harder, running with the low-to-the-ground gait common to his kind. He raced along the park's main road toward the campsite, gasping for air as if he would collapse.

A circle of flattened grass marked where the big blue tent

had stood. The Sticks' bread-bag tent had vanished, too. The Boykin spaniel finished with a fantastic burst of speed.

"Hershey!" the Chappy Daddy called as the dog ran up. But instead of running to the man, the dog scooted underneath the van.

"Hurry!" Sunny called. Her family hurried to them.

"Where have you been?!" Mom demanded. "We were supposed to leave an hour ago! We'll be lucky if—"

"Shut it!" Sunny yelled. She lowered Lizzie onto the grass.

Mom, Dad, and Ups all crowded around. To Lizzie, their wide-eyed faces bobbed around, going out of focus and sharpening again. He couldn't remember how he knew them.

Mom put her hand over her mouth. Lizzie lay in tatters. Parts of him looked like lace. His shin had split open again, worse than before. Pieces of clothing and flesh were missing. His glue had been stripped.

"Let me know if you need me again," Hershey panted, then crawled away. Lizzie caught a glimpse of his paws, bloody as raw hamburger.

"Oh, my!" Mom whispered.

"Lizzie Lou? Can you hear me?" Dad asked.

Words that should have been soothing made no sense.

"Honey, I'm so sorry, I didn't mean those stupid things, I—"

"What happened?" Mom asked, turning to Sunny.

"The Fire Empire swarmed her," Sunny said. "Right after

she fell into the falls and nearly drowned."

They all stared in silence. Mom touched the Stick boy's face, but that only brought a wince of pain. Then Ups noticed the worst part. "Oh, no, her glue!"

Mom snapped her fingers at the Stick dog. "Go, run get Mavis and Thoma. We need all the magnolia sap they have."

Lizzie blinked. Nico's moms were there. Everyone was talking, their words running together.

"We don't have enough sap."

"It'll never dry in time."

"Superglue, that's our only option."

"But that's terrible!"

"What other choice do we have?"

"It's the only way."

"And it'll work."

Nico's face appeared. "Maybe we should ask him."

"Him who? Lizzie? She doesn't even know where she is."

"She didn't know me," the Stick dad said. "My little girl didn't even know me."

"Boy," Lizzie whispered, but no one heard him. They weren't even looking at him now. He tried to raise his head. "Ask me... what?"

A Stick man's face appeared. "Hey, sweetie." There was something odd about it. New lines. Lizzie had never seen creases on his forehead. *His name starts with a D.* Other faces crowded in.

"We're gonna get you all better," Mom said.

"There's no time for the sap to dry," Mavis explained. "You'd fly Off Glass."

"But me and Ups can overlap you," Sunny put in, "I told them we'd hold you down, but—"

"But then we'd lose all three of you." Mom stroked Lizzie's face. Instead of comfort, he felt fire.

Nico edged in close. *The boy with the fancy face.* "They want me to go for the Superglue. I can do it, no problem. I'm an Insider, remember?" Lizzie didn't remember.

All that detail, he thought. *Eyelashes. Fingernails. Lips.* Something about a barrel. Someone trapped.

Lizzie looked at Nico and his moms. "Aren't you supposed to be—" He searched for the word *gone*. It was gone.

"We have a flat tire," Mavis said. "Our Mobiles are changing it now. Someone poked a hole in it."

"Our car, too," Ups added. "That boy, he had a Swiss Army knife and—"

Lizzie tried to hold up his hand. "What dries fast?"

"Nothing, sweetie," Mom said, "you don't have to worry about that."

"You're gonna be okay," said Dad.

"But—" Lizzie started, but Dad placed a finger on his lips.

"Shhhh."

"I think Lizzie should decide," Nico said.

Pain passed through Lizzie like bitter cold. "Decide?"

"About the superglue," Nico said.

"The…"

"Superglue."

"To hold you On Glass. To keep you safe," Mom and Dad added.

Lizzie looked at each face, lastly at Ups. He couldn't remember the Stick dog's name, but he knew that he had never seen that look before. Then it hit him. Superglue. The stuff that made you stuck forever.

"No," he said. He began breathing hard. "No, no, no, no nooooo!"

"Just a little dab on your hands and feet," her dad said, "maybe a drop on your head. Just 'til we get you home."

"No!" Lizzie struggled to sit up, but couldn't. "Mom!" he pleaded, remembering the name. "Please, no, please!" He found Sunny's eyes. "You. Girl! Tell 'em! You can't, no, no, no, you can't!"

Sunny took his hands. Tears rolled down her face. "I can't lose you," she said.

Lizzie pushed her away and began scuffling, kicking. Other hands held him down. Out of his raw fractured mental state came clarity. *No Superglue.* He wouldn't let them, whatever it took.

In the end, Mom sided with him. It was Lizzie's life, she said. Lizzie calmed down. The hands released him. No one said anything. In the silence, a buzzing sound grew until it filled the space beneath the van. A trio of black-and-yellow fliers landed —Sojourner, Cynthia, and Seth.

"We heard about the attack," Sojourner said. "How is she?"

"She—" Mom began. She glanced at Lizzie. "He's in bad shape."

"This van's going to pull away any minute," Dad added. "We need to get her On Glass."

Thoma turned to Nico and Ups and handed them several empty acorn shells. "Fill these to the brim with sap and get back here fast," she said.

"Sap?" Sojourner asked. "That won't dry."

Thoma nodded grimly. "It's all we have."

"Not all," Sojourner said. Just then a sound like a roomful of electric fans filled the air. Dozens of honey bees landed and surrounded them. The Sticks stared at them. Lizzie couldn't see their faces yet, only a sea of antennae.

"I called in a favor," the yellow jacket explained. "Our cousins here have agreed to make a donation to the cause."

"A donation?" Dad asked. "What kind of—"

He fell silent as a drone stepped forward and laid a golden capsule in the grass. "For Lizzie Lou," the honey bee said. "For the barrel." And he flew away. One by one, the bees stepped forward and lay golden capsules at the Sticks' feet. Lizzie stared at each face. Each one the same. Each one different."For Lizzie Lou. For the barrel," each bee said. Soon they were all gone. Only the yellow jackets and the Sticks remained. Lizzie looked up at a circle of faces.

"That's a lot of nectar," Dad said, glancing at the capsules.

Ups pulled at his whiskers. "Will it work?"

Thoma shook her head. "Hard to say. That stuff won't won't dry for days."

"Thicker than sap," Mavis pointed out.

"It'll have to work," Mom said.

"It *will* work," Sunny added. "I know it will." She gave Lizzie a brave smile.

"Wha—?" Lizzie didn't know what they were referring to.

Nico leaned over and whispered. "No Superglue."

Thoma carefully painted the back of Lizzie's body with the sticky golden nectar. And she again tried to repair the slash to his right leg. Lizzie blacked out, then awoke face down. Thinking *fire ants* and *Superglue*. He began to resist.

"Shh, shh, it's alright," Sunny said. She smoothed down the Stick boy's tangled rainbow hair. "It's just honey."

Lizzie lay still again.

Mavis began coating the back of his head. To see, Lizzie melded. "I'm..." He licked the corner of his mouth and tasted sweetness. "Sticky."

"And sweet," Sunny said, stroking his hair. This time her touch didn't burn. "Sweeter than ever."

Looking through honey was like wearing gold-tinted prescription glasses. With the wrong prescription. The honey also coated his nervous system, so the shocks faded. The stinging from all the holes in his body subsided, too, leaving instead an all-over ache. But Lizzie wasn't any stronger. And random images kept jumping out in his mind's eye, making him flinch.

He heard the mechanical clacking of the jack. Turning, he saw that a scaffold-like apparatus had been placed beneath the minivan. One side of the vehicle was rising in small increments. He saw hairy pale legs as the Mobile dad began changing the flat tire. Light flooded the underside of the vehicle as the tire came off. Then, as the man struggled to line up the spare, he dropped a lug nut in the grass. Lizzie heard him curse, and watched the steel nut roll beneath the van. The Chappy Daddy's hand groped for it.

"Down!" Mom commanded. Everyone dropped to the grass, except Lizzie who was already there.

He heard the giant girl, Sophia, say, "I got it." Her feet appeared, one of them barefoot. The Sticks all froze as Sophia's face came into view. She grabbed the lug nut and disappeared, but not before stealing a glance toward the back of the vehicle.

As the group got to their feet, a hushed discussion broke out.

"She saw us!"

"You sure?"

"How do you know?"

"She looked right at us!"

"What's gonna happen?"

"What does it mean?

"It's over, we're all gonna die!"

"We'll get scraped off."

"We're already off. They'll never let us back on."

"She didn't see us," Sunny said. Everyone looked at her.

"Are you sure?" Ups asked.

"She stared a hole in us!" Mom said.

"But she didn't notice."

"Are you positive?"

"Absolutely, one hundred percent," Sunny said. "Her mind was...on something else." She hesitated.

"On the boy?" Nico prompted.

"Yes. The boy. Joaquin," Sunny said. "She was thinking about her crush. She didn't see us." She cast a worried look at her injured twin. Their eyes met.

Thoma finished spreading honey on Lizzie's feet. "I'm done," she said.

Ups pointed. "But you didn't use it all."

Thoma shook her head. "No, but it's already dripping off."

Lizzie's parents turned to her. "Thank you," they said. The

Stick mom stroked Lizzie's face. "We'll just have to hold on to our...boy, like our lives depend on it."

Not our lives, Lizzie thought. *Just mine.*

The two families said hurried goodbyes. Nico's family wished Lizzie luck.

"Be kind to yourself," Thoma told him.

Nico bent down and kissed him gently on the cheek. "Bye, Lizzie Lou from the barrel."

"Bye." Lizzie searched for a name. "Fancy face." The Subaru's engine started. Nico and his moms sprinted away. For the first time in their lives, they would travel as Outsiders.

Above Lizzie's family, the minivan suddenly dropped to its normal level. The jack rattled out from beneath it.

"The Chappies are moving out, too," Dad said. "It's time."

The yellow jackets followed Lizzie and his family. With the honey still dripping, they all helped him up onto the van's back windshield. He didn't stick like normal; it felt slippery.

"You're not bad for a sticker," Sojourner said, hovering before the Stick boy. Cynthia and Seth nodded in agreement.

"You're not bad for a...bee."

"Hey!" Sojourner buzzed her wings. "You mean wasp."

Lizzie grinned, then scowled because it hurt. "My bad." The jackets waved as they flew away.

The Sticks assumed the pose a little differently than normal. Sunny took one of Lizzie's hands. Ups took the other. None of them smiled. The hatch went up as the Mobile dad stowed the jack and lug wrench and the last of the camping gear. The Stick family was upside down for only a few seconds, but Lizzie felt himself already sliding. Then the hatch came back down with its usual boom. Lizzie slid back into place with a little help from his sister and dog. At the same time, thunder boomed. A white bolt streaked skyward. Then oversized raindrops began speckling the glass.

"Here it comes," Mom sighed. She peeled her head up long enough to make eye contact with the others. "Hold tight!" Lizzie heard something unfamiliar in the Stick Mom's voice. Fear.

Sophia and Ups nodded.

Lizzie heard the minivan's engine rumble to life. He could feel his memories twining together like vines on a fence. Beneath the layer of honey, inside Lizzie's semi-unglued mind, things were coming back. Sometimes memories were like a friend with kind green eyes. Sometimes a monster pointing an accusing finger. Memory melded between grace and cruelty. Now, the worst memory of all lay in wait, the one Lizzie had long battled. On the drive to come, it would once again take up arms against him.

Fifty-three

Before Mr. Chapman could back the minivan away from the campsite, an ambulance rolled by. A red supernova burst through a cloud of brown dust. Seeing it, Lizzie recalled the accident. *Red lights on a rainy night.* For a moment, he couldn't distinguish then from now.

Then the Subaru passed by as well. The fancy-faced boy and his moms all waved. Only now, their faces had become simple, their features once again hidden. The bumper sticker characters waved too: Hello Kitty, the Louisville Cardinals, Mother Earth, the chrome lizard creature, Darwin, Gandhi with no legs. Ringo, the hand, waved his peace sign.

A new character that had joined Nico's family. Above the left tail light, stood a small pirate with a grim expression. As the Subaru followed the ambulance's dust cloud, Cap'n Nobeard unsheathed his sword and saluted. *My pirate friend,* Lizzie thought. With difficulty, he raised his hand and saluted back. Then he noticed the face of a black-and-white cat staring out from the Subaru's back windshield. Only then did the Stick boy understand. Nico's people had adopted both the cat and the little pirate. The ambulance carried the old woman. They all disappeared in dust.

The van pulled out. The Chapmans and the Sticks were on their way home.

Lizzie heard the wind before he felt it. It invaded the treetops, then swirled the van's trail of dust. A moment later, the sky let loose. Raindrops assaulted the Sticks.

"Oh, boy," Sunny said.

Back in the Lowcountry, the family had endured many storms, even a hurricane. They had never been afraid of rain. Their glue was strong enough to keep them stuck through a car wash. But today, Lizzie was clinging to the glass with nothing but honey. He was weak.

"Don't let go of me," he said.

"We won't," Sunny and Ups both promised.

Lizzie melded to see inside the vehicle, but the cargo compartment had been filled with trash bags. The Mobile mom and dad had promised the rangers to haul out as much trash as they could. Lizzie melded back to face the rain.

"How's..." Lizzie searched for a name, "Soapy?"

Sunny let out a half-laugh. "Sophia."

"Right. Her."

"Not great."

"Upset about…Wha-what's-his-name?"

"Joaquin? No. She's worried about you."

"Oh."

"Besides, I got their license plate and Nico gave me their address."

Lizzie nodded. He lifted his hand from the glass, to test how easy it would be to fall off. Everyone's life would be easier if he did, he thought.

Ranger Frowns-a-lot stood on the porch of the Visitors Center as they passed. He raised a hand, waving goodbye to each carload of campers. The eagle belt buckle gave Lizzie a feathered wave as well.

As the rain intensified, Lizzie's mind struggled to make sense of the moment. He felt the bending trees, the raindrops in their mad dash, beams of headlights cutting through the rain, the splash of individual drops as they exploded on metal or glass.

The Chapmans had almost reached the paved road when suddenly a flying squirrel, Jayla, landed on the front windshield. Everyone in the car screamed. The minivan swerved and braked. Its tires dug trenches in the mud. The Stick family peeled their heads up and looked at one another in confusion. Lizzie couldn't see Jayla, but felt his friend's claws as he clung to a moving wiper blade. The Stick boy felt cold rain on damp fur. Something about losing his glue had caused him to become temporarily hyper-sensitive to others and to his surroundings, in some bizarre way.

Mr. Chapman laid on his horn until the rodent leapt away. As the minivan rolled on, Lizzie watched the little flier pick himself up. Their eyes met as they vanished from each other's lives.

Soon, the minivan turned onto blacktop, and Lizzie's surreal experience of the storm faded. That didn't mean he was safe. As they rounded the first mountain turn, the Stick boy slid a little, and gripped his sister's hand and his dog's paw even more tightly.

The rain continued to pound. The mountain roads that linked Gorges State Park to the highways, and then to the Interstate, coiled around the Appalachian foothills like a timber rattler. Again and again, Lizzie collided with Sunny and Ups, smearing honey across the glass.

"It's coming off!" he shouted.

"Sunny, Ups, scoot together!" Mom commanded. "Everyone shift in!"

The family bunched up so that Lizzie wouldn't have anywhere to slide, but it didn't work. He just slid on top of them. The family became a sticky tangle.

"I can't stop!" Lizzie screamed.

"Just hold on!" Sunny shouted. "It's gotta let up soon."

The thunderstorm did weaken, but the rain continued. There were many twisting miles to go. Lizzie could already feel his strength begin to falter. Sunny and Ups reached over Lizzie and clasped hand-to-paw, pinning him down. This worked pretty well until they reached the Interstate.

As the van merged with the faster traffic, the wind tried to rip Lizzie's dog and sister from the windshield. Reaching over was now too risky. Mom barked orders. They let go of each other and once again took Lizzie's hands. Unfortunately, the honey had grown very thin.

As the wind fluttered Lizzie's edges, he wanted to cry out, "Hold me down!" But there was no way he would put his sister and dog at risk.

"How're you doing?" Dad called.

"Good, I'm good," he lied.

"Tight grips, but not crazy tight," Mom ordered. "There's hours of road ahead. Don't wear yourselves out before the first exit."

"Maybe we'll stop soon," Ups said.

"Full tank," Dad replied.

"Well, maybe they'll have to stop to take care of—" Sunny began. "What did she call it?"

"Business," Lizzie answered. *That, I remember.*

"What's that?" Dad asked.

"Nothing," the twins said. Then Sunny added, "Does anyone's Mobile feel pressure in their stomach?"

"You mean like right before Hershey marks territory?" Ups asked.

"Exactly like that," Sunny answered.

"No," they all said.

Then we're not stopping anytime soon, Lizzie thought.

Some days it seems like night falls in the middle of the day. This was one of those. The clouds hung so low, Lizzie wondered that the big trucks didn't scrape them.

As traffic grew heavier, it also got faster, despite the rain. Lizzie tried to hold tight, but he knew that it was their strength, Sunny's and Ups', holding him on. He didn't mention that the wind was lifting his edges more and more. Or that he had felt an icy trickle of rain beneath his back. Worrying them wouldn't help.

Then Lizzie's head suddenly flapped up. Scared more than he had ever been, he summoned all of his strength and flattened again. Sunny shot him a horrified look, but Lizzie said nothing. A moment later, there was a commotion in the cargo area. Sophia, having sensed the fear of both Sunny and Lizzie, pushed between the black garbage bags and stared at the Sticks. The whole family quickly melded to face her.

"What are you doing?" Sunny yelled. "Get back!"

"Get back in your seat!" Lizzie screamed.

Dad, Mom, and Ups gasped.

Sophia's muffled voice filtered through the glass. "I shoulda brought you inside," she said. "I'm so sorry, I don't know what I was thinking!"

"Sit down!" Lizzie yelled. "Now!"

And Sunny pleaded, "Please, please buckle up!"

The thirteen-year-old said something else, but the *whoosh* of a passing big rig drowned it out.

"Please!" the twins yelled.

Lizzie got deja vu. An uncanny feeling like she had been here before. It had been raining. Elizabeth had unbuckled and leaned into the back of the van. An eighteen-wheeler had blown past them—a green one carrying a load of logs, just like the one Lizzie saw only seconds ago. If the scene played out the same as last year, a car in front of them would brake suddenly. The Mobile dad would slam on his brakes. And a white SUV—like the one behind them right now—would crash into them.

Sophia tilted her head. In the grayness of the day, her green eyes stood out to Lizzie as the only color. The honey had become so thin that he no longer saw things with a golden tint. Elizabeth had tilted her head just like that. Lizzie closed his eyes. Then the van suddenly lurched. He heard the screeching of tires.

Elizabeth's head had smashed against the glass. Her neck

had bent. Her eyes had blinked wide. Lizzie had heard the snap. A splinter of glass had torn across his leg. And his beloved Mobile had collapsed, broken forever.

Now Lizzie's eyes blinked open. Sophia braced herself against the glass with one arm. Her giant hand filled Lizzie's vision. The Stick boy quickly melded to face the trailing traffic. *This* white SUV didn't hit them. The minivan had braked, but was again accelerating. There was no broken glass. Lizzie unpeeled his head to look down at his leg. A mistake.

The wind bent back his head and lifted his torso from the glass. What was left of his rainbow hair danced like serpents on Medusa's head.

"I killed her," Lizzie screamed at Sunny. "Tell Sophia it was me. I killed Elizabeth!"

"No!"

"Just tell her!"

"It wasn't you, Lizzie! She was getting a water bottle out of the cooler. For Sophia."

"No, no, I distracted her! It was me!"

As Lizzie hung halfway off the windshield, he now understood that Sophia, too, blamed herself for Elizabeth's death. But clinging to guilt felt easier than clinging to glass right now. As the wind lifted his lower half, Lizzie flapped like a hurricane flag.

"Lizzie Lou!" cried his dad. "I'm sorry!"

"Hold on!" Mom shouted.

The voices and bodies all jumbled together as the Stick family scrambled to pull Lizzie back. Still, he felt himself slipping. He saw a wide-eyed Sophia yelling at her dad to stop the car. But there was no way to stop. The van was hemmed in. Cars in front and behind, and an eighteen-wheeler in the next lane.

Lizzie's body was already broken. What happened next nearly broke his heart. Dad peeled up and reached across, and was nearly torn from the windshield. Then his sister and dog lunged for him, both of them also peeling halfway off the glass. Sunny cried Lizzie's name. Ups howled like a wolf. Lizzie saw that the wind would rip them all away. "Mom!" he shouted. "Stop them!" With a look of sorrow on her face that Lizzie had never seen, Mom launched herself, tackling Sunny, Ups and Dad to the glass.

"Lizzie! Lizzie, no! Lizzie Lou!" they shrieked.

I couldn't save Elizabeth, but I can save them, he thought. And Lizzie let go. As he did, he finally released his guilt, as well. He felt it rush out of him, even as the van holding everyone he loved rushed away. In the violence that followed, a detached sort of peace rested on him, which almost made up for the pain.

The wind swept him down near the pavement, then up. Tumbling, he watched the minivan and his family recede through the rain. The last piece of his memory from the car wreck flashed by. He saw himself reflected in that shard of headlight glass, falling like now. This present moment seemed to have always been hidden in the memory, in that piece of glass.

Through a blur of water, Lizzie saw the world roll: sky, horizon, road, sky again. The white SUV passed beneath him. Then something much bigger. He felt a hot blast, smelled something foul and oily, and shot skyward as a blue-black cloud propelled him. He glimpsed the taillights of a big rig. Then he was falling again.

Lizzie spread his limbs, trying to glide. His tumbling slowed. He was able to level out, wobbly. But the rain pummeled him earthward. The highway grew quickly in his vision. He had no time to look around, to aim for a place to land. He winced as he hit the rough pavement, felt it scrape his entire body. Water filled his face and mouth. From deep inside, a scream tried and failed to escape.

Lizzie had long imagined what it would be like to fall Off Glass. He had visualized being spun through the axles and wheel rims of big trucks. Of bouncing off the undercarriages of cars. He had once dreamed of being blown around the dirty inside of a dump truck bed. The reality was much different. The first car that ran over him smashed him—a weight so forceful that he never would have believed it. For an instant, splashing water buoyed him. Then a rear wheel ground him again into the blacktop. Darkness and unimaginable pressure.

Fire ants had inflicted searing cuts. Traffic now gave him a brutal beating. Initially, he had landed face-down. With each vehicle that ran over him, he melded from seeing the black pavement to seeing the underside of the car and then the sky. Road-car-sky, road-car-sky strobed before him. The weight of the tires was beyond pain. He felt his being crushed, and at the same time, pieces of his body disintegrate. Then he no longer felt. The sky and cars flickered like an old-time movie, then faded to nothingness.

Fifty-four

Relentlessly, the rain pelted the pavement. Lizzie's body gradually drifted out of the wheel-worn path, but not off the highway. Out of a black night and the storm, marched a column of black ants—an anomaly, since their kind take shelter at such times. The Stick boy heard their strange language, distant, punctuated by his own name. If he had spoken Black Ant, he would have heard something like this:

"Circle up. Let's get him out of here."

"But he's dead. Why are we disposing of a dead Stick?"

"Show a little respect. It's Lizzie Lou of the Barrel."

"*The* Lou?"

"The real one?"

"Of course it's him. And I don't think he's dead, not yet anyway."

"But look at him. There's no way."

"Either way, we've got orders. Some of you get under his head."

"What a shame. Better if he had died quick like."

"The rest of you line up along the arms and legs. Move it!"

"Yes, sir!"

Then someone speaking Black with an accent. "Where do you want us?"

"Where'd you guys come from?"

"From our tunnels. Same as you."

"Well, we could use the help. Have your men fall in line."

Lizzie lifted his head to see, or thought he did. In reality, the ants lifted his head. The Stick boy saw smeared images: heads and legs washed by waves of car headlights. His body moved a little, then he fell to the asphalt again. He heard commands being barked in both Red and Black. Then confusion and angry words. It sounded like a fight might break out. Then he glimpsed something incredible. Two captains, one black ant and one red, face to face. Wars between them was the stuff of history lessons. Tonight, they battled only the rain.

The sound of running water ran through Lizzie's strange dreams. His entire body felt on fire. He felt thinner. Frayed at the edges. To force his mind away from the pain, he focused on his surroundings. But there were few clues. It was dark, earthy, and cold. And there was an echo. Sometimes he heard voices. Whether they were real or imagined, he couldn't have said. They were both.

He felt a cool cloth pass over his face. Even that hurt. He opened his eyes, but still saw nothing.

"Hold on, young feller," said an old-sounding voice. "Gimme a minute. A little road grime in the way, that's all."

The old man rewet the cloth, wrung out the cloth, then rubbed Lizzie's eyes. A face came into view, a man's face, but unlike any Lizzie had ever seen. He was ancient, with thinning white hair and a small white beard and mustache. He was flat, mostly, with a lumpy face creased with deep lines. He wore a bow tie and wire-framed spectacles. He removed a stethoscope from around his neck, stuck the ends in his ears, and placed a shiny flat piece on Lizzie's chest.

"I'm Doc Rockwell," he said. "Now, take a deep breath."

As Lizzie did so, the air seemed to scald the inside of his lungs, as if lava had been poured down his windpipe. He groaned.

"Again."

Lizzie winced through another deep breath. The old doctor looked into the distance and listened. Then he lifted the Stick boy's head and shoulders.

"Ow, ow, ow!"

"I know, I know, I'm sorry." The old man placed the listening device on the Stick boy's back. "Again, deep breaths."

Lizzie did as he asked, squeezing tiny tears from the corners of his eyes.

"Once more. I promise it's the last time. For now."

Lizzie inhaled again, then trembled as the old doctor eased him back down. He removed the earpieces and wore them like a necklace again.

"You're a tough kid. Lucky thing you were pretty much flat to begin with."

Lizzie started to ask, *Am I dead?* but realized how stupid that would be, and switched gears. "How long—" He didn't get it all out. Talking hurt more than he expected. He sounded like he was gargling nails, his voice almost as cracked as his body.

"Well, let's see…" The old man removed a pocket watch from his vest pocket and flipped the device open. "It's half past four on the Lord's Day." His wild, bushy white eyebrows arched in response to Lizzie's questioning look. "That'd be Sunday," he explained, pronouncing the word *sun'-dee*. "It was pert near midnight when they brung you in, so… 'bout sixteen hour."

Lizzie tried to turn his head. On the edges of his vision, he saw orange light flickering off a curved ceiling. He opened his mouth to speak again, but couldn't.

"You wanna know where you're at. Hm. No mystery there. You're at the end. I could say you're at mile marker fifty-two on

I-26 just west of Hendersonville, but that's beside the point. You've hit the ditch. Which, every soul knows, is the end of the line. Unless you count the landfill, which I don't. That's death. And you're not quite dead. Almost." The old man shuddered. "This here—" he patted the ground, a peculiar surface with diamond-shaped holes in it, "—is a tray from a bread truck. Somehow it got stuck here in this drain pipe, and God bless whoever lost it because it keeps our butts out of the water."

Oh, Lizzie mouthed and fell back asleep.

Awake, asleep, awake again. Time passed like a slow-moving freight train with the boxcar doors open on both sides. Lizzie caught glimpses of weird broken characters, some of them real, some not. Sometimes even glimpses of daylight.

A sun-faded GEICO Gecko, named Martin, came by and explained enthusiastically how Lizzie could save fifteen percent or more on car insurance.

"You're about...fifteen minutes late," the Stick boy replied, then laughed until his ribs hurt.

An Energizer Bunny visited. A kind gesture, but his constant drum-beating worsened Lizzie's headache. Once, Lizzie woke to see a cheetah peering at him over a pair of cracked sunglasses. "Crunchy," said the feline and slunk away. A tiny and not-so-jolly Jolly Green Giant sat with Lizzie for hours. The Giant complained bitterly that Santa Claus had stolen his "Ho, ho, ho!"

For the most part, they were a depressed bunch. This was, as the old doctor had pointed out, the end of the line.

Doc Rockwell said that ditch people often showed up tattered, crumpled, even burned. Many didn't make it. Lizzie couldn't help feeling a tinge of guilt. Until the Barrel, whenever he had seen people like that, he had usually just looked away.

One exception to this gloomy community was Evan, a huge human-drawn man wearing a hard hat. He had been part of a door magnet on a truck owned by Evans Construction, LLC. Like Lizzie, the wind had torn him from his home. The other ditch people had worked for days to free him from his background, cutting him out with a soda bottle top and sharp rocks. Evan was literally rough around the edges. He had to bend himself to fit through the drainpipe to visit Lizzie. In a steady, soothing voice he told the Stick boy not to give up, to hang in there. No great speeches, but the Stick boy drew strength from his words.

One day Lizzie woke to find Doc painting his arms with a blackish paste. "That feels...awesome," the Stick boy managed.

"Blackberry," the old man said. "It stains, but this poultice takes away the sting, as the saying goes. Won't help with your voice, I'm afraid. You may always sound like that."

Lizzie grunted. "So I've been told." His hands were so worn that he could see through them. The Stick boy wondered if they would fall off if he tried to grasp something. But below his wrists, the part already covered with sticky paste felt stronger.

Doc Rockwell explained that blackberries weren't in season, but he always kept a stash of dry ones, which he had mashed up and mixed with puddle water. It reminded Lizzie of Nico's moms and their magnolia sap. When the Stick boy had been coated from head to toe, the doctor left him to dry. Several hours later, the old man returned. He touched Lizzie's forehead.

"Am I done?" Lizzie asked.

"Not yet," Doc replied, "but you're gettin' there. Go see for yourself." He pointed to daylight at the mouth of the tunnel.

Lizzie crawled to the edge of the pipe and examined himself. "I'm *purple!*" he called to Doc. "Permanently stained?"

"Yep," the old man replied, "but only on the outside. Not the part of you that matters."

Later that day, Evan, the magnet man, visited again.

"What's the deal with the Doc?" the Stick boy asked. "He's amazing and...weird. What is he?"

According to Evan, Doc Rock, as many in the ditch called him, had escaped from a Norman Rockwell painting. "Claims he got stuck in a museum and that wasn't no kinda life for a person. Wanted a real home."

"How'd he get out?"

"Some crazy dude cut him out, long time ago. Not a print, an original. Whoever did it took their time. He's real precise." The magnet man ran a hand over his own rough-cut shoulder.

"Unlike me."

"An original. What does that mean?"

"Far as I can tell," the big guy replied, "he's made of oil paint and canvas. A little sun-faded, like the rest of us, but still kickin'."

As the blackberry paste did its work, the Stick boy's memory returned, more vivid than ever. He thought a lot about Elizabeth, and remembered stuff he thought he had lost for good. Not just her face, or the raspy sound of her voice, but a hundred little things she had done. Blowing dandelions, digging in the dirt, funny things she had said. Blackberry paste for the heart. Nothing had ever been easy for Lizzie. Finding Elizabeth inside his mind, reconnecting with her through moments that could never happen again, was painful and delightful in equal measures. He didn't have much of her, but it would have to be enough.

Fifty-five

Tuesday Morning

Early in the morning on the third day, Lizzie rose from his bed and limped out of the drain pipe. *I ache like an old person,* he thought, clutching his hip. Sometime in the night, the rain had finally let up. The sun had just risen. He shielded his eyes from its glare, and in doing so discovered that his hair had been bludgeoned off of his scalp by the traffic. The wind had no doubt scattered the last multi-colored strands all over the Interstate. Lizzie was a baldy. In time, his hair might grow back. But he wasn't so sure he even wanted it.

A muddy, litter-strewn trench ran alongside an access road beside the Interstate. Dozens of characters called the ditch home. Evan, the magnetic construction dude, waded in the brown water, scavenging. He looked up and waved. Lizzie waved back. Then, the big man stooped down and pulled a plastic water bottle from the muck. "You're gonna need this," he called, and waded over.

As they sat on the bank, Evan tipped the bottle and dampened a Subway napkin. Lizzie began scrubbing the film of blackberry paste off his arms and legs, with no success.

"Wasting your time," Doc called. He stood on the opposite bank, fishing for who-knew-what, using a broken plastic fork and real fishing line.

Lizzie stared at him. *What does an old dude made out of canvas and oil paint eat, anyway,* he wondered?

"Scrub all you want," Doc added. "That berry stain ain't goin' nowhere."

Lizzie kept at it.

"Don't mind him, he's a stick in the mud," Evan said. "No offense."

Lizzie smirked. "Like I never heard that one before. Ow!" He clutched at his throat. It still hurt to talk.

"But he's probably right," Evan added. "You're purple now."

Lizzie winced as he cleaned around the old slash wound on his leg. The surgery that Mavis had performed would need to be redone.

"Not to mention," Doc Rock called, "that blackberry stain is the only reason you can think straight."

Lizzie stopped scrubbing and looked up at Evan. "Really?"

The magnet man shrugged. "He's the Doc."

Just then, Chester Cheetah approached. "Say," he said. "you're that cat, aren't you?"

Lizzie got painfully to his feet. "Do I look like a cat?"

"Naw, man, you're that Lucy Lou I keep hearing about," said the cheetah. "Or maybe it was Lazy Lou. Just doin' the math, two and two makes three, if you know what I mean."

"Not really, no." Lizzie began circling around the ditch to say thank you and goodbye to Doc.

"Whoa, brotha," the feline said as he walked alongside the Stick boy. "You're just kinda famous, that's all."

Lizzie laughed. "Must be some other Lou. I'm Lizzie Lou, if anything." He waved a finger at the cheetah. "But nobody calls me that, got it? Just my dad."

"Suit yourself, barrel boy," said the cat. "So what should I call you? You don't look like a Lizzie."

"Call me outta here," Lizzie replied. "I'm going home."

"We could call you Lou," said the big magnet man. Lizzie and Chester both turned to see Evan. "You look like a Lou."

Lou, Lizzie thought.

"So, Lou," asked the cheetah with a devious purr, "how ya gettin home?"

"Rideshare," the Stick boy grumbled. "Walking. Obviously."

The three reached Doc, who gave them a grandfatherly smile.

"You're looking pretty good for someone who's been run over by a truck," the old man said.

"More like a dozen of 'em," Lizzie replied. "I swear, tire tread is permanently stamped on my nervous system."

"I 'spect you'll be sore for a long time," Doc said. "Maybe a touch of arthritis, too." He arched his back and Lizzie could hear it crack. "Welcome to the club."

Lizzie nodded. "I just wanted to say thank you before I go."

"Go?"

"Crazy dude thinks he's walking home," Chester put in. "Crazy like cheese that goes *crunch!*"

"Is that a fact?" Doc planted his fishing pole into the mud and crossed his arms. Lizzie could see the brush strokes where Norman Rockwell had painted white hair on his forearms.

Lizzie nodded.

"Well, good luck to you, young feller." The doctor extended his hand and the Stick boy shook it. Lizzie began walking away. "How far you gotta go?" Doc called.

"Charleston."

"Oh, dear!" The old man sighed. "Oh my. You can barely walk, you'll never make it."

Lizzie made it all the way across the grassy area between the access road and the Interstate. He turned around to see Doc, Chester, Evan, and more than a dozen others following the trail he had cut through the tall grass. He was touched. *They're coming to see me off.* Many of them had watched over him during his hours of delirium. He didn't even know some of their names. So he waited at the emergency lane.

A little girl ran up. She held an umbrella overhead and had a box of salt under the other arm. "Can I go with you?" she asked. "Please?"

"Yeah, Lou," said several others. "We're sick of this ditch."

Then someone at the back of the group—Lizzie didn't see who—yelled, "What does he care? He's famous. We're just trash."

Famous, Lizzie thought. *They've got me confused with someone.* He watched as several turned and walked away.

"You can share my umbrella," the girl promised. "Please?"

Lizzie knelt down beside her. "What's your name, sweetheart?"

"Sally."

"Well, Sally, it's a very long journey and you're just an itty bitty thing. Are you brave enough?"

The little girl bit her lower lip. "I'll try to be."

Lizzie stood up and watched as the crowd began trudging away. "Hold up, everybody," he called, but no one heard him. "Everybody? Hello?"

Then the little girl with the umbrella stuck two fingers in her mouth and let out an ear-splitting whistle. Every face turned. *Didn't expect that,* Lizzie thought. He cleared his throat.

"I owe you folks my life. You and the ants. And I know I don't look—" He looked down at his arms and legs, in some places as thin as cheesecloth. "I don't look like much. But if you're crazy enough to follow a half-dead berry-stained Stick down a road that might not ever end, I'm not gonna stop you." *Dog, I sounded like Sunny.* He closed his eyes and tried to feel the moment, then shook his head like a dog drying off.

"If you come with me, we do this as one," he went on. "Like everyone matters. Nobody's better than anyone else."

He searched their worn faces and was struck by their grim determination to keep living, even in squalor. Despite being tattered. The Jolly Green Giant had a hole through his shoulder. Chester's sunglasses were cracked and askew. Sally seemed unaware of the holes in her umbrella. Others were muddy or torn or creased.

"I don't care who tossed you out or how you ended up in the gutter," Lizzie continued, his gravelly voice rising loud enough for all to hear. "You're not trash. Not to each other. Not to me. Nobody is."

He thought of the Team Sticks. How they made fun of anyone not like themselves.

"I used to see myself that way, like trash, because I'm different. But it was a lie I told myself. Or sometimes I believed it because of how people looked at me."

He thought then of the little pirate, Cap'n Nobeard, waving

from the back bumper of the Subaru. And of the black-and-white cat peering from the back windshield.

"There's a home somewhere out there for all of you, I know there is. At least...I hope so. I can't promise we'll find it, but we gotta try. I do, anyway. And if we don't ever get there, then we'll make a home together. Somewhere better than here. One thing's for sure, every one of you deserves better than this ditch."

Chester pumped the air with a velvety fist. "Right on, Purple Haze!" No one else cheered, but they looked at one another and nodded.

"Well, alright then," said Doc. "I'm in. We can shelter in drain pipes from here darn near to the ocean."

Lizzie lifted up his eyes to the hills from where he had come. Then he looked down the long highway that led to the sea. He started walking. Limping. Feeling pain with each step, but free from the past.

The group fell into a zigzagging line, not at all like a column of ants. Evan, in his hard hat, brought up the rear. Sally, the Morton Salt girl, marched proudly up front, holding Lizzie's hand and twirling her tattered umbrella.

"Think others will join us, Lou?" she asked.

Lizzie glanced behind at the ragged group. Then he gazed into the distance. Both the Interstate and the access road ran to the horizon. *That's one long ditch,* he thought. He looked down at the girl and shrugged.

"You know what it says on the box, don't ya?" the little girl persisted.

"What box is that?"

Sally giggled. "The salt box, silly."

"Oh. No, what's it say?"

"When it rains, it pours!"

That brought a real smile, although a crooked one, to the Stick boy's face. Which hurt. He looked closer at the caption on Sally's salt box.

"So it does, Sally, so it does."

They walked on and on. Traffic was light. Sometimes they flattened themselves soon enough. Sometimes a fast car or truck surprised them and blew them into the grass.

Lizzie closed his eyes and felt the sun on his face. *Sunlight heals.*

Somewhere in the world, he imagined, an electronic dude moonwalked for kids at a crosswalk. And hopefully, back in the mountains, near Rainbow Falls, Serena Williams and other trash barrel refugees were making a new home in Sophia's lost boot.

But far ahead, near the end of this highway, he supposed, a human girl now stared at a blank space on a windshield and mourned yet another loss. In that same town, grass grew over Elizabeth's grave. *But not her Essence,* Lizzie knew. *Not the real her. And I'm not gone, either.*

Deepest of all in the Stick boy's memory, lay those unchosen Sticks. The ones left in darkness, in a box, in an attic. There, they waited, barely alive, like Lizzie at the bottom of the river. The Stick boy stared down the long highway. *I'll get to them, somehow.*

Lizzie's family was wounded and divided. Or maybe it only looked that way. Looking back, his eyes rested on each person from the ditch. Maybe *Lou's family* had actually grown. Maybe they just needed someone, anyone, just one person, to believe in them. *I'm someone,* he thought, *maybe that can be me.*

Fifty-six

The endless ditch alongside the Interstate, a dumping ground for the broken and the dying, was littered with homeless souls. News of *Lou's Caravan*, as it became known, often reached them before he did. Hundreds hobbled out of drain pipes, the grass, the muck, sometimes dragging broken friends. They had few, if any, belongings. Lou, who owned only his clothes and a pair of sandals he had made, offered them nothing more than respect. He turned none of them away.

Doc Rockwell patched them up as well as he could. Some had to be carried, some dragged on makeshift litters made of twigs, but others were too far gone to travel. On a dark night long ago, Lou had watched the light go out of Elizabeth's eyes— a true horror. Now, his heart broke over and over again as he held hands with characters drawing their last breaths. More horror, to be sure, but also an honor. They whispered his name in cracking voices, as though he, a worn, stained, un-sticky sticker, was someone important. The Stick boy cried more tears than he thought possible. In the fading eyes and brave smiles, he saw stubborn hope, as they passed from their hard lives to whatever lay beyond.

Some newcomers were well known: Tony the Tiger, the Pillsbury Doughboy (aka, Poppin' Fresh) with his gentle laugh, M&Ms who never stopped joking around, dozens of tiny Keebler Elves, and a pair of Coca-Cola polar bears. Most had already been freed from their packaging. Others were still trapped. Using a gem of broken glass, Doc Rock surgically freed many, including Lucky the Leprechaun and a Honey Nut Cheerios bee named Buzz.

Toucan Sam, the long-beaked tropical bird from a Fruit Loops box, insisted that everyone call him Zazu, after the Lion King character. He claimed that his original brand name just reminded him of a painful past. It was his life, so why not? Zazu, it was.

Others who joined the Caravan were either less famous or outright generic: the Clif Bar rock-climber, a paper cricket, french fry people, a blocky ice-man from a bag of ice.

At night, each one told his or her story on the dark roadside. They made no fire, of course, since nearly all of them were flammable. And they had no funny-fire.

The road stretched ever before them. The bigger people carried those too small or wounded to keep up. Evan carried dozens of Keebler Elves. Zazu rode on Lou's shoulder. Sally—quick as a little sandpiper—walked always at his side, spinning her porous umbrella and trailing an infinite line of salt.

Looking like strewn trash, a long line stretched out behind the Stick boy. They hurried past exit ramps and entry lanes, making every effort to stay together. Whenever cars sped by, the characters lay flat, avoiding both the wind and the attention of puzzled travelers. But when a big rig passed, some usually got swept up, often with rough landings. After this had happened dozens of times, it finally occurred to Lou that most of his followers were light enough to glide. Maybe this should have been obvious, but, other than being fun, for the Stick boy, gliding had never been proved useful. Both times when it might have saved him from danger—first, when he fell off the cliff and into Rainbow Falls, and second, when he slipped Off Glass and was run over by traffic—gliding had failed him. Then again, in both instances, water had weighed him down. That wouldn't always be a factor. On the journey ahead, the Caravan might encounter situations where controlled gliding and landing came in handy. And they could use a little fun. So he taught them.

They climbed mile markers and practiced floating, turning, and landing. Some excelled, while others struggled, but most got confident in their ability to glide safely to the ground from small heights. The magnet man, Evan, tried it once, but weighed too much and fell with a thud. And Sally, with her Morton Salt box tucked under one arm (she refused to put it down) and her umbrella in the other hand, could only glide in a spiral. Still, it astonished Lou that such a simple diversion boosted morale as much as it did. Characters who had been dragging behind, either tired or doubtful about their trek, practically raced to the next marker.

The next challenge came in the form of a towering green road sign, which announced the next exit. Watching row after row of characters leap from its top edge, Zazu observed to Lou that the Keebler Elves tended to glide in groups of three or four, mimicking one another. That afternoon, the Caravan began experimenting with gliding in formation. First they tried pairs, then groups of three, four, and so on. It seemed that even numbers had the most mistakes. Then Doc Rock pointed to a flock of geese on the horizon, winging its way south. From that point on, they adopted the V formation, with everyone in a group following the point person. This seemed to work great in groups of up to ten.

Eventually, Lou conducted a "gliding master class" at a deserted overpass. Here, they honed their skills at diving. Why they might ever need to dive, no one asked. The Mobiles' world was a dangerous one for characters.

Lou's band of discarded misfits didn't have much going for them, but if they ever needed it, many could now glide. Lou appointed Chester Cheetah, Tony the Tiger, and the chief Keebler Elf to train newbies as they joined the Caravan.

Characters always ate more for taste than for hunger. Now Lou discovered just how little food he needed. As the sun baked purple blackberry stains deep into him, it also gave him energy. He had no idea how this worked. Neither he nor any of his followers were plants. Even the Jolly Green Giant was made of paper. So they ate very little, mostly from discarded junk-food bags. They didn't find any yellow Skittles in the breakdown lane.

Two weeks in, they reached a Black Army outpost. Using their network, Lou sent word ahead to his family: "I'm alive and coming home. And I'm bringing friends." But then for weeks, the Caravan passed through Red territory, so he had no idea if his message had gotten through. He tried to send it through the Red network, as well. Chester spoke Red. But their kind was preoccupied with an invasion from the Fire Empire. Communication was iffy. *My family must think I'm dead,* Lou thought, which worried him. He didn't want Sunny, Ups, and his parents to live with the same kind of guilt that he had.

One day, as the Caravan hurried past what appeared to be a pile of clothes beneath an overpass, they noticed the pile move. They all gathered around. A pair of eyes blinked open. A mouth concealed by bushy, gray whiskers let out a laugh.

"Am I dead?" the Mobile asked.

Lou stepped forward. "Nah. You're dreaming."

The old man looked around at the ragged characters. "Dreams are weird."

"Okay, you're not dreaming and you're not dead," Lou admitted. "But if you're sleeping under a bridge, I guess no one will believe you if you tell them about us."

A smile appeared through the beard. "I don't even believe it."

"Are you hurt?" Lou asked.

"Well…" The man's wild eyebrows bristled like excited mice. "Sleeping on pavement don't exactly help my back. But, no. No more than usual. Guess my feelings are the only thing that always hurts."

Lou glanced around at his friends. Chester Cheetah shrugged. Doc stared ahead at the highway. "Sorry to interrupt your nap," the Stick boy said. "We'll be moving on." Then Sally tugged at Lou's hand. He bent down so she could whisper in his ear.

Grinning, Lou turned to the man. "Sally here just reminded me that we don't turn anyone away. So if you want to come with us…" He glanced all around. A few shrugs, a few nods from the crowd. "You can."

The man sort of laughed, sort of coughed. "Wouldn't be the

craziest thing I ever done. Where ya goin'?"

Sally spoke up. "We're marching to the sea!"

"Are you now? Hm. You wouldn't be planning on burning Atlanta, would you?"

Chester Cheetah laughed. "Dude. That's way out of our way."

"Just checking. In dreams, anything can happen."

"We're on our way to Charleston," Lou said. "My family's there. But we voted. Everyone wants to see the ocean first."

"The beach, huh? Been a while since I put my toes in the surf. Which one, Sullivan's Island or the Isle of Palms?"

"First one we get to," Lou said. "Isle of Palms, I think. I'm Lou. This here's Doc, Chester, Tony, Zazu, Sally."

"Baker," said the old man, "Gene Baker." He reached out a grimy hand, but, of course, it was too big for Lou to shake. One by one, many of the characters introduced themselves. For everyone except the Stick boy and Doc, it was the first time they had spoken to a Mobile. And that was how Lou's Caravan acquired a human.

Gene Baker couldn't really come *with* them, since walking along the Interstate is illegal and he didn't need to get picked up by the State Patrol. Again. Nor did Lou want that. If the Po-Po showed up, they might send someone to clean up all the "trash" along the highway, meaning them. So Baker hiked alongside I-26 through the nearby woods, only coming out to talk with his imaginary trash friends when traffic seemed particularly light.

One night when it rained, the group all crowded into the old man's leaky tent—he actually had one—and listened to his story. Then he made them an offer: he'd stuff everyone in his duffel bag and hitchhike to Charleston, saving them tons of time on the road. They discussed it amongst themselves. The characters could all smell the stench on him, and his duffel bag didn't seem any better than a ditch, so they politely declined. Plus, they thought it unlikely that anyone would give him a ride.

Then, one day, they could no longer see Baker's tent through the trees. Lou figured they would never see him again.

As their numbers grew, the Stick boy organized the Caravan into groups of ten, which they called tents, even though few of them had one. Each character, in turn, would act as spokesperson for their tent for a week. Each morning, the tent leaders huddled with Lou to voice concerns, complaints, and suggestions. Every evening, the tent groups met internally, where they discussed problems and told stories.

As summer came on, Lou expected the blistering Carolina sun to be the Caravan's worst enemy. But no, that was the wind. Whenever they saw a big truck approaching, some dashed into the tall grass while others allowed the updraft to propel them skyward, and then glided down.

One afternoon, Evan, the tallest, spotted an enormous industrial lawn mower in the distance.

"Mower!" he yelled.

Deep creases etched into Doc Rock's already wrinkled forehead. "Oh, boy," he said. "That's bad."

Lou peered up and down the road. "We've gotta cross to the median! Now, before traffic gets here!"

Word quickly passed to those in the back. Shouting and screaming, the Caravan rushed across the highway like a paper army charging across a wide field. Not long after they reached the grassy median, a line of cars streamed by.

"How is everybody?" Lou called. They were all okay. One guy had lost a shoe.

Tony the Tiger summed it up with his signature line: "They'rrrrrrrrre GREAT!" That brought a cheer.

Moments later, a sound like a fleet of helicopters filled their ears as the giant mowing machine rumbled past on the opposite side of the road. Watching its blades buzz through the tall grass, Lou could only imagine what the mower would have done to his friends.

Sally's mouth dropped open. Her salt box slipped and a pile of salt spilled out.

"It's okay," Lou assured her, "we're safe."

That was the first of five mowers they encountered. Each time, they crossed the highway. Once, a few stragglers were tossed skyward by traffic, unharmed.

One day, they spotted a construction zone far ahead. Lou

held up a fist and the Caravan halted.

Chester Cheetah lowered his sunglasses and whistled. "That's a lot of heavy metal."

"Buzz!" Lou called. A moment later, the honey bee hovered before them. "You and Zazu fly ahead. See what you can find out."

"You got it." The bee buzzed away with the toucan flapping behind him.

Lou turned to the magnet man. "Evan, you're the construction pro. What do you think?"

The big guy took off his hard hat, wiped his forehead, and squinted into the distance. "They're working both sides of the Interstate. Could be bridge repairs, but my guess is they're putting in new ramps. A new exit. That's why it's on both sides."

Doc said, "Gonna be tricky gettin' past."

Lou nodded. "After dark?"

"Ain't gonna help," Evan said. "They'll be working around the clock. When that crew quits, there'll be another one coming in."

The scouts returned and confirmed the bad news. "It's a no-go," Buzz said. "Workers were talking about a night shift."

Lou peered into the dense woods that flanked both sides of the highway, then glanced back at the crowd. "It'll be hard to circle around," he said. He waved everyone forward. "Huddle up!"

The Caravan bunched up for a discussion. They could make a wide circle and fight through the brush, or double back to the previous exit and look for an alternate route. Their grueling journey, with no assurance that life would be better somewhere else, was already hard enough. But the woods looked pretty much impassable. No one was happy about it, but they decided to turn around.

Two days later, they stared up at a sign. Several people groaned. Sally, the little Morton Salt girl, lowered her umbrella and closed the lid on her salt box to keep it from spilling.

"What's it mean?" she asked.

"Half a mile to the next exit, then another four miles to the town of Anglewood," Lou said. "It means a long detour."

"And we'll have to sneak past that town," Doc added.

Sally looked down. "Oh." Then she looked up with a bright smile. "But we're still going to the ocean, right?"

Chester gave her a thumbs up. "Exactamundo!"

She raised her umbrella and gave it a twirl. "And we still have each other!"

Lou looked around. Everyone was grinning.

"Yes, we do, Sally." The Stick boy patted her on the head. "Yes, we do."

Fifty-seven

They decided to travel through the small town of Anglewood at night. Just before dawn, as they hurried past a Dunkin' Donuts, a collective *Mmmm* rose from the Caravan. They could see workers setting out fresh donuts.

"Bah!" scoffed one of the Keebler clan riding on Evan's shoulders. "Cookies are the real deal."

Lou stared at the glazed sweets. Elizabeth had been lukewarm about donuts. Instead, she had craved the Thin Mints she had sold as a Girl Scout. The Stick boy kept his thoughts to himself, though. The Elves considered the Scouts their mortal enemies.

The next night, the Caravan reached Anderson Mill Road. From here, they would head south again. One more night of travel, then they would turn back toward the Interstate. At the corner, Lou stared up at an electronic Walk/Don't Walk sign. Unlike the one that Nico had once described, this guy didn't moonwalk. Instead, he waved silently as they passed.

Most Caravan characters, like Stick people, relied on the sun for energy. Having walked all night, they were exhausted. Just before dawn, they reached an elementary school. Lou halted at a crosswalk. Summer had ended. A crossing guard would soon be here shepherding kids across the road. There was no electronic sign, just a diamond-shaped yellow one with the silhouette of a person walking, frozen in mid-stride.

A voice came into Lou's mind. "It is not time to cross," it said.

Sally tugged his hand. "Did you hear that?" The Stick boy nodded, as did Evan and the Elves on his shoulders. Doc glanced at Lou and crinkled his bushy eyebrows. From Lou's shoulder, Zazu squawked.

Lucky the Leprechaun came running up. "The sign around the corner is talking," he reported. "It said—"

"It's not time to cross." Lou pointed. "This one, too."

"They're all talking," whispered the salt girl. "All over town."

"Maybe all over the world," Doc added.

"Freaky," said Chester. "I like it."

"We are one," said the faceless walker on the sign. Again, just in their heads. Everyone hushed.

After a long pause, the sign spoke again. "You'll find trouble on the road. Don't be afraid." Lou could hear an echo from the sign around the corner, even though it was making no audible sound. Sally stared up at Lou and mouthed the word *trouble*. She nervously twirled her umbrella. "Follow the nose," the voice said.

Zazu flapped his wings. "That's me!" he squawked. "Follow the nose! It always knows!"

The characters all stared at the sign for another minute or so, but it said no more.

"I'm not sure if the dang thing was promoting breakfast cereal," Doc said, scratching his head, "or just fear."

"It said trouble's coming," Lou said, raising his voice for everyone to hear, "but that we don't need to be afraid."

The old paint-man pointed to the horizon. "I'll tell you what's coming. The sun."

"Doc's right, we need a place to camp," Lou said. He looked at Zazu. "So, can we cross the road, yet? And which way?"

The toucan closed his eyes. "Yes, it's time," he replied. He swung his long beak around like a divining rod until it pointed in a steady direction. "Not far. Behind some kind of...something. I think."

"Always knows, eh?" Lucky quipped.

Lou waved them all forward and the Caravan lurched into motion. Trouble was coming, the signs had said. Real trouble. But what kind?

Fifty-eight

The Caravan hurried into some woods behind a nearby grocery store. As they made camp, a light rain began to fall.

"Great," said Tony, not in his happy voice.

One of the store's loading-doors flew up. A worker wheeled a cart onto the loading dock and began throwing stuff into one of the dumpsters. The whole Caravan stared.

"What's all that?" Sally asked.

"Expired food," Chester answered.

Others nodded. Although most characters in Lou's Caravan had been on products that had been bought—and, eventually, tossed in trash cans—others had spent their entire lives on store shelves, before ending up in a dumpster. The "Best By" date on their packaging had been a death sentence. Millions, maybe billions of them, lay decaying in landfills. Those who somehow made it out were rare exceptions.

"Buzz, Zazu, go check it out," Lou said. The bee and the toucan flew across the parking lot, then quickly returned.

"He's dumping bread," they reported.

Lou looked around. "Those bags would make great tents," he said. He didn't bother with the obvious: if the drizzle kept up, the cardboard folks in the Caravan would have to dry out for hours before traveling again. So, the Stick boy devised a plan to send rescue parties in three waves: climbers, cutters, and transporters. Word passed through the Caravan.

Next, the store worker began tossing out boxes of expired Keebler products. Outraged, the Elves in the Caravan raced to the edge of the woods, with their Chief shouting, "He's killing our kin!" Lou and others had to restrain them from attacking the worker.

Cookies were just the tip of the icing. Cart after cart, the worker flung jugs of milk, tubs of yogurt, and boxes of unopened stuff that no one could identify. When he began throwing out breakfast cereal, the whole Caravan groaned.

"In my day," Doc Rock said, "we didn't waste nothin'."

Finally, the young man went inside and lowered the overhead door. Lou turned to his fliers. "Go," he said. Buzz and Zazu flew to the loading dock, peered through its foggy window, and nodded to Lou.

The Stick boy ran out of the woods. "For the barrel!" he shouted. The first wave sprang after him, shouting the same. Again, as when they had rushed across the highway to escape the giant mower, they charged like an army.

The Clif Bar rock climber scaled the dumpster first, secured his rope, and threw down the other end. Lou shimmied up next, followed by a long line of characters, who then scrambled down through the debris into the cavernous dark bottom.

At first, the metal walls rang with confused voices. The characters recently discarded from the store had never heard of Lou's Caravan. They couldn't imagine that anyone cared about them. They did understand, however, that the landfill meant death. This was their chance to live.

Whispers of hope spread through the steel prison as the Caravan excavated boxes and bags of expired food. The dumpster divers rummaged through every inch of the pitch-black bottom and worked their way up. Clinging to the metal sides, Evan pulled out package after package as the divers hauled them up.

Leading the second wave, Doc Rockwell set up an emergency surgery unit on the loading dock. There, they cut the new characters free of packaging using fragments of glass.

Chester led the third wave, rushing the newcomers across the pavement and back to the woods.

When every trapped soul had been extricated, the first wave

climbed to the rim, then glided down to the loading dock.

As drizzling rain turned into a downpour, Lou's team began the final task of emptying bread bags and hauling them back to the woods. Some bags pictured Little Miss Sunbeam biting into a slice of bread. These had no bodies and were too flimsy to walk, so the "Sunbeams" became part of the new tents.

The forest rang with happy voices. The Caravan now boasted seventeen Lucky the Leprechauns, twenty-two Tony the Tigers, thirty-six Snap, Crackle, and Pops, fifty-two Little Miss Sunbeams, seven Trix Rabbits, fourteen Cap'n Crunches, nine Dig'em Frogs, a flock of cuckoo birds (all named Sonny), and hundreds of Keebler Elves. Surveying the crowd, Lou pointed out those who were still one of a kind: Doc, Evan, and Sally.

"Doc and Evan weren't mass-manufactured, so that makes sense," he mused. "But one Sally? Wonder why?"

"Easy," Zazu answered. "Salt never expires."

When it seemed that everyone had had enough time to mingle, the original Tony climbed up on a stump and introduced Lou.

"We didn't exactly elect him our leader," the Tiger said. "We didn't need to, he just is. Anyway...Lou?"

Standing in the rain, the Purple One told the story of the Caravan, how they had left the ditches and followed the Interstate. How their numbers had grown. How some had died in their arms. How the black ants gave them intel. How the crosswalk sign had instructed them to follow Zazu's nose (and predicted trouble ahead). And that they were walking to the sea, hopefully to find homes.

"The sea sounds grand!" said one of the Cap'n Crunches.

Lou left out parts of his own story: how a depressed Stick girl named Lizzie had found the courage to reveal herself to a Mobile. How he had lost Elizabeth. How he found his true self. He said nothing about that first rescue at the Barrel, or about being attacked by fire ants, or being left for dead on the highway. Others would tell the new people Lou's story—or a glorified version of it—along with stories of their own journeys.

One of the new Snaps (of Snap, Crackle and Pop fame) asked, "What makes you think the Eaters will give us a home?"

"Eaters?" Lou asked. "You mean Mobiles? Mobiles, that's what we call them. Though I guess Eaters fits, too." He stood still for a moment as raindrops pelted his face, and thought about Elizabeth and Sophia. "I know they seem awful, throwing you in the trash, but they don't know any better," he said. "I knew one who was very kind. I knew another one who was...kind of full of herself, but then she changed. Once they see us as people, they're not cruel." He shrugged. "That's our hope."

The chilly rain kept coming. Using sticks as poles, and pebbles to weigh down the corners, the Caravan erected the bread bags. Evan acted as foreman. The Little Miss Sunbeams provided rays of hope, literally singing in the rain.

There weren't nearly enough tents for everyone. That should have precipitated arguments, but Lou and his inner circle volunteered to sleep out in the open. Others saw their example and volunteered as well. Everyone had the good kind of chills.

Late in the afternoon, the rain let up. The sun shone through the haze. Most everyone was too wound up to sleep. Evan stood watch while Lou, Zazu, Sally, Doc, Chester, and Tony walked from tent to tent, listening to stories and answering more questions. The grocery store folks had a lot to learn, not all of it pleasant.

Lou finally bedded down a couple of hours before sunset. He had passed the word that they would start late, so that people could get a little more rest before hitting the road. Before he shut his eyes, he stared at his forearms for a few seconds. In some ways, this journey was wearing him out. In others, it was making him strong.

Next to him lay Zazu, his head tucked under one wing. According to the toucan, their days of walking along the Interstate were probably over. He could feel it in his nose. A lot of towns lay between here and Charleston—lots of stores, restaurants, and fast-food places. The Caravan was likely to keep growing. Their camp would get harder to hide. Eventually, the Stick boy knew, something would have to give.

Fifty-nine

Traveling at night didn't mean there weren't hazards. Every time a car passed, dozens of characters would get caught up in the swirling air current. No one got seriously injured, but some were always pulled into the lane and a few were run over. Lou knew how it felt to be crushed by wheels. His tattered body was mending, but he still felt aches from the night he had been pummeled on the Interstate.

Zazu's nose led them next to a convenience store. Then another, and another. Then, to a fast-food restaurant. At each stop, they rescued more characters from dumpsters and litter-strewn parking lots. They added Ronald McDonalds, Icee polar bears, and pigtailed Wendys.

As his following grew, Lou worried that they would be discovered. At any time, a crew of Mobiles might show up with rakes and death sticks to clean up the trash. Many in the Caravan found it hard to sleep during the day, but Lou insisted they travel only at night. Every dawn, they camped as far off the road as possible.

One day as they rested, a landscaping worker came through with a leaf blower, scattering hundreds. When he left to go get a leaf bag, the Caravan quickly hid. That was a wake-up call. From then on, Lou got little resistance about walking at night.

Lou's family and Sophia seldom visited his thoughts anymore. Were they still trying to find him? Or grieving? Was Sunny depressed? Had Sophia moved on, distracted by her social life? Did Ups and Hershey run around sniffing for *Lizzie's scent?* Each time the Caravan reached a major black ant colony, Lou accessed their system of communication tunnels, and sent the same message: *I'm alive and coming home, with lots of friends.* But he never got a reply.

Zazu's nose zigzagged the group through South Carolina. At each little town they passed—Jonesville, Carlisle, Clinton, Kinards, Newberry—they raided dumpsters at grocery stores, gas stations, and apartment complexes. Once, they hit a row of garbage bins in a neighborhood. Pantry dwellers who had been rescued revealed some amazing facts about Mobiles. One detail caused the Snaps, Crackles, and Pops to snap, crackle, and pop with excitement. "When the Eaters pour on the milk," they said, "you can hear the cereal calling our names!"

Their route didn't follow any pattern that Lou could figure out, but meandered toward the coast. Ditch people continued to stumble out of the muck alongside the highway. One morning, some of them brought Lou a strip from a palmetto frond—the slender leaves that the ant armies often used to send long messages. Lou couldn't read the tiny handwriting. Neither could Chester, who read Red. But TurTur (a turtle from a Turtle Wax can) spoke and read Black.

The Palmetto strip told the story of Lou's Barrel. Of Lou (not Lizzie Lou, just Lou) rallying characters and insects to empty the trash barrel to save Serena. TurTur read the whole thing aloud to the Caravan. When he reached the part where Lou had demanded help from a human (Sophia), the listeners cheered. It reminded Lou of how people used to cheer whenever he and Sunny did a gymnastics trick. Only the story on the leaf was no trick. Overly dramatic, sure, but in its essence true. Throughout the reading, his throng of followers stared at him—a frayed, glue-less, purple-stained Stick boy—with a kind of reverence that helped to balance all the shame he had felt.

Lou himself never spoke about what *he* had done, or *his* vision of finding home. It was always *our* journey, *our* mission, where *we* are headed. *Us*. Never me or mine, never I.

After TurTur finished reading, others spontaneously told of their own first encounters with Lou. Or how Doc had repaired them. Or how awestruck they had been the first time they saw

Evan lift something heavy. Studying their faces and listening, the Stick boy was impressed by how closely these random strangers had bonded, and by how selflessly they acted when helping others worse off. The stormy evening when he had fallen Off Glass seemed so distant now.

At the crowd's insistence, TurTur reread the story, since many of them had been standing too far back to hear it all. Lou watched Sally trace the lettering on the Palmetto frond with her finger. And he thought, *It was worth it. I would go through it all over again.*

The Morton Salt girl pointed to a funny little symbol on the frond. "What's that say?" she asked.

The turtle glanced at the Stick boy. "That's their word for Lou."

Sally scooped a handful of salt from her box and rubbed it over the word. The crystals stuck to the ants' odd ink, making "Lou" sparkle.

Each tent group in the Caravan took turns carrying that scroll of palmetto frond. The Little Miss Sunbeams, printed on the tents and not having a lot else to do, memorized the story. This started them memorizing the stories of everyone in their tents. Whenever new refugees joined them, the Little Miss Sunbeams would recite Lou's story, plus the stories of their tent mates. This was how multiple characters—the Tonys, for example—could be introduced as individuals, and how the many Keebler Elf clans expressed their uniqueness.

Everything wasn't always laughter. People argued about how fast or slow some of them walked, or about getting the best camping spot. And just about everyone complained about the prankster M&Ms, who would often run ahead, set dog poop on the path, and call it chocolate. "They're… not so great!" boomed Tony.

Some characters were competitors: the Icee and Coca-Cola polar bears, the Leprechauns and Elves, the Nesquik Bunnies and Trix Rabbits. But, mostly, the Caravan fussed over who would be called by what name. With multiple Tony the Tigers, Dig'em Frogs, Ronald McDonalds, and so on, they all wanted to go by their original brand name. "I'm not just some guy named Frank," a new Chester Cheetah told another from the ditch. Eventually, most of them agreed that they could go all by their original name. Or they could make up new names. The Crunches all wanted to be Cap'n, but would adopt new first names—Cap'n Ryan, Cap'n Patti, Cap'n George, Cap'n Don. And they only kept one ship's wheel, which the "Cap'n of the Week" carried. This way, only one of them at a time could pretend to steer their imaginary ship.

The bickering didn't bother Lou. Usually, he allowed people to sort things out on their own. What did concern him was a growing threat from the Fire Empire. One afternoon, he followed a frantic Keebler Chief to a demolished tent at the edge of camp. Fire ants had attacked them for bread crumbs. The bag lay in tatters. Four Elves and a Little Miss Sunbeam had been injured. Doc patched them up and surgically removed the Sunbeam.

The tent leaders met and decided to get rid of anything that Fire Ants might see as food. The Caravan then trekked to a small creek, where they washed out the bread bags and set them up to dry. Any character who still had traces of food, such as cereal dust or powdered sugar, bathed.

Many from the ditches took this opportunity to clean up as well. Afterwards, they shone as if fresh off the shelf.

Lou, too, rid himself of weeks of road grime, but not the blackberry stain. To everyone around him, he would always be the Purple One. But as he washed the top of his head, he felt stubby hair growing. That made him laugh.

And just when I got used to being bald, he thought.

That first attack by the Fire Empire actually improved morale. But it wasn't the last.

Sixty

One dawn in early September, as the Caravan stopped for the day, a Black Army patrol marched up carrying a leaf with writing on it. Zazu looked at it, then raised his beak and called out, "Anyone named Lizzie?"

"Um, me," Lou replied. He accepted the leaf and, as best as he could, thanked the black ant leader.

The message, written in both Black and the Common Tongue, said, "We're so thrilled that you're safe! We love you, Lizzie! When will you get here? We'll be waiting!" At the bottom, the names of Mom, Dad, Sunny, and Ups.

Friends had gathered around and read over Lou's shoulder. "Is that from your family?" Sally asked.

Lou nodded, too choked up to reply. After a moment, he tucked the leaf under one arm and rubbed his face to erase some tears. "Let's all get some sleep. We have a big night coming up."

Tonight they would travel into Columbia, the state capitol. Although it seemed like a no-brainer to go around, Zazu's nose had pointed them right at it. The Caravan now numbered over a thousand people. Keeping out of sight in the burbs had been tricky enough. Lou had few ideas how to hide such a large group along city streets. A couple of hours before nightfall, while the rest of the Caravan packed up, the Stick boy and the tent leaders stood on a hill and looked out on Columbia's modest skyline.

Lou gave each leader a serious look. "I gotta be honest," he said, "I don't know how we're gonna get through without being attacked by sanitation workers."

"We Elves have a solution," said the head Keebler. Lou turned to him.

"Whatcha got, Chief? Show me."

"Prepare to be amazed!" The Elf pulled a french fry person to the middle of the group. Then he dipped his hands in a bag of dust, sprinkled it on the fry, and said, with a flourish of his hands, "Blickle!" Slowly, the french fry faded until he was partially see-through.

"See?" said the head Elf. "We'll disappear the whole Caravan. If no one can see us, we can go wherever we want, whenever we feel like it."

The french fry guy examined his hands. "Hey," he objected, "change me back!"

The Chief cracked his knuckles. "Er, we're working on that."

"Amateur," mumbled Lucky the Leprechaun.

Lou reached out to touch the french fry's arm, but his hand went right through. "Interesting," he said. "Can you do this to a thousand of us? All the way invisible?"

The Elf squirmed. "Possibly. But we'll need to gather lots more ragweed, like a whole dump-truck full. That's the magic ingredient."

"I'll take that as a no," Lou sighed. "And you gotta be able to change them back. Work on that part first."

"Invisible? Bah! What we really need is sparkles," said Lucky, loosening his green scarf, "shaped like me marshmallows. Pink hearts, yellow moons—"

"Orange stars and green clovers," Lou finished. "I've seen your ads. Show me."

Lucky produced a smattering of colorful sparkles that danced and quickly faded. "Sparkles be both beautiful and distracting at the same time," he said. "If a Mobile sees us, we'll dazzle them." The green-clad fellow plucked a star from the air and popped it in his mouth. "Plus, they're magically delicious!"

Lou grunted. "We need something practical."

Evan and Chester stepped forward. Neither was a tent leader. They had been lingering at the edge of the group, listening. "We made this map," the magnet man said, offering a crumpled piece of paper.

Lou spread it on the ground. It showed major roads, parks, and some of the larger buildings in the city. He looked up at Evan and Chester. "This is amazing. Where'd the intel come from?"

"The Reds," the cheetah replied. "They let us copy their charts, as long as we left out their own tunnels and forts. And we promised to never share it with the Black Army."

"We gotta tear it up once we're on the south side," the magnet man added.

Cap'n Patti (one of the Cap'n Crunches) pointed at a pond. "There's an ocean!"

"And a creek and a river," said an Icee polar bear.

"Trix are for maps!" the Trix Rabbit quipped. The rest looked at him. "Trix are for *fill-in-the-blank*," was about all he ever said.

Lou pointed at numbers written beside many of the intersections. "What do these mean?"

"That's the number of seconds at each stop light," Evan said.

Chester tapped the map with a claw. "And look. All the local parks. Lorick, Riverfront, Granby."

"Places we can bed down for the day," Lou nodded. "Perfect. Assuming that Zazu's nose doesn't lead us somewhere else. If we move fast, we can get through town in three or four nights.

And what's this?" He indicated a large area labeled *USC*.

"University of South Cackalacky," Chester answered.

Lou glanced at him. "Oh right, South Carolina. That space in the middle looks perfect for hiding."

"That's the Quadrangle," Evan said. "They'll be quick to clean it up, so best not to pitch tents."

"Plus, we can hide under the pine straw or ivy," Chester added.

Lou made eye contact with each person around the map. "We'll have to split up into smaller groups at a lot of these parks. And there'll be traffic, even at night. Getting separated is what I'm worried about most."

Cap'n Patti nodded. "Aye, a captain worried about his crew."

Chester Cheetah said, "We'll need to keep a low profile. Those M&M cats could blow this for everyone."

The Stick boy nodded, then pointed at the Elf. "Tell the Ms, 'No mischief.' Any pranks before we get through the city, and you Elves have authority to turn them invisible."

The Chief Elf grinned. "We'll tell them that disappearing would be like melting in someone's hand."

"Perfect," Lou said. He looked up at Evan. "You have signal flags ready, right?"

"Yep." The big guy held up three plastic straws: one green, one orange, one red.

Lou folded up the map. "Then, let's get going."

Sixty-one

As the sun disappeared, the Caravan set out. Columbia, South Carolina wasn't one of the biggest cities on earth, but to characters who had lived their lives on store shelves and in ditches, it seemed that way. Compared to the small towns, more businesses stayed open late or all night. Someone drove the streets at all hours.

They marched through the night without incident, with Lou, Doc, Sally, Chester, Zazu, Tony, and Evan, as usual, up front. They passed a homeless person sleeping on a bench, but he didn't stir. At sunrise, they made camp at Hyatt Park, a green space the size of a city block. Having kept up a fast pace, they were worn out. But with dogs barking, doors slamming, and construction crews hammering, it was past noon before Lou finally dozed off. Even then, he didn't sleep well.

The next night, they crossed their first major intersection, Monticello Road and North Main Street. A Walk/Don't Walk signal did what they usually do–displayed an electronic hand indicating don't walk, then a person in mid-stride, meaning time to proceed. No moon-walking. Lou and those close to him ran across first. When they reached the other side, Evan waved a green signal straw and hundreds of characters scurried across the pavement. Perched on the magnet man's tilting shoulders, dozens of Keeblers leaned one way, then the other, as if on a rocking boat.

"Don't stop, folks, keep moving," Doc urged, as the crowd poured into the grass.

"Wow, that timer is fast," Zazu squawked, "and that's with no cars waiting at the red light."

"You're right, birdie bird," Lou replied, "but at least we know the map is accurate." He turned to Evan. "Switch to orange." The big man lowered the green straw and waved the orange one. The Caravan kept moving, many of them staring up at the glowing yellow timer as it ticked toward zero.

"Now, red," Lou instructed.

Evan waved the red straw. On the far side of the intersection, people halted. Those still in the road sprinted off the pavement. Up on the steel post, a Don't Walk Hand replaced the Walk Person. The traffic light changed from yellow to red.

"Great job!" Lou called those on the far side. "Sit tight."

He glanced down at Sally. The girl twirled her holey umbrella as a mound of salt grew behind her. Half of the time she forgot to close the lid, but somehow the navy blue box never ran out of sodium crystals. Whenever Lou began to doubt their mission, the wonder of Sally's salt—like her relentless faith in him—brought him comfort. A trail of salt marked their path, from here all the way back to where it had last rained. Sometimes this bugged him. If someone was trying to find the Caravan, all they needed to do was follow the salt. *Or maybe leaving a trail is a good thing,* he thought. *If one of us in the Caravan gets lost, they can follow it.*

It took five light changes for the entire group to cross. From there, they stayed with North Main and continued into the heart of the city. When night ended, they hunkered down at the edge of Earlewood Park. On the other end of the broad lawn stood a cluster of sun-bleached, human-sized tents. While the rest of the Caravan bedded down, Lou huddled with his friends. He unrolled the Red Army map and pointed to a patch of green on it.

"That's us," he said, then moved his finger an inch. "And that's them." He nodded at the tattered tents across the way.

Doc shrugged. "Probably still asleep."

Lou nodded. "Probably, but they're still Mobiles. Who's got the first watch?"

Tony the Tiger raised a clawed finger. "I'm south-side. I think Lucky's got the north."

"Well, anyone seen him?"

"I'm here," said the Leprechaun, walking up. "Don't get your britches in a bind, lad. What's going on?"

"Don't want to be paranoid," the Stick boy said, "but did you notice the tent city?"

"Of course," said Lucky. "If they give us any trouble, I'll dazzle them with me pink hearts, yellow moons—"

"Yeah, yeah. Just keep an eye on them, that's all." He sent the group away to find places to rest.

After meeting with the tent leaders, Lou strolled amongst the Caravan's hidden campsites, as was his custom. Characters had tucked themselves beneath ground cover or pine straw. The bread bags, though not in use, were folded in such a way that each Little Miss Sunbeam could participate in conversations. At one such group, Lou met Cocky, a garnet-colored rooster that the french fry people had freed from a discarded stadium seat cushion. Lou listened to the story of how Cocky had attended football and baseball games with a university student. The Stick boy had the tact not to ask what it felt like (or smelled like) to be sat on for hours at a time.

"I was there when we won the College World Series, two years in a row!" Cocky said. The rooster then craned back his head and let loose with an "Ur-ur-ur-ur-urhhhhh!" crowing so loudly, it knocked Lou and the fries off their feet.

"Whoa!" Lou laughed. "I never realized so much sound could come out of a rooster."

Cocky puffed out his chest. "Rooster? Ha! *I* am a Gamecock!"

Lou took the other's outstretched wing and got to his feet. "Okay, Gamecock. Just remember we're trying to hide, right?"

"Oh. My bad."

When Lou got back to his own campsite, Sally rushed up. "Did you hear that animal?" she asked. "Do you think it's dangerous?"

"Relax, it's just a chicken."

Tony and Chester looked at one another and smiled. "Hm," Chester said, "I could go for a little chicky-chicky."

Lou wagged his finger the way his mom used to. "I see where this is going. One, neither of you eat meat, you're made of cardboard. Two, he's not a real chicken, he's made of vinyl or something. And three, he's about five times your size, he could squash you."

Chester shrugged. "Doesn't hurt to dream."

The next night, the Caravan set out with the goal of making it to the Quad, the park-like space at the heart of the university. But almost every intersection in the center of the city had a stop light and all of them were short. Barely a hundred characters could cross before Evan began waving the orange straw. If cars were waiting at the light, none of them could cross. And here, where stores and office buildings met broad sidewalks, the Caravan found little cover. At one intersection, it took twenty light changes to get through.

"This is taking forever," Doc complained.

Lou stared at his wrinkled face. "I thought old people were supposed to be patient," he said. But he thought, *he's right, we're wasting the night.*

A few minutes later, the Stick boy noticed the GEICO Gecko doing cartwheels across the road. It reminded him of how he and Sunny used to compete to see who could do the most cartwheels. And gave him an idea.

At the next vacant lot, Lou halted the Caravan and announced a new strategy. If cars were stopped at a red light, members would no longer scatter and hide. Instead, they would tumble or roll across the intersection, mimicking wind-blown trash.

At the very next light, they tested it. Sure enough, the Mobiles either didn't notice the acrobatic litter or didn't care. No one jumped out of their vehicle. No one pulled out their phone to record it. The Caravan reached the Quad with an hour to spare before dawn. Within minutes, everyone had disappeared beneath shrubbery or pools of ivy.

But hiding was easier than sleeping. Hundreds of students came and went from the surrounding dorms and lecture halls.

Skateboards and electric scooters rumbled by. In the afternoon, some students even spread out beach towels nearby and listened to music as they sunbathed. So when the Caravan took to the road again that night, most were sleep deprived and grumpy. There were also angry comments about wanting to "roast some chicken." Cocky had woken up everyone repeatedly with his ear-splitting crow. After the eighth time, the french fry folks had taped his beak shut.

Zazu's nose told the toucan that they should travel through Five Points, a cluster of bars and restaurants popular with the locals. Lou and his tent leaders had gathered around the map to discuss their options, when Doc Rock approached.

"Sorry to interrupt," the old man said.

The Coca-Cola polar bear scooted over to give him space. "Not a problem."

"I always welcome input from my subjects," the Burger King king added, then dodged everyone's eyes. He was still adjusting to the idea that his realm wasn't universal.

Doc made a fluttering motion with one hand and did a funny little bow. "It's just—I can't see how we're gonna get through Five Points without being caught," he said. "There'll be dozens of people walking around this place. Maybe hundreds."

"How do you figure?" Lou replied.

Doc shrugged. "You kidding? Saturday in a college town. Game day!"

The Pillsbury Doughboy nodded his head. "Hehehe, that's right. I heard the loud chicken say that the Gamecocks are playing the Bulldogs."

A little ways away, Sally squealed. The group at the map turned to see her struggling with her umbrella, which had nearly blown away.

"Not to mention, it's windy today," Doc added.

Lou grunted. "Yeah, but maybe we can use it. You know, the whole tumbling-in-the-wind-act. What do you think, Poppin' Fresh?" He poked the Pillsbury Doughboy in the tummy. People did it all the time; it was irresistible. The doughy guy let out his gentle laugh.

After more discussion, the leaders voted to stick with the plan. After all, the toucan's nose had guided them so far without incident. The Caravan entered the Five Points area by Gervais and then Harden Streets, tumbling and twirling like crazy, and keeping to grass whenever possible. The stiff breeze helped sell their act to dozens of pedestrians and passing motorists. No one made an effort to clean them up.

Flapping above them, Zazu sang, "Follow the nose...It always knows!"

All thousand-plus of them reached a pentagon-shaped fountain and climbed into the planters that surrounded it. "So far, so good," Lou said. He and Zazu popped their heads above the greenery to scope things out. Less than a block away lay the intersection of Harden, Devine, and Santee that gave Five Points its name.

The Stick boy turned to the bird. "Zazu?"

"Yes?"

"Which way?"

The bird pointed a wing toward Santee. "There."

After everyone had a chance to catch their breath, the Stick boy led them toward the intersection. But just as they began crossing Devine, blaring horns split the night. Instinctively, everyone looked around for a speeding car, but there was none. Instead, a line of people playing trumpets and trombones filed out of a tavern. A sign over the door identified the place: Yesterdays.

"Lordy, it's a pub crawl!" Doc yelled.

"Keep moving!" Lou called. But as an endless line of Mobiles staggered out of the bar, some stepped on or kicked Caravan members along the sidewalk.

"What's with all the trash?" asked a man in a Gamecocks jersey.

Then from somewhere back in the Caravan, Cocky let loose with a hearty "Ur-ur-urh-ur-urhhhhhh!" Some of the Mobiles stopped and turned toward the sound. The pub crawl jumbled up, causing one of the trombone players to swing his instrument, which hit a guy in the face. As giant feet stomped everywhere, characters dove for safety. Then, a Volkswagen

Beetle sped through the intersection, sending some of them airborne. Lou, standing in the road and trying to direct Caravan traffic, shoved Doc out of the way of the giant tires. Turning, the Stick boy saw Sally floating in the air. "Nooooo!" he shouted. The girl landed on the car's windshield like a snowflake.

Anyone but Sally, Lou thought.

Sixty-two

Someone knocked Lou off his feet. Zazu went rolling. For a moment, the Stick boy could only see people's legs. Then he was on his feet, racing after the Volkswagen, with Evan at his side. As they gained speed, the Keebler Elves clinging to the big guy's shoulders flew off.

"She's stuck...in the wipers!" the magnet man panted.

"I know!"

They sprinted after the red taillights, with little chance of catching up. Lou felt the limits of his stamina. Then the VW screeched to a halt at a traffic signal, just one block away.

"Yes!" the magnet man shouted.

Lou dug deeper for more speed, but it wasn't enough. He watched as the light changed from red to green, and the VW lurched forward.

But with one last burst of energy, the magnet man launched himself at the Beetle's rear bumper, and stuck. As the car sped out of sight, Lou slowed to a walk, then halted. Out of breath, out of gas, he rested his hands on his knees. As he did, he noticed something—many somethings—glistening in the street. He bent down and picked one up. Examined it, tasted it. A crooked grin spread over his face. *Salt.*

Holding a stitch in his side, the Stick boy once again began running, following Sally's trail. Several blocks later, he spotted the Beetle in a driveway. A young woman got out, plucked something from her windshield, and walked toward a small house. A tree obstructed Lou's vision, but he heard the door close.

He found Evan unpeeling from the bumper. After climbing up the front steps, they discovered Sally on a bench, next to the front door. Evan helped her down.

"You're alright!" Lou exclaimed, as the three hugged.

Evan put a finger to his lips. "Let's get out of here."

At the bottom of the steps, Sally stopped to close her salt box. "She didn't throw me away," she said, glancing back.

"You're lucky she didn't rip you in half," the Stick boy whispered. "C'mon, let's hurry!" *The Caravan must be a wreck,* he thought.

Evan bent down to Sally's level. "What d'ya mean?"

"Well," the girl explained, "the whole time I was on the

windshield, she kept looking at me. Once, I almost flew off and she made this face." She showed Lou and Evan a look of shock. "She even rolled down her window and stuck out her arm, but she couldn't reach me."

The magnet man grinned. "Well, you are pretty cute."

Sally twirled her umbrella. "Aw."

Lou bit his tongue. *We're wasting time!*

"How come she tossed you on the bench?" Evan asked.

"I don't know."

Hanging from a tree branch, wind chimes rioted in the wind. Sally turned at their tinkling, then took a long look at the small house: rocking chair on the porch, flower boxes in the windows, homemade decorations dotting the yard. Next to the steps bloomed a bed of pansies. Atop a metal rod stuck in the dirt, a glass frog winked at her.

"Hiya, kiddo," he said.

"Well, hi there," Sally replied.

"I see you've met the Beetle girl."

"Who?" Sally, Evan, and Lou all asked.

"Emma," said the frog, "the Volkswagen Beetle girl."

"Oh." Sally showed a timid smile. "Is she...?"

"Nice? Oh, yeah. Kind? Creative? Don't you doubt it. Not to mention, pretty. We're all in love with her. Least..." the frog gave a bashful look, "...I am."

"We?" Lou and Evan asked.

"Hey there, sticky boy, big magnet dude," the frog said. He pointed a webbed finger at Lou. "You're wicked fast for a—whatever-you-are. And determined. I like that. And you—" He raised some froggy eyebrows at Evan. "Very clever, hitching a ride on the bumper. Funny, I always thought it was plastic."

"The cover is, but there's metal underneath," Evan clarified.

"You don't say."

Lou tapped his foot. In his mind, he saw the Caravan running around dazed, some lying hurt in the street.

"Can you go back to that part about love, Mr. Frog?" Sally asked.

"Oh, yeah." The other smiled and let out a little croak. "We all got a crush on Emma. Although I'd like to think I'm one of her favorites, seeing as how she made me."

"Really?!" the girl gushed.

"Oh yeah, she's a crafty one," the frog said. He thumped his glass chest. "When the sun's out, I throw colors all over the ground."

"I'll bet you pretty-up the sidewalk," Sally said.

Lou cleared his throat. "You were saying?"

"Oh yeah. Emma's got quite a collection. We're all over the yard, but some live in the house, too. Mostly on the fridge." He pointed at Evan. "You'd be perfect there."

Evan looked away for a second, then shook his head. "I got places to be."

"What about me?" Sally squealed.

"You? Oh, well that goes without saying. Emma found you, so it's meant to be."

Lou took Sally's hand and scowled at the frog. "Then why'd she leave her outside?"

"Eh, no big deal. She'll come out and get her in the morning. Emma's not in a hurry. She's different that way."

The Stick boy nodded at the car. "Hard to tell, from the way she drives."

The frog grinned. "What can I say? She's complicated."

Lou glanced at his wrist as if he was wearing a watch, then at Sally. But for some reason, he couldn't look her in the eyes. "We need to go," he said. "People are counting on us."

Evan put a hand on his shoulder. "Nope, they're counting on *you*." He patted the girl on the head. "Not her."

"Oh yeah? How's everyone gonna find each other without her salt trail?" Lou asked.

"We'll figure it out," Evan said, and winked at Sally.

The girl tugged on the Stick boy's arm until he met her eyes. "It feels right being here."

Lou felt a lump in his throat. He had lost Elizabeth, then his family. He squatted down. "You're sure about this?" Sally just smiled and nodded.

"C'mon, Purple," Evan said, and taking Lou by the hand, pulled the Stick boy toward the road.

"You be careful," Lou called. Then to the frog, "If anything happens to her, so help me, I'll hunt you down and—" But it sounded angry and petty, so he just shut up and turned to go. He only made it a few steps, before Sally ran up and hugged his legs.

"Thank you for getting me out of the ditch," she said. Her salt box had jostled and was leaking again.

He tugged one of her pigtails. "Thanks for believing in me."

She released him and stepped back. "Now, go find the ocean!"

"Will do. First I gotta find the others."

As he and Evan reached the end of the driveway, Lou heard the frog call, "You wouldn't happen to be *the* Lou, would ya? From the Barrel?"

"Well, of course, he is," Sally replied.

"Oh wow, I heard about him. I'm Scott, by the way. Oh, and close your lid, sweetie, you're spillin' salt."

"That little bit?" Sally replied, "That's nothing. You should see what happens when it rains!"

And together, Lou and Evan said under their breath, "It pours."

Sixty-three

As the two walked back toward Five Points, Lou's urge to hurry had been replaced, at least for the moment, with a peace that usually escaped him. At the end of the Beetle girl's street, a very stretched-out Caravan met them. Doc carried a rumpled Zazu.

"Birdie-bird!" Lou called. "What happened?"

"Billions of careless feet," the toucan replied. "Then a car."

"Ouch."

"I must say, boss, I have a whole new appreciation for what you went through."

Doc laid the bird down on the street. Lou knelt beside his feathered companion. "Is there anything we can do for you?"

"Well," the other said with a weak voice, "I'd love a bowl of Froot Loops."

"Fresh out," Lou said. He gave Doc a questioning look.

"Busted wing," the old man said. "I can fix him up, but not right here. Not with what I got with me."

Chester wiped his broken sunglasses with his tail. "It's that freakin' chicken's fault. Once he started crowing, the humans went crazy. Dancing in the street, dodging cars, stomping our people."

As more Caravan members caught up, they hugged Lou and Evan and offered their own opinions on who was to blame for the scene at the intersection.

"Stop it," the Stick boy said, raising his hands. "Just stop. It wasn't anyone's fault. Blame me if you want to. I led us here."

"Thank you," said Cocky.

"Where's Sally?" someone asked. "Did we lose her?"

"Not exactly," the Stick boy replied.

Doc scratched his head. "What exactly does 'not exactly' mean?"

"She's okay," Lou said. "She's not hurt."

"Better than okay," Evan added. "She's great."

Tony the Tiger repeated the phrase, loudly and with his usual enthusiasm.

"Then, like, where is she?" the cheetah asked.

Lou glanced down the street. "She found a home."

A collective "Ah" went through the crowd.

"What do you mean, a home?" asked the Clif Bar climber.

Lou grinned. "Sally's with a young woman named Emma. She's gonna live on a—" He looked to Evan for help. "What'd the frog call it?"

"A refrigerator," the magnet man said.

"A milk house!" Tony declared. And when others looked at him funny, he added, "According to a cow I know."

Lou nodded his stubby head. "Sally will be living inside a people-house with a bunch of other refrigerator people."

"Nice," said one of the Keeblers, as a clan of them climbed back onto Evan's shoulders. "Can we be defibrillator people, too?"

Several in the crowd laughed. Evan said, "I don't think it works that way."

Cap'n Crunch crinkled his white eyebrows. "But then...how *does* it work? I thought we were hiking to the sea to find homes. Or better yet, a home on the sea."

The Doughboy raised his hand. Lou pointed to him. "Yes?"

"I kinda thought we were going to the sea to die. I mean—" he gestured to those around him, "—we all look pretty bad, you know." He let out a soft giggle. One of the Coke polar bears put an arm around him. The other one straightened the chef's rumpled hat.

"We're not going anywhere to die," Lou declared. "But honestly, I don't know how we're going to find homes. I've been up front about that. The signs–the crosswalk signs–wanted us to follow Zazu's nose. As we saw tonight, that's unpredictable."

"And broken, I believe," Zazu said, touching his beak.

"Some of your friends died in ditches or dumpsters and never even started the journey," Lou went on. "Maybe some of us will get run over, get torn apart, I don't know. It's rough out here. Mobiles see us as trash. I can't promise to keep you safe, but I'm still walking to the beach."

TurTur gave a thumbs-up. "Slow and steady."

"That's easy for you to say," said one of the M&Ms, pointing at Lou. "You have a home down there. A family and that Mobile girl. We got nobody!"

"You've got me," Lou said. "You've got each other. And I can promise you this: I'm not going to leave anyone behind."

The crowd looked from Lou to the M&M guy and back again. One of the french fry people shouted, "Amen, brotha!"

Lou was about to get the group moving again—sunrise was fast approaching—when from the back came a rumble. The crowd parted as something big made its way through. A moment later, a paper cup rolled up, pushed by Snap, Crackle, and Pop .

"Hi, what can I get started for you?" asked a green mermaid printed on the cup.

What was left of Lou's eyebrows went up. "Huh?"

"Will that be for here or to go?" she continued.

"Will what be?" asked the Stick boy.

Cap'n Crunch removed his hat. "Well, hello, gorgeous!" he said.

"Hi, welcome to Starbucks. What can I get started for you?" she repeated. "Will that be for here or to go?"

"Forgot to tell you," said Doc to Lou, "we picked up a stray."

The other looked closer at the mermaid. "What's she talking about?"

The old man shook his head. "No idea."

"Okay, where'd you find her?"

"Welcome to Starbucks, what can I get started for you?"

Doc removed his spectacles and polished the empty lenses. "Remember our friend Gene Baker, the feller sleeping under a bridge? He was in that tent city back at the park. Followed us."

Snap filled in the details. "When the brass band marched through Five Points, Baker started dancing in the street. He tossed this cup on the ground, so we figured he wanted the fish girl to come with us."

Lou looked off in the distance. "Where's Baker now?"

"Dunno," Snap said.

"Hi, welcome to Starbucks. What can I get started for you?" the mermaid asked again. "Will that be for here or to go?"

"Wow, that's annoying," Lou said. He examined her. Her long hair seemed to sway as if underwater. "What's she supposed to be?" he asked, pointing at her crown.

"Queen of the sea?" Poppin' Fresh ventured.

"Queen of my heart!" Cap'n Crunch declared.

"And these?" The Stick boy pointed at two scaly appendages. "Are these her hands? She looks like she's either about to take off her crown or put it on."

Doc stepped closer. "I think it's part of her tail. It's a double." He pointed around her circular border. "I've seen her kind before. Folks say she leads some kind of cult. They say her partners—whatever that means—call her the Siren. You know, like the kind who lure sailors to crash on the rocks?"

"She's soooo beautiful!" Cap'n Crunch exclaimed.

"Hi, welcome to Starbucks. What can I get started for you?"

"Does she say anything else?" Lou asked.

Snap said, "She speaks Italian. Sort of. We think." He snapped his fingers.

"Tall, grande, or venti?" the Siren asked.

Chester looked over his sunglasses. "Freaky."

"Lovely!" Cap'n Crunch moaned.

Lou nudged the cup. "This thing won't roll in a straight line, will it?" Snap, Crackle, and Pop shook their heads. "Okay, let's cut her out, but make it quick. Night's almost gone." Several Elves descended from Evan's shoulders and ran forward with bits of glass.

Doc said, "She ain't got legs. Somebody's gonna have to carry her."

Cap'n Crunch jumped up and down. "Me, me, pick me!"

Lou laughed. "Okay, she's with you, Cap'n. But remember, she's a queen. I expect you to be a gentleman."

The mariner stood to attention and saluted. "Always!"

Lou pointed at Tony. "Keep an eye on him."

The Tiger covered a toothy yawn. "Aye-aye."

Once the Elves freed the sea queen from her paper cup, the Caravan moved on. Soon they reached a vacant lot hiding the remains of a burned house. Again making do without tents, they bedded down amongst overgrown weeds and broken beer bottles. While Doc tended to Zazu, Lou and Evan walked around, counting everyone and checking them off on their master list. For weeks, the Stick boy had been scratching everyone's names onto the magnet man's back.

As the sun rose, Lou finally lay down, dead-tired. Like an unknown road, life had taken a turn, he reflected, and Sally had found a new home. He stared at his paper-thin hands. In this light, his berry-stained fingers looked lilac instead of purple. His toes too. Doc Rock could only do so much to repair him. If they didn't make it to the ocean soon, the pavement might wear him down to nothing. Somehow, this didn't upset him.

Sixty-four

The next night, as the Caravan made its way out of Columbia, they passed a place that many had only dreamed of: a Krispy Kreme factory. The characters peered through an expansive window at a conveyor belt, which rolled out thousands of glazed donuts.

Evan shook his head. "I don't get it," he said. "How can Mobiles eat so much? How come they don't get giant?"

From his shoulder, an elf proclaimed, "They *are* giant!"

The magnet man grunted. "Okay, more giant. Where's all that food go?"

"Well," Lou explained, "they use some of the food for energy, just like we do with sunlight and crumbs." Everyone turned to listen. Many of them had never been face to face with a Mobile, other than Gene Baker.

"Blimey," said Lucky the Leprechaun. "What do they do with the rest of it?"

A smile sneaked its way onto Lou's face. "It's called...*doing their business.*"

Chester peaked over his sunglasses. "Like Frito-Lay? That's a business."

"And Keebler," added an Elf. His clan all agreed that Keebler was the best business to do.

"The supermarkets!" Dig'em Frog shouted. "I did my business in a Publix!"

Lou covered his face to conceal his laughter.

"Don't forget Quality Bakers of America," a Little Miss Sunbeam added.

One of the M&Ms cleared his throat. "Not sure about bakers, but, for candy companies, you can't beat Mars. Those people *love* doin' their business."

As they made their way out of the city, the whole Caravan debated which business was best of all. Recalling the stench in the Baby Bear Trading Post restroom, Lou just let them go. *They're better off not knowing,* he thought.

Watching the moon rise, the Stick boy's thoughts often wandered into bizarre territory. He wondered if he had imagined talking with Sophia. And this journey. Was he really lying dead on the side of the Interstate? Was this the afterlife? At one time, Sophia had thought that he and Sunny were imaginary. He glanced around. Were these *his* imaginary friends?

He found himself staring at the painted stripe that marked the edge of the road. *What makes a person real,* he wondered? *Those Sticks that Elizabeth left in the box. They're lying in darkness right now, in the attic. Are they people, too? And where in all the Universe did she go? Gone forever, apparently. But where?*

The Stick boy gasped as he felt a hand on his shoulder. He looked up to see Doc Rockwell. And noticed for the hundredth time or more the fine brush strokes: wrinkles, white hair, wire-rimmed spectacles. "This ole road just keeps a-goin', don't it?" the old man said.

"Right you are, my friend."

With the next sunrise approaching, they camped, pitching their Little Miss Sunbeam tents in a spot far from the road. Just as the Stick boy nodded off, a fine mist began tickling his face. Sometime in the middle of the afternoon, during a dream about whitewater rafting, rain began coming down for real. In his dream, the raft passed beneath a waterfall.

Many in the camp hopped up to bring their belongings into their tents. Lou barely opened his eyes. He had been sleeping out in the open for so long now, he preferred it. The rain was chilly at first, but then it stopped and the sun came out. He slept soundly.

Doc patched Zazu's wing, but the nose that "always knows" had gone haywire. For direction, Lou relied on advice from those around him, and on his own instincts. They stuck to backroads whenever possible.

Every night, characters from dumpsters and ditches still joined them. Some new folks brought drama. Colonel Sanders and a trio of Chick-fil-A cows, for example, had a beef with Ronald and the Burger King king. Others brought an upbeat vibe. Little Debbie, having lived through the Great Depression, encouraged everyone to keep going. The cheerful Sun-Maid woman carried a bowlful of California Raisins, who sang *Heard it Through the Grapevine* and other R&B oldies. A fabric softener bear named Snuggle thanked his rescuers with hugs. Little Caesar delivered cheesy jokes.

Around the beginning of November, the South Carolina autumn finally turned cool. Surpassing three thousand in number, the Caravan swept over the countryside like a flock of birds, flowing from road to ditch to woods as one. They crossed neighborhoods and parking lots in unison that, to an outside observer, might have looked instinctive. In fact, it took loads of planning and continuous adjustment. The Keebler Elves—those quick little fellows—relayed Lou's orders front to back and side to side, enabling a high degree of real-time coordination.

By this time, word of Lou's heroics at the Barrel had spread to every ditch and dumpster along the way. Not only did the Caravan carry out nightly rescue operations, characters now wandered to them on their own: a Kool-Aid man, the Michelin man, Sugar Bear, Charlie Tuna, dozens of little Scrubbing Bubbles. A mustachioed Pringles man had only a head, so others dragged him around on a maple leaf. A bald guy calling himself Mr. Clean had only half a body, but a buff half. He walked faster on his beefy arms than most people could on legs.

Some of the new folks—Mrs. Butterworth's, Aunt Jemima, Uncle Ben, a bunch of Chiquita Banana ladies—had been created as stereotypes—but lived on, despite having been discontinued by their brands. They were the last of their kind. The Chiquita women, who only had heads, found new homes on the tent bags with the Sunbeam girls. Mrs. Butterworth's, although elderly and also without feet, remained independent, somehow scooting around as if on skates.

A salty pirate named Captain Morgan drew crowds, telling bawdy tales of the sea, waving his sword and tipping his bottle. Lou thought, *That's the kind of pirate Mom always warned us about.* Cap'n Crunch made sure to keep the Siren far away.

Newbies were always astonished to see how big Evan the Magnet man was. They marveled, too, as they ran their fingers over the oil paint brushstrokes of Doc Rockwell. All of them wanted to meet Lou.

But the Purple One had work to do. Fire ants began raiding almost daily, always hitting while they slept, consuming anything edible and even stuff that wasn't. The Stick boy understood better than anyone how insanely fire ants craved sticker adhesive. Although few people in the Caravan were stickers—and even those had little or no stickiness left—apparently the Fire Empire hadn't gotten that memo.

Lou established a security force. During the day, while everyone slept, they patrolled in shifts. At night, they walked on the outskirts as the Caravan moved. He met frequently with the tent leaders, and relentlessly walked the perimeter of the camp, checking with the guards. Usually the sun was well above the tree line by the time the Stick boy bedded down. Even then, he often lay awake, worrying about attacks and thinking about his family. Ever since that first message delivered by the Black Army, he had heard nothing further from them.

Sixty-five

The Caravan stretched longer and longer. To Lou, the miles blurred. His feet hurt, his back hurt, seemed like everything did. But, at least, he wasn't alone in his aches and fatigue. There were always more injured people than Doc Rock could tend to, and some too far gone to help. The old fellow worked non-stop, but every blackberry bush between Orangeburg and Charleston had been picked clean by birds. He soon ran out of the purple poultice.

One morning, Lou slipped out of camp and sat by himself on what passes for a hill in South Carolina's Lowcountry. Here in the suburbs of Charleston, subdivisions and traffic stretched endlessly. The Stick boy wondered how they could make it to the beach without being caught. Even if they made it, what could he possibly do to find homes for all these people?

A chilly breeze ruffled the rainbow bristle brush that his hair had become. Below him, the Caravan shimmered like a lake. He longed for another message from his family. But these days, his idea of family had evolved. His biological family, if that concept made any sense for Sticks, was still hugely important, always would be. But these many lost characters were no less precious. They were family, too.

The Stick boy squinted into the sunrise. Last night, Zazu had spotted seagulls. That had prompted the Purple One to declare today *We're Almost There Day*. And so now, while he sat apart, the Caravan partied, and would continue to do so until almost noon, most of them dancing and singing and playing music as if they had never known a moment of sorrow. As if this moment was all that mattered.

The Isle of Palms lay just twenty miles away. Getting there posed a challenge, made harder by an increase in fire-ant attacks. The Interstate was no longer an option, since much of it was elevated and would provide no cover.

Instead, Lou and the tent leaders chose Highway 61, which wound through suburbia under a canopy of live oak branches. He remembered this road from back when he lived On Glass. It wasn't near the Chapman's neighborhood, Vinylville, but they had driven out here several times to attend swim meets.

As December ticked by, holiday lights appeared on more and more homes and yards. Dazzled, some in the Caravan assumed that Charleston always looked this way. Those who had seen Christmas decorations in stores, though, now understood their purpose. Neither Santa, his reindeer, nor any of the blow-up characters cared to join Lou's growing troupe. They already had homes.

"Reminds me of Vegas," Chester said, gazing at an elaborate display, "only not as bright." No one thought to ask the cheetah how he knew of the gambling capital.

For Lou, the festive lights brought back a memory of Elizabeth and her family shopping for a Christmas tree. He recalled the fragrance of the Douglas fir they tied to the top of the minivan. A happy memory, but painful, too. He embraced it like the cold.

On Christmas morning, as the Caravan lay down to rest, Doc Rock told stories of what it was like in the homes where he had hung decades ago, when he was still *In Frame*. And before that, of Norman Rockwell's studio, where a vast community of characters—dogs, chickens, boys playing baseball, grand-folks in rockers, and so on, had lived—never aging—eating the same apple or sandwich or Thanksgiving dinner each night, until a fire in the studio tore apart their world.

Shortly after sunset on the day after Christmas, the Caravan funneled into the pedestrian and bike lanes of a soaring bridge, enormous even by Mobile standards. Although a concrete wall concealed them from drivers on the traffic side, only a steel rail and cables stretched between them and a dizzying drop to the water on the other. With wind constantly whipping in multiple directions, they took it slowly, holding hands, heads down, low to the ground. It didn't matter that nearly all of them could glide skillfully. No one wanted to glide into a river.

Near daybreak, human runners and bikers appeared. Again, the Caravan pretended to be trash. Many got trampled underfoot or ran over, but none were seriously injured.

It took two more nights to reach the Isle of Palms. Along the way, Lou saw places that woke sleeping memories. He pointed out landmarks to anyone close enough to hear: "That's where the twins used to take gymnastics," or "That's Shem Creek, where my Mobile first saw dolphins." And finally, "That's Sophia's school. Elizabeth would have gone there, too."

During these last days, alarming messages came in from both the Black and Red Armies, longtime enemies that had now begun to cooperate. For miles around, Empire mounds had emptied out, the reports claimed, as fire ants began to converge on the Caravan.

The Black- and Red Armies had formed a corridor to protect Lou and his friends. But the Fire Empire outnumbered them and were better trained. Messengers warned Lou to expect a major assault soon.

On the day before their last night of walking, Lou couldn't sleep. He climbed atop a mailbox and stared at the horizon. On either side, he knew, lay unseen encampments of their ant allies. And somewhere beyond them, the fanatical Empire, hating his kind for no reason that the Stick boy could see.

Chester Cheetah climbed up and stood beside him. "You smell that? Something funky," said the spotted cat. "A little salty, but not at all like a bag of Tostitos."

"That's the salt marsh," the Stick boy replied. He pointed. "See that intersection?" The other purred, meaning yes. "That's the Connector. Leads straight to the beach."

"How far?"

"Couple of miles."

The cheetah's tail twitched. "That's just a night's walk."

Lou shrugged. "It's a causeway. Runs over the marsh, then over a big waterway to the island, over a bridge. It's out in the open. Nowhere to hide until we reach the dunes. Plus, there'll be a headwind."

Chester inspected his claws. "We won't get caught."

Lou grunted. "If we do, it's all for nothing."

"We got this, purple dude." The cheetah whipped off his dark glasses and stared at him with penetrating yellow eyes. "Like cheese that goes crunch." He sounded like he believed it. They climbed down.

All afternoon, characters came by to see their leader. Some to thank him. Others just wanting reassurance. When Lou's voice went hoarse, his close friends tried to hold the crowd back. But the Purple One overruled them. The Caravan washed over him like road dust. He sat Zen-like, allowing anyone who wanted to, to touch him, no longer bothered by it.

People stopped trying to tell or ask him anything. Instead, they simply spoke one phrase and stepped away. He looked each one in the eyes, unable to tamp down a crooked grin.

"For the Barrel," said the tiny Jolly Green Giant.

"For the Barrel," said the Energizer Bunny.

"For the Barrel," said the M&Ms guys, although Lou could tell they were itching to crack a joke.

"For the Barrel," said the Little Miss Sunbeams.

"For the Barrel," said oodles of french fry people.

"For the Barrel," said Cap'n Crunch. And from his arms, "For...the...barrel," said the Siren. Lou gave her a wink, knowing that she had struggled not to welcome him to Starbucks.

"For the Barrel," said bees and bears and geckos and rabbits.

"For the Barrel," whispered Poppin' Fresh, giggling softly.

"For the Barrel," said Evan. Looking around at the crowd, he raised a huge magnetic fist, and his powerful voice. "And for the ditches and the dumpsters and anywhere else people don't feel wanted!" A cheer went up. Then he bent down, gave Lou a hug, and added quietly. "Even minivans."

The Stick boy's grin broadened to a smile. "And construction trucks, big guy. Can't forget about the trucks."

Sixty-six

They were calling this final night on the road the Last Dash. Ants now visibly lined the roadside, twenty rows deep, the Black Army on the left, the Red on the right. The Fire Empire was still nowhere to be seen. Tony the Tiger, always an optimist, took that as a good sign. Lou, not so much. His skin itched.

As the sun dipped below the horizon, the Stick boy set out at a furious pace. On one side marched Evan, with Elves clinging to his shoulders. On Lou's other side, Doc and Chester. A legion of characters followed.

Zazu, Buzz, and a flock of Cocoa Puffs cuckoo birds soared overhead.

The Caravan now included many who had been wounded in fire-ant attacks. These they transported on stretchers made of anything they could find—straws, napkins, drink-cup lids. Several people rode on TurTur's back. Still, the Turtle Wax mascot lumbered along faster than anyone had expected.

As they moved out onto the open causeway, a headwind hit them. Soon afterward, several vehicles swished by. Fighting for every step, no one needed to pretend to tumble in the wind.

About a quarter mile onto this stretch, a Keebler Elf caught up with Lou and ran alongside. "The Red and Black Armies have barricaded the road behind us," he reported. "They'll only open up to let cars through. And still no contact with the Empire."

"Perfect!" Lou replied.

The Elf then joined the clan riding on Evan's shoulders, while another of his kin jumped down and ran to the back of the Caravan.

A few minutes later, Lou raised his hand and halted. "Ten-minute rest!" he called. Behind him, the Caravan fell like dominos. Nearby, the Energizer Bunny banged his bass drum one last time and slumped. The fliers landed.

"This wind is cuckoo!" one of the Sonnys huffed. Others around echoed his complaint.

"Zazu," Doc said, "how's that wing holding up?"

"A little clunky, but manageable." The toucan waddled over and allowed the old man to examine the gold star that he had used to patch his wing.

"Sure you don't want to ride on my shoulder?" Lou asked. The bird shook his head.

"There's a time to ride and a time to fly," he replied. "But I'll let you know if I need a tad bit of rest."

Then everyone turned their heads as TurTur plodded past them, hauling a load of the wounded. Someone called out, "You should sell batteries!" The turtle smiled and kept going. *He might start slow,* Lou thought, *but he's got a hard-shell finish.* Inwardly he grinned, thinking it sounded just like one of his dad's jokes.

Sometime in the night, they reached the incline where the road vaulted up over the Intracoastal Waterway. Lou called another halt. Thousands of characters collapsed onto the concrete, both from exhaustion and to stay out of the wind. The Stick boy turned to Doc.

"What time you got?"

The old man drew out his pocket watch. "Eleven forty-three," he said. They had been going for over six hours.

Lou turned to his friends. "We might make it over by morning, if we don't keep stopping."

"That's a big if," Evan said, staring up at the bridge. As the Caravan rested, hundreds of Scrubbing Bubbles scooted up onto the magnet man's shoulders and clustered there with the Elves. Despite their usual energy, the Bubbles had struggled against the wind.

Many in the Caravan had brought pebbles to weigh them down from that same wind. These turned out to be a burden. Pea gravel now littered the Connector. They hadn't lost anyone, but a paper cricket had flown away into the marsh. Buzz, the Honey Nut Cheerios bee, had air lifted him to safety.

They resumed their march.

Halfway up the bridge, the wind shifted and a crosswind scattered the Caravan into the vehicle lanes. Each time headlights appeared at the crest, everyone raced to the sides. In the hours just before morning, they became too exhausted to scatter, and just flattened instead. Dozens of characters took the weight of the wheels. Lou had to call halts to help them up.

At the crest of the bridge, a wave of cheers went through the Caravan. Spread out before them, house lights dotted the dark barrier island. Beyond that, moonlight sparkled on the sea.

Running downhill had its own challenges. Characters who ran too fast stumbled and fell. But when the pavement flattened out and they started the final stretch of the Connector, the Stick boy thought, *We're going to make it!* As the eastern horizon blushed from gray to gold, Lou heard Cocky, somewhere behind him, crowing. No one bothered to object.

When the road ended, they crossed a parking lot, veered around a cluster of buildings, and down a narrow sandy path that led through a small palmetto forest. Hopefully, to the ocean. The loose sand seemed to drain Lou's remaining energy.

Whenever the Chapman family had gone to the beach, the Sticks had remained on the windshield. Lou had only seen the ocean from a distance. Now, fighting for each shifting step, a barrage of vicarious memories flooded his mind: laughter, beach toys, sandy feet, the smell of sunscreen, the feel of salt drying on his skin. The wind gusted and the Stick boy rubbed grit from his eyes. As he blinked away tears, a vision flashed before him: the soft pink insides of eyelids, then the sky, as if he were not running along a path, but lying on the sand. He gave a shudder as he felt warm water rush underneath his back. *I'm lying on the beach,* he thought. The vision quickly passed.

He glanced over his shoulder and saw the throng of characters struggling to walk. "Keep going!" he shouted. Ahead, the path led over a rise. What if nothing lay beyond? What if they reached the top of the dunes and discovered another highway? Another ditch?

The scrubby forest thinned out. Ahead, sea oats bent in the breeze, a peaceful contrast to the Caravan's gasping and shouting. When Lou crested the dunes, a wide beach stretched before him. The Atlantic sparkled with the sun's first rays.

The Caravan surged forward, then fanned out onto the flat expanse. Some sailed or tumbled in the stiff breeze. A few exhausted ones sat down in the sand, but most sprinted toward the water. The sound of crashing waves washed over them. Woven through it, the cries of seagulls.

"Whoa, this wind is freaky!" shouted Chester, fighting the sea breeze.

Eventually, they all found their way to the water's edge. There, they watched the sun emerge from the sea. Giddy laughter rippled through them. The roar of the ocean flooded their conversations. The Scrubbing Bubbles scooted to and from the surf. The Starbucks Siren splashed her double tail in a tidal pool.

Standing perfectly still as the morning sun spread gold over the world, Lou felt as if he might never speak again. Like the ocean contained everything that had ever existed. *Maybe that's where life comes from,* he thought, *maybe where Elizabeth is.*

Other than thousands of characters, the beach was nearly deserted. Several hundred yards away stood a Mobile family with a dog and a big plastic bin—too far away to worry about. Lou stared down as the surf rinsed his sand-speckled feet. He had a new worry now: finding homes for all of these people. The Stick boy closed his eyes for a few seconds, felt cool salt water on his sore feet. He held out his arms and let them flutter in the breeze. The moment slipped away like the sand under his toes.

"Lou!" a voice shouted.

The Stick boy looked up to see Evan waving frantically.

"The dunes! Look! They're here!"

Lou hurried to where he could see through the crowd. Evan, Lucky, Tony, Doc, and Chester met him.

"What's going on, what's wrong?" they shouted.

"Buggers must've circled around, days ago," Evan said, pointing. "They were here the whole time!"

Lou peered into the distance. The dunes rippled, not unlike the sea. He couldn't see in any detail, couldn't hear anything yet. He didn't need to. From one end of the beach to the other, fire ants raced onto the sand. An invincible empire attacking a sleeping village.

Sixty-seven

When the Caravan saw millions of fire ants advancing, some characters plunged into the water. But most in the Caravan were either made of cardboard or paper, or couldn't swim. Even those who were waterproof still had no way to escape. The surf washed them back onto the beach. Only a few Goldfish, Charlie Tuna, and the Siren made it through the waves.

The Stick boy looked around at thousands of fearful faces. They could veer left or right and try to outrun the Empire. But fire ants stretched as far as he could see in either direction.

"Fliers to me!" Lou called. A moment later, Buzz, Zazu, and several cuckoo birds hovered before him. "I need your eyes. How deep are they? Are there any gaps? Anything! Go!" The fliers disappeared on the wind.

Peering into the distance, Lucky asked, "But why would they attack us?" Even he understood that they weren't after his Lucky Charms.

"Glue," the Stick boy answered.

"Oh, no," said TurTur, and drew into his shell. Since leaving his Turtle Wax can, he had never quite lost his stickiness. And not just him. Hundreds in the Caravan either still smelled of adhesive, or were still a little sticky.

"But—" Evan turned in a three-sixty, "—look around. There ain't enough glue here to stick a stamp!"

"What if we lie down?" asked the Pillsbury Doughboy. "When the ants don't find any glue, maybe they'll leave."

"Playing dead won't work," the Stick boy shouted. "The Empire will just tear us apart! Stay near the water. Form a semicircle. Stay tight. Don't let them get behind us!"

The Caravan closed ranks in a half-moon formation, as close to the surf as possible. Lou's closest friends surrounded him, ready to defend their leader. "We won't let them get you, again!" Tony declared. He and Chester unsheathed their claws. Doc Rock removed his spectacles and took off his belt. Lucky drew from his vest a dark jagged wand that he had never shown to anyone.

Everyone got ready. The Coke and Icee polar bears reared up on their hind legs. Fangs and claws came out. The Clif Bar climber uncoiled a whip. A GEICO Gecko, hissing, bared his sharp little teeth. The Cap'ns, Crunch and Morgan, drew their swords. Everyone else, from the smallest elf to the fluffiest bunny, balled up their fists and dug their feet into the sand. Evan towered above them all.

Out of breath, Zazu landed. "They're spread out, about a half mile…either side…and closing in!"

"How deep?"

"A hundred feet or so."

Evan bent down to Lou's level. "The ants can't hurt me," he said. "I can flatten 'em. Let me bust through, make a path for the injured." He nodded toward a group of characters lying on stretchers.

"But there's millions out there," Lou replied. "You'll never get through."

"Send us!" called a girl's voice. "We'll carry the wounded!"

Lou looked around. "Who said that?"

The Nesquik Bunny ran up, carrying a folded tent. Printed on it, a Little Miss Sunbeam said, "Unfold us. Load us up with the injured. We'll carry them away on the wind."

Lou glanced around at the Caravan, all of them bristling to fight and fluttering in the wind. "Sunbeam, you're a genius," he said.

As the ants closed in, the smallest and weakest in the Caravan were rushed to one spot, along with all the Sunbeam bags. "Spread 'em out flat," Lou ordered, "but don't let them blow away!" The bread bags flapped in the wind as the wounded were helped inside.

"Our bag is full," called one of the holders. "Do we let 'em go?"

"Not yet!" yelled Lou. "Too soon and they'll land in the middle of the Empire." He turned to Evan. "How long do we have?"

The magnet man peered over the crowd. "Maybe half a minute."

The Stick boy could hear the Empire's eerie, high-pitched screams. His skin crawled as if they were on him already.

Buzz, Zazu, and the cuckoo birds landed. "There's no way out!" the bee shouted.

Lou turned to Zazu. "You all get out of here while you can!" he ordered.

The toucan spread his wings. "They'll feel my beak from above!"

"And my stinger!" shouted Buzz. The two of them took flight, along with all but one of the toucans.

The remaining Cocoa Puffs mascots, raised a wing. "Uh, I did something cuckoo!" he said. "I asked a furry thing for help! His name was Seamus."

"Who?!" Lou demanded. But without answering, the bird flew away.

As the last of the wounded crawled into the bread bags, a

Little Miss Sunbeam called, "Is it time?"

"Hold steady!" the Stick boy replied.

Hysterical fire-ant calls filled their ears. With grim expressions, the Caravan stared toward the charging Empire. Lou could see their glassy eyes and sharp mandibles. The sand beneath his feet began dancing from the weight of the onrushing army.

"Not yet...almost...almost..." the magnet man called. "Now!"

"Now!" Lou yelled.

The holders let go. The Sunbeam bags filled with wind and swept skyward, their wounded passengers clinging to the insides. An "Ah" escaped the crowd. Then the insane cries of the Fire Empire obliterated all other sounds—the surf, the wind, the Caravan's own voices.

Evan ran forward and body surfed through fire ants, smashing thousands underneath. Millions more swarmed the Caravan. Characters batted, clawed, and clapped the insects to pulp, but they kept coming, running up their legs, along their arms, over their faces, through their hair or fur—frantic for the same sticky nectar that their kind had stripped from Lou.

The Stick boy's vision filled with chomping mandibles and stinging abdomens. Finding little glue on their prey, the ants began tearing at the cardboard, paper, or plastic bodies in a frenzy of hatred and frustration. For the second time in his life, Lou found himself lying beside the water as tiny pieces of his flesh were ripped away. *They won't get my sanity this time,* he thought, *just my life.* At that moment, he heard a bark. Smearing hundreds of ants from his arms and legs, Lou flipped over onto his stomach, then got to his knees.

He looked around at anarchy: characters being dragged to the ground, others writhing in agony. A huge cluster of the enemy tore at an upside-down dome shape—TurTur being stripped of glue, of who he was. The sight made Lou's heart sink. Then, a golden shape swept by him, followed by something broad and sharp. He stared after a palmetto frond being dragged by a puppy. Then another puppy, then another, and another.

Still brushing off ants, the Stick boy made it to his feet. Six golden retriever puppies ran back and forth—seemingly unfazed by ant bites—each of them dragging something heavy: a stick, a sand shovel, a towel. The smallest, with a green ribbon around his neck, dragged the palmetto branch, raking through the Empire and carving furrows in the sand.

Lou continued fighting off ants until a blast of air–stronger than any he had ever felt–lifted him into the air. Hundreds in the Caravan and thousands of ants went airborne as well. But as the attackers tumbled to the ground, the Stick boy and other Caravan characters quickly recovered from the sudden gust and began gliding.

"Formations!" he shouted, and the airborne Caravan

members formed into groups, a fleet of jet fighters made of paper and plastic.

Looking down, searching for the best place to attack, Lou glimpsed a vision that lifted his heart: dozens of humans marching across the beach—through the main force of the Empire—each holding a long device, which they swept back and forth. *Leaf blowers,* Lou thought. *Who are these people?* Before them, a multitude of fire ants became a swirling cloud of bodies and sand.

"Don't land, bomb them!" Lou yelled.

On either side of him, Tony and Chester pointed to the same spot, a stretch of sand littered with tiny seashells. "There!" they yelled.

The Purple One pointed himself like a missile and screamed, "Dive!" The formations followed, swooping just above the surface of the sand, plucking up hundreds of tiny shells. A moment later, the wind carried the group aloft again. On the next dive, the gliding characters aimed at the enemy. Dropping their payloads of sharp little shells, they tore into the fire-ant lines.

The roar of waves and leaf blowers, and the cries of the Empire, filled Lou's hearing. The Caravan air force soared skyward again, then swooped down and reloaded with shells for another run. Over and over, they blasted the Empire's army, trying to protect their Caravan friends still on the ground.

One by one, Lou's air force ran out of updrafts. Unable to pick up shells, they landed and began battling the Empire hand-to-hand. One of the last still gliding, Lou took in the scene. As fire ants scattered in chaos, the Caravan reformed into a semi-circle before the lapping surf. Sunlight bathed the beach and sea. The golden, runt puppy, wearing the green ribbon, now ran in circles, digging a trench around an island of stranded ants. Humans splashed into the surf, plucking out characters before they went under. In the distant dunes, bread bags alighted and the wounded began pouring out.

The Stick boy felt a familiar tug on his heart as he spotted the only Mobile in the world crazy and brave enough to organize such a weird, leaf-blower army: a caramel-haired teenager. And on her shoulders, Lou's sister, Sunny, her pigtails flying behind her, waving her fists like a warrior.

Sixty-eight

Sunday Afternoon, One Month Later

A red Jeep Cherokee sat in the Chapmans' driveway. It still had that new-car smell. What it didn't have were any stickers. No AAA oval on the bumper, no reminder for the next oil change on the front windshield. No Sticks on the back. Sophia's parents had finally traded in the minivan.

In a bedroom overlooking the driveway, Sophia and Holly sat at a desk. On it stood the Chapman Sticks—Lou, Sunny, Ups, and the Stick mom and dad. An open laptop sat on Sophia's desk. The faces of Joaquin and Nico filled the screen.

"Hola, linda!" Joaquin said.

"That's you," Holly said, and poked Sophia.

Lou thought, *He's right, she is beautiful.*

"You have no idea how weird it is to be standing here talking to humans," the Stick mom said. "And yet, the world hasn't ended. Right, hun?"

"Yes, dear," said the Stick dad.

"Yeah, well, I could say the same thing," Joaquin said from the phone. "I mean, when Nico here first showed himself to me, I thought I'd gone nuts."

"You are nuts," Nico cracked.

"That must have been hard for both of you," Dad replied.

"The hard part was getting him to call Sophia," Nico said.

"Girls are way more scary than talking Stick people," Joaquin added.

Sophia and Holly elbowed each other and giggled.

"Did you get that thing I sent you?" Sophia asked.

"Yep." The boy held up his arm, displaying a pink scrunchie on his wrist. The girls giggled again.

Gimme a break, thought Lou.

"So, anyway, Mr. and Ms. Sunny's parents," Joaquin said. "I think you're gonna love this new virtual world I built."

"We can't wait," the Stick mom said. The Stick dad nodded vigorously. "And, young man, that's Mr. and Ms. Stick to you. We have names, you know."

Really? Lou thought.

"Sorry, Ms. Stick," Joaquin amended.

"If you want to stay in this world," Sophia said, patting her viola case, "there's a place for you here."

From the case, Tony the Tiger roared, "That would be GRRREAT!" Beside him, stuck to the instrument case, stood Lou's other close friends.

Zazu bobbed his head. "I most heartily agree."

"You could cohabitate with the coolness," Chester added.

Lou smiled to himself, thinking: That wouldn't last long.

Holly spoke up. "Or on my violin case. You'd hang out with Dig'em and Snuggle and Buzz and some M&Ms. They're so cute."

But the Stick mom shook her head. "Not going to happen. I don't put up with foolishness."

"There's still room over here."

Everyone turned. The offer came from the Chiquita Banana women, adhered to Sophia's dresser mirror. Others lived there, too—Poppin' Fresh, Lucky, the Icee polar bear, a clan of Keeblers.

From another wall, a Little Miss Sunbeam said, "We've got a place for you, too." A collage of bread-bag girls—freshly cut from their bags—had been pinned to a cork board.

Sunny turned to her mom. "See? Anywhere you want. Even the Jeep."

The Stick mom glanced out the window. "Hm, new glass. Tempting." She gave her husband and Ups each a long look. "Thank you for your kind offers, all of you, but the new neighborhood looks perfect for us. Right, hun?"

"Yes, dear," said Dad.

From Sophia's laptop, Joaquin said, "You're gonna love it. The Crossing is a great place to live. Me and Nico have been working on it for months."

"That's Nico and I," Mom corrected.

"Yes, Ms. Stick." Joaquin winked at Sophia.

The Stick mom took Sunny and Lou's hands. "Just because you two are staying behind, doesn't mean you don't have to do what I tell you."

They grinned their crooked and perfect grins. "Yes, Mom."

She hugged them. It lasted about five seconds longer than Lou wanted, but he endured it.

The Stick dad embraced Sunny and kissed her on the top of her head. "Keep shining, Sunflower. And take care of your...your sibling. We don't want to lose her—him—again." He started to hug Lou, hesitated, then shook his hand instead. "Wow, that's some grip you got there."

The Stick boy grinned. "The ditch makes you tough." His dad laughed and started to say more, then lost his breath as Lou pulled him into a fierce hug. "Bye, Dad. See ya on the other side, okay?"

The Stick dad patted the other's bristle-like hair. "I'm proud of you, Lizzie." He took a step back. "Lou."

Ups stepped forward, wagging his tail. The Stick boy

squatted down and scratched him behind the ears. "You can lick my face. Just. This. Once."

The Stick dog did so, then asked, "Sure you won't come with us? Looks pretty awesome. Nico says there are whole fields full of tennis balls!"

"Not for me." Lou pressed his face into the Stick dog's shoulder. "But I'm gonna miss petting your nose."

Ups pulled back. "Enough with the mushy-gushy, I got places to be. Hey, Hershey, in this new world, I'll be the big dog. How about that?" The brown canine just looked up and shook his floppy ears.

"All done with good-byes?" Sophia asked. "Good. You can talk to them later, anyway." She flipped open the lid of a scanner. "Who's first?"

"Me." The Stick mom climbed onto the glass and lay down. "Just don't shred my body, in case I want to come back."

From Sophia's laptop, Joaquin said, "Well, um, remember we're still working on that, ma'am. For now, you'll be stuck there."

"Figures. I've been stuck somewhere all my life," Mom answered. "Zap me."

Sophia said, "Stay perfectly still," then closed the scanner lid and nodded at Holly.

Lou watched as a sliver of light traveled from one end of the device to the other.

"Uploading…" Joaquin said. "Looking good…there, got her!"

Holly clicked some keys. "This is so cool," she whispered.

After a few seconds, the pixelated image of a woman's body began to form on the screen. Details slowly filled in. Holly moved her finger back and forth on the touchpad. A three-dimensional Stick woman rotated on a pedestal.

"Finalizing your crossing," Joaquin said. "And…done."

Onscreen, the Stick mom's eyes blinked open. She stepped off the pedestal, examined her arms and hands, then looked around. "I can't see," she said.

"What?!" everyone said at once.

"I mean you, I can't see any of you," Mom clarified. "Don't blow a fuse up there in giant land."

"Oh," said Joaquin. "Just swipe up."

"What do you mean, young man? I've never swiped anything in my life!"

"No ma'am, of course not."

The girls laughed. "Not that kind of swipe," Holly said.

Sophia added, "Just do a little flick of your wrist. Swish up with your fingers."

The Stick mom did so, then smiled. "Oh, that's easy. Girls, I can see you two, but where's everyone else?"

Sophia tilted the laptop screen down a bit. "Better?"

"Affirmative." She waved. "Hi, kids."

Sunny and Lou waved back. "Hi, Mom."

Then to her husband, "Honey, get in here."

"Yes, dear."

Holly raised the scanner lid. Everyone watched as she carefully placed a lifeless Stick mom sticker in an envelope. The Stick Dad climbed up and lay down on the glass. They scanned him. Then, he rendered according to the specs he had requested: tall, with broad shoulders.

"Well, look at you!" Mom said as he materialized in 3D.

"Is that you, Dad?" Sunny and Lou asked.

He looked himself over. "Oh, yeah! Hi, dear." He stepped off the pedestal and took his wife's hand. "Where'd everyone go?"

"Swipe up, dear. Like this."

"Oh. Oh, there you are. Hi, kids!"

"Hi, Dad."

The old Stick dad went into the envelope.

After many kisses from the Stick twins, Ups lay down on the scanner. He looked up at Doc Rock, who now lived on a Norman Rockwell poster on the wall. "My dear doctor," he said, "thank you, again, for fixing— No, wait, I don't like that word. Thank you for healing Lizzie, I mean, Lou."

"Nothin' to it," said the old man. "Now, go have yourself an adventure."

"You know it!"

A moment later, the digital version of Ups rendered into the Crossing, the online world that Joaquin had built. The 3D dog ran around a virtual yard. "Hey, check this out, I'm marking my territory!" He hiked his leg by a tree. "Finally!"

Sunny, Sophia, and Holly said, "Ew!" and looked away.

The Stick mom said, "Not to be rude, but we're going for a walk around the block. You know, see what kind of weird, inefficient people we have for neighbors. Then I have a list of chores to start on. Right, hun?"

The Stick dad took his wife's hand. "Maybe," he said, staring into her eyes. "Or maybe your list can wait awhile."

"See ya tomorrow," Sunny said.

"See ya," Dad said with a wave.

"Oh, say hi to my moms and Papa Gandhi for me," Nico called. "Three doors down from you."

"Of course, we will," Dad said.

Mom gave a little salute. "Roger, that."

Once Mom, Dad, and Ups had disappeared from view, Sophia turned to Holly. "What's the count?"

The girl checked the laptop. "The Crossing population is now four thousand and twenty-six. And—" She scrolled down. "And nine hundred eighty-seven adopted in real life."

"Cool, like me," Joaquin said. "So are we done for today?"

Sophia picked up her phone "That's all for now. A hundred or so are still waiting."

"Hey!" Joaquin exclaimed, as black fur replaced the boys' faces. "Get down, Boo! I swear, that cat's into everything."

No sooner did the cat get out of the way, when a giant dog's nose filled the screen. "Daisy May!" Joaquin scolded, as he pulled the retriever back. "Lie down and you'll get a belly rub. There ya go, good girl." The teenage boy reappeared. "She only does that when I'm on a call with y'all," he said. Then added in a whisper, "I think she's got a crush on Hershey."

In Sophia's room, the Boykin spaniel looked up from his spot on the floor and wagged his stubby tail.

Nico nudged into the corner again. "You were saying, Sophia? A hundred characters are waiting? Waiting for what?"

"For adoption in real life," Sophia said. "Don't worry, they're all spoken for. They just need to heal up."

"How about you guys?" Holly asked.

"Digitized the last of ours this morning," Joaquin said. "You should have seen that little pirate guy. We gave him and all those Cap'n Crunches their own ships. They were having races."

"I'll bet they're remarkable vessels," Lou said. "But wait, if you're done digitizing—" he pointed at the screen. "—we all know what you two will be up to tonight."

"Dumpster diving!" The boys pumped their fists.

Holly said, "Gross."

Sophia wagged a finger at them. "Stay out of trouble."

"No problema!" the boys answered together. Followed by another round of laughter.

"Um, Soph?" Lou interrupted. "I just heard your mom's

keys."

The teenager glanced at the door. "Hold up, Mom!" she called, "Holly and I'll go with you." Then to Joaquin and Nico, "Grocery store. Gotta go."

"Bye," the boys replied. Sophia's laptop went dark.

From the Norman Rockwell wall poster, Doc said, "Don't forget my berries this time. I'm almost out of poultice again."

"Blackberries, got it," Holly said. "That's why we're going."

That started a flood of requests. Chester wanted a bag of Cheetos, saying, "I just need to hear that cheese go crunch!"

The Chiquita women wanted bananas. Poppin' Fresh wanted crescent rolls. Lucky wanted pink hearts, yellow moons, orange stars, and green clovers. The Elves wanted every kind of Keebler cookie and cracker ever made.

"Check, check, check, and...we'll see," Sophia said. The Mobile lowered her shoulder to the level of the Sticks. "Hop on." Sunny did, but Lou didn't.

"Think I'll hang here with these guys," the Stick boy said. "Had enough of the road for a while."

The other shrugged. "Suit yourself." Sophia bounded downstairs with Holly right behind her and Sunny hiding in her hair. Lou watched from the window as the Jeep pulled out of the driveway.

"That new car's so quiet," he said. "I barely heard it start."

"That red machine purrs like a cheetah," Chester said.

From the poster, Doc lowered his spectacles and peered down at the Boykin spaniel. "Hershey Bob, you may continue."

The brown dog jumped up on the bed, turned in several circles, and curled up. "Where was I?" he asked.

"Wait for us," said Lucky. The Leprechaun and others made their way to the bed, with Poppin' Fresh and the Icee polar bear carrying the Chiquitas. Lou stretched out on Sophia's pillow. Zazu circled the room and landed beside him.

"You were telling us about time travel in a phone booth," Doc said.

Lou grinned. He had heard these stories before, but it was nice to hear them from the beginning.

"Ah, yes," Hershey said. He shook his head, making his long, lush, floppy ears bounce like a woman's locks in a hair-color commercial. "After the Doctor fled Gallifrey in the TARDIS, the time machine somehow got stuck in the form of a British police box," the spaniel began.

"A what box?" asked the Pillsbury Doughboy.

"A police box. Like a phone booth." Hershey waved a paw. "Oh, but you wouldn't remember."

"I do," said Doc.

"Like a Lucky Charms cereal box?" Lucky asked.

The dog tilted his head. "Perhaps. Anyway, by its rather small outer appearance, you'd never guess that the TARDIS was really quite enormous inside...."

Sixty-nine

Monday Morning

The Stick twins clung to Sophia's book bag as she pedaled her bike to school. Tony, Chester, and Zazu bounced along on the viola case, strapped to the back.

"Isn't school glorious!" Sunny exclaimed.

Lou started to reply, "Doesn't suck," but said, "Sure," instead. *The Sunflower is in full bloom today,* he thought. Then they hit a bump in the sidewalk and he almost lost his hold. The Stick boy grabbed Sunny's hand as she offered it, her fingernails now bright red to match her lips.

A few blocks later, Holly pulled her bike alongside. Everyone exchanged good mornings.

Sunny leaned out toward Holly's passengers. "How's everybody on this glorious morning?" she asked.

From Holly's violin case, Dig'em, Buzz, Snuggle, and several M&Ms replied that they were tired but okay. Tony loudly declared that he was GREAT. Chester just let out a kind of purr-snore. Lou yawned and waved. After weeks of nocturnal travel, he couldn't quite adjust to being awake in the daytime. The Stick boy covered his eyes to hide from the sun, now cresting the rooftops.

"Hey, Chester, can I borrow your sunglasses?" he mumbled.

"Sure, dude," the big cat replied, "when I'm dead."

Soon other bicyclists joined them, all with characters on book bags or stuck to the bikes themselves: Cap'n Crunch and the Siren, Icee, Tricks, Clif, lots of Elves, Bubbles, and fries. They would see dozens more at school—the Coke bears, Little Debbie, the Burger King king, Ronald.

At first, Sophia and Holly had sneaked around, sticking them on desks and lockers. Then they became a trend. Now there was a waiting list. Some kids even brought their own characters from home. But humans didn't own them or rule them. The characters themselves always decided when and if to reveal themselves to their Mobiles. Dozens of middle-schoolers were now in the know—most of them oddballs, nerds, freaks. Almost none of the popular kids.

Everyone in the Bike Caravan greeted Lou like he was still their leader. They asked about TurTur, who had been slow to mend since the battle on the beach.

"Blackberries didn't help at all, but Doc says Turtle Wax is doing the trick," the Purple One replied. "TurTur's getting stronger. His memory's back."

"I heard he's being adopted," said the Nesquik Bunny.

"Yeah, by me," said a Mobile boy. He slapped his saxophone case. "Going right here." Out of habit, most of the characters froze. The boy said, "It's okay, it's me, Dorian. I'm a recycler." *Recycler* was their code word for a Mobile who knew about them.

"Everybody chill," Lou said. And they all relaxed.

"Ever hear from Sally?" a french fry person asked.

"Oh yeah, I almost forgot," Lou replied. "The Black Army just delivered a note from her. She sends hugs and kisses and a shout-out from her new peeps on the refrigerator." He went on to say that the Morton Salt girl's new human friend, Emma, had patched her umbrella and drawn polka dots on it.

Several blocks from school, the other kids rode on while Sophia and Holly stopped their bikes beside a bucket truck— one of those with a long mechanical arm. The two girls peered up through the branches of a tree.

"Morning, Mr. Baker," they called.

From the bucket high above them, Gene Baker paused in his tree-trimming work. The three of them made small talk.

Stuck to the door of the truck, Evan gave his friends a smile. "Hey, fellas."

The characters all greeted him. Glancing up, the Stick boy asked, "How's Baker?"

The magnet man gave a thumbs-up. "Second week on the job. Sober. Living at the shelter while he saves up. That recommendation from Holly's dad helped a lot."

"Good for him. You're looking good, too."

"Yeah? I feel great." Evan ran a hand around the smooth edge of his hard hat. "Check this out, I got trimmed up with an X-Acto knife."

"Nice!"

The girls rode on. At the traffic signal by their school, Sophia and Holly again stopped. Holly pointed at an electronic Walk/Don't Walk sign at the corner. "That thing's busted. The little man just keeps flickering."

"Not broke," laughed Lou, "he just woke up."

Sunny leaned out from behind Sophia's hair. "Wait for it..." she said, "wait for it..." After a moment, the electric character began moonwalking. When he was done, everyone applauded and he took a bow.

A few minutes later, the humans parked their bikes by the school and unstrapped their instrument cases. "Coming over later?" Sophia asked.

Holly gave her a look. "Are you kidding? I can't. I'm getting my puppy today! Remember?!"

"Oh, right, the one from the beach. Think up a name?"

"He already has one. Seamus. I'm so excited!"

Sophia wrinkled her nose. "You're keeping that name? Sounds like *shame us*."

"It's the perfect name," Lou said. The other characters all agreed that, no matter what it sounded like, the little runt had been a hero in the Battle on the Beach. No shame in Seamus.

Holly took Sophia's hand. "Come over to my house, instead. You can meet the puppy."

Sophia glanced at Lou. "I would, but there's something important we gotta do."

"If you say so."

"Can I go, instead? Can I, can I?" Sunny pleaded.

Sophia turned to the Stick girl. "Sure, I guess. If you want, just stay over and we'll see you in the morning."

"A sleepover!" Sunny squealed. She cartwheeled over to Holly and hid beneath her hair.

All through the first two periods at school, Lou dozed. He rallied for Ms. Curry's biology class, his favorite. They were studying microbes. The Stick boy had read the material, so it was a little frustrating that he would never get called on to answer her questions. This teacher was the coolest, but for now they were all sticking to a rule that no adults could find out about the characters.

Other than band class, when Lou and his friends got to socialize in the instrument room while the Mobiles learned

Bach, the rest of the school day passed in the usual way, with characters staying unnoticed.

First thing when they got home, Lou and Sophia checked on the injured people hidden in the garage. Doc, having sneaked off of his poster, spread a new coat of wax on TurTur. The old man still wasn't sure what to do about one of the cuckoo birds, who had lost a wing in the battle. Unless he figured out how to make him a new one, the Froot Loops mascot would have little choice but to move online. Either that or fly in circles.

But tending to wounded characters from the Caravan, though important, wasn't the task that the Stick boy and Mobile girl had set for themselves this afternoon.

Lou stared into pitch black as Sophia rummaged around in the attic. *It's dead quiet up here,* he thought. *Quiet as a river bottom. Or as a grave, I guess.*

Minutes later, back in the bedroom over the garage, the Stick boy and his friends gathered around as Sophia opened a dusty box and slid out sheet after sheet of leftover Stick people. As their years of darkness ended, Lou thought, *I remember this. The light's so bright they can hardly stand it.*

"Why, there's a whole village of 'em," said Poppin' Fresh.

Chester nodded. "Look at them all. It's, like, the deluxe set."

"They're GRRRREAT!" Tony proclaimed.

Lucky wasn't so thrilled: "They'll be after me Lucky Charms!"

Sophia leaned her freckled face close to the newbies. Green eyes stared down, big as moons. "They're still so clean," she said. "In such good condition."

"Uncommonly good," agreed an Elf.

Lou imagined what was going on in their heads. Their instincts told them to remain perfectly still, so that's what they did. They didn't squint or blink their black eyes. They didn't stretch or yawn. They didn't wiggle the fingers on their four-fingered hands. They just stared at the ceiling. They were all connected. Lying on their backs, they couldn't see each other, but they felt one another's presence. They had memories of being in a dark place. Their noses itched, but they resisted the urge to scratch. They lay flat and motionless, waiting for the world to tell them what they were. Not that anyone would. Not this time.

"Hi there," or "Hello," Sophia said to each one as she separated them.

That stings, Lou thought, rubbing his hands.

The Mobile lay them on her desk, but none would move.

"Come on, it's okay," Lou said, walking amongst them. "Wake up, get to your feet. You can walk, you can talk. Everything's gonna be alright. Jeez!"

"Rise and shine, fellows!" added Zazu, nudging some with his beak.

Hershey's short tail thumped the carpet, like a drum

cadence calling them to attention. One by one, silently, the Sticks stood up.

"There ya go," said Sophia. But once standing, they remained as still and expressionless as a batch of new robots.

Tony, Chester, Poppin' Fresh, Lucky, and the Keeblers mingled with them. The cheetah waved a velveted paw in front of one's face. No response. "Curious," he said.

Finally, a Stick girl in the back walked forward and faced Lou. She brushed a hand across his bristle-like rainbow hair, then ran her fingers over his weathered, purple skin. When she touched a corner of his crooked grin, an audible *Ahh!* rippled through the rows of Sticks. They stirred and began whispering to one another. The Stick girl examined Lou's tank top, his pants. She even put a finger into the hole in his belly, where Cap'n Nobeard's sword had gone through. "You're like us," she said, "only different."

"Yes," he replied. "Just two minutes out of the box and you're already gettin' it." He gave her pigtails a gentle tug.

Outside, a mockingbird on a branch launched into song. The new Sticks shuffled toward the window, their manufactured smiles rounding into looks of astonishment.

"Oh yeah," Sophia said, "there's a whole other world out there."

Lou pointed toward the red Cherokee in the driveway. "It's time for their Peeling," he said.

"Excellent!" squawked Zazu. "I've always wanted to see that." He fluttered onto the window sill. "But I'll watch from inside, if you don't mind." The other former Caravan members climbed onto the sill as well. "Us, too," they said. They had had enough of the outdoors for a while.

A moment later, Lou clung to the back windshield wiper as Sophia placed the new Sticks *On Glass*. "Good thing I hid the scraper!" she said as the windshield filled up.

"And good thing that a Mobile can bond with more than one Stick," Lou said. "Oh, don't forget to leave an empty spot." He pointed toward the middle of the windshield. "Right about there."

Sophia looked puzzled. "For the driver to see out?"

"No, silly, for me and Sunny. Your folks can use their backup camera."

"Oh, right. Right!" Then after a pause. "In the middle, huh? I thought you were more edgy than that, dude."

Lou and the Stick village all groaned. "You've been spending too much time around my dad," he said.

"Wait. You're not sticky. Aren't you afraid of flying off?"

The Stick boy looked out at the road. "What's the worst that could happen? I end up in a ditch and make more friends? I think Sunny and these guys can hold me on."

Lou watched as the freshly-placed Sticks adjusted to their new home: grown-ups and children of every size. Dogs, cats, birds, a hamster. They made no attempt to stay still. They peeled up, looked around, conversed. The kids and animals climbed up top and explored the roof of the Jeep. The two smallest held hands and danced in a circle. Lou felt joy radiating off of them, like heat from sun-soaked pavement. Their nightmare of darkness had vanished. Only a dream of light remained, for uncountable miles ahead.

Seventy

Turning to Lou, Sophia said, "How 'bout some just-us time? Somewhere special."

The Purple One shrugged. "Works for me."

Looking back at the Stick Village, he started to say something more. Maybe to let them know where to find the User's Manual, or to give instructions like his mom might have done. But he held his tongue. *Eh, they'll figure it out.*

Hiding behind Sophia's hair, he rode back inside. The girl's parents sat in the great room, streaming some show. They didn't look up. Without a word, Sophia walked straight to a bookcase and drew out a huge leather-bound book.

"What's that?" Lou whispered.

"Shh. You'll see."

As the teenager slid open a glass door to the backyard, her

mom asked where she was going.

"Just...back...you know...to the, uh—"

"Back where?"

Sophia pointed. "The treehouse."

"Aww." Her mom shook her dad's shoulder and said something into his ear. A moment later, both human parents were hugging their daughter, so close that Lou could feel their breath.

"I thought you had outgrown that thing," her dad said softly.

"I kinda did," Sophia replied, "but don't you ever tear it down. We built it together—you, me, and 'Lizbeth. Well, mostly you two."

"Yes, we did." He kissed her forehead.

As they released her, Sophia's mom stroked her hair. Lou felt the giant hand from head to foot. *Good thing I'm glueless,* he thought.

In a back corner of the yard, Sophia climbed a tall oak tree, using wooden two-by-fours that served as a ladder—slowly and one-handed, because she carried the big book. "Did you know about this place?" she asked.

"I've felt it," the Stick boy replied. He hopped from Sophia's shoulder and got a good look at the place. Built in a three-way fork, the treehouse formed a triangle. Overhead, a tattered, faded, blue-and-yellow canopy flapped in the breeze. "She used to cry up here," Lou said.

"Uh-uh!" Sophia protested. "She was tough as nails, she never cried. She came up here to read horse books." She searched the swaying branches, as if they would back her up.

"Yeah, but not just to read." At the other's sad look, Lou added, "Sorry to burst your bubble."

They both sat on the rough, wooden floor. The Mobile set aside the leather-bound volume, then dug something out of her pocket, but kept her fist closed around it. "Show me your belly?" she said.

Lou wrinkled his forehead. "Uh, what?"

"Just do it."

With an embarrassed grin, the Stick boy lifted the bottom of his tank top, revealing six-pack abs and, a little off-center, the hole where he had been stabbed by a pirate's sword.

"I got you something," Sophia said. "Sorta." She unfolded her hand, revealing a small, silver earring in the shape of a crescent moon and two stars. The thirteen-year-old inserted the sharp part through Lou's midsection and attached the clasp in the back. The Stick boy ran his hand over it. "It's kinda plain," Sophia added, as if to apologize. "No little diamond chips or anything, but it's—"

Lou silenced her with a raised hand. "It's perfect," he replied. "Couldn't be more perfect."

Sophia stared up at sunlit leaves. "Really, it's not from me. It's from her." Their eyes met. "It was Elizabeth's. Remember?

Back in the sixth grade, when she was into–"

"Astronomy. Yeah. She had glow-in-the-dark stars on the ceiling of her room, right?"

Sophia nodded. "I gave her these earrings for her birthday. The only time I ever got her to wear them, she lost one."

"Figures." The Stick boy stared at his reflection in the polished surface for a moment, before covering it with his shirttail. He looked up. "Thank you."

The giant girl placed the heavy book in front of them.

"So, what are we reading?" Lou asked.

"We're not. It's a photo album." Sophia opened it.

Oh.

Baby pictures filled the first few pages. Lou couldn't tell which twin was which. Further on, it became obvious. Sophia smiled and curtseyed, while Elizabeth pulled her hair; one girl put on her mom's lipstick, as the other drew a mustache on herself with mascara; one showed off new shoes, the other displayed muddy, bare feet.

"She was such a character!" Lou laughed.

"Ha!" Sophia replied. "You're one to talk."

The Stick boy grunted. "Too bad these pictures aren't alive." He noticed a quick glance from the other. "But they aren't and never will be," he added. "They're never gonna start walking around like Tony or Doc or Lucky or me. They're just pictures. They're dead. I should know. Out on the road, I saw people die.

Characters, I mean. Ones that were too far gone for Doc to help."

Sophia wiped at her eyes. "Really?"

"Yeah. When you're gone, you're gone."

"What about, you know, heaven?"

Lou shrugged. "Could be. I mean, Joaquin found a way to scan zillions of us into a computer. So, maybe the Universe has a way to fling you into the stars or something."

"I hope so," Sophia said, and now tears were streaming down her face. She turned page after page. The twins getting their heights marked on a doorpost. Performing gymnastics. Wallowing on the floor with Hershey as a puppy. A vacation at the Grand Canyon—Elizabeth wearing a cowboy hat and riding on a mule. Camping. Cartwheeling. The two girls smiling, cheek-to-cheek. Always together, always so different.

"I just...miss her so much!" Sophia blubbered, and melted into serious boo-hoos, her hair becoming matted and snot running. She covered her face. Tears dripped through her fingers.

After a long moment, Lou said, "Here," and handed her a leaf.

"Thanks." Seconds later, a wet leaf floated to the ground. "That sucks as a tissue."

"Yep. I'll get you some more."

"No, I got it."

While Sophia plucked leaves and dried her face, Lou studied a small photo in the corner of the page. A close-up: Elizabeth at eleven, her chin resting on a softball glove, her face tilted into the sun, green eyes shining, a big grin, crooked of course.

"That's a good one," he said, tapping the photo. "I remember so much more than I did, but I don't remember that day. Fact, I had forgotten that y'all even played softball." He ran his hand across Elizabeth's face. "Sometimes I wish..." He trailed off, not sure what he had meant to say, or if he could say it.

"Move back a sec," Sophia said, and Lou did. The Mobile girl peeled back the clear laminate that held the photos in place. "Now try."

Lou lay down on the photograph, his face to Elizabeth's. As he rested there, that moment—the sunshine, the sounds of the ballpark, the taste of a hotdog, the smell of leather—came flooding back. He recalled her laugh, her voice. *Like sandpaper.* He felt that quirky, lost, tomboy more deeply right now than at any time since her death. Soreness swelled his throat. His body trembled. Tiny tears wet the page. In them, a year and a half of sorrow washed away like road dust. Eventually, he raised himself and looked up at Sophia as she offered him a leaf big enough to use as a blanket. "When I'm gone—" he started.

"Gone?"

"I mean, when life's gone out of me, like it will one day, like it does for everybody, *this* is where I want you to put me, okay?"

The other nodded. Together, they burst into fresh sobs.

Several minutes and a pile of leaf-tissues later, Sophia asked, "Would you go with me...to visit her grave? Someday soon?"

What will it be like to run my hands across her name engraved in stone, the Stick boy wondered? As he nodded, his tear-rimmed eyes shone like a pair of stars; his sliver of a smile tilted like a new moon. The giant girl smiled back, displaying a fortune of orthodontic railroad tracks.

She'll get those braces off one day, Lou laughed to himself. *Some things are not forever. Others stay with you, even through unbearable nothingness.*

THE END

Acknowledgments

Thank you, Karen my love, for your patience while I write. And for believing in me, despite all evidence to the contrary.

To my children, Deoni and Cady, for your courage to be yourselves. You make me proud. To JM, David, Sarah, Sabien, and to all of those seen by the closed-minded as less-than; you are worthy.

To my "grammarholic" editor, Deborah, for cleaning up my messy manuscript. To my beta readers, Hillary, Justin, and Garrett, talented writers all, for your insights into story and character. To the "critters" at critique.org who sampled and critiqued with honesty. To the writers' workshops in Mt. Pleasant and Frisco, the first for wading through so many speculative short stories, the second for crystalizing my cast of characters. To Terian, for your artist's eye.

To my friend, Scott, for insightful opinions on controversial subjects. To my TKD buddies Rick, David, Denis, Hannes, and Peter, for all those years of kicking my butt, followed by brunch.

To my siblings, Patti, and George, for loving me even when we don't agree. To Ryan, for not hating your uncle in his long absences. To my cousin James; you were never a black sheep to me for loving who you love. To my mom, Eleanor, for modeling kindness and acceptance, no matter what.

To Zazu, my little, green birdie-bird. I left you beneath a cairn in the shadow of Buffalo Mountain. You left beak marks on my life.

And because no story of mine will ever come to life without a good dog at my feet, to Daisy, Seamus, and Josie Posey, for your unconditional love.

Finally, thank you to Hershey and to Beth. I carry the two of you in my heart like a beautiful, sad song, with equal parts of fondness and regret. If I could go back, I would have given you more time, would have been a better dog dad and a better brother. I miss you.

About the Author

D. Austin Walker is a writer and graphic designer with a bachelors in Journalism from the University of Georgia. His career includes news production, post-production editing, on-air promotion, digital marketing, web design, and content development. He lives in Central Florida.